Praise for *Cowboy Trouble*

"A fresh take on the traditional contemporary Western… There's plenty of wacky humor and audacious wit in this mystery-laced escapade."

—*Library Journal*

"Contemporary western fans will enjoy this one!"

—*Romantic Times*

"Refreshing and different… Ms. Kennedy's debut novel is a winner… A little romance, a little mystery, good looking guys and wide open spaces are a perfect combination."

—Night Owl Romance, Reviewer Top Pick

"Held my attention from the first page to the last. The chemistry sizzles."

—Allison's Attic of Books

"A fun and delicious romantic romp… If you love cowboys, you won't want to miss this one! Romance, Mystery, and Spurs! YUM!!"

—Wendy's Minding Spot

"Fun, sexy, with a little mystery to boot, this was a sure fire winner in my book and a true can't miss. That cowboy charm alone won me over."

—Book Junkie

One Fine
COWBOY

JOANNE KENNEDY

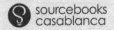

sourcebooks
casablanca

Published by Sourcebooks Casablanca, an imprint of Sourcebooks,
Inc.
P.O. Box 4410, Naperville, Illinois 60567-4410
(630) 961-3900
FAX: (630) 961-2168
www.sourcebooks.com

Printed and bound in Canada
WC 10 9 8 7 6 5 4 3 2 1

To Scrape McCauley, with love.

Chapter 1

THE COWBOY BOOT WAS THE MOST PATHETIC PIECE OF footwear Charlie had ever seen. Upended on a fence post, it was dried out and sunbaked into dog-bone quality rawhide. She glanced down at the directions in the dude ranch brochure.

After pavement ends, go 1.6 miles and turn right. Boot on fence post points toward ranch.

The boot's drooping toe pointed straight down toward the ground. Evidently, Latigo Ranch was located somewhere in the vicinity of hell.

No surprise there.

Still, the boot was a welcome sight, signaling the last leg of the weird Western treasure hunt laid out in the brochure, and putting Charlie one step closer to getting done with this cowboy nonsense and going home to New Jersey where she belonged. Back to New Brunswick, with its crowded streets and endless pavement; its nonstop soundtrack of whining sirens; its Grease Trucks and commuter buses. Back to the smog-smudged brick of New Jersey and the slightly metallic, smoky scent of home.

Wyoming, on the other hand, smelled disturbingly organic, like sagebrush and cowflops, and offered nothing but endless expanses of featureless prairie with a few twisted pines wringing a scant living out of the rocky ground. If this was home on the range, the deer and the antelope were evidently taking the summer off. She hadn't seen so much as a prairie dog at play since she'd crossed the Nebraska border.

Cranking the steering wheel to the right, Charlie let her back end spin up a plume of dust, then winced as the Celica jerked to a halt. Yanking on the emergency break and flinging open the door, she stomped around to the front of the car to watch the right front tire hiss out its life in a deep, jagged pothole.

She pulled in a long breath and let it out slow. She could handle this.

Reaching under the seat, she hauled out the jack and climbed out of the car. After a fair amount of fumbling around, she managed to set the jack handle and start cranking, ignoring the itch that prickled between her shoulder blades as the sun leached sweat from her skin. The car rose, then rose some more. Then it shifted sideways, groaned like a tipping cow, and slammed back onto the ground, its wounded tire splayed at a hideously unnatural angle.

This was no ordinary flat tire.

Charlie knelt in the dust, staring at the crippled car. What now? She was in the middle of nowhere with a screwdriver, a roll of duct tape, and a 1978 Celica hatchback that looked as if euthanasia would be the only humane solution.

She pressed the heels of her hands into her eye sockets to push back the tears. She wasn't scared. She really wasn't. That couldn't be her heart pounding. Couldn't be. It was… it was…

Hoofbeats.

Hoofbeats, drumming the road behind her. She turned to see a Stetson-topped silhouette approaching, dark against the setting sun. Lurching to her feet, she fell back against the car as a horse and rider skidded to a stop six feet away, gravel pinging off the car's rear bumper.

The sun kept the horseman's features in shadow, but Charlie could see he was long-boned and rangy, with pale eyes glimmering under a battered gray hat. She could almost hear the eerie whistle of a spaghetti Western soundtrack emanating from the rocky landscape behind him. She'd have been scared except one corner of his thin lips kept twitching, threatening to break into a smile as he looked her up and down.

It had to be her outfit. Saddle Up Western Wear called it "Dude Couture," but she was starting to think "Dude Torture" would be more appropriate. The boots were so high-heeled and pointy-toed she could barely drive in them, let alone walk, and she was tempted to follow local tradition and upend them on a fence post for buzzard bait. Then there was the elaborately fringed jacket and the look-at-me-I'm-a-cowgirl shirt with its oversized silver buttons. She cursed the perky Saddle Up salesgirl for the fourteenth time that day and straightened up, squaring her shoulders.

"Whoa," the rider said, shifting his weight as the horse danced in place. "Easy there, Honey."

"I'm not your honey." She tossed her head and her dark hair flared up like a firecracker, then settled back into its customary spiky shag. The horse pranced backward a few steps, then stilled, twitching with restless energy.

"I know. Easy, Honey," the rider repeated, patting the horse's neck. "Tupelo Honey. That's her name," he explained.

"Oh." Charlie looked up at the animal's rolling eyes and flaring nostrils and blushed for the first time in fifteen years. "I thought you meant me."

"Nope. The horse. So you might want to calm down. You're making her nervous, and she's liable to toss me again." Honey pitched her head up, prancing nervously in place as he eased back on the reins. "It's her first time."

"Her first time," Charlie repeated blankly.

"First time in the open under saddle," he said. "Doing just fine, too." He bent down to fondle the horse's mane. "Doing just dandy," he crooned softly.

Charlie watched him rotate his fingers in tiny circles, rubbing the horse's copper-colored pelt. Honey's long-lashed eyes drifted shut as she heaved a hard sigh and loosened her muscles, cocking one hind leg.

"Niiiice," the rider purred. Charlie felt like she'd interrupted an intimate encounter.

"Sorry." Dammit, she was blushing again. "I'm trying to get to Latigo Ranch. My car broke down." She gestured toward the crippled Celica.

"Latigo? You're already there," he said. He swung one arm in a slow half-circle to encompass the surrounding landscape. "This is it. You a friend of Sandi's or something?"

"A customer," she said. Sandi Givens was listed as "your hostess" in the glossy dude ranch brochure that lay on the Celica's front seat.

He straightened in the saddle and widened his eyes. "You came all this way for Mary Kay?"

"Mary Kay?" Charlie shook her head. "No way. They do animal testing. I came out here to do some research on horse whispering." She attempted a smile. "I'm a grad student. Psychology."

The rider bunched the reins in his fist and backed the horse a step or two. The horse moved cautiously, one foot at a time, nodding her head and laying back her ears. "Well, Sandi could sure use a shrink, but she's not home. And don't let her tell you she knows anything about horses. Whispering or otherwise."

Charlie shrugged. "Well, duh. She's just the hostess."

"Hostess of what?"

"The dude ranch. I'm going to a Nate Shawcross clinic."

The cowboy narrowed his eyes. With his battered hat and the two-day growth of stubble on his chin, he bore an uncanny resemblance to the young Clint Eastwood. That eerie, fluttering whistle pierced her subconscious again.

"Nate Shawcross doesn't do clinics," he said.

"Yes, he does. I have a reservation." She set her fists on her hips and squared her shoulders. "Is there some kind of problem?"

"Kind of." He leaned forward and pointed a thumb at his own chest. "Because I'm Nate Shawcross, and I don't know a damned thing about any clinic."

Charlie stood stunned, her mouth hanging open. "But... but I'm Charlie Banks. From Rutgers. I came all the way from New Jersey. My boss sent a deposit."

"To Sandi, I guess," he said. He looked down and fiddled with the reins. When he lifted his head, a muscle in his jaw was pulsing and his gray eyes glistened. He swallowed and looked back down at his hands. "Sandi's my girlfriend," he finally said. "She up and left, though. Went to Denver. I guess that makes her my ex-girlfriend."

He shook his head, still looking down at the reins. "Sorry. She didn't tell me anything about this."

"I'm supposed to stay here for three weeks," Charlie sputtered. "And my boss expects me to come back with enough notes for a paper. There's a conference…" She shook her head and blinked fast, pushing back tears. "I got lost, and now the car's broken down and…" A single tear welled up in one eye and she flicked it away, praying he hadn't seen it. She was angry, not scared, but she always cried when she was mad. And the madder she got, the harder she cried. It made her look weak, and she didn't want to look weak in front of this stupid cowboy.

Because that's what he was—a cowboy. No matter what the brochure said about "horse whisperers," the man in front of her was a cowboy.

And she didn't like cowboys.

She'd tried to explain that to Sadie Tate, but Sadie really didn't care what Charlie liked.

Three days earlier, Charlie had parked her butt in an orange vinyl chair and devoted a solid half-hour to convincing Sadie Tate that the trip to Latigo Ranch was a bad idea.

The orange chair was part of the psychology department's sixties vibe—a decorating concept as attractive and up-to-date as Sadie herself. The woman looked like an advertisement for *What Not to Wear* in her shapeless gray sweater and high-water pants.

"So you want me to spend the summer on a dude ranch, harassing innocent animals with a bunch of cowboys." Charlie grimaced. "Please. I'm begging you. Don't make me do this."

"But it's perfect." Sadie's nasal voice meshed perfectly with her appearance. "You love animals. And this is valuable field research." She pushed her heavy glasses up the long slope of her nose and glanced down at the research proposal on her desk. "You'll be assessing the parallels between the training techniques of Western livestock managers and the nonverbal cues with which humans communicate their wants and needs."

Charlie snorted. "You can't fool me with your academic double-talk, Tate. I know what a Western livestock manager is. It's a *cowboy*." She shoved the glossy brochure under Sadie's nose, tapping one crimson fingernail on a color photo of a man in Wrangler jeans and a Stetson. "I'm a PETA member in good standing, Sadie. That's 'People for the Ethical Treatment of Animals.' I won't 'bust a bronc,' and I don't want to deal with anyone who does." She sighed. "Can't we just experiment on a few more freshmen instead?"

"Times have changed, Charlie." Sadie dismissed her last question with an imperious wave of her hand. "They're not called 'cowboys' anymore. They're called 'horse whisperers.' They use nonverbal cues to communicate with another species. They soothe them and gain their confidence by mimicking the body language the animals use to communicate with their own kind. It's exactly the sort of thing we need to understand."

Charlie sighed. Her summer was ruined, but she'd stand on her head and whistle Dixie for Sadie Tate if she had to. Sadie was the only professor who'd been interested when Charlie shopped around for grad schools.

The others figured out that her choice of psychology as a field of study was an afterthought. She'd majored in biology with an eye toward veterinary school, but she'd never make it with her mediocre grades. She'd spent too much time at PETA protests and not enough at her desk.

At least a degree in psychology would lead to some kind of meaningful work. No way was Charlie going to end up like her mother, sacrificing her life to making a living in a succession of dead-end jobs. Waitress. Receptionist. Hostess.

Mom.

Charlie knew her mother loved her, but being saddled with single motherhood at seventeen had been the equivalent of a life sentence to New Jersey's minimum wage gulag. Mona Banks could have escaped, but she'd saved every penny she earned for her daughter's education. That's why she was still waitressing herself half to death on the night shift at the All-American Diner, still pushing Charlie to succeed at something, anything. *There'll be time enough for fun later, after you get your education,* she'd said. *Make some sacrifices.*

But cowboys?

That was going too far.

"Do you realize what you're asking me to do?" Charlie demanded. "You're asking me to spend half my summer with men who make their living subjugating helpless animals. Men who think getting ground into the dirt by angry bulls is the ultimate proof of manhood. Who swagger around in chaps and cowboy hats, chewing tobacco and looking for 'buckle bunnies.'"

"Exactly," Sadie said. "I'm glad you have such an

accurate grasp of the concept. Your flight leaves in three days."

"Flight?" Charlie blanched. "Oh God, Sadie. Don't make me fly. I hate flying. Can I drive? Please let me drive. I'll take my own car."

Sadie smiled and slit her eyes like a satisfied cat. "Why certainly, Charlie. I'm so glad you've agreed to go."

Charlie cursed herself silently. She'd fallen right into Sadie's trap.

"But you'll need to leave tomorrow since you're driving," Sadie said. "It's at least a two-day trip, and I arranged for you to arrive early in order to receive some individual instruction."

Individual instruction? That meant Charlie would be on her own—all alone with a cowboy who would no doubt try to tell her what to do. She pointed a finger at Sadie and took a deep breath, preparing to plunge into verbal battle.

Sadie stared back, calm as a Buddha, and Charlie felt her anger fade into hopelessness.

"I need to pack," she mumbled and slouched out of the office.

Reaching the doorway, she turned. "But if they abuse their horses, I'll—"

"You'll observe and report," Sadie said, raising her eyebrows and stabbing the air with a ballpoint pen. "As a student of psychology, you will maintain an objective perspective and will eschew any personal involvement with your subjects."

"Yeah, that's just what I was about to say," Charlie muttered.

"Good." Sadie shoved the pen behind her ear and nodded sharply. "I'm glad we understand each other."

Charlie's mother tossed a plastic-wrapped package into Charlie's suitcase.

"Here," she said. "I got you these."

Charlie scanned the model on the cover. "Mom, these are granny panties," she said. "Yuck." She flipped through her underwear drawer and pulled out a pair of polka-dotted hi-cuts and a matching bra. "I wear pretty stuff."

Her mom flipped her waist-length gray hair over her shoulder and peered into the drawer, picking through the satin and lace pretties. Pulling out a flimsy scrap of lace, she held it at arm's length and eyed it as if she'd found the decaying corpse of a dead trout.

"What is *this*?"

"A thong," Charlie said, snatching it out of her hand. "It's so you don't get panty lines." She tossed it into the suitcase, but her mom immediately snatched it out and flipped it back into the drawer.

"Don't you have any *regular* underwear?"

"This *is* regular," Charlie said, holding up a scanty bikini panty with lace panels in the side. "I like pretty things, Mom. It's not a big deal."

"How do you expect to be taken seriously in your career when you dress like that?"

"I'm not going around in my underwear, Mom," Charlie said, rolling her eyes. "It just makes me feel good to be pretty underneath, you know? And I'll be wearing jeans and stuff the whole time. I need a little pick-me-up."

"Just don't let anyone *else* pick you up."

"They're cowboys, Mom," Charlie said. "I told you. I'm not going to fall for some dumb bronco buster."

"I didn't think I'd fall for a football jock either." Her mom sat down on the side of the bed. "But it happened. And you know what it got me."

What the football jock "got" Charlie's mother was Charlie herself. Then he moved away a year later, never to be heard from again. Charlie barely even knew what her father looked like. If she passed him on the street, she'd probably walk on by—and he'd probably run away. He'd never paid a dime in child support.

"Just don't get involved with anybody until you finish your education."

"I know."

"Because men are different. They can just walk away, even from their own child." She slipped the panty package back into the suitcase. "Men don't love like we do. Just remember that."

"Maybe they're not all like that," Charlie said. "Maybe there are a few good ones out there."

"Maybe," her mom said. "But it's not worth the risk. Not for you. Not now."

She set her hands on Charlie's shoulders and looked her daughter in the eye. Charlie looked up and offered a quick prayer for patience, then met her mother's gaze.

"What's The Plan?" her mother asked.

It was their own private catechism, and Charlie had the answers down pat.

"Get my degree."

"And after that?"

Charlie sighed. "Get meaningful work. Work that

fulfills me. Work that helps people."

"Right." Charlie's mother patted her shoulders twice and beamed at her. "Just keep your eyes on the prize, and you'll be fine."

"Okay," Charlie said.

"And keep everyone else's eyes off your underwear."

"No problem." Charlie grinned. "They're cowboys. I'm not interested, and anyway, I've heard they only have eyes for sheep."

Chapter 2

NATE EYED THE CRIPPLED CELICA AND SHOOK HIS HEAD. THE right front tire was completely flat, angling the front end into a painful twist, and the left rear wheel was perched up on a rock, accentuating the car's absurd position.

"How were you planning on getting up to the house?" he asked.

"I'm going to walk," the woman said decisively. "It can't be far."

She was unconsciously mimicking the pose of the car, with one hand fisted on a cocked hip and her torso twisted to survey the wide expanse of prairie. She was a tiny little thing, with short black hair hacked into a ragged, choppy shag. She'd rimmed her green eyes in thick black eyeliner, and her lips were painted a deep shade of crimson. Any self-respecting Mary Kay lady would faint dead away at the sight of her, but Nate thought she looked exotic, like a strangely attractive alien from Planet Jersey.

"Ranch house is ten miles that way," he said, pointing down the road. He looked down at her boots and stifled a smile, picturing her teetering across the rugged landscape in her fashion footwear. "It's getting dark. Don't you think you'd better ride?"

"I don't ride," she said. "I'll call the ranch." She tugged a cell phone out of the back pocket of her painted-on jeans. "They'll send somebody."

He watched, amused, as she flipped the phone open and stared in dismay at the "No Service" notice that lit up the screen.

"Shit," she said.

"Those don't work here," Nate said. "And besides, who's 'they'? Don't tell me Sandi made out like we had a staff or something." He swung a leg over the horse's back and eased himself to the ground.

"Okay. I won't tell you." She glanced over at the car, then flicked her eyes back to him. He followed her gaze and spotted a glossy brochure in the passenger seat. "Live the Western Dream at Latigo Ranch," it said. Dang. It had Sandi written all over it. He wondered how many more of them were out there.

Sighing, he jerked his stirrups short and looped them over the saddle horn.

"What are you doing?" she asked.

"Taking Honey's saddle off. Can I put it in your car?"

"Why? The car's stuck."

"Right. And that's why." He turned and met her eyes. "Honey'll carry us bareback, no problem."

"I told you, I don't ride," she said.

"It's up to you," he said. "Either you ride, or I leave you here and the coyotes pick your bones." He shrugged. "Your choice."

"But I can't," she said. "It's morally wrong, forcing animals to serve us. Nobody has the right to…"

"Look." He wedged one finger in front of the bit and lifted Honey's upper lip into a horsey snarl. "See those teeth? And look at those feet." As if to emphasize his point, Honey stamped one heavy hoof. "She weighs almost a thousand pounds. If she didn't want to carry me, she wouldn't." He stroked her muzzle and she nosed his ribs, snuffling at his shirt. "Honey and I have a deal. I keep her warm and fed and spend a fortune on vet bills, and once in a while she takes me somewhere."

The woman studied the horse, then turned to survey the featureless expanse of land surrounding them. "Okay," she said uncertainly.

He heaved the heavy Western saddle into the Celica's hatchback, then tossed a thick saddle blanket into the front passenger side. The blanket released a puff of white dust onto the black leather upholstery, and the brochure rose into the air and flipped out the car window. As Nate and Charlie watched, it fluttered across the landscape on a gust of wind, resting briefly against a clump of sagebrush, then continued on its random, breeze-blown journey across the plains.

"Oh, well." Nate hadn't really wanted to read what Sandi had written anyway. Swinging up onto the mare in one easy motion, he tightened the reins and backed up until Honey stood right next to the car. "Step up on the hood and I'll help you up."

Charlie looked down at her boots, then up at Nate. "I can't. The boots will scratch my car." He wondered why she cared. The car looked to be ninety percent Bondo and ten percent rust.

"Take 'em off," he said. For some reason, the phrase summoned up a picture of Charlie Banks taking off a lot more than just her boots. He gave himself a mental slap. Women were nothing but trouble—this one more than most, he was willing to bet. As far as he could tell, she was just a bad attitude in a pretty package.

He'd better keep his wayward imagination under control.

The bad attitude rested her shapely ass on the car's fender while she jimmied off the boots and tossed them into the hatch with the saddle. Rummaging around on the floor behind the driver's seat, she found a pair of sparkly flip-flops and slid into them.

"Now, up on the hood," he said. "Give me your hand."

"I don't know," she said, hoisting herself onto the car. "I don't even know you."

His lips twitched again, and this time he let them curl into a smile. "You want an introduction?" He held out his right hand. "Hi, I'm Nate Shawcross."

"Charlie Banks," she said. "Nice to meet you." She reached up for a handshake and yelped as he grabbed her right hand, tucked his other palm under her left armpit, and swept her up onto the horse's hindquarters in one smooth, practiced motion.

Honey snorted and danced sideways as Charlie flailed her legs and struggled for balance. Nate reached back to steady her and felt some soft, yielding body part give way beneath his hand. Good thing she was behind him, he thought. He could feel his face heating in a blush.

"Okay?" he asked.

"Sure." She sounded breathless, and he wondered if she was scared of horses.

Maybe she was scared of him.

He hoped so. He wasn't scared of grizzly bears, rattlesnakes, or charging bulls, but he was definitely scared of women.

"Hang on around my waist," he said.

She set one hesitant hand on each of his hips. Honey pawed a front hoof and snorted again.

"No, I mean really hang on." Nate grabbed her wrists and pulled her arms around his waist. She clasped her hands tight, her knuckles whitening. Good thing he was wearing his granddad's old rodeo buckle. If it weren't for that two- by three-inch plate of chased silver, she'd have hit the danger zone.

Honey bunched her hindquarters and gave a little hop to the right, bouncing his passenger up into the air and back down hard on her tailbone.

"Ow!" she said.

"Shhhh." Nate stayed firmly in place and patted the horse's shoulder. "It's all right," he said.

"Oh, I know," Charlie said. "I mean, I've ridden before. When I was a kid." She sighed. "Before I realized how wrong it was."

Nate glanced back at her, then returned his attention to the horse. "I figured that."

"You did?" She sounded pleased.

"Yeah. It's Honey I'm worried about."

He felt her stiffen against him. That probably wasn't what he was supposed to say, but heck, if the woman had ridden before, it must have been a birthday party pony ride. She sat the horse like it was an electric chair on death row.

"Honey's just new to all this, so try not to be nervous. She can feel it."

"Okay."

Nate murmured a few sweet nothings in Honey's ear and felt her blow out her tension in a long, slow breath. At a click of his tongue, she stepped out briskly, nodding her head in time with each step.

The woman squeezed him tighter and tensed up despite Honey's easy gait.

"Just relax," Nate said. "Relax your thighs."

He fondled the crest of Honey's mane and tried not to think about Charlie's thighs. She was squeezing the mare's flanks so hard she was liable to urge the horse into a jog, and that would probably land both of them in the dirt. With any luck, he'd land on top of her. He shut his eyes tight, banishing the image of the two of them wrestling in the dust.

"Don't worry, Honey," he murmured. "We'll take this real slow. There's nothing to be afraid of."

"I know," Charlie said. She hung on a little tighter, and he felt an involuntary flood of warmth wash over more than just his face this time.

He didn't like this woman. He wished she'd go away. But some part of him was glad she didn't mind being called Honey anymore.

Unfortunately, it was the wrong part of him, and it was harder to control than a hungry horse hell-bent for the barn.

Chapter 3

CHARLIE SHIFTED HER HANDS AWAY FROM NATE'S BELT buckle, but that left them flat against his stomach, where she could feel his muscles tensing under her fingers. To make matters worse, every move of the horse made her breasts brush against his back. Between that and the rocking motion of the horse under her pelvis, she was in serious danger of enjoying the ride a little too much.

She tried to concentrate on the horse. She could feel repressed energy pulsing in the animal's flexing muscles as if the animal was holding back, trying not to break into a run. Maybe horses didn't mind being ridden. Maybe the partnership worked out for everyone, like Nate said.

"You rode before?" he asked. He sounded doubtful.

"A long time ago. I went through one of those horse-crazy phases as a kid. Got over it, though, and it's been a while."

"Well, you're working way too hard at it. You need to relax. Just hang on to me and forget about staying on. I don't plan on falling off."

"Okay." She relaxed, shifting her pelvis forward and letting her legs dangle, but that only brought her into closer contact with Nate. When she sat up straighter, her breasts pushed into his back, so she slouched again and gave in to the pleasure of the horse's rhythmic gait.

"Good job," he said. She felt a rush of pride, then

realized he'd offered the praise in exactly the tone he'd used on Honey—except his voice lacked the silky, intimate tone he used with the horse.

"Just relax and do what feels right," he said. "That way, we'll all work together—you, me, and the horse."

Unfortunately, what felt right was her hands laced across his stomach, his back warm against her breasts, and the gentle rocking motion of the horse. She pushed her libido aside and let her mind go blank—a skill she'd perfected in late-afternoon seminars on sparkling topics like "Cognitive, Affective, and Social Aspects of Behavior" and "Qualitative Research Methods."

Once she stopped thinking about the cowboy and the horse, she could appreciate the scenery. Somehow, what had looked bleak and featureless from the front seat of her car looked completely different from the back of a horse. The late afternoon sun streaked the grass with golden highlights and cast deep blue shadows under every rock and tree. A bird started up from under the horse's feet and flew away with a high, piping call, dipping and rising in eccentric flight. The ground stretched ahead of them, broken by rills and escarpments and speckled with brown and white cattle grazing serenely on the hillsides. In the distance, a single light sparkled near the horizon.

"Is that the ranch?" she asked.

"Yup."

"It's still a long way away, isn't it?"

"A ways. You okay if we jog a little?"

With a jolt of surprise, she realized she was. She'd forgotten to worry about her riding skills, and they'd somehow improved dramatically.

"Sure," she said.

Nate clicked his tongue and Honey broke into a smooth, easy trot. Charlie tightened her grip, then caught herself and relaxed. For a minute she was off rhythm, and her pelvis punched into Nate's Wrangler butt at every downbeat. Centering herself, she took a deep breath, and suddenly they were moving in perfect harmony, the three of them merged into one graceful being.

"There," Nate said. She couldn't see his face, but she thought she heard a smile in his voice. "Now you're getting it."

"Go faster," she said, breathless.

He pressed his heels into Honey's ribs and the mare rose into a graceful lope, her long stride eating up the terrain, her hooves thumping out a rhythmic tattoo. Charlie laughed, delighted, as her hair swept back from her face.

"Feels good, doesn't it?" Nate said.

"It's wonderful." Without thinking, Charlie clutched him a little tighter in a grateful squeeze.

Nate steered Honey up to the top of a rise and pulled her to a reluctant stop. The sun hung inches above the horizon, and the sky was tinted with luminous jewel tones of aquamarine and amber.

"That's the ranch down there," he said, pointing toward the west. Beneath the golden flare of the setting sun, Charlie could barely make out a cluster of buildings nestled in a shallow valley, surrounded by a network of fences delineating various paddocks and pastures that held an assortment of cattle and horses. A row of spindly cottonwoods bordered a shallow creek that mirrored the sky's subtle colors.

"It doesn't look much like the brochure."

As a matter of fact, the place looked almost deserted, like a movie set from a B Western that had been abandoned to the elements. A few horses grazed in the surrounding pastures, but not a single human enlivened the landscape. Charlie was alone in the back of beyond with a total stranger.

She wasn't afraid, though. Partly it was because of the way he'd treated the horse, but mostly it was because she was from Jersey. The only things she was afraid of were mobsters, five o'clock traffic, and the prices at the Menlo Park Mall. A lone cowpoke was nothing compared to the dangers Jersey had to offer.

"I'm going to have to take a look at that brochure," he said. "See what Sandi promised you."

"It blew away, remember? But never mind," Charlie said. "I'm starting to think Sandi made a lot of promises she never intended to keep."

"Yeah." Nate clicked his tongue and steered Honey down the rock-strewn slope that led to the ranch. "I'm starting to think that too."

As they descended the slope at a slow walk, Nate leaned back, adjusting his posture to the angle of the horse's back. Charlie tried to parallel his stance, but with her arms around his waist, the position felt strangely intimate, as if he was lying in her arms. She was relieved when they reached the end of the slope and straightened up to head across the flat.

As they neared the weathered buildings, Charlie realized the place looked even worse from close up. The buildings in the brochure were unpainted and aged to a quaint chestnut color, like old-fashioned cabins. The actual ranch buildings were unpainted too, but the sun had leached all the life out of the warped gray siding. The only signs of life were a few chickens pecking in the barnyard and an impressively overweight dog lying a few feet away, its belly swelling like bloated roadkill. As they approached, the dog lifted its head and whuffed out a half-hearted greeting, then settled back to sleep.

Honey strolled up to the barn with no guidance from Nate and blew loudly through her nose, impatient for rest and food. The barn was by far the biggest building of the bunch, and by far the best kept. Its doors sported shiny new hardware, and it appeared to have been painted sometime in the past decade.

Reluctant as she'd been to mount the horse, Charlie was even more reluctant to dismount—especially since she couldn't figure out a graceful way to do it. She swung her right leg out and back over Honey's hind end, but the motion flung her forward against Nate and her left breast pressed into the hard muscle of his arm as she slid to the ground.

"Nice," Nate said. She wondered if he was referring to her dismount or the breast-pressing incident. He seemed like a pretty straight-laced guy, so she decided he was just being polite.

He swung down from the horse's back in one fluid motion, then flipped the reins over the horse's head. "I've got to take care of Honey," he said. Without another word or a backward glance, he turned and led the horse into the barn.

It was a good thing he couldn't see Charlie's face, because a pout wasn't her best look. She was the damsel in distress here, but she might as well be a stick of wood for all he cared. It was all about the horse.

Charlie was starting to understand why Sandi, whoever she was, had bailed out. Still, it was nice to see a man who cared more about animals than women, even if the woman was her. And it was surprising to find a guy like that under a cowboy hat.

She glanced around at the surrounding buildings, trying to distinguish the house from the chicken coop. All the structures were in similar states of disrepair, but Charlie decided chickens probably wouldn't have much use for a front porch or a chimney, and they wouldn't have lights on at this hour either. She didn't know a lot about farm animals, but she remembered roosters crowed at dawn and figured they'd want to hit the sack by sundown.

She thought the front door was locked at first, but it was just stuck, warped into place by the sun. A hard shove popped it open, revealing an old-fashioned kitchen that looked like it was stuck too—in time. The fifties, to be exact, judging from the red and white color scheme and the wallpaper, where bright red cherries burst from a black-and-white checked background.

Charlie felt something fill up her chest and give her heart a quick tug. She knew that wallpaper. One of the apartments she and her mother had shared was decorated with the same tacky stuff. Looking at it, she could almost smell her mother's baking and hear the rush of traffic outside the window. For just a second, she felt ten years old again.

Shaking off the memories, she scanned the rest of the room. Sandi had apparently left some time ago, judging from the stack of dishes teetering in the kitchen sink. A wastebasket overflowing with empty Hungry Man boxes and bent aluminum trays showed how Nate had solved his culinary issues. He was evidently partial to Roast Turkey Dinner with Stuffing.

Thanksgiving every day.

That would be a psychological study for you, Charlie thought. Could you judge a man's personality by his choice of TV dinners? The roast turkey might mean Nate longed for home and family.

More likely, it meant he got sick of Salisbury steak and was too lazy to cook. Or maybe he didn't know how. There was a distinct odor of burnt toast about the kitchen, and a peek into the refrigerator revealed the decomposing corpses of several unrecognizable entrees.

That didn't bother Charlie. As a grad student, she'd eaten her share of overcooked ramen noodles and cold Spaghettios. She just hoped Nate had some other selections in the freezer, because she didn't eat meat.

And besides, Turkey Dinner didn't come with dessert.

Chapter 4

THE UNINVITED GUEST WAS STANDING AT THE SINK STARING out the window at the last remnants of the sunset when Nate strolled inside.

"Don't bother with the dishes," he said. "I'll get to them later."

"Don't worry, I won't," she said. "I might have been born a girl, but I didn't inherit the tidy gene."

He caught the sarcasm in her tone and gave himself a mental pat on the back. Sandi always said he wouldn't recognize sarcasm if it bit him in the butt, but he'd caught it that time. Maybe Sandi was just too subtle. Maybe it wasn't his fault.

Charlie Banks sat down at the kitchen table, a chrome-and-Formica dinette set his grandmother had bought with green stamps. A glass tumbler filled with daisies and bright purple dame's rocket sat on a white doily in the center. She reached out and adjusted one of the daisies.

"We always have flowers on the table," he said. "I make sure they're always there, in case... oh, never mind." He frowned and turned away, busying himself with his boots, stamping off the muck on the doormat and wishing he could use one to kick himself in the ass. This woman didn't want to hear about his family traditions. She probably didn't want to hear about anything but dinner.

"There are TV dinners in the freezer. I could make you one."

"Got macaroni and cheese?"

He shook his head. "Nope."

"How 'bout fettuccine Alfredo?"

"Nope. Just Turkey Dinner."

"The gravy on that one's gross. Like congealed snot," she said. "Besides, I don't eat meat. Got any cereal?"

He set a box of Lucky Charms on the table, along with some milk. He glanced at the kid in the photo on the side of the milk carton and decided she didn't look any more lost than he felt. He'd hardly even looked at another woman since meeting Sandi in high school, and now he was sharing his home with an alien creature.

New Jersey? She might as well be from the moon. Hell, he didn't even know what to feed her. It was like getting some exotic pet without a chance to read up on how to take care of it.

Fortunately, the woman seemed happy enough crunching on her shamrocks and pink marshmallows while Nate nuked his frozen dinner. He sat down across from her and picked at the slabs of meat with a bent fork.

"I never thought of that before," he said. "About the gravy."

Just the sight of it turned his stomach now. He pushed his chair back. "I don't think I can eat this."

"Sorry." She spooned the last of the pink-tinted milk out of her bowl and stretched. "I'm bushed. Where am I sleeping?"

"You can have my room."

"You don't have a place for guests?"

He shook his head. "There's a bunkhouse, but it's a mess."

"No other bedrooms?"

Nate stiffened. "Just in the attic," he said. "And that's—you can't use that one."

"What's wrong with it?"

He shrugged. He didn't have to explain himself to this stranger. The attic was off-limits. That was all she needed to know.

"I'm probably not the only one who got that brochure, you know. If it got all the way to Jersey, your girlfriend must have gone nationwide. You're going to need every bedroom you've got."

"It'll be okay," he said. "I doubt anybody else will come. It's hardly deluxe accommodations."

"Yeah, but she made the place look like a luxury dude ranch. You're going to end up with a full house."

He doubted that. It would take a feat of magic to make Latigo look luxurious. Maybe Charlie's professor or whoever had sent her here just wanted to get rid of her. She seemed like she might be a little hard to get along with. Difficult.

"So if I sleep in your room, what'll you do?" she asked.

"I'll sleep on the sofa."

"I could do that," she said. "It's your place. And I'm not picky."

Maybe she wasn't so difficult after all. "No," he said. "Butt sleeps on the sofa. It's gross."

"Who sleeps there?" She looked puzzled. "Did you say Butt?"

"My dog. Sandi named her Buttercup, but that sounds stupid, so I call her Butt."

"Bet Sandi loved that." She laughed. "I don't mind dogs."

"Butt likes to roll in the cow patties," he said. "I try to catch her and hose her down, but she's wily."

"Okay," she said. "You can have the sofa."

He shrugged. "I haven't slept in the bed since Sandi left anyway. It's—big."

Charlie stretched and yawned, lifting her arms high above her head. Her top hiked up, revealing a tanned stomach accentuated by a rhinestone belly button ring. The tantalizing edge of an unidentifiable tattoo peeked out from the top of her jeans.

Nate looked away and tried to think about his great-aunt Martha. Aunt Martha was usually good at chasing pretty girls out of his head.

"I'll get your stuff out of the car in the morning," he said, faking interest in the back of the cereal box. Actually, he'd read it every morning since Sandi left. He could probably guide the leprechaun through the maze with his eyes closed, and he knew the answers to all the riddles.

"No rush." She rolled her shoulders and rubbed the back of her neck. "I've got most of what I need in my purse."

"You'll need your clothes."

"Yeah. Eventually. I always carry emergency panties, though. Just in case."

In case of what? he wondered. That got him wondering what the panties looked like, and next thing he knew, Aunt Martha had gone back to Dubuque and he was picturing Charlie in black lace and garters.

He looked at the purse dangling from the back of her chair. It was small, not much bigger than a wallet, and decorated with so many zippers and buckles that there

wasn't room for much else. The cell phone had come
out of there, and she probably had makeup with her too.

Those had to be really tiny panties.

A thong, maybe.

She saw him looking at the purse. He hoped she
couldn't read the expression on his face.

"Sorry," she said. "Too much information."

Too much? Now that she'd sparked his curiosity,
Nate was thinking it wasn't nearly enough.

Sandi might have kept the fifties-era furnishings in the
rest of the house, but she'd released her inner Miss Kitty
in the bedroom, decking it out like a Victorian bordello.
An ornate brass bed dominated the room, draped in red
velvet and mounded with pillows fringed with white fur
and feathers. A carved chest of drawers was covered
with candles, and Charlie could picture a forest of bright
flames reflected in the dresser's gilt-decorated mirror,
casting a romantic glow over the room.

Anybody would look good in that kind of light. She
remembered the feel of Nate's muscles under her hands
as they rode, the way his shoulders flexed when he lifted
the saddle from Honey's back, the glimpse of tanned
skin when his shirt rode up.

He'd look better than most.

Obviously Sandi thought so. The cowboy seemed
like a quiet kind of guy, but the bedroom appeared to
be a celebration of some pretty impressive interpersonal
skills. Either that or all the ruffles and flourishes were
compensating for something that had been lacking in
the relationship.

A stack of magazines and books occupied the night-stand, and Charlie couldn't resist checking them out. They were obviously Sandi's—fashion and style maga-zines, along with a book on makeup called *The Perfect Face*. Charlie flipped through the pages, scanning the parade of flawless features inside, then glanced up at the mirror. Too wide at the cheekbones, too sharp at the chin—her own face was far from perfect, but at least you'd never mistake her for anyone else. Certainly not any of the generic, vacant-eyed blondes in the book.

Setting it down, Charlie shimmied out of her jeans and shucked off her T-shirt, then took off her bra and slipped the T-shirt back on. Turning back the comforter, she poked her feet under the sheets, propped herself up on the pillows, and closed her eyes.

She could still feel the rocking motion of the horse, and that heightened the memory of Nate's warm back against her breasts and the feel of his muscles under her clenched hands. She could feel her body coming alive at the thought of him. It was going to be tough to fall asleep knowing he was sprawled on the sofa in the next room, probably with his shirt off. Maybe he'd get un-comfortable and unsnap the waistband of his jeans, and then... She looked over at the candles again and decided he probably didn't need to compensate for anything.

Other than the fact that he was a cowboy, of course. She didn't like cowboys.

She needed to keep that in mind.

There was a tap on the door.

"Come in," she said. She didn't bother to get up—just opened her eyes halfway.

Nate's eyes widened at the sight of her sprawled

among the pillows. The guy was obviously shy, and it was fun to watch him get all flustered. She stretched and arched her back, then gave him a come-hither smile.

Yup. She'd found his blush button.

"Toothbrush," he stammered. "In the bathroom. And towels. Clean ones."

"Okay." She patted down a yawn. "Sweet dreams."

Nate stared a moment, then shut the door. She heard his boot heels hitting the hall floor as he fled to the safety of the sofa.

Charlie drifted off into a blissful state of slumber spiced with randy dreams starring her hard-riding host. Evidently her subconscious liked cowboys just fine.

It was after midnight when the bedroom door eased open and a shaft of light fell across the bed. Charlie thought she was awake, but she wasn't sure. Maybe she was still sleeping. She could hear heavy breathing, but it could have been her own. She was pretty charged up from that ride, and the thought of having a nocturnal visitor got her amped up all over again.

Something thudded to the floor a couple times— boots?—and then a heavy weight settled on the bed beside her. She didn't think she was dreaming, but she kept her eyes closed, just in case. After all, she couldn't help it if she indulged her impulses in her sleep, right? Besides, the guy seemed really miserable. Let him cozy up for some comfort if he needed it. She'd be leaving soon, so it wouldn't matter. There was no point in staying if he wasn't doing the clinic.

A warm body cuddled up against her and heaved a

long, satisfied sigh. She made a little sleepy noise and snuggled closer.

The distinctive scent of cowflops assaulted her senses, along with the heady perfume of wet dog. She jerked her head back, then pulled her arm out from under the covers and stroked the furry hide of her unexpected guest.

"Buttercup," she said. "You slut."

The dog grinned and panted, wriggling closer.

"I know." Charlie sighed. "It takes one to know one."

Chapter 5

NATE SHOOK A FLAKE OF HAY INTO JUNIOR'S STALL AND watched the stallion paw his bedding and toss his head, ignoring the tasty alfalfa.

"I know just how you feel, buddy," Nate said. "I couldn't eat breakfast either." Not only had he lost his appetite; he'd gotten about two hours of sleep, thanks to the emergency panties that danced in and out of his restless dreams. He'd spent most of the night imagining various types of risqué lingerie that might be lurking in the depths of Charlie's purse. He could have revolutionized Victoria's Secret with the designs he dreamed up.

Junior kicked the stall and shrieked out his frustration in a long, nervous whinny. The noise would have been alarming coming from any other animal, but it was Junior's normal decibel level.

"Let's use our inside voices today, okay?" Nate said. "You're going to scare our guest."

He didn't want to turn out the mares until Junior had worked out his kinks in the round ring and was safely confined to his own paddock. The stallion didn't go out of his way to bite and kick anymore, but Nate still wasn't sure he had the kind of temperament that would justify breeding him. Right now his bad boy personality was manna to the mares, but slightly off-putting for humans.

He sure had the looks, though, and the pedigree too. If Junior could behave like a gentleman, the stud fees would go a long way toward supporting the ranch. Nate led the stallion out on a lunge line and admired his conformation as the animal bucked and kicked his way around the circular pen. Focusing his attention intently on the horse, Nate heeded him around the ring, working him until he calmed, then asked him to walk, trot, and lope until the horse forgot the mares and became docile and obedient as a circus poodle.

Nate was trying to concentrate on the horse, but the panties drifted through his consciousness again and his mind wandered into the house and through the bedroom door. Charlie was probably sleeping in, he thought, sprawled in his bed like she was last night. Or maybe she was up, taking a shower. She'd arch her back as the warm water pelted her bare skin, then step out in a wreath of steam and caress her naked body with a towel. His towel. Then she'd step into those tantalizing undergarments...

A scream from Junior brought him back to earth. The horse reared up, striking his front hooves against the high walls of the pen. Nate glanced left and right, wondering what had startled him. Everything was normal. Then he looked up and saw Charlie's tousled head peering over the top of the wall.

"Get down off of there," he barked. The pen's walls were six feet high. Charlie must have climbed up the hay bales he'd stacked against the fence, and her head probably looked to Junior like the crest of a seven-foot monster hovering above him.

Nate didn't want to yank the lead rope or bully the horse, so he eased over to the edge of the ring and picked up his lunge whip. Returning to the center of the circle, he raised the whip's long handle in the air. Junior stopped and stood quietly, breathing hard.

Then all hell broke loose. Charlie vaulted over the wall, landing hard, then dashed across the ring and threw herself at Nate. She grappled with him, struggling to wrench the whip out of his hand.

"No!" she shouted, digging her nails into his arm and grabbing for the whip. Junior screamed again in panic, galloping around the ring, his eyes rolling in fear as the whip jerked back and forth in the air.

"Take it then," Nate shouted. He let go of the whip and Charlie fell over backwards just as Junior reared again. The stallion's hooves crashed to earth inches from her head.

"Dang it! Get out!" Nate bent over and scooped her up, flinging her over his shoulder in a fireman's carry while she kicked her feet and tried to club him with the whip handle. Ignoring her thrashing, he dodged out of the pen, swung the gate shut, and dumped her on a stack of hay bales against the fence.

Tumbling onto her back, Charlie raised one knee and brought the whip handle down hard across her shin with both hands. She was trying to break it, but it just flexed and bounced away from her, landing unharmed a few feet away. She turned over, punched a clenched fist into the hay, and burst into tears.

Nate stood and watched her, his hands on his hips, waiting her out as if she was a spoiled pony. Finally, she sat up and faced him, doing her best to shoot daggers with her red, puffy eyes.

"You bastard," she said. "Horse whispering, my ass."

"What the hell is your problem?" Nate splayed his

hands. "You scared the crap out of my horse. He could have been hurt."

"By me? You're saying he could have been hurt by *me*?" Charlie clenched her fists. "You were going to whip him."

Nate shook his head and rolled his eyes.

"Don't try to deny it," she said. "I saw you raise the whip." Her eyes welled with tears. "I won't allow it. I won't let you hurt that horse. Goddamn cowboy." She wrenched a fistful of hay out of the bale she was sitting on and flung it at him. It fell harmlessly at his feet, scattering in the breeze.

Nate picked up the whip and slowly extended it toward Charlie, his eyes never leaving her face. Eye contact worked with horses; hopefully it would work with this insane, irrational woman. If he broke the gaze, there was no telling what she'd do. Attack him, probably.

"Go ahead," she said, her voice shaking. "It figures you'd whip women too. No wonder your girlfriend left you." She folded her arms across her chest. "If she actually did. You probably whipped her to death and hid the body in the attic."

He almost laughed at that idea. If anyone in his dysfunctional relationship with Sandi was whipped, it was him.

"Go ahead," Charlie said. "Do your worst."

Setting his mouth in a grim line, he lowered the whip toward her. Bringing it down slowly, he touched the tip to her thigh.

She winced, and he knew she expected him to raise the whip and lash her in earnest. Their eyes met, hers challenging, his steady and stern. He lifted the whip in

the air and held it there, his lips curling in a grim smile
that didn't alter the flinty expression in his eyes.

"That's my worst," he said. "That's it. If I touch the
horse at all. When I hold it up, they stop. When I drop
it, they go. I don't whip horses, Charlie. Nobody does,
except sociopaths. Now if you'll excuse me, I have a
frightened horse to deal with—thanks to you."

He turned and stalked back to the pen, breathing
slowly and deeply in an effort to calm his anger so Junior
wouldn't sense it. As he lifted the latch, he turned.

"Junior was abused before I got him," he said. "Your
screaming and yelling probably brought it all back for
him. So the only one hurting a horse here is you."

He eased the gate shut, resisting the urge to slam it.
Junior stood across the ring, trembling, his sides slick
with sweat. He started when Nate walked into the pen,
as if he expected to be hit, then darted his head at Nate's
arm, his lips drawn back to bite.

He hadn't bitten anybody in a month. And it would
take at least that long again to get over this setback.

Just as Nate expected, it took almost an hour to calm
the stallion to the point where he'd allow himself to be
led back to his stall. Eyes wild, the horse backed into a
corner and stayed there, ready to defend himself with
slashing hooves and nipping teeth. He wouldn't move
even when Nate shook out a flake of hay.

Nate scowled as he put the mares out to pasture
and went to work cleaning stalls. Between Sandi and
Charlie, he'd learned his lesson. He was going to keep
his life simple from now on. Simple, and female-free.

The steady work calmed him, and by the time Charlie
showed up again, he was able to be civil.

"I need a ride to my car," she said. All her bravado was gone and she hung her head, staring at the ground when she talked, avoiding his eyes. She had straw in her hair from her tumble onto the hay bales and dark smudges streaked her jeans. She reminded him of an abused horse cowering in the pen at a livestock auction.

He chased the image out of his head. Those animals were innocent. This woman deserved to be miserable after what she'd done to Junior.

"I had it towed," he said. "Ray Givens came out and got it first thing this morning. I grabbed your stuff out of it, though." He waved toward the house. "Your suitcase is in the hall."

"You what?" She stared at him as if she couldn't grasp the concept of towing a wrecked car.

"I had it towed." He took his hat off and ran his fingers through his hair. "Ray can fix it, but he's got to order parts. Your axle snapped." He settled the hat back on his head. "That little sissy car just wasn't made for these roads."

"How much is it going to cost?"

Nate shrugged.

"You didn't get an estimate?" She didn't look so whipped now. She looked mad.

"Nope. Ray won't cheat you. It costs what it costs. You want it fixed, right?"

"Of course I want it fixed." She stamped her foot, and he was almost relieved to see her acting herself again. "I need to get out of here."

"That's what I thought. So I had Ray order the parts. They should be here in about a week."

She stood motionless, staring at him with her mouth

half-open, looking like one of those goggle-eyed gold-
fish you see in the fish tanks at Wal-Mart.

"But I need to go," she said. "This was all a mistake."

"I know," he said. "I want you out of here too."

She turned away, but not before he saw the glisten of
rising tears in her eyes. He felt a brief spasm of sympathy. She was just getting what she deserved, he reminded
himself.

She still hadn't been hurt as badly as Junior.

Chapter 6

CHARLIE SWIPED AT AN END TABLE WITH A RAG, THEN PUMMELED a flaccid throw pillow to life. Removing a row of plastic horses from each windowsill, she swabbed at the grit that had seeped through the crevices. The wind seemed to have swept every loose speck of the Wyoming plains right into Nate's living room. It was a wonder there was anything left of the landscape outside.

She replaced the toy horses in their prancing rows, wondering why a grown man would collect such things. There was an old rocking horse in the corner too, with leather reins and a mane and tail of woven rope. The guy was obsessed with horses. It was odd, and kind of endearing, really. She shoved that thought out of her mind, calling up the image of him standing over her with the lunge whip.

There was nothing endearing about that.

And then there was that business with the attic. If he had an extra bedroom up there, why wouldn't he let her use it? What was he hiding? She paused at the door and tried the knob.

Locked.

Nate Shawcross didn't seem like the criminal type, but it was a little unnerving to be alone on an isolated ranch with a man who had a locked secret chamber in his house. If he'd made any effort to lure her into his bed, she'd have been worried about becoming the next victim of the Wild West version of Bluebeard—but serial killers generally make some effort to charm their victims into submission, and he hadn't so much as smiled at her all day.

She filled the kitchen sink with hot water and a squirt of soap, rattling dirty plates and silverware around and scrubbing them before stacking them haphazardly in the dishwasher. The machine was full, so she stabbed a few buttons until it whirred to life. Then she danced a quick and dirty tango with a battered O-Cedar broom, unearthing the respectable hardwood floor that was hiding under all the mud and straw the dog had dragged in.

She cursed herself silently the whole time. *Observe and report*, Sadie had said. *Maintain an objective perspective*. If Charlie had taken that advice she might have waited before reacting and saved herself a lot of embarrassment. Nate's defense of the whip rang true, so he was probably right: the only person hurting the horse had been her.

But she wouldn't apologize. Not after catching the hard glint in Nate's eyes while he stood there with the whip raised. She remembered how exposed and vulnerable she'd felt, cowering in the straw. Apologizing would give him an advantage, and she couldn't let that happen. So she'd help out. Clean his house. That ought to count for something.

The place sure as hell needed cleaning. The pile of dust and dirt from the kitchen floor looked like she'd just cleaned out a stall in the barn. The man lived like an animal. Worse, actually. If he made his horses live this way, she'd sic the wrath of PETA on him and have them hauled away.

She was scraping the last of the dirt into a dustpan when she heard the heavy tread of boots hit the porch outside. Folding her arms across her chest and setting her jaw, she leaned against the sink and waited for his reaction to her efforts.

"Hmf." Nate forced out a noncommittal grunt as he strode past her, scattering mud and straw across the clean floor. He kept his head down and his hat on, hiding his eyes under the wide brim while he prepared a rudimentary lunch. All she could see of his face was his clenched jaw, square and stubbled, set in a stony scowl.

The man ate like a farm animal too. Fisting a spoon like a toddler, he shoveled Fruit Loops and milk into himself until the last loop was scooped, then upended the bowl and slurped up the last of the sugar-laced milk. He wiped his mouth on his sleeve and glanced around the house, taking in the shining counters and the empty sink. She was prepared for a thank-you, maybe even an apology, but he just stared up at her for a moment, his pale eyes expressionless. Turning away, he walked out without a word. She watched him go with her teeth painfully clenched.

Had she ever been this angry in her life? She thought back to every bad breakup she'd ever had, every fender bender, every fight. She hadn't felt this kind of rage since Teresa Grummond stole her boyfriend in seventh grade.

"Bastard. Son-of-a-bitch bastard," she mumbled. She stormed into the bedroom and changed her pants, kicking her feet into clean jeans so angrily she tripped herself and hopped around the room like a palsied rabbit before she managed to poke her foot through the leg-hole.

She'd call Sadie. That was what she'd do. She'd call Sadie and demand a rental car. She wasn't spending an entire week of her life with Nate Shawcross. He was dangerous, for heaven's sake. He'd brandished a whip at her, right? Well, sort of. Anyway, she was going home.

Sadie picked up on the first ring. "Tate," she said.

"Get me out of here, Sadie." Charlie's resolution to act poised and professional hadn't even survived the dialing process.

"Charlie, I never would have suspected you were a bigot," Sadie said. "I am so disappointed in you."

"Bigot?"

"This problem you have with Westerners. Now just because someone isn't quite as sophisticated…"

"It has nothing to do with sophistication!" Charlie's knuckles whitened on the handset. "Sadie, there's no dude ranch here. The whole thing's a bust. The place is a broken-down dirty hole, and I need to leave."

"Charlie, I'm looking at the brochure as we speak, and…"

"I don't know where those pictures were taken, but it wasn't here. The brochure is a freaking hoax."

"Then there are no horse whisperers there?" Sadie sounded like she'd just found out there was no Santa Claus.

"There's just one guy and he's a cowboy, not a horse whisperer." Charlie explained about Sandi and the brochure.

"But there were all those recommendations from other trainers. Satisfied clients. Admiring colleagues."

"She made them up," Charlie said. "She made up the whole thing."

"No." Sadie sounded so sure of herself that Charlie felt a spasm of doubt. "Those were endorsements from top trainers, Charlie. Buck Brannaman. Clinton Anderson. And I called for confirmation."

"They were real?" Charlie's mind was racing, trying to figure out how elaborate a hoax Sandi had managed to put together.

"Definitely. They were surprised to hear Mr. Shawcross was running a clinic—he's evidently somewhat, er, antisocial—but they were unanimous in their praise. Unanimous."

Charlie didn't want to believe it, but the antisocial comment certainly rang true. "Well, he's not teaching a clinic," she said. "So however talented he is, it's not doing us any good."

Sadie sighed. "You'll need to get our deposit back," she said. "Then I guess you might as well come home."

"I don't think he has it. The deposit, I mean. I think his girlfriend took the money and ran."

Sadie cleared her throat. She always cleared her throat when she had something unpleasant to say.

"He'd better have it." Her nasal voice jumped into a higher register. "We can't afford to lose it."

"I know," Charlie said. "And I need a rental car. Mine broke down."

There was a long silence.

"Sadie?"

"Charlie, our funding is limited. We need to conserve our resources."

"It'll be a week before the car's fixed. I can't stay here for a week."

The silence again, and then the throat-clearing.

"I'm looking at my budget right here, Charlie," she said, "and I don't see a line item for 'rental car.' Besides, you can't just leave yours there."

"I'll get it back somehow. That's my problem. Listen, I'll even fly if you want. I just need to come home. Now." She took a deep breath. "This isn't a good situation you've put me in, Sadie. He definitely doesn't want me here."

"Good. We'll use that for leverage. Tell him you're not leaving until you get that deposit."

Charlie hated to bring out the heavy artillery. It didn't seem fair to Nate somehow, but she had to get Sadie to pay for a ticket. "Sadie, you don't understand. He's dangerous. He brandished a…"

The door swung open and slammed against the wall. Nate staggered inside, holding a bloody cloth to his forehead.

"Oh my God," Charlie said.

He bent over the sink and pulled the cloth away. A bloody gash on his forehead sent a rivulet of blood down his pale face.

"What?" Sadie sounded panicked. "What was that? What did he brandish? A knife? A gun? Charlie, are you all right?"

"I have to go."

"But if he's dangerous…"

"I was—I was joking, Sadie. I have to go."

"That's not funny, Charlie."

Charlie looked over at Nate. The side of his face was streaked with blood.

"I know," Charlie said. "It's not funny at all."

Chapter 7

CHARLIE HUNG UP THE PHONE AND TURNED TO NATE. "KEEP
pressure on it. I'll get some antiseptic."

She ran to the bathroom and rummaged through the
medicine cabinet. She found every substance known to
Mary Kay, but no peroxide. No Neosporin. No Band-
Aids either, but she suspected he needed more than a
strip of plastic to close that wound anyway.

"Peroxide. In the barn," Nate said. He was rocking
back and forth, his jaw clenched, still holding the rag
to his head.

She dashed out to the barn. Unlike Nate, the horses
had a full first aid kit at their disposal. Charlie carried
the whole thing inside along with a brown plastic bottle
of peroxide.

She set the bottle on the counter and reached for a
paper towel. Apparently, horses didn't use cotton balls.

"Thanks."

Nate didn't use cotton balls either. Leaning over
the sink, he grabbed the bottle and poured a stream of
peroxide into the wound, clenching his eyes shut and
grimacing as the liquid hissed and bubbled.

"Whoa." He teetered a little as Charlie pressed a
handful of paper towels to the wound. "Gotta siddown."
She took his arm and supported him as best she could
while he stumbled to the table.

He pulled the paper towel away, then dabbed at the

cut. The flow of blood was slowing. Resting his elbows
on his knees, he held his head in his hands and stared
at the floor, looking so hurt and helpless that Charlie's
heart softened a little. Maybe if she helped him they
could get along somehow.

Unless this injury was her fault.

"Was it…" She paused. "Was it Junior?"

"What?" He turned toward her, puzzled. "Oh. No.
You thought Junior kicked me? No." He tried to laugh,
then grimaced with pain. "If Junior kicked me in the
head, I'd probably be dead."

"Oh."

It wasn't fallout from the scene this morning, then.

"I pulled a hay bale down from the top of the
stack," he explained. "Forgot I'd piled some lum-
ber on top. Piece came down and clonked me in the
head." He tried to smile. "Just a stupid cowboy thing,
that's all."

Maybe the blow on the head had done him some
good. He'd actually admitted he was a stupid cowboy.
She poked around in the first aid kit and finally found
a packet of sterile gauze. Pulling his hand away, she
dabbed gently at the cut with one last paper towel and
pressed the gauze to it, adhering it with two strips of
Red Cross tape.

"Thanks," he said. "I'll be all right now."

"Do you want…"

"No."

"I could…"

"No." He glanced up at her. "Look, I appreciate the
whole Florence Nightingale thing, but you can go back
to whatever you were doing. I'm fine." He grabbed

the edge of the table and pulled himself up, wobbling slightly as he caught his balance.

"Fine." She folded her arms across her chest and set her jaw so he wouldn't see he'd hurt her. "Then I guess you're okay to talk business."

He sat back down, and she thought he might have turned a half-shade paler, going from ghost-white to almost transparent.

"I need a refund for my deposit," she continued. "I can't get home without it."

"I don't have it," he said.

Charlie sat down across from him. "You have to have it. You owe it to me."

"Sandi owes it to you."

"Well, where's Sandi, then?"

He stared down at the table. "I don't know. Somewhere in Denver. It's a big town."

"Then I'll have to get it from you. Come on, Nate. Two hundred dollars will get me out of here."

"I don't have it," he repeated. He looked up, meeting her eyes for the first time since the whip incident. "I don't have anything, Charlie. I don't know how I'm going to pay for my next load of hay, for God's sake."

"This is a class-A operation, isn't it?"

"It used to be. Well, it was going to be." Nate dropped his head again. "She emptied the bank accounts. Checking, savings—it's all gone."

Charlie shoved her chair back from the table, suppressing a twinge of pity that threatened to overwhelm her anger. "Well, I can't leave until I get my money back. And I know you don't want me here."

He didn't respond.

She turned to the sink, picking up a rag and wiping the counters. They were already clean, but she had to do something so he didn't see her crying. She was just mad, dammit. He was pissing her off. That's all it was.

A series of heavy thumps made her turn back toward the table. Nate was staggering to his feet, pulling himself off the floor with a trembling hand on the tabletop. One of his knees gave way, and he fell back into his chair.

"Holy shit," Charlie said.

"I'm okay. Slipped," Nate said, hauling himself to his feet again. "I'm fine."

"Sure you are. Nate, your pupils are huge and you can hardly stand up. You have a concussion."

"It's nothing." He took a few steps toward the door, supporting himself on the counter, then reeled back to the chair and sat down. "Things are flickering a little, though. Just around the edges."

"I'll bet," she said. "You need to go to the emergency room."

"What emergency room? The closest one's Cheyenne, and it's a fifty-minute drive."

"I'll take you."

"I can't afford it," he said. "I told you, she took everything."

Charlie gave him a long look. Maybe he'd be okay. He was starting to get some color back.

Arguing seemed to do him good.

"Okay. But you have to lie down, and you can't go to sleep," she said. "And we ought to ice that."

"What's this 'we' stuff?" he said.

"We, as in you and me. Hey, I don't like it either, but I'm all you've got."

"I'll call Ray."

"Ray's busy. He's fixing my car."

"Not yet he isn't. And somebody needs to feed the horses and check their feet. Peach needs her bandage changed too."

"Peach?"

"One of the mares."

"I can do that."

He lifted his head and looked her in the eye, his pupils dark and dilated but still managing to express his utter disdain at her horse-handling skills.

"I can," she protested. "Look, I'm good with animals. This morning—well, that wasn't me. Not really."

"Who was it then?"

She sighed. "My evil twin, the PETA activist," she said, letting a smile tip her lips. "Really, she causes so much trouble for me."

"Seems to me she causes trouble for everybody."

"Well, yeah. You might say that. It's kind of a hobby of hers. She even got me arrested once."

"Arrested?"

"Long story," Charlie said, wishing she could bite back the words. It definitely wasn't a story she wanted to tell. Not to this guy.

He looked at her a long moment, then let it go with a shrug. "Can you do me a favor, then?"

"Sure." She nodded eagerly. If he let her handle the horses, she might get a chance to make up with the stallion. Undo the damage she'd done, and prove herself in the process.

"Keep your evil twin away from me. And bring me the phone so I can call Ray."

She glowered, hands on hips. "You don't need Ray. You have me."

He rolled his eyes.

"What is your problem?"

He shrugged. "Look, I'm sorry, but Sandi was 'good with animals' too, and I wouldn't trust her with a gerbil. You have to be really focused to work with horses, and you girls always have something else on your mind."

"Like what?"

"God knows. Mary Kay, I guess. Clothes. Girlie stuff."

"I'm not Sandi, Nate. I'm not like that. And I don't know if you've noticed, but I'm not exactly a girlie girl."

Charlie stood with her feet apart, jaw jutting, fists clenched, obviously trying to look tough, but all Nate could think about when he looked at her was her panties. And her red lips. And all the other parts of her that lay across his bed last night.

She sure looked girlie to him. She'd felt pretty girlie too when she'd dressed his head wound with surprisingly gentle hands.

He shook his head, trying to shatter the image of her bending over him. Her breasts had been inches from his face, pressing into the cloth of her T-shirt, and she'd smelled sweet and clean.

"You look pretty girlie to me," he said, hoping she wouldn't notice the weird strangled quality of his voice. "I mean, look at your fingernails. You can't groom a horse with nails like that."

"I can so. I've done it before. Lots of times."

"When?" he asked.

Charlie looked up at the ceiling as if she was probing her long-term memory. She probably couldn't remember the last time she'd so much as seen a horse. "All right, it was a long time ago. I was maybe fourteen. But still…"

"You've grown your claws out since then."

"In more ways than you know," she said, tossing her head. "But I can do stable work. I don't care if I break a nail." She sat down beside him. "Come on, Nate. At least let me feed them."

He looked at her a long time. There was an element of pleading in her expression, as well as determination. The combination was a little unsettling, but he finally interpreted it as desperation and gave in.

"All right," he said. "You can feed them. Stay out of the stalls, though. There are a couple customers out there that have a bad history with humans so far. And try to calm down. They'll mirror your mood, and you're kind of… well…"

"Kind of what?" She tossed her hair, eyes flashing, obviously on the defensive.

"Kind of type A," he said. "See if you can think happy thoughts or something."

"Oh, I'll be fine," she said. "I'm happy when I'm with animals. You'll see." She shot to her feet with a speed that would send a nervous horse into conniptions. "I'll do a great job."

She'd try. He had no doubt of that. But succeed? Probably not. Sending this woman out to the barn was like sending a mouse into the elephant house at the zoo.

It wasn't likely to end well for anybody.

Chapter 8

ONCE CHARLIE LISTENED TO HIS INSTRUCTIONS AND LEFT FOR
the barn, Nate stood up. He still needed to call Ray about
that bandage for Peach. The little roan mare was half
Junior's size, but she'd cut herself up in an apparent
effort to get at the stallion. She was one feisty female—
kind of like Charlie. He took a few steps toward the
phone, then sat down again.

Things were still flickering around the edges, but at
least the throbbing in his forehead was fading a little.
Finally, he managed to make the call and drag himself to
the sofa without passing out or falling down.

He flicked on the TV. He'd just sit down for a minute—
only a minute. Then he'd go check on Charlie.

Animal Planet was on, and he didn't bother to change
the station. They were showing dog agility trials, and he
watched a sheltie vault over a fence and crawl through
a tunnel at top speed, then leap up onto a table into a
down-stay. Pretty impressive.

The dog door thwapped and Buttercup waddled in.

"Watch this, Butt," he said.

A dog barked on the show and Buttercup plopped
down and stared at the screen, watching a saluki leap in
graceful arcs through the course.

"See?" Nate said. "You could do that."

Buttercup turned and grinned, then trotted to
the sofa. Placing her front paws by Nate's feet, she

struggled to hoist her bulk up beside him, snorting with effort.

"Or not," Nate said. He patted the dog's flat head and sighed. "I guess you're past that, aren't you? You're an old lady now."

The dog grinned and panted, clearly relieved that she wouldn't be climbing ladders or jumping through hoops anytime soon.

A documentary on alpaca farming followed the agility trials, and Nate soon drifted off to Magic Panty Land.

He woke with a start when the sun dropped low in the sky and threw a patch of golden light across his closed eyes.

"Shoot." He looked out the window. Long shadows stretched across the prairie. "Why didn't you wake me up, Butt?"

Charlie, he thought. Where the hell was she? For all he knew, she'd done something stupid out there and got herself hurt. And that was the best-case scenario. The woman apparently had a criminal record, for God's sake. He stood up, tottering a little as pain stabbed into his forehead, and headed for the barn.

He heard her as soon as he cracked the barn door open. She was singing some old blues song, low and slow, in a husky, whiskey-laced alto. It was pretty, and he stopped in the doorway so she wouldn't see him and quit. He could hear the horses shifting in their stalls, munching their dinner rhythmically, soothed by the sweet, slow song. Heck, it even made his head feel better.

He eased the door shut and snuck around the corner to see what she was doing, then clapped a hand over his mouth before he could call out.

Yelling at her would only make things worse. And things were bad enough.

Charlie stood in the box stall beside Junior, working a currycomb over his bright bay coat as she sang. The open door cast a slash of sunlight across the horse's face and Junior shifted, the white of one nervous eye showing as he scanned the barn for intruders. Charlie glanced up, her singing stopping mid-note when she spotted Nate.

Junior bobbed his head and pawed the straw with a forefoot. Nate put a finger to his lips and widened his eyes, signaling her to be quiet, but she straightened up and set her fists on her hips in her typical combative stance.

"What?" she said. "We're fine."

"Step away from the horse," he said, holding his hands up in what he hoped was a calming gesture. "Move really, really slow."

"What are you, an equine security system? 'Step away from the horse,'" she repeated in a nasal, mechanical tone. She laughed. "I'm not trying to jack your stallion."

Junior tossed his head and stamped a heavy hoof.

"See?" she said. "You're making him nervous."

She turned back toward the horse, tossing her hair. It flared up in angry spikes right in the animal's face.

Junior stumbled backward. Slamming his rear into the stall door, he lifted his front feet from the straw and lashed out, one heavy hoof striking Charlie's knee. She grimaced, but she didn't fall down and she didn't yell.

"Get out of there. You need to get out," Nate said, trying to keep his tone level. "He's dangerous, Charlie."

Charlie eyed him from the far side of the stall. "He was fine until you got here," she said.

"He was fine until you got all uppity and tense," Nate retorted.

"You mean he was fine until you pissed me off."

The horse whinnied a warning and they both lowered their voices.

"Whatever. We can argue later." He had to give the woman credit. She had guts. The kick had to have hurt. Her face was pale, and tears stood in her eyes, but she wasn't about to back down.

Sandi would have passed out by now.

Junior snaked his head out; his lips pulled back from his teeth and he snapped the air inches from Charlie's shoulder.

"Oh, shit," Charlie said. She kept her voice soft and calm, making the curse sound strangely out of place. "You might have a point. But I can't get out, Nate. He's in front of the door."

The flickering around the edges of Nate's field of vision intensified, and he set one hand against the wall for support as he struggled to tamp down his emotions—anger at Charlie for being so cocky and careless, and fear that Junior would stomp her into the straw at any moment. "We're going to have to calm him down," he said. "Take some deep breaths. Think good thoughts. Try to send some his way. Maybe talk to him, or sing. He seemed to like your voice."

Charlie glanced at Nate, then flicked her eyes back to the horse. He was breathing hard, trembling slightly, and his eyes were wild.

"A green meadow," she said softly, letting her voice drop into the low tone of her singing. "Grass, waaaaving in the sunshine. Yummy grass. Mmmm."

Junior stamped a foot and shuddered.

"No fences," she murmured. "Miles and miles of hills. You can gallop up and down. Up and down." Her voice was low and slow, mesmerizing. Nate's headache was starting to ease, but Junior only snorted.

"A mare," she said. "She's beautiful." She drew out the word like it tasted good. "She has a nice round rump. A perky tail." Nate's eyes shifted down to Charlie's own perky rump as she took a step to the right. The horse shifted slightly away from the stall door. "She likes you, Junior. That mare really likes you."

Junior tilted his head to one side and blinked, swiveling his ears forward with interest. Something in Charlie's voice had struck a chord.

"Put your hands behind your back," Nate said. His tone echoed hers, gentle and slow. "You're less of a threat that way. Now don't look at him, and don't face him. Angle away from him a little bit."

Charlie did as she was told, moving a little stiffly.

"Good. You're doing great," Nate said. "Now breathe down your nose. You've seen horses greet each other? Like that."

Charlie expelled a shaky breath.

"Easy," Nate said. "Do it slow."

Charlie breathed out again, smoothly. Junior stretched his neck toward her, but slower this time, and whuffled the air in front of her face. Charlie responded, leaning toward him, her eyes half closed, black lashes brushing her pale cheeks, her lips slightly parted. She seemed totally immersed in the moment.

Nate caught his breath. They were two of a kind,

he thought. Both full of fight. In Junior's case, it came from fear.

He wondered where Charlie's combativeness came from.

She took a cautious step forward and the horse mimicked her, bridging the gap. Finally, the two of them stood face to face, sharing breath, Charlie's nose almost touching the stallion's muzzle. Her eyes were bright and Nate held his breath, praying she wouldn't speak and break the spell.

She didn't.

Nate held his breath as Junior turned his head and explored Charlie's ear with his soft, mobile lips. She backed up a step and the horse followed, fascinated by this strange being. A few more steps and his hindquarters swung away from the stall door.

"Now," Nate breathed. "Just ease over and open it real slow. Don't move too fast."

"He's okay now," Charlie said. "It's okay."

She slowly lifted her hands from behind her back and stroked the horse's neck. It wasn't a smart move, but Nate could understand it. Communicating with another species could dissolve your rational side, make you act from impulse—like an animal.

Fortunately, Junior didn't mind. He continued his exploration, working his way down Charlie's neck, mumbling her shirt collar between his lips. Charlie smiled.

Sandi would have run away screaming by now, Nate thought.

"I can finish up, I think," Charlie said. "He's okay now."

He couldn't believe it. She was looking around for the currycomb.

"No," he said. "Listen to me. Get out of the stall. Please."

"But look. He's fine." She rubbed Junior's chest and he stepped forward, hanging his big head over her shoulder and leaning into her.

"He's a big baby," she said, stroking his neck.

Nate stared at the tiny woman struggling to stand under the weight of the horse's affection.

"Okay," he said. "I give. You win. You're good with animals. If I had a gerbil, I'd give it to you. Just please, please get out of the stall. Please."

Charlie ducked out from under Junior's head and limped toward the gate, giving the horse a quick good-bye kiss on the tip of his muzzle. Nate half-expected the horse to flare up again, but Junior only blinked.

"I'm sorry," she said softly as she stepped out of the stall. "But he's hard to resist." She stepped through the gate, then turned back toward the horse. "You're just a hunka hunka burnin' love, aren't you?"

As she closed the gate, Nate's dizziness returned. It might have been the head wound, or it might have been relief at Charlie's escape. When he grabbed her shoulders as she turned toward him, he realized it might have to do with something else about Charlie. She met his eyes boldly, amused by his stern expression and still elated by her encounter with the horse.

Nate shook her slightly, his mouth working, trying to form the right words. Part of him wanted to yell at her for being so reckless. Another part wanted to praise her for her courage. And another part—the biggest one, he had to admit—wanted to wrap his arms around her and kiss her until she felt as dizzy as he did.

Charlie smiled up at him and laughed, her eyes bright with triumph. A picture of what could have happened, of her body bruised and broken in the stall, flashed through his mind and he pulled her close, squeezing her in a quick, hard hug. She squeezed back with surprising strength, and he felt her heart pounding against his chest.

"Oh, he's beautiful, Nate," she said, her breath warm on the side of his neck. "Did you see…"

He took her hand and dragged her down the alleyway, away from Junior's stall. She stumbled behind him, but she didn't resist. Once they reached the door, he turned and grabbed her shoulders, pushing her out to arm's length. "Don't ever do that again," he said, giving her a slight shake. "You knew from this morning how he could be. You could have been hurt."

"But I wasn't, was I?" Her eyes gleamed triumphantly. "Who's the horse whisperer now, cowboy?"

"There's more to it than that," Nate growled.

"Oh, that's right. I'm not a horse whisperer. I'm just a dumb girl, all clothes and makeup, right?" Charlie said. "And Junior's vicious."

"Hey, I never said you were dumb," Nate said. "It's just that you're not used to horses, and you don't know…"

"I didn't know Junior was dangerous," she said. "That's what I didn't know. And that's why I could handle him." She folded her arms. "If I'd believed that, I'd have been nervous, and I probably would have gotten hurt."

"No," Nate said. "You would have stayed away from him."

She narrowed her eyes and hardened her expression.

"You think I stay away from everything that's danger-ous? Think again."

Nate backed away. Maybe it was the woman who was dangerous.

"No wonder he's bad," she said. "And no wonder Sandi left you. They're just living up to the labels you go slapping on everything. She's girlie, and Junior's vi-cious. What's Buttercup? Stupid?"

His head was spinning, and he was pretty sure it wasn't from the concussion. "What the hell are you talking about?"

"If you label things, they're liable to perform right up to your expectations."

"I don't label things."

"You labeled me. City girl, all hair and makeup. Well, I just cleaned up your monster killer stallion for you." She tossed her head, and that crazy hair flared up again. "Label me now."

Chapter 9

CHARLIE PLANTED HER FEET SOLIDLY ON THE BARN'S WORN floorboards, daring Nate to contradict her. Her face felt warm, flushed with excitement from the encounter with the horse.

Nate stared back, meeting her eyes with his own steely glare, and suddenly she felt an electric current flow between them—a deep, primal connection not unlike what she'd felt with the horse, but with an additional component she didn't want to identify. She stepped forward, lips parted, then caught herself and looked away. It broke the bond, but the moment remained, throbbing between them like a promise.

Nate's gaze dropped from her face and swept up and down her body, assessing every detail like a wealthy buyer at a livestock auction. She felt herself come alive under his scrutiny and wondered if he was noticing her bone structure, the length of her legs, the swell of her breasts.

She gave herself a mental slap. *Cowboy*, she told herself. *Stupid cowboy*.

But wasn't that a label too?

That was different, she told herself. Sometimes you had to label things. You had to remind yourself of the facts when your impulses got the better of you. Sometimes a label was all that stood between you and sure disaster.

Because any connection between her and this cowboy was sure to end badly. They had nothing in common. Nothing. She was educated and determined to finish her degree. He obviously knew horses, and as a rancher, he was probably well versed in weather and crops and agriculture—but he was hardly dedicated to higher learning. She was sociable, loving parties and get-togethers with her girlfriends. He seemed perfectly content to commune with the horses and the sagebrush—anything that didn't require words. Sure, there had been something between them for a minute there—a visceral connection, man to woman—but you couldn't base a relationship on sexual attraction.

Sometimes it was fun to try, though.

Nate's eyes finished their exploration of her finer points and rose to meet hers. She could feel him fishing for the connection, but she closed her heart and glared.

"So what am I now?" she repeated, hands on hips.

"Hm," he said, putting a finger to his lips and squinting, pantomiming deep thought. His eyes widened when he hit the answer. "Pissed off?"

Charlie laughed in spite of herself. "You got that right."

The tension drained out of his face, and she could swear the air cooled a little as he rested his shoulder against the wall. With the gauze taped to his forehead, he looked like a hero returning from a war. "And pretty crazy about the monster killer stallion," he added. "Am I right?"

She tilted back against the wall herself, then glanced over at the tall, dark, handsome horse and smiled.

"Oh, yes," she said.

"So." He leaned forward a little, so she had to look up to meet his eyes. "Do you always like them dangerous?"

His tone was quiet, caressing, and she felt her pulse quickening. She could tame him too, she thought, just like the horse—but she shook her head and pushed that notion to the back of her mind. Looking down, she concentrated on sweeping a clear space in the dust and straw-specks with the toe of her boot.

She shrugged. "I guess I do have a thing for the bad boys," she said. It was true. She always gravitated toward difficult men. That way she could have her fun and walk away unscathed. "That's probably why I'm still—well, never mind."

His lips quirked up on one side. "Single?"

She stepped back. "I prefer 'independent.'"

"That would about cover it," he said. His voice was low, almost a growl, and she took another step back. She was starting to think he was more dangerous than the stallion.

No wonder mares were so jumpy.

"How's that knee?" he asked.

"It's okay," she said. "Throbbing a little."

"You want me to look at it?"

"No. It's fine." She had some other throbbing parts that might need some attention, though. She wiped that thought out of her mind and pasted a polite smile on her face. "So," she said. "Are you going to show me how to change that bandage?"

"No," he said, but there was a note of humor in his voice. "I've got enough trouble without getting you and Peach together."

"What do you mean?"

"She's—a lot like you."

Charlie cocked her head. So the guy already thought he knew her. "Like me how?"

"Difficult."

Maybe he did know her.

"And she's in heat," he added.

She gave him a sharp look, but he didn't seem to realize what he'd said.

"Peach can wait 'til tomorrow," he continued. "And anyway, I already called Ray. We have to leave something for him to do."

She pouted, disappointed. "But you said—you said I could have your gerbil."

He laughed. "You're impossible. And Peach is no gerbil. Besides, it's dinnertime, don't you think? How 'bout some turkey and snot? Or maybe something new. I found some macaroni and vomit in the back of the freezer."

"Mmmm," she said. "Vomit. My favorite." She grinned. "Hey, is there someplace around here I can use a cell phone? I need to call my mom."

"Up the hill behind the barn." He walked her past the stalls and swung open both halves of a Dutch door. "There's kind of a path."

He gestured toward a flat channel where the grass had been pressed down. It wound its crooked way up a gentle slope toward a twisted pine that arched over a weathered park bench. Charlie trekked up the hill, then sat down and dialed home.

"Honey?" Her mother sounded worried. "Did you make it? I thought you'd call yesterday."

"I should have." Charlie felt a stab of guilt. She'd promised to call as soon as she reached the ranch. "Sorry. I've just been so busy."

"With the cowboys?"

"No." Charlie sighed and rolled her eyes. She felt like a teenager again, defending even the slightest encounter with a boy. "Well, kind of. But not in a friendly way. There's only one, and he's a jerk."

"Well, good."

Charlie laughed. "You're the only mother I know who hopes her daughter *doesn't* find a nice guy and settle down."

"No, I hope you do," her mother said. "I just hope you don't do it *now*. Don't forget The Plan."

"No worries," Charlie said. "The guy's a jerk, the place is a dump, and I can't wait to get home."

"I thought this was some kind of fancy dude ranch."

"So did I. But the brochure exaggerated." She looked down the hill at the ramshackle barn, with its sagging roof and weather-worn paint. "It exaggerated quite a bit."

"Have you learned anything?"

Charlie thought about her encounter with Junior. "Yeah, I have, actually."

"Good. You'll be bringing back lots of information for your advisor, then?"

"I think so. I'm working on it."

"Good. That's what matters. Eyes on the prize, Charlie. Remember that."

Charlie watched as Nate stepped out of the barn, pushing a wheelbarrow full of straw. He'd taken off his shirt, and Charlie couldn't help admiring the way the sun glossed the tops of his shoulders and shadowed the muscles of his back.

"I know, Mom," she said. "Eyes on the prize."

—ᴍᴍ—

Charlie twisted a soapy sponge into a tumbler while she mooned over the view from the window over the sink. Nate had protested when she set the table with plates and silverware, but she was pretty sure he'd liked eating like a real human being for a change. There was a nice, calm vibe over dinner—a feeling of family.

Not that she knew what family felt like. She'd never really had one—just an absent father and a mother who was always working, always stressed, struggling to raise a daughter alone. Her grandparents had pretty much ignored her since they'd put up a wall of holier-than-thou disapproval between themselves and their wayward daughter. If Charlie had learned one thing from her mother, it was to go it alone. You might love your family, and they might love you back as best they could. But that didn't mean you could rely on them. It didn't mean you could trust them to be there when you needed them.

And men? Men were even worse—users and opportunists, intent on their own pleasure, their own goals. Still, it had been kind of nice, sitting across from the table from a man, eating... well, eating macaroni and vomit.

Dinner wasn't always about the food. Sometimes it was about just sitting down with somebody. Feeling connected.

But she'd feel a lot more connected if they were eating something they could actually look at without making distressing connections between the food and various unpleasant bodily functions. Maybe she could cook something.

She opened the pantry cupboard. It was neater than the rest of the house, with snacks and cereals lined up on paper-covered shelves. There were five different kinds of sugary cereal, several jars of peanut butter, a box of animal crackers, and two containers of Nestlé's Kwik. The guy ate like a kid.

Hopefully there was something nutritious in the freezer. She opened the top compartment in the ancient fridge and sorted through an assortment of packages wrapped in white butcher paper. If some animal had died to feed Nate, there was no point in wasting the sacrifice. Charlie herself would never eat meat—not ever—but she tried not to be prejudiced against carnivores. They just didn't know how animals were treated at the factory farms and slaughterhouses that provided their meat. They were uninformed.

Unenlightened.

She peeled back the paper on one packet and stared down at an angry red hunk of frozen flesh. It was obviously some part of a cow. She winced and pulled the paper back over it, reading the description slashed in magic marker across the front.

Brisket.

What the hell was a brisket, and what did you do with it? It looked like the kind of thing you saw centered on a platter, browned and surrounded by potatoes and carrots, but she had no idea how to get to that result. She shoved it back in the freezer and pulled out a slightly smaller bundle.

Another slab of meat. This one was rounder, kind of a bread-loaf shape. She pictured a cow she'd seen once at a PETA protest. Someone had spray-painted lines on

it so it looked like the diagrams you see in cookbooks—
a walking meat-cutting guide. It had been an effective
image, the living, walking beast, with its soft brown
eyes, crisscrossed with harsh black lines. The guy leading it had worn an executioner's costume, with a black
hood, and carried an axe decorated with fake blood.

She shuddered and flipped the corner of the paper
over. *Boneless Shoulder Roast*, she read.

Boneless shoulder? She'd heard they were breeding
genetically altered cows these days, but how did the
poor thing walk?

She sighed and pulled out another package.

Ground beef. She never thought she'd be so glad
to see an animal chopped up beyond recognition. This
she could deal with. She could make spaghetti—with
meatballs for Nate and whatever other students might
show up.

Because they were bound to show up. Nate seemed
confident no one would opt to stay at Latigo Ranch, but he
hadn't seen the brochure. Wherever Sandi had taken those
pictures, it had been gorgeous—rustic, yet comfortable,
with rough-hewn log furniture and open-beam ceilings.

She glanced around the kitchen, taking in the worn
linoleum floor, the scarred countertops, and the chrome
dinette set. Then she looked at the wallpaper and felt a
rush of happy, homey familiarity. The place definitely
worked for her—but the other students were in for a
very rude surprise.

———

Nate's head was pounding by the time he'd finished the
after-dinner chores. He practically staggered to the sofa,

then fell onto the cushions, letting his head loll on a pillow. Sleep. He needed sleep.

Blessed, blessed sleep.

"You can't sleep," said a voice behind him.

Nightmares already?

He turned to see Charlie standing in the doorway to the kitchen. There were times he might call the woman a nightmare, but this wasn't one of them. Her hair was smoothed down, the spikes calmed to sleek layers, and her face was freshly scrubbed. Without the red lipstick and dark eyeliner, her face looked softer, more approachable.

More kissable.

He chased that thought away. It was totally inappropriate—but he couldn't help moving his eyes down that body, lured by the pale skin of her bare legs. She was wearing only an oversized white T-shirt that barely covered those mysterious panties, and Nate was sure he could see faint round shadows where the fabric peaked over her breasts.

Damn right he couldn't sleep. Not after seeing that. He licked his lips, then pulled his gaze back up to her face, flushing guiltily.

"You have a concussion," she said. She seemed totally unaware of the fact that he'd just stripped that T-shirt off her in his mind, savoring the curves and valleys of the body underneath. Her skin would be smooth, he thought—smooth, warm and yielding.

Totally unlike her personality.

"You can nap for maybe an hour," she continued, stern as a drill sergeant with a new recruit. "But you need to wake up every once in a while. Maybe you could set an alarm."

"I'll be fine," he said, looking away. He could feel himself shifting, stirring with arousal, and he squeezed his eyes shut, calling up Aunt Martha from the depths of his subconscious. "It's nothing serious."

She plopped down on the sofa beside him and peered into his eyes. He turned away. He knew what she was looking for, and he knew she'd find it. He'd looked in the mirror earlier, and his pupils were still dilated. But he was fine. In fact, judging from the way his body was responding to the sight of Charlie in her skimpy night-clothes, he was perfectly healthy.

She reached up and took his head between her hands, turning his face toward hers. Her eyes met his with an intensity that set his pulse to pounding, and he could swear his temperature spiked a good three degrees. Maybe she was only looking for concussion symptoms, but it felt like she was looking deep inside him, search-ing his mind—maybe even his soul. He swallowed hard, wondering if she could see his thoughts: The faint outline of Aunt Martha, fading behind an ever-changing series of images. Images of Charlie, naked as she stood there in the doorway. Naked on the sofa. In his bed. In his arms. On his lap.

He needed to put something on his lap, that was for sure. Charlie didn't need to look in his eyes. All she needed to do was look down and she'd know exactly what he was thinking.

"Your pupils are still huge," she said.

She hadn't caught his thoughts then. Or noticed the growing bulge pressing at the fly of his jeans. He breathed a sigh of relief and let his eyes meet hers.

The same connection he'd felt in the barn zinged

back into being, stretching between them, pulling them together. Charlie's eyes widened in surprise. She looked away, but then her eyes flicked back to his, as if she couldn't help herself, and now he felt like he was looking into *her* soul, into *her* heart, past the brittle façade she presented to the world to a softer version of Charlie hidden behind it. The flickering lights around the edge of his vision intensified, giving her a shimmering halo, and he closed his eyes and gave in to the inexplicable force that was drawing them together.

When their lips touched, the pull intensified. It was instantaneous, thrumming like a lariat stretched taut in the moment where the roped calf balks and the horse backs, pulling the rope tight—but when he went to haul her in, deepening the kiss, she slipped the noose and pulled away.

Chapter 10

HE COULDN'T SAY HOW LONG THE KISS HAD LASTED. HAD IT been seconds? Minutes? Maybe hours? It wasn't duration that mattered; it was the intensity of it, the feeling he'd given in to a fixed, unalterable destiny that had been waiting for him all his life. The feeling was almost overwhelming—overwhelmingly *good*—but when he opened his eyes, the look on Charlie's face said otherwise. Her expression was easy to read:

Sheer, stark terror.

"Oh shit," she said.

It wasn't quite the response he'd hoped for, but it was pure Charlie. He couldn't help smiling.

"I love it when you talk dirty," he said.

"No, really." She jerked to her feet, pacing the room and swishing her hands together as if dusting flour from her palms. "That didn't happen, okay? Didn't happen." She turned to face him, narrowing her eyes, and soft, sweet Charlie was gone, replaced by the Charlie she wanted the world to see.

"It's just been too long, I guess. Or something," she said. "I just—I don't know what I was thinking."

Well, good. If she didn't know what she was thinking herself, maybe she hadn't figured out what was going through his mind either.

"But you can't sleep," she said. She was all business again, as if nothing had happened. "You can take a nap, but I'm waking you up in an hour." She grabbed the remote and powered up the television. "You can use the bed if you want to."

"I'm fine right here." No way could he sleep in the bedroom. Not after seeing her sprawled on his bed the night before. His dreams were randy enough without being fueled by that vision, and by the scent of her that no doubt lingered on the pillows.

He pulled off his boots and dropped them to the floor, then set a throw pillow in Charlie's lap and lay his head on it, bending his knees and pulling his stocking feet onto the sofa. He felt her stiffen and glanced up to see her staring down at him, her expression changing from confusion to anger to tenderness and back again. She settled on pissed off, which seemed to be her default expression.

"Get off," she said, jiggling her legs.

"This way you can wake me up easier," he said, closing his eyes. "'Night."

She might have responded, but if she did, he missed it. Exhaustion from the day's events hit him like a knockout punch. He didn't just fall asleep. It was more like he blacked out.

Charlie braced herself, staring down at the man in her lap. He looked less hard-edged and masculine in sleep—more boyish. His hair was short and lay close to his head except for a stubborn cowlick at the crown. She lifted a hand to smooth it down, then stopped herself.

No touching. Touching led to kissing, and God knew what that would lead to. Certainly not that "objective perspective" Sadie had cautioned her to maintain.

In fact, she was feeling less and less objective about Nate Shawcross. She was starting to see him as a human being—not just a cowboy. That was the problem with stereotypes—once you got to know people, those preconceptions were no defense.

And the stereotype—the "stupid cowboy" label—was all she had to protect herself from the guy. As long as she believed he was a rude, crude, steer-rasslin' ignoramus, she was safe. But so far, he'd shown compassion for the horse, courage in the face of danger, and a surprising willingness to forgive and move on despite her stupid mistake with the whip.

Maybe she should wake him up so he could do something to piss her off. He was a man, after all. He was bound to screw up somehow. She tensed her thighs, getting ready to shake him awake, but he mumbled in his sleep and creased his brow, clearly feeling the pain of his head wound even in his dreams.

Sighing, she muted the sound on the television so as not to wake her patient. He'd been watching Animal Planet. Well, they had that much in common, anyway. Nature documentaries were about all she ever watched.

She settled down to watch one on Japanese snow monkeys. The monkeys were adorable, frolicking in a hot spring, playing in the snow, grooming each other…

She felt her eyes drifting shut and blinked herself awake. No sleeping. She had to stay alert so she could wake Nate up in an hour. She didn't know what happened if you slept too long with a concussion, but she remembered some vague warning. She rubbed her eyes and tried to concentrate on the monkeys. They were showing a mother and baby now, the baby snuggled in its mother's arms, warm and safe and sleepy… sleepy…

She flicked the channel to a UFC fight on the Spike network where some neckless behemoth was making mincemeat of a guy covered in tattoos. Who could sleep through that?

She could, apparently. Her eyes just wouldn't stay open.

What she needed was some caffeine. A Coke.

She put both hands under the pillow and gently lifted Nate's head. He mumbled a sleepy protest and she froze, then scooted out from under him when he subsided back into sleep. Sliding a second pillow beneath the first to prop his head up, she padded out to the kitchen for a can of Coke from the fridge.

Perching on the edge of the sofa, she sipped her soda and watched the rest of the fight. Next came a series of commercials for beer, pheromone-laced deodorant, condoms, and energy drinks. The kind of guys who watched the Spike network probably used all four products at once.

The next fight was between two short, stumpy men who tumbled to the mat and stayed there, flailing around on the floor in an effort to grapple each other into submission like two spiders fighting in a jar.

Boring. Her eyes drifted shut, and this time, she was too sleepy to stop herself.

The birds were just beginning to greet the morning when Nate awoke. The house was quiet, the only sound his own breathing and Butt's, their sighs alternating in gentle counterpoint. He smiled, feeling the warm body snuggled against him. Butt had to be the homeliest mutt God ever made, and possibly the most useless, but she was his partner, for better or for worse. He reached down to stroke her coarse fur.

But it wasn't coarse. It wasn't even fur.

It wasn't Butt.

He propped himself up on one elbow and opened his eyes. Charlie lay spooned against him, her body curled close to his. She was sleeping, her face gentle in repose, the perfect lips slightly parted, the dark hair tousled into freeform disarray.

His hand hovered above her hip. He hadn't meant to touch her. He'd thought he was petting the dog. But now that he realized what he'd done, he wanted to do it again.

Slowly, he lowered his hand and traced the tuck of her waist, the swell of her hip. He drew back when she shifted her weight and let out a tiny moan—or maybe it was more of a purr. She settled back into sleep and he stroked her again, savoring the graceful curve of her body.

He shouldn't be doing this. She wouldn't let him touch her if she was awake.

Would she?

She'd let him kiss her. More than that—she'd kissed him back, giving him a taste of a need that matched his own before she'd caught herself and pulled away.

He stroked a lock of hair away from her face, tucking it behind her ear, then stroked his fingers through the thick dark strands at the nape of her neck.

Oh, no. This was so wrong. He savored the feel of her hair running through his fingers one last time, then clutched the armrest to avoid temptation. Lifting his other hand from her hip, he clenched it on his own thigh and looked down at her, stretched across his couch, so quiet, so peaceful.

Watching her sleep was almost as good as touching her.

———

Charlie rolled onto her back and opened her eyes.

Nate.

Uh-oh. He was staring at her.

She squeezed her eyes shut, then opened them again.

Still Nate. But now he was watching a documentary on penguins as if he was thinking of breeding the damn things.

Too late. She'd seen how he was looking at her: softly, gently, but most of all, intently, as if he was memorizing her features. It was a look as intimate as a touch—and just as unsettling.

He might as well have kissed her again.

She jerked upright and bounced off the sofa as if the cushions had suddenly burst into flames, then glanced around the room in search of an excuse for her sudden flight.

"Uh—hungry," she said.

Nate kept his eyes on the screen but the corner of his mouth tipped up, the same way it had when he first saw her at her car, stomping around in a temper tantrum in those ridiculous cowgirl clothes.

"For food," she blurted out. "Breakfast." She practically ran for the kitchen.

Ten minutes later, she was standing at the sink scooping the last spoonful of cereal out of a plastic Pebbles and Bam-Bam bowl she'd found in the cupboard. Lifting it to her face, she tipped the bowl up and slurped the milk from the bottom. Let him look at her now. This was the real Charlie. This one.

Not the one he'd seen on his sofa just now.

Judging from the look he'd given her, she must have relaxed in her sleep. She'd probably had her mouth open, maybe even snored a little. And for some reason, that had charmed him—probably because she looked totally, utterly defenseless. He'd caught her with her guard down, and now he thought he knew the real Charlie.

She never should have let him catch her like that.

She looked down at her distorted reflection in the steel faucet and narrowed her lips into a thin line. The curved steel emphasized her jutting jaw, making her look like a cartoon thug. Now *that* was the real Charlie.

She heard a rustle behind her and turned to see Nate standing in the doorway. How long had he been there? Had he seen her slurping up her breakfast, rivaling Butt for sheer piggishness?

She hoped so.

He strode into the room, making a beeline for the fridge. Swinging it open, he grabbed the milk carton and upended it, tilting back his head and downing what was left in three long swallows. She watched his throat convulse, once, twice, three times.

Setting the empty carton on the counter, he wiped his mouth on his forearm and grinned, his eyes teasing.

"Cretin," she said, struggling to keep a straight face. "Try using a glass next time."

"Yeah," he said, still grinning. "And why don't you just lick that cereal bowl while you're at it? You've got worse table manners than Butt."

He gave her arm a gentle punch and swung out the front door, heading out to the barn.

Charlie was smiling in spite of herself as she turned to the window and watched him go, the long vista of sage-strewn prairie dwarfing his departing figure in spite of his confident cowboy swagger. It was amazing how he transformed the minute he stepped out of the house. Inside, he seemed a little lost, clumsy, out of place. Outside, he was in his element.

He disappeared into the barn and she scanned the ranchland spreading out around the outbuildings, admiring the way the sage receded into a misty blue-green blur toward the horizon. It was so quiet out here, so serene. So empty, except for—what was that?

A dust cloud appeared in the distance, moving steadily closer. Charlie squinted and leaned toward the window. It had to be a vehicle. Someone was coming. Ray? Or a new student? With her luck, it would be another cowboy to join forces with Nate. She'd be surrounded by them. And men in packs were always exponentially more annoying than individuals.

As she watched, the wind swept the dust away, parting it like a stage curtain to reveal a mud-caked white Ford pickup bouncing up the drive. It sure looked like a cowboy truck. Sighing, Charlie wiped her hands on a ragged dish towel and stepped out onto the porch as the truck lurched to a stop and its lone occupant slid down from the driver's seat.

It wasn't a cowboy. It was a woman. Her pouf of gray hair, dry and fine as cotton candy, fluttered in the wind as she strode up to Charlie and offered a ringless, calloused hand. Her arms were tanned and sinewy, the muscles ropy from hard work, and there wasn't an extra ounce of flesh on her anywhere. She was skinny as a soup chicken, with sharp, bird-like eyes behind her wire-rimmed glasses.

"You Sandi?" she asked. Her voice cracked on the upturn of the question. She sounded like a boy hitting puberty.

"No." Charlie took the proffered hand and had her own crushed in a steel-hard grip. "I'm Charlie Banks," she said through teeth gritted in pain.

"Doris." The woman grinned and released her grip. "Doris Pedersen. Rocky Head Ranch." She looked Charlie up and down. "Danged if you don't look like a city girl, honey. No offense."

"None taken," Charlie said. "I am a city girl. A grad student at Rutgers."

Doris looked left and right, then peered over Charlie's shoulder toward the house.

"Nice to meetcha," she said. "But hey, this place looks like a dump. And where's the staff? I'm looking forward to getting some cowboy time here." She winked. "I put my luggage toward the front of the compartment so they'll put on a show gettin' to it."

Charlie furrowed her brow. "A show?"

Doris cocked her hips and grinned. "They'll have to bend over and scrabble around a while to reach it. I like those Wrangler butts, don't you?"

Charlie thought of Nate's neat, compact backside and grinned. "Well, yeah," she said. "But I'm afraid there's not much of a staff here."

She explained how Sandi had sent out the brochures, collected the deposits, and left. Doris chuckled.

"That's one way to get a man moving," she said. "So

are we out of luck here, or is he gonna live up to the hype?"
She pulled a Latigo Ranch brochure out of her back pocket
and held it up, glancing from the glossy photos of rustic
ranch buildings to the sorry shacks that surrounded them.

"If he's as much of a disappointment as the ranch,
he'd have to be one ugly son of a buffalo," she said.

"No, he's—he's not ugly," Charlie said.

Doris narrowed her eyes, a teasing grin plumping
her cheeks.

"You think he's cute," she said.

Charlie swallowed hard, hoping she could somehow
choke back the blush she felt rising to her own cheeks.

"Only looks-wise," she said, trying to sound casual.
"That Wrangler butt seems to have taken over his entire
personality."

"Just a big ass, huh?"

Charlie shrugged. "Sometimes."

"So where is he?"

Charlie gestured toward the barn, her mouth tightening.

"He's out there, taking care of the morning chores,
I guess. He hurt himself, so I offered to help, but he
doesn't seem to think a woman can handle anything
more challenging than a broom and dustpan."

"I'd say that girlfriend of his handled his money and
his ranch for him, wouldn't you? Left him in a world-class
mess." Doris glanced around at the ramshackle buildings.
"I'm thinking maybe I ought to just head home."

Charlie felt a surge of panic. She had to get Doris to
stay. Nate needed the money.

"It'll be okay," she said. "I've planned dinner, and
there's a bunkhouse we can fix up just fine, if you don't
mind a little rustic atmosphere."

We? What was this *we* stuff? And why did she care if Nate needed money? For some bizarre reason she'd just allied herself with a cowboy.

What was she thinking?

She knew the answer to that. She was thinking the same thing she'd been thinking ever since she'd woken up. Her mind kept drifting back to the morning, remembering the warmth of Nate's hand on her hip, the tender look she'd caught in his eyes before he'd realized she was awake. What would it be like to wake up to that look every morning? To know, first thing every day, that somebody…

No. There was nothing behind that look. They'd both been half asleep. He was probably just trying to figure out who the hell she was.

And if she was going to start making the situation into something more, she'd better get out of here and head home—the sooner, the better. She had The Plan, after all, and hooking up with a cowboy was definitely not on the agenda. In fact, hooking up with anybody was a bad idea. The course of her relationships was always a rocky road—one that generally led both parties off a cliff. That was okay when the guy deserved a long fall with a hard landing, but Nate seemed like a good guy.

Maybe Doris would pay the rest of her portion in cash, and Charlie could get her deposit back and skedaddle back to Jersey before she made some stupid mistake and hurt somebody.

"Rustic's fine," Doris said, interrupting Charlie's reverie. "That's the way I like it. But I'm not just here for dinner and digs. Can the guy handle horses? Or did I waste my money?"

"He's good, I think," Charlie mused. "Really, I wouldn't know. I'm a psych student, not a cowgirl. I'm here to study inter-species nonverbal communication."

Doris chuckled. "That's the fanciest way to say horse handling I ever heard," she said. "But it's good we've got a trained professional on the premises. With all his troubles, it sounds like Mr. Broke-heart's going to need a lot of counseling."

Charlie laughed. "I'm not really a psychologist yet, though," she protested. "I'm just studying—"

"I know," Doris interrupted. "Nonverbal communication. That's probably exactly the kind of counseling our lonesome cowpoke needs."

Charlie looked down at the ground, suddenly shy. The verbal contact she'd had with Nate had mostly consisted of arguing, but the nonverbal moments they'd shared had been infinitely more successful—if having your insides turned into a throbbing mass of warm, gooey pudding was any gauge of success.

Doris put a motherly arm around Charlie's shoulder.

"So that's how it is," she said. "I thought so. We're not just going to be training horses here." She gave Charlie's shoulder a squeeze. "We're going to be doing some cowboy whispering, too."

Chapter 11

NATE STEPPED OUT OF THE DIMLY LIT BARN AND BLINKED IN the sunlight. His eyes didn't seem to be adjusting to the bright light like they should, so he could barely see the outline of a big white truck, with Charlie and someone else standing beside it. Maybe another one of Sandi's so-called customers had turned up. Either that, or Charlie had gotten somebody to pick her up and get her out of here.

Both possibilities gave him a sinking feeling in his gut.

"Nate." Charlie trotted toward him, that crazy hair flaring out, then settling, over and over like a candle in a stiff breeze. It made him want to reach out and muss it up. 'Course, she'd probably hit him if he did. For some reason, that realization made him smile.

"You've got company," she announced.

She grabbed his arm and towed him toward a little old lady who had parked one foot on the running board of a customized F-450 Super Duty that looked like it could take on anything the West could dish out. The bumpers were cast steel, the headlights and side windows were protected with metal grills, and half of Wyoming seemed to be spattered over the sides and rear window.

It was some truck. Almost hot enough to distract him from the warmth of Charlie's hand on his arm.

Almost, but not quite.

"Doris Pedersen." The lady stepped up to him, hand extended. Nate took it, and she squeezed his hand so hard he thought she'd break it. She wasn't very big, but she had a grip like a WWE wrestler.

"From Rocky Head Ranch," she said, pumping his hand up and down. "I'm here for your clinic. Hope you don't mind I came a day early, so I can rest these old bones. That Ford's been bouncing my butt for six hours, and I feel like I just got off a shit-kickin' bronc." She put a hand on her back and grimaced. "So what's the schedule?"

"I, uh, yeah." He sounded like a real smooth operator, he was sure. "We'll start tomorrow, I think."

"You think?" The lady's eyebrows were so light you could hardly tell when she raised them, except her eyes got bigger and her forehead wrinkled up even more than usual.

"I mean, yeah. Tomorrow."

"What's the agenda for the first day?"

"The agenda?" Nate could feel his own forehead wrinkling up. He couldn't widen his eyes, though. The light hurt too much. Charlie had definitely been right about the concussion.

"I chose Package B," Doris said.

Nate just stared at her. He had no idea what she was talking about. Sandi had offered packages? Heck, she'd never wanted much to do with his package. Not near enough, anyway.

"The three-week deal," Doris said.

Three weeks! What was he going to do with a stranger around the place for three weeks? He remembered the brochure on Charlie's front passenger seat. He should have taken a look at it before the wind took it. Figured out what he was in for. Now it was gone and he was flying blind. He had half a mind to saddle up Honey and set off in search of it. If he couldn't find it, he could just keep going. Maybe ride off a cliff or something.

"You know," she went on. "The 'Green Horse, Green Rider' program. I spend a lot of time on horseback, but I never got to start from scratch like that."

"I picked that one too," Charlie said. Her eyes slid over toward Nate, and he breathed a sigh of relief. She was going to help him out.

"That's the one where we break a mustang to ride," she said. She winced. "Not 'break' it. Gentle it, right?"

Nate nodded, squelching a sudden rush of excitement. The Bureau of Land Management held mustang sales a couple times a month. He'd been cleared as a registered bidder, but Sandi would never let him buy. Said the wild horses were too dangerous.

Now he'd have to. She must have figured out he'd run the customers off the property before he'd let strangers handle his own horses.

"Right. Package B." He hitched up his belt and stood a little straighter so they wouldn't know he'd only just come up with a plan. He was pretty sure there'd be a sale on Saturday, maybe as close as Wheatland or Riverton. He could teach the students about conformation and temperament for the next day or two, then have them put the knowledge to work selecting a mustang at the sale.

It would actually be a great experience for them. For the first time, the clinic idea seemed like it might work.

"So where's the bunkhouse?" Doris looked right and left, taking in the tipsy shacks behind the house.

Nate felt his throat tighten up.

"There," he managed to say, gesturing toward the dilapidated disaster that had once been a bunkhouse. "I—I'll need to do some fixing up, though. It's not quite ready." He flailed an arm toward the house, wondering how the hell he was going to make that abandoned shed into living quarters for anything more civilized than a homeless field mouse. "You're welcome to come into the house while you wait."

"Well, I'd like to get my luggage unloaded," Doris said. "Can you get me that one out of the back of the truck, at least? It's got most of what I need to pretty up."

He wondered if the bag held a full array of plastic surgeon's tools and a Hollywood prosthetics kit. It would take all that and more to pretty Doris up.

Ouch. That wasn't nice. Nate would have smacked himself upside the head for being so mean if he hadn't been hurting so much already. The woman couldn't help the body God put her in. And she seemed nice enough. Kind of demanding, a no-nonsense sort of person, but nice.

"I'll be glad to get that for you, ma'am," he said, tipping his hat. Maybe a dose of cowboy etiquette would help distract her from the condition of the ranch. After all, she was getting an authentic Western experience here. The place Sandi had shown in the brochure was one of those phony dude ranches, but Latigo was the real thing—a working ranch. Falling down all around them, but still working.

Doris popped the pickup's tailgate, and Nate reached in for the bag. It was pretty far toward the front, so his fingers barely brushed it and he wound up pushing it farther away.

"Sorry." He grunted and leaned farther into the truck, but he still couldn't reach the bag. Charlie made a choking sound, and he turned around to see her covering her mouth with her hand. Her face was red as a side of beef.

"You okay?"

"Sure." Her voice sounded kind of strangled. "Just—just inhaled some dust."

Now Doris was coughing too. Must have been something in the air. Nate wriggled out of the truck and patted Charlie on the back. He tried not to smack her too hard, but her eyes got all teary and she bent over double.

"Sorry," he said. He patted her more gently, and she seemed to get over whatever it was that got her going. Doris too.

Man, his head was pounding. He closed his eyes tight and squeezed his temples, trying to force himself back to normal so he could go after the luggage again. When he opened his eyes, Charlie was hopping up on the tailgate and scrambling into the truck, scuttling to the front on all fours. He couldn't help noticing how lithe and strong she was, and how her jeans stretched tight over her butt as she made her way to the suitcase.

Junior's dream mare wasn't the only one with a perky tail.

"Thanks," he muttered as she handed him the suitcase. He put a hand to his head, wishing the throbbing would go away. He was perfectly capable of unloading the truck himself if he could just get the laser light show in his head to shut down.

"You okay, son?" Doris asked.

He nodded. "Fine. Hit my head earlier. But it's getting better."

"Well, I'm sorry to cause so much trouble," she said. "I'll just go inside, if that's okay."

"Sure," he said. "Fine."

Doris trotted up the front steps, toting the heavy suitcase in one hand like it was Charlie's dinky little purse. She stopped and turned at the door.

"So what's for dinner?" she asked.

Nate froze, wondering what the heck he was going to do about feeding her. He rummaged through his freezer in his mind, trying to remember what was in there. There was a brisket, he was pretty sure, and a shoulder roast, but he had no idea how to cook either one.

"Turkey dinner," he finally said. "It's real good."

Chapter 12

"TURKEY DINNER?" DORIS MADE A FACE. "WHAT, LIKE Stouffer's or something?"

His mind scrambled. She was on to him. When Charlie put the frozen food on plates the night before, it had looked almost like homemade. He'd thought maybe he could get away with it again, but Doris was too sharp for that.

He did a quick mental inventory of the pantry.

"Spaghetti then," he said. He could do that. Just boil the pasta, he was pretty sure, and then heat up a can of sauce and dump it on top.

"Oh, yum," Doris said. "I love spaghetti—'specially when it's seasoned right."

Seasoned? You had to season it? With what? He watched Doris stride into the house, slamming the screen door behind her.

"Guess I'd better get to work on that bunkhouse," he said. He shifted his eyes toward Charlie. "Gee, I'm not sure where to start."

"Go get a broom and dustpan," Charlie said. "I'll dust."

He could have fallen at her feet and kissed those ridiculous high-fashion cowboy boots in gratitude. She was going to help.

"And get some linens," she continued. "Sheets, and all the pillows you can find. I'll try to add some girlie touches, make it pretty. You'll see. It'll be fine."

Pretty? Hell, he was just hoping they could get the bugs out. His head was spinning again. "It's awful in there," he said. "Nobody's slept there in years. The mattresses…"

"Take them out and beat them with a broom," she said. "And open the windows. Let some air in." She glanced toward the house and her expression grew crafty. "Maybe you've got some stuff up in the attic we could use. You want me to check?"

"No," Nate said. He wished she'd get her mind off the attic. He didn't want anybody poking around up there, touching stuff, moving it around. Sometimes he liked to go up there and just sit, remembering. Hoping.

It was none of her business.

"Okay. Just linens then," Charlie said.

Nate turned toward the bunkhouse, humbled by his helplessness. He and Sandi had gotten together right out of high school, and she'd always said he just got in the way in the kitchen. He could barely cook for himself, let alone a bunch of strangers.

"One more thing," Charlie said.

She was standing with her fists on her cocked hips, her head tilted to one side. Uh-oh. Nate swallowed. "Sure," he said.

"I'll help you for a day or two," she said. "We can make this work. Make sure Doris is a satisfied customer, along with whoever else shows up. I'm willing to do all I can to get you started."

"Great," Nate said, honestly grateful. "Thank you so…"

"But you need to get the rest of her payment right away," she interrupted. "Then you can refund my deposit, and I can get out of here."

Nate nodded, but the motion set his head to hurting

and his ears started to ring. Next thing he knew, a dizzy spell hit him so hard he almost collapsed in the dirt. Must be the concussion.

That, or the realization that he was on his own, playing host to God-knew-how-many aspiring cowboys and cowgirls. How was he going to feed and clean for a bunch of strangers when he could barely take care of Butt?

He shook his head, and the ringing intensified. Closing his eyes, he pressed the heels of his hands into the sockets, struggling to get the pulsing lights under control. When he opened his eyes again, there were two Charlies staring at him.

He stumbled to the steps and sat down hard. His forearms rested on his knees, and he hung his head low, staring at the toes of his boots.

Charlie sat down beside him and heaved a heavy sigh. "Oh, geez," she said. "You're in bad shape, aren't you?"

He nodded.

"Do you want me to stay?"

A thick, strained silence stretched between them while he struggled to answer. Of course he wanted her to stay. Hell, he wanted her, period. He wanted to reach up right now and pull her close, rerun that kiss on the sofa one more time, just to make sure he got it right. But all he could do was sit there, staring at the ground.

"Dammit," she said. "Don't cowboys ever talk?"

Truth was, no, they didn't—not this one, anyway. That was probably why he was so comfortable with horses. Horses communicated all the important stuff with looks and gestures. Body language.

Touch.

That he could handle. He could *show* Charlie he

wanted her to stay. He could take her in his arms and kiss her with all the desperation he felt when he realized she could just take off down the driveway, head back to New Jersey. Or he could just look her in the eye, communicating his need that way. Twice now that had worked, forging a connection that bound them stronger than words ever could.

Heck, why did she need him to talk, anyway? Couldn't she see just from the way he was sitting there, shoulders slumped, staring at the ground, that he was beat? That he needed help?

But women liked words.

He looked up at her. Talking was hard enough when it was just about the weather, or crops. Asking a woman to come to his rescue was about as bad as it got. In his world, men were self-sufficient. They didn't ask for help unless they were desperate.

Nate reviewed his situation in his mind.

Yup. He was desperate.

"Yes," he said, finally. "Please." His voice sounded tight and strangled, so he cleared his throat and tried again. "Please stay."

"Okay," she said, her posture relaxing. "I guess that's about all I can hope for. Cowboy eloquence, right? But we need to set some ground rules."

He nodded, swallowing.

"First of all, no kissing," she said. "No touching either. And no looking at me like you're thinking about me naked."

Shoot. She'd noticed that after all.

"You are *so* not my type," she said, drawing her brows low over her eyes. "And I'm going back to Jersey when this thing is over. So we might as well stop the shenanigans right now."

Shenanigans? Was that what they called it in New Jersey?

He'd have to remember that.

"And I'm not staying for you," she continued. "I'm staying because I want to learn horse training, and I guess I'll let you teach it to me."

She took a deep breath, like she was going to make some kind of confession.

"And besides," she said. Then she muttered something he couldn't quite hear.

"What?" he asked.

"I think I'm in love," she mumbled.

Danged if he could figure out how to react to that. A minute ago she'd said he wasn't her type; now she was saying she loved him. He'd always had a strange effect on the ladies, but this was the weirdest yet. He hadn't done a thing right with Charlie—well, except maybe that kiss—and here she was already in love with him.

He was going to have to dial down the charm—if he could just figure out what he'd done that was so darned attractive.

She saw his stricken face and laughed.

"Not with you. With Junior." She shoved his shoulder, joshing him like a kid sister. "I told you, you're not my type. I mean, you're a cowboy, for God's sake. But I liked what happened with that horse. I want to do it again. I think I might like to work with horses more—see if Sadie will let me write this paper, maybe even present it at the conference. I always wanted to work with animals, and I think this might be my ticket."

She pulled a blade of grass out of the lawn at their feet.

"I think the things you know about horses—about communicating with them—could help people learn to communicate better with each other."

She looked over at him and gave a little snort of laughter. It sounded a lot like her coughing.

"Not that it's doing you any good," she said. "I mean, if you'd paid half as much attention to Sandi's moods as you do to your horses', I bet she'd still be here."

Nate thought about that, then shook his head.

"Sandi didn't like this life," he said. "She didn't like the ranch, the dirt, or the critters. She never would have been happy."

"I don't necessarily like those things either," Charlie said. "But if I had a man who loved me and treated me right, I think I'd be happy most anywhere."

She stood up and stretched, lifting her arms high above her head, totally unconscious of the way the setting sun outlined her silhouette in amber and peach. With her spiky hair and lithe figure, she looked like a heroine from a Japanese cartoon.

One of the sexy ones.

She looked down and caught him staring. His jaw was hanging open, and he probably looked like a lovesick hound dog.

"Of course, it would have to be the right man," she said. She spun on her toes and trotted past him up the porch steps. "No cowboys, that's for sure."

Chapter 13

THE BUNKHOUSE HAD BEEN UNOCCUPIED FOR DECADES, unless you counted the dust bunnies that patrolled the floor beneath the iron-framed beds. Charlie was now liberating said bunnies from the confines of the bunkhouse in droves. They leapt to freedom as she wielded the broom like a weapon, creating a wide fan of dust that spread from the open door.

She hummed a line or two of "Born Free," then set to work on the flimsy blue-ticked mattresses, dragging them out the door and draping them over the split rail hitching post by the door. Clutching the broom handle like a Louisville Slugger, she whacked half a dozen home runs into each one, venting her frustration.

Doris had snagged Nate the minute he returned to the house for supplies, and now he was out there playing host, showing the woman around the ranch like the lord of the manor. Charlie glanced over at the paddock, where the two of them stood side by side, each with one booted foot on the bottom rung, watching two of Nate's mares munch the evening ration of hay.

She cursed under her breath. It was nice to see Doris getting her "cowboy time," but Charlie had offered to help the guy, not be his slave. Giving the last mattress a final wallop, she dragged it inside and pitched it onto one of the old iron bed frames, then tossed herself on top.

She looked around the room, a cavernous space with rough paneled walls and an open-beam ceiling. Even in the half-light from the grimy windows, she could see silver-white cobwebs festooning the beams, with swaddled fly mummies dangling from them like ghoulish Christmas ornaments. Sighing, she lurched to her feet and grabbed the broom. If she was stuck here, she might as well make it livable.

Two hundred cobwebs and half a bottle of Windex later, the place was starting to look habitable. She set her fists on her hips and looked around.

Not bad.

Now for the girlie touches.

She opened a rickety old cabinet that leaned up against the wall in one corner and found a cache of mason jars—picturesque old blue ones with bubbles in the glass. She gathered up a half-dozen of them and carried them out to the yard.

Halfway between the barn and the house, a rusty spigot arched from a crooked pipe that jutted out of a concrete block. Charlie cranked the knob and water splashed out over the cement onto the grass. Humming to herself, she rinsed the jars, then filled each one with water.

Half an hour later the jars decorated the bunkhouse's rough wooden windowsills and crude nightstands, each one filled with a bouquet of asters and daisies gathered behind the barn. They added a homey touch, and the flowers coordinated with the faded blue and white coverlets Nate had brought before he'd taken off to play tour guide.

Charlie puttered around a while longer, rearranging,

perfecting. She folded the coverlets back in neat trian-
gles, making the beds look uniformly welcoming, and
fooled with the flowers, touching up the arrangements.
She couldn't wait for Nate to see what she'd done with
the place. She couldn't wait to…

Uh-oh.

She backed away from the windowsill, lifting her
hands in the air like a hold-up victim. *Step away from
the flowers*, she told herself. *Step away.*

She was nesting, settling in, subconsciously making
herself at home, like a dog turning in circles before lying
down. It was her biological clock going off, she was
sure. After four years of college and two of grad school,
something inside her wanted to settle down. It also
wanted to find a man, have babies, and shop at Dress
Barn. Fortunately, she had her mother as an antidote,
along with her own good sense.

She clasped her hands in front of her and resisted the
impulse to move a daisy just a hair to the right. There
would be no more nesting.

No more kissing either, or touching. The whole incident on the sofa came back to her in a rush of memory
and she shoved it into the back of her brain. No more
pressing her body against his, feeling her breasts yield
to the solid muscle of his chest. No more breathing in
the scent of him, clean straw and fresh grass, with that
subtle hint of leather and sage. No more fantasies about
what it might be like to share his bed, to light those
candles on the dresser and strip off her clothes while he
watched, his pale gray eyes sweeping down her body
like his slow hand stroking her skin.

If she let that happen again, she'd lose herself—lose

her purpose. She was supposed to be a dispassionate observer, a student of human and animal behavior. *Observe and report*. That was her job. *Eschew personal involvement*. If she didn't stop this nonsense, she'd end up like her mother, sacrificing her dreams and aspirations for a man who could walk away any time he pleased without a backward glance.

It was a damn shame. Usually, a little casual sex would be a good thing—and with Nate, she had a feeling it would be a whole lot better than good. But there was something about the guy that made her wary. He made her feel something more than the zing of sexual attraction—something deeper. And she was definitely staying in the shallow end when it came to relationships.

Footsteps hit the floor behind her, and she turned to see the cowboy in question stepping through the door.

"Hey, this is amazing," he said. "It looks great. Need any help?"

"No," she said. "I'm done." She injected a heavy dose of sarcasm into her tone. "Thanks for all your help."

"Oh, you don't have to thank me," he said graciously. "All I did was get the comforters and stuff." He looked around. "But it looks good. I think we're going to be okay."

Charlie looked right, then left. "We?" she said, cocking her head. "I didn't see any 'we.' Not while all the work was going on."

"No, I guess not," Nate said. "Sorry." He backed out of the room, looking at her like she was some kind of slavering wild animal he'd cornered by accident. "You're right. There's no 'we.' Just you and me, here alone with these…" He waved a hand around the room.

"These what?" Charlie asked.

"Beds."

Charlie followed his eyes. The beds were set in a neat row against the wall, blankets neatly turned back in an almost irresistible invitation to climb inside. They could play "Goldilocks and the Three Bears," she thought. Test out each one. See if any of them were "just right."

She looked back at Nate just as he glanced at her, and the room felt suddenly hot and close. His eyes darted away, flashing around the room in search of a new topic of conversation.

"Sorry," he said again. "I didn't mean—I won't kiss you again or anything. I mean—never mind."

Nate wiped a hand over his brow. The bunkhouse looked great, but it sure was warm. He glanced at Charlie. She was staring at him, biting her lower lip. If he didn't know better, he'd think she was disappointed.

Looking at her mouth made him remember that kiss, and he took an inadvertent step toward her. She glanced up at him, and despite the laws she'd laid down earlier, he could swear there was an invitation in her eyes.

Only one way to find out. But did he dare to take the chance? He needed Charlie—needed her to help him with the clinic. If he overstepped his bounds, she might take off. He was starting to think she was as flighty as Junior, ready to flee or fight at the slightest little thing.

But he needed her in another way too, and he was willing to take the gamble. After all, what was life without a little risk?

He stepped toward her just as she stepped back. The bed hit the back of her knees and she sat down hard. He was suddenly conscious of that stirring again, his body betraying him, and this time she noticed. She had to. His belt buckle was an inch from her face.

Flushing, he sat down beside her. The two of them stared straight ahead for a heartbeat, and then they turned—maybe he turned first, maybe she did, he really couldn't tell—and she was in his arms, tilting backward onto the bed as he kissed her with all the fervor he felt. He didn't hold anything back. When he finally took a gamble, he always went all in.

And so did Charlie. There was no mistaking the message in her kiss. She wanted him as much as he wanted her—maybe more.

It had never been like this with Sandi.

He felt the full length of her body yielding to his. There was no way she could miss his arousal now. He started to pull away, but she flexed her hips against him and deepened the kiss, pulling him closer.

He didn't know how long it lasted, but for one long moment there was no clinic to teach, no angry ex-girlfriend, no troublesome ranch woman waiting for horse-training instructions. There was only him and Charlie, and all those beds.

Finally, he pulled away—or maybe she did—and their eyes met. He scanned her face, trying to read her emotions in her eyes. Was he only seeing what he wanted to see—or was that a faint hint of regret crossing her face now that the kiss had ended? He could sense the slightest hint of hesitation in a horse, but danged if he knew how to read women. He sat up, figuring he'd give Charlie a chance to escape, but sitting up only made his feelings more obvious.

She didn't seem inclined to run away. In fact, she smiled up at him with a teasing light in her eyes, as if she was egging him on. Her face was flushed, her hair in disarray, and her shirt had somehow hiked up to display the edge of that tantalizing tattoo, along with a hint of black lace peeking out from the waistband of her jeans.

The panties. Without thinking, he reached down and stroked one finger across her belly, tracing the line of lace from one hip to the other. A tiny red bow peeked out just above her hipbone. He fingered it, watching Charlie's face as her eyes eased closed and her lips parted.

He stroked her again, with two fingers this time, and tugged the bow playfully. To his amazement, it came undone in his hand. He expected Charlie to tense, to push his hands away, but she only opened her eyes, meeting his in a clear challenge, and reached down to unsnap her jeans.

Charlie felt a ripple of need cross her skin as Nate's fingers gently traced her waistband. She needed more. She'd been holding back for some reason, resisting the weird connection between them, and for the life of her, she couldn't remember why.

She reached down and undid the snap on her jeans, watching his face as he realized what she was doing, and what it meant. Bending down, he kissed her again, and this time it wasn't an all-out, go-for-broke festival like last time. It was sweet, a gentle joining that made her ache with need. His hand slid lower, dipping below her waistband to stroke the sensitive skin where her lace-up panties had come undone.

She tucked her hands under his T-shirt and swept them upward, savoring the muscles that flexed under her hands, the warmth of his skin, the slight gasp as her fingertips brushed over his chest.

His lips left hers and he looked her in the eye.

"I don't have anything," he said. "I mean—you know. Nothing—safe."

She felt like a swimmer surfacing from a warm ocean, fighting for breath, her limbs heavy. "We can't then," she said—but her eyes flicked over to her purse, perched on the nightstand. She had what they needed. She always did. Her mother made sure she always carried protection, just in case. She was determined her daughter would never derail her life with an unplanned pregnancy. "It's okay. It's—it's just as well." She didn't mean it—she didn't mean it at all. But what could she say?

"But could I just see…" He bit his lip and flushed.

"See what?"

This was different. He was no smooth Lothario, that was for sure. The poor guy could barely speak. The fact that he was trying told her how much he wanted her. Needed her.

He hooked a finger in the waistband of her jeans and tugged it down just an inch or so, revealing a matching red bow on the other hip. The ribbon seemed to call him like a red cape draws a bull, adding to his urgency and giving him courage. He tugged harder, revealing a swath of translucent lace.

"Your panties," he said. "I just—I just want to see what you're wearing."

His face was red, and no wonder. Hers probably matched. It was an odd request. What, was the guy interested in *fashion*? And why did the fact that he wanted to see her panties make her so hot she could hardly breathe?

He was hardly Tim Gunn, but she suddenly wanted his honest opinion on the merits of her black Victoria's Secret lace-up low-rise bikini briefs more than anything in the world. Fumbling with her zipper, she tugged it down and hooked her thumbs in the waistband of her jeans, shimmying them down her hips. Nate had undone one side of her low-rise bikini, and it snagged on the denim and revealed the tattoo on her hip. It was a tribal-style image, a horse made of streaming flames inked in black on her pale skin.

Nate traced the image with one finger, stroking the arch of the horse's neck and trailing down its spine to its flaming tail.

"Looks like someone I know," he said.

"I know," she said. "Junior. I thought so as soon as I saw him."

He traced it again, slowly, but his eyes rose to meet hers. His gaze was as intense as it had been that morning, but she didn't look away this time.

"Maybe you're meant to be here," he said.

She didn't answer; she just lifted her arms and laced her fingers behind his head, pulling him down for another kiss. The moment felt serious, almost ceremonial, as if they were sealing some claim on each other. Something in the back of her mind blared out a warning, but the rest of her softened and gave way as he tugged her jeans away and dipped his fingers under the silky black fabric.

There was no hiding now. He had to know, the minute he touched her, how ready she was and how much she wanted him. She pulled him down for another kiss, partly to taste him again, partly so he'd close his eyes. Her body was telling him enough. She didn't want him reading her mind.

His hands were rough, but his touch was so gentle she pushed her hips up off the bed, asking for more, and he caught on, stroking her harder, then faster, making her body hum as her heart quickened and need pulsed through her veins and fed her desire. Breaking the kiss, she tossed her head back and arched her back, opening herself to his touch. Through half-shuttered lashes, she could see him staring down at her—not at her body, but at her face, as if he was searching for directions, reading the flashes of ecstasy and changing his pace as he read her unconscious signals. His pupils were still dark, and his gaze was so enraptured she felt possessed, dominated, almost owned—but instead of being afraid or pulling back, she felt a flood of relief as she gave herself up to him, closing her eyes and losing herself in a whirl of sensation and emotion. That warning in the back of her mind was still sounding, but she'd made up her mind. She wasn't going to listen. For once, just this once, she was going to do what she wanted and to hell with the consequences. Focusing on the thrill of his touch, she pulsed her hips and moved with his rhythm.

He kissed the corner of her mouth, then moved down to touch her jawbone, her throat, the blade of her collarbone. His hand slipped under her shirt and cupped her breast, his touch warm through the thin cotton of her bra. The touch seemed to ignite the slow flame between her legs, and as he stroked her with new urgency she felt herself ignite and explode. The room was gone, the bunkhouse, the ranch, the past, the present. The sensation of his touch was all that mattered, all that existed as her world fell apart and spun away into space.

As the hum in her blood subsided, she opened her eyes and looked up at him. She was limp in his arms, her head pressed against his chest as she waited for the aftershocks to subside. She expected to feel loss, shame, maybe horror, but what filled her mind when she looked at him was something like triumph. In giving herself away, she'd somehow tapped into her own power. She'd given herself to him, let him into the most private part of herself. She should have felt diminished, but for some strange reason, she'd never felt stronger.

He closed his eyes and kissed her again, and she wrapped her arms around him and flipped them over so she was sitting on her knees, straddling him. Somehow her jeans had wound up crumpled at the bottom of the bed, and God knew where her panties had gone.

"Not fair," she said, tugging at his belt. "Too many clothes."

Nate grabbed Charlie's hands, stopping her determined assault on his belt buckle. "I told you," he said. "I don't have anything."

She grinned, rubbing the heel of her hand up the bulge behind his fly. He closed his eyes and gasped. He'd never been the kind of guy who carried a condom everywhere just in case an opportunity came up. He'd never wanted to be that kind of guy.

Until now. He'd give anything to be that kind of guy now.

"Oh, you have something, all right," Charlie said. She flipped his belt away and went to work on his button fly, the touch of her fingers making him ache and throb with need.

He took a deep, shaky breath. "No. We can't. I don't..."

"Shh." She scrambled off him and lunged for her purse on the nightstand. "Hold on." She unzipped one of the compartments and held up a small square package.

Evidently, Charlie was that kind of girl.

He shook his head. No, she wasn't. He hadn't known her for long, but somehow, despite the fact she sparked desire in him with every casual wave of her hand, he knew she was no floozy. He'd seen her face when she let herself go and lost herself to his touch, and he'd seen the stunned amazement on her face when she opened her eyes afterward.

This wasn't business as usual for Charlie. What was happening between them meant something to her.

The touch of her hand turned off his thoughts as if she'd thrown a switch. She was on top of him again, tugging his clothes away, taking him in her hand and meeting his eyes as she tore the package open with her teeth and sheathed him with trembling fingers that sent lightning shocks flickering through his veins.

"Now." She straddled him again and rubbed herself against him, once, twice, and then he was inside her, feeling her warmth all around him, watching her close her eyes and throw her head back as she flexed her thighs and moved in slow circles above him.

Reaching up, he lifted her shirt and cupped her breasts, her perfect breasts, small and pert, peaking under his touch. He wanted this to last forever. He wanted to explore every inch of her, to know her like his own body—but his body wanted release. They moved together and he felt like a river, like a smooth-flowing stream of sensation running around her and through her as the pace increased and they both started to breathe in harsh, urgent gasps.

She tensed around him and he clenched his jaw, trying to hold back, trying to wait, but something inside him broke and a surge of pure sensation overwhelmed him. He was hers, all hers, she was everything, he couldn't stop himself.

He was gone.

He let go and felt them flow together into one being, one flame, one flower exploding into bloom.

—◊◊◊—

Charlie collapsed, letting her body cover Nate's, resting her head in the hollow of his shoulder. He wrapped his arms around her and she closed her eyes, feeling nothing but the warmth of him and the pulse of his heartbeat against her chest. The world was perfect.

Perfect.

She lay there a minute or two before her life gradually swirled back into focus. What had she done?

The world wasn't perfect. It was gravely flawed—because she had to get up now and finish cleaning the bunkhouse. And then she had to go out there and face Doris. And then she had to learn everything she could about communicating with horses so she could go back to Jersey and put it in a research paper.

In New Jersey.

Not in Wyoming.

She shifted and peered up at Nate. He'd fallen asleep,

his face serene, his mouth slightly open. She felt a stab of tenderness and turned away.

She couldn't afford to fall for this man. She was leaving, no matter what happened between them, and she didn't want to take any baggage with her when she left. She wanted to go home free and unencumbered, with nothing but happy memories of her stay on Latigo Ranch.

No regrets. No broken hearts.

She ran her fingers through her hair and let out a long, shuddering sigh, then grabbed for her panties, pulling them on and fumbling with the ribbon he'd undone. Her fingers were shaking and she kept her eyes carefully averted until Nate reached over and flicked the ribbon with one finger. She flinched and turned around. His eyes were open, but just barely, and a lazy grin crossed his face.

"Hey," he said. "Leave those off."

"No." She shook her head, refusing to look at him. "We're done here. Sorry."

"We're done?"

She nodded. "Sorry."

He grinned. "Me too."

"It's just that I have to go home."

"Now?"

"Eventually."

"Well, that's okay. You're here now, right?" He flicked the ribbon again and ran the back of his hand up the side of her thigh, sending a shimmer of heat straight to her center. "Come here. Lie down with me a minute. Let's talk."

"No." She reached down and grabbed his jeans, then

tossed them hard against his chest. "There's nothing to talk about. Come on. Get dressed."

"Okay." He stepped into the jeans and stood up, fastening his belt, then sat down again. She turned away from him and tugged her own jeans up over her hips, then slipped into her T-shirt.

"Charlie," he said. "Wait. Sit down a minute. I…"

They both spun as the door creaked open and Doris's face appeared in the opening.

"Hey, are you—oh. Damn. Sorry."

Nate caught a quick glimpse of the woman's grinning face as she ducked back outside.

"Oops," Nate said. He couldn't help grinning. He still hadn't put his shirt on, so Doris had probably figured out what was going on. It was embarrassing, but somehow, he knew the old cowgirl would understand.

"It's okay," he said to Charlie.

"No, it's not." Her voice was shaky as she smoothed her shirt. "It's not okay. I lost it, all right? You're very—attractive. Very—I don't know, persuasive or something." She raked her fingers though her hair again. "It was just a once and done thing, okay? Forget about it."

"I don't think so," he said. "Not likely." His voice had lost its light tone. He sounded stubborn. Determined.

Charlie turned away and started fooling with one of the pots of flowers she'd set around the bunkhouse. "I'll finish up here," she said, hunching her shoulders. "You'd better go."

Chapter 14

NATE SHUT THE BARN DOOR BEHIND HIM AND LEANED AGAINST Junior's stall, wiping his forehead. Something about Charlie had his hormones amped up into the red zone. He couldn't believe he'd actually asked her to show him what she was wearing. To show him her—dang, he couldn't even say the word to himself, but he'd said it right out loud to her. *Your panties*.

And she'd said yes. To everything. Said yes, and yes again, showed him just how miraculously *right* they were together, and then shut down the minute it was over as if she regretted what she'd done.

She seemed angry. He needed to fix things between them—but how? He didn't even know what he'd done wrong. Maybe she felt used. Maybe he should have taken it slower.

What had she said? He was too persuasive. He'd have to watch that.

But he wouldn't say he was sorry, that was for sure. He knew better than that. Apologies always revved Sandi up into a rage. Just saying he was sorry was bound to get him in trouble, and he wasn't going to blow it with this girl like he had with Sandi. He might be a little slow on the uptake when it came to women, but he'd learned a few things. *Don't tell me—show me*, Sandi always said. *Words are easy*.

He didn't exactly agree with that, but he knew what she meant. Words were easy for *her*.

What worked for Sandi was jewelry, or a new pair of shoes. Sometimes she went for flowers if his offense wasn't too bad, but they had to be real flowers, like roses. *Bought* flowers. He'd tried gathering wildflowers for her one time, and that hadn't gone over well at all.

And this last time, nothing had worked. All Sandi had wanted was out.

He wondered what he should do for Charlie. Obviously, she was perfectly capable of gathering her own flowers. And it would hardly be appropriate to buy her jewelry.

So what would be appropriate? Shoes?

No—*boots*. He could get her some cowboy boots— real ones, to replace those ridiculous high-fashion wannabe boots she'd brought from Jersey. Boots would be perfect. Not only were they practical, but they'd show he wanted her to stay. Sure, boots were pretty expensive, even plain ones without a lot of tooling, but—

But nothing. He almost groaned aloud. He couldn't buy Charlie boots. He couldn't buy her anything. He was broke.

He froze. Broke.

He didn't have any money at all. Sandi had cleaned him out.

Presents for Charlie were the least of his problems. He couldn't even take her and Doris to the mustang auction. He'd need money to buy the horses.

His stomach balled itself up and clenched tight as a fist. What the hell was he going to do?

Breathe, he told himself. *Breathe. Don't panic. Slow*

down and think. It was the same ritual he used when a horse acted up—only now he was trying to tame his own crazy life, and it was tougher than any screwed-up stallion he'd ever faced.

The door opened and Doris strode into the barn.

"There you are," she said. "Thought I'd spooked you, you took off so fast. What were you two up to in there?" She gestured toward the bunkhouse.

"Nothing." He could feel a blush heating his face. Doris noticed.

It seemed like Doris noticed everything.

"Why, you're blushing! You blush just as easy as Charlie," she said, a wicked glint in her eye.

"Charlie blushes?"

"Sure." Doris winked. "Mostly when we talk about you."

Nate looked away, squinting toward the horizon. "That's not blushing," he said. "She's just mad. I can't do a thing right where she's concerned."

"Oh, I don't know," Doris said. "I think you were doing something right back there in the bunkhouse."

Nate shook his head. It had sure felt right. But judging from Charlie's response, what they'd done was wrong in her eyes.

He'd moved too fast. Spooked her.

"Can you show me that stallion now?" Doris bounced on the balls of her feet like an eager ten-year-old.

"Sure." Nate thought he might show her some other horses too. Maybe he could sell her on the notion of using one of his horses instead of a mustang. Kind of lead her into it, make her think it was her own idea. She had the walk of a real horsewoman, and a calm vibe about her that most likely served her well with animals. He could probably trust her with his horses. In fact, he had a feeling he'd have to be on his toes to teach her anything.

"Charlie says you can tame that stallion down 'til he's sweet as a baby," Doris said. "I can't wait to see that."

It wouldn't be hard to distract Charlie from the mustang idea. All he'd have to do was let her work with Junior—but that was impossible. He'd pretty much staked the ranch on that horse, and he wasn't about to let a greenhorn handle him, no matter how much he needed said greenhorn's help. No, he'd have to hope he could steer Charlie toward one of the other horses. She'd probably like Boy, the handsome black gelding he was finishing for a rancher up in Story, but he couldn't let a student handle a client's horse either.

Maybe she'd like Razz. Yeah, that would do it. The flashy paint was saddle-broke and fully trained, but he had a few spunky mannerisms that might convince Charlie she was working with a genuine wild pony. He was a handsome devil too.

Yeah, she was bound to fall for Razz. He'd just tell her the horse was a mustang. He wasn't much for lying, but sometimes you had to. Sometimes you didn't have a choice.

— ∿ —

A half hour later, Doris clomped up the steps to the bunkhouse and surveyed the accommodations, hands on hips.

"Not bad."

Charlie started. She'd been staring out the window, lost in thought.

"Now that you've got our digs all fixed up, I think I'll get myself a little shut-eye, if that's okay with you," Doris said. "I generally nap in the afternoons." She cocked a thumb over her shoulder toward the house. "Your boyfriend's in there dithering over supper. You know he was going to feed us TV dinners? I set him straight, though. With what he's charging, the food oughta be better than that."

"That's all he knows how to cook," Charlie said.

"I know. That's why I told him it just wouldn't do," Doris said. "He's a mess. Needs you to rescue him." She grinned. "What's the girl equivalent of a knight in shining armor?"

"A fairy-tale princess, I guess." Charlie looked down at her clothes. She'd changed out of her jeans and T-shirt—they were dusty and dirty from cleaning the bunkhouse, and besides, those panties had to go—but she was still dressed like a farmhand. "I'm not sure that's me."

"I don't know—I think you're a damn good kick-ass princess." Doris punched a fist in the air in a girl-power salute. "Go save his butt like a good princess should."

"A kick-ass princess," Charlie said. "I like that."

"He'll figure it out," Doris said, patting her shoulder. "It might take him a while, but he'll get it."

"Get what?"

"That you're the girl for him." Doris grinned. "You should have seen him blush when I talked about you."

"He should blush," Charlie said. "He's done nothing but screw up since I got here." She felt her own face heating. That wasn't quite true. Nate had done something right back there in the bunkhouse.

Something very, very right. She shoved the memory out of her mind.

"He likes you," Doris said. "I can tell."

Uh-oh. Doris obviously had the matchmaking bug. Charlie had a sudden flashback to seventh grade, when an overzealous girlfriend had tried to fix her up with half the football team just because she'd made a comment about how hot they looked in their pads. Charlie didn't like football players any better than she liked cowboys. She meant they looked warm. Overheated.

Kind of like her libido ever since she'd hit Latigo Ranch. She flushed, remembering what had happened with Nate. It would be easy to blame him for the incident if she hadn't grabbed for that condom like it was the holy grail or something. What had she been thinking? He was a cowboy. A stupid cowboy.

And she was leaving.

"You don't have to play matchmaker, Doris. I appreciate it, but Nate's not my type."

Doris smiled and shook her head.

"Really," Charlie protested. "I don't like cowboys. I'm no buckle bunny, you know."

"And Nate's no rodeo rider," Doris retorted. "I saw how he handled the horses. He's very good at what he does." She tipped Charlie a sideways smile. "He's got a nice, gentle way with him."

Charlie thought of Nate's hand stroking her hair, touching her skin. The tenderness of his touch had sent a tingling thrill through her body, but the way he'd looked at her afterwards had sparked an amber caution light in her subconscious. He thought he knew her now. He thought he'd seen through all her defenses, when really all he'd seen was her panties.

Well, not really. They'd gone way beyond the lingerie

fashion show he'd requested. But what kind of guy wanted to look at a girl's panties, anyway?

And besides, there was that locked attic. Who knew what was up there? Until she found out, she needed to stay away from the guy. For all she knew, he was a serial killer and it was full of severed body parts from his many victims.

Or panties.

Yeah, right. More likely, he kept the rest of his plastic horse collection up there and played Barbie Horse Show when no one was around.

"It doesn't matter," she said, with a toss of her hair. "I'm going back to Jersey, soon as I get what I came for."

As she said it, she knew that was what she needed to focus on. Get in, get the information she needed, and get out. She was on a mission, with a clearly defined goal: observe and report.

She'd deliver that paper and hopefully steer Sadie toward letting her do more research comparing animal and human behavior. Then she'd do her practicum, and after that, who knew? She'd find some kind of meaningful work—something with kids, maybe. Or, better yet, with animals.

Maybe both.

Long-term, she didn't really know where she was headed. But she did know one thing: there was no man in the picture. Certainly no cowboy.

"We'll see." Doris kicked her shoes off and plumped up a pillow. "I'm pretty sure you're going to get what you came for, Charlie Banks. I'm just not sure you realize what it is you want."

Chapter 15

FROM THE KITCHEN WINDOW, CHARLIE COULD SURVEY THE front of the barn, most of the outbuildings, and the long, winding driveway. She knew Nate was in the barn cleaning tack and Doris was napping in the bunkhouse, so she was the only person who saw a car sweep up the drive and deposit Nate's newest client. The car was a genuine redneck taxi—a beat-up El Camino with a checkerboard paint job that had obviously involved a can of spray paint and a homemade stencil.

Charlie supposed you might call the apparition that stepped from the passenger's seat a cowgirl—but she was definitely a cowgirl with a twist. The girl was a symphony in black—black leather cowboy boots, a black lace bustier revealing a swath of pale tummy flesh, black jeans, and a long black duster like the bad guy in a Kevin Costner Western. She wore plenty of black eyeliner too, and even black lipstick and black polished fingernails.

Charlie laughed aloud. This was going to be good. If there was such a thing as a Goth cowgirl, she was looking at it. She couldn't wait to see Nate's reaction.

The creature stood in the dust of the departing taxi, staring after it like it was her last chance for salvation. Then she squared her shoulders and turned toward the house.

Charlie recognized that gesture. She'd squared her

shoulders exactly the same way half a million times. It was how she steeled herself to deal with a situation she didn't want to face.

It was how she dealt with fear.

She stepped out onto the porch and waved at what appeared to be the Satanic Cowgirl of Doom. "Welcome to Latigo Ranch," she said, as the new guest mounted the steps at a dirge-like pace.

Dead Cowgirl Walking, Charlie thought. She fought off an urge to giggle.

"Yeah." The girl wasn't much for talking, but then she'd apparently spent all her eloquence on her appearance. Besides the black clothing, her hair was the flat black of a bad dye job, and her skin was pasty pale, as if she'd lived out her life in a cave. The whole effect screamed misfit. There wasn't much left the kid needed to say.

"Did you want to clean up? Stow your stuff in the bunkhouse? There's another guest in there napping, but I'm sure she won't mind. I mean, it's your bunkhouse too." Charlie stopped her jabbering, aware that the girl's silence had unnerved her into babbling incoherence.

"By the way, I'm Charlie," she said. "I'm—I'm sort of Nate's assistant, I guess."

The girl stared at her, the gray eyes expressionless.

"And your name is…?" Charlie lifted her eyebrows expectantly.

"Phaedra."

"Phaedra…?"

"Just Phaedra."

"Oh, I get it. Just one name. Like Madonna."

"No, like Cher. Cher's cool. Madonna's a bitch."

"Right. Like Cher."

Stifling a chuckle, Charlie trotted down the steps and grabbed the girl's duffel bag, wondering if everything inside was black.

Probably.

"Come on—I'll show you where you're staying." She trotted off to the bunkhouse without looking back.

The girl traipsed behind her, stepping into the bunkhouse doorway a moment after Charlie had hoisted her bag onto a bed by the window. Doris lay sprawled on the next bed over, deep in slumber, a gentle but unmistakable snore issuing from her open mouth.

"I'd rather be over there." Phaedra pointed toward the far corner of the room, toward the only bed and nightstand that lacked a jar of flowers.

"Oh, no you wouldn't," Charlie said. "It's nicer here by the window. Plus it'll be easier for our pajama parties."

"I'm not into nice," Phaedra said scornfully. "Or pajama parties. I want that one over there. Where I can be alone."

Doris sat up, rubbing her fists into her eyes like a sleepy child.

"Alone?" She shook her head, then fluffed up her hair on the side where it had been flattened against her pillow and squinted at the new arrival. "You'll be alone in the grave, child. Best take good company when you can find it."

Phaedra shook her head and hauled her gear over to the corner bed.

"Or not." Doris shrugged and turned to Charlie. "How's that cowboy's butt doing? You save it yet?"

"Well, dinner's almost ready," Charlie said. "You can come on in if you want. You too, Phaedra."

The girl looked up from where she was arranging a pile of books on the nightstand. Sartre's *Nausea* topped the stack.

"Not hungry," she said.

"Come anyway." Charlie gave her a look that had cowed many an underclassmen during her stint as a teaching assistant. "It's part of the deal."

"All right." Phaedra rose, mumbling under her breath, and trailed behind the two women like a reluctant haunt.

"Smells good," Doris said as they mounted the porch. "Terrific."

"I probably can't eat it, whatever it is," Phaedra announced. "I'm a vegetarian."

"No problem," Charlie said. "It's spaghetti and meatballs. Meatballs optional."

The table was set with a blue gingham cloth and blue paper napkins Charlie had found in the pantry. A drinking glass filled with black-eyed Susans was flanked by an earthenware bowl of pasta, a saucepan filled with rich, red sauce, and a pyramid of plump meatballs stacked on a plate.

"Sit down and help yourselves," Charlie said. "I'll go get Nate."

"No need."

She turned to see the cowboy standing in the doorway, his hat in his hand.

"Well, dinner's ready." She gestured toward the table like a game-show hostess, waiting for his reaction to the homey atmosphere she'd managed to wring out of his bare-bones kitchen.

But Nate was staring across the table at their newest guest. He squinted, then put a hand to his forehead.

"Hello?" he said.

"That's Phaedra," Charlie said. "A new client."

"Thought I was hallucinating," he muttered. He stared down at the table, that muscle in his jaw working. "I'll go wash up," he said and strode out of the room.

Charlie watched him go with her hands on her hips. She'd cleaned the bunkhouse, cooked his dinner, played hostess to his spooky new student, even shown him her panties, and then some—but he had nothing to say. She was starting to think he couldn't be much of a horse trainer. Didn't animals need positive reinforcement?

"Guess he didn't realize his ass was in trouble," Doris said.

"Guess not." Charlie shrugged and sank into a chair. If Nate didn't shape up, she'd be gone sooner rather than later, that was all. She swallowed a lump that was closing off her throat and wondered what that was all about.

"Well, let's not wait on the cowboy," she said. "Eat up, girls."

Doris pulled out the chair across from Charlie and sat down, making a production out of tucking a paper napkin into the neck of her shirt. Phaedra hovered behind her.

"Sit, child." Doris motioned toward a chair at the far end of the long farm table. "Over there, if you want. Where you can be alone." She gave the words a goofy Greta Garbo inflection.

Phaedra slid wordlessly into the indicated chair and

took a tiny serving of noodles when Charlie slid them her way. Dipping into the sauce, she topped them with a dab of red.

"This looks terrific." Doris forked a huge pile of noodles onto her plate, topped it with four meatballs, then ladled the sauce generously over the top. Nate re-entered and sat down, scanning the table with about as much expression as a peeled potato.

"Got us another vegetarian," Doris said, nodding toward Phaedra.

"Oh." He considered Phaedra, his gaze taking in her bizarre outfit. "Which package did you buy?" he asked.

Phaedra shrugged. "Don't know."

"What do you mean, you don't know?"

"My dad did it. He said I'd get to ride horses, though."

"Well, how long you here for?"

She shrugged again.

"Guess you'll do Package B with the others, then."

"Whatever."

"What's your name again?"

"Phaedra," she said, drawing the name out as if he was an idiot for asking.

"Phaedra who?"

She heaved a heavy sigh and looked over at Charlie.

"Just Phaedra," Charlie said. "She just has the one name. You know, like Madonna."

"Cher."

"Madonna."

"No. Like Cher."

Charlie laughed. "What do you have against Madonna, anyway?"

Phaedra shrugged. Charlie watched her a while, but

the girl lapsed back into silence, studiously twirling her spaghetti onto her fork a strand at a time.

"Phew," Charlie said, swiping her brow in mock relief. "For a minute there, I thought we were going to have a conversation. You know, you're going to make a great cowboy." She glanced over at Nate. "They don't talk either."

Nate had watched the exchange like a spectator at a tennis match, his head bobbing from one side to the other. Now he ducked his head and squeezed his eyes shut, lifting a hand to his forehead.

"Sorry," he said. "Headache."

Despite her anger, Charlie felt a stab of pity. She could never resist a wounded animal, and Nate, with his silence and his stoic endurance, seemed more animal than cowboy sometimes.

"Let me see your eyes." She leaned over and pushed his hair off his forehead. His eyes were still unnaturally dark, a narrow border of gray edging the dilated pupil. Without thinking, she reached up and ran her free hand through his hair, stroking him like an injured pet. He swallowed hard and glanced toward Phaedra's watchful eyes and Doris's delighted grin. Charlie pulled her hands away and he stared down at his plate.

"You should probably go lie down," she said.

"No, I want to eat," he said, sounding surprised, as if he'd noticed the spaghetti for the first time. "You made real food."

"Sure did," she said. "There wasn't much to work with."

"I'll take you into town to restock if you want," he said. "Later. After, um… after I do the dishes."

"I'll do the dishes," Doris said. "You two go on to town."

Charlie flashed her a glare. "You're a guest," she said. "Nate should do them."

"Well, you're a guest too," Doris said. "And it seems to me you do all the work around here." She looked expectantly at Nate, who was looking down at his plate and chewing his spaghetti like a meditative cow savoring its cud. He didn't seem to hear her.

Charlie sighed. "Whatever," she said.

The four of them turned their attention to the food, twirling the pasta onto their forks in awkward silence. Charlie could feel Phaedra's eyes watching her every move. She set down her fork and turned toward the girl.

"You have a question?"

"No," Phaedra said. "I mean, yes."

Charlie sat back. "Well, ask it."

"Why are you here?"

Charlie shrugged. "Same as you, probably."

Phaedra kept watching her with those spooky kohl-rimmed eyes. Charlie wondered if she ever blinked.

"But you're cool," Phaedra said. "I like your hair. And your clothes."

"Well, thanks." Charlie almost laughed at the unexpected compliment. She might have to rethink her style if Goth Girl approved.

"You don't belong here," Phaedra said.

A loud clatter at the other end of the table pulled their attention to Nate. He'd slammed his fork onto his plate, spattering spaghetti sauce across the front of his shirt and onto the floor.

"She does so," he said, giving Phaedra a hard stare.

Charlie looked up, startled, a forkful of spaghetti halfway to her lips. "What?" she said.

"You belong here," Nate said, shifting the fork to one side. His voice was too loud, his tone defensive. "You belong here just fine."

Charlie stared at him a moment, then followed his gaze as he looked around at the table loaded with food, and at the black-eyed Susans in their water glass, then back at her.

"Oh," she said. "You're welcome."

Chapter 16

NATE'S PICKUP WAS A NEST OF FAST-FOOD WRAPPERS AND horse tack and smelled faintly of Butt. Embarrassed, he rolled down a window, then tossed some of the junk onto the back bench of the crew cab to make room for Charlie.

"Watch the potholes," she said, climbing in. "You'll break an axle, like I did."

"No way." Nate patted the truck's dashboard as if it was a faithful cow pony. "Sally's made for these roads."

"Sally?" Charlie grinned and Nate felt his face flush. "You named your truck? And it's a *girl*?"

Nate cranked the ignition and revved the engine, ignoring her. She was a city girl, he reminded himself. She didn't realize how important a good pickup was to ranch work. You had to treat it right, like a woman.

Not that he had any clue how to treat a woman. He glanced over at Charlie. He'd made her clean the whole bunkhouse by herself, and then he'd stepped over the line and kissed her again.

And then he'd taken advantage of her. Or something. Obviously, he'd crossed some invisible line.

She didn't seem mad anymore, but the air in the pickup felt hot and close and he couldn't meet her eyes. He needed to apologize to her, but he couldn't figure out how. It seemed like she'd forgiven him but probably for all the wrong reasons. It wasn't because she knew he couldn't help himself when she looked at him a certain way, and it wasn't because she realized he was up against it with this clinic thing, and desperate for help.

It was because she thought he was ignorant and didn't know how to behave.

He glanced down at her hip. The red ribbon had disappeared. She'd retied the bow. Probably with a double knot—or a padlock.

"Is there anything you need for yourself? In town?" He still had a credit card. Maybe he'd just charge those boots and hope for the best. Sandi wouldn't have minded a bit that there was nothing in the checking account to back up the plastic. She always acted like a credit card wasn't real money. Like stuff you bought that way was free.

As a matter of fact, he'd better call the bank and see if she was still using her card. Who knew how much she'd charged since she'd left? Being broke was probably his best-case scenario. Most likely he was in debt up to his neck. He ought to shut the account down.

No, he couldn't do that. Sandi wasn't the only one depending on him.

"I'm okay," Charlie said. "I don't need anything."

If it hadn't been for the pebbles pinging off Sally's undercarriage, the truck cab would have been totally silent the whole rest of the trip. He just couldn't think of a thing to say.

They passed the grain elevator, then Bucky's Feed and Seed, and finally turned right onto Main Street. Nate had always enjoyed coming to town, but with Charlie by his side, the thriving metropolis of Purvis looked small and dusty—kind of pitiful. The biggest building was the three-story sandstone Masonic Hall on the corner, and the business district consisted of a hardware store, a tack shop, and five bars.

Charlie was from Jersey, where they probably had a Super Wal-Mart and a shopping mall in every town. Purvis must look to her like the back of beyond.

And what did he look like through her eyes? A redneck? A hick? He already knew she didn't like cowboys. She probably thought he was a real yahoo.

She was wrong. He was no yokel. He read a lot and watched documentaries all the time. He had opinions on all kinds of things outside the limited world of Purvis.

But she'd never know it if he didn't learn to carry on a conversation.

———

Charlie watched the town flash past. It took about three seconds for the businesses lining the main street to peter out, giving way to occasional gas stations and minimarts. As far as she could see, Purvis was just a handful of bars and a hardware store.

"Well, if you want to get drunk and fix stuff, this is the place to be," she said.

"We have a bowling alley," Nate said, his tone defensive.

She smiled and let her hand dangle out the window, feeling the air rush through her fingers. Nate had barely said a word the whole trip—just stared straight ahead like an all-night trucker on his last leg home. It should have felt awkward, sharing the truck cab with such a silent companion, but for some reason, Charlie felt comfortable. There was no need to clutter up the drive with small talk.

But that could get old, long-term. She wondered how Sandi dealt with Nate's reticence. She'd have had to be one of those self-possessed women who didn't need a lot of fussing and petting—a woman who was complete in herself.

Somehow, Charlie didn't think that was the case. She remembered the magazines scattered around the house—all about movie stars and fashion—and the "Perfect Face" book in the bedroom. There were self-help books too, about how to be happy.

How could you learn to be happy from a book?

Charlie was pretty sure Sandi was looking for something in Denver that was lacking in her life here at Latigo. It must be something to do with Nate, because the ranch had plenty to offer. She thought of Junior, pressing his soft muzzle to her neck; the long view of the plains from the kitchen window; the fresh, smog-free air scented with sagebrush and pine. She felt closer to nature here than ever in her life—more a part of the world, more whole and complete. Maybe she and Sandi had just been given the wrong lives.

Maybe they should trade.

Yeah, right. She could find fulfillment out here. She wouldn't miss civilization. She could do without ethnic food and pedicures and nightclubs and the shore.

Not.

And her mother would be thrilled to hear that her hyper-educated daughter was giving up on school to clean house for a cowboy.

Yeah, right.

Nate swung the truck into a lighted parking lot,

pulling up in front of a long, low clapboard building with large windows bearing hand-lettered sale signs.

"Holy crap." Charlie was halfway out of the truck before Nate pulled to a stop. "Veggie Burgers half price." They pushed through the swinging door. "I wouldn't think they'd even carry them around here."

"We don't." A heavyset man at the cash register tipped his straw Stetson as they stepped inside. With a bucking horse tattooed on his bicep and a bandanna knotted around his neck, he'd have looked more at home riding in a roundup than clerking in a corner grocery. "Got 'em in on accident. That's why they're on sale." He turned to Nate. "Hey, Nate. How's Sam?"

Sam? Charlie wondered who that was. Since Nate had named his truck, she figured it was probably his tractor, or a combine or something.

"Fine," Nate said. "I think."

"You think? A looker like that, you'd better keep track of her." The cash register cowboy slapped a hand over his heart and put on a theatrically pained expression. "She's a heartbreaker, that one."

A looker? A heartbreaker? Charlie narrowed her eyes at Nate. Surely the natives didn't take the personification of farm machinery that far, although it was possible Nate had a closer relationship with that pickup than he'd ever had with a woman.

No, it sounded like Sam was a flesh-and-blood female. Had Nate had a little something on the side—something besides Sandi? It seemed incredible that he could have found enough words to woo another woman. After all, that would involve having conversations beyond his usual Neanderthal grunts.

Nate shrugged and grabbed a cart. Apparently, the mysterious Sam didn't even merit a grunt.

"What should we get?" Charlie asked. "You want to do burgers tomorrow? You have a grill, right?"

Nate nodded.

Charlie pitched a bottle of ketchup into the cart, along with a jar of mustard. Burgers were always good—ground beef for Nate and Doris, and the on-sale veggie patties from the frozen food department for herself and Phaedra. She was dithering over the rolls when a tall man in a felt hat pulled his cart beside theirs.

"Nate," he said. Nodding to Charlie, he tipped his hat, revealing a bald pate rimmed by a fringe of gray hair. Wyoming was paradise for bald guys, Charlie thought—if only they'd ditch the hat-tipping tradition.

"Ma'am," he said.

"Len." Nate nodded.

The man lifted his eyebrows, still regarding Charlie.

"This is, ah, Charlie Banks," Nate said. "She's kind of helping out at the ranch."

"Nice to meetcha." The man turned back to Nate. "How's Sam?"

Whoever Sam was, she was hardly a secret. Maybe this guy thought Charlie was girlfriend number three.

"Fine," Nate said. "Gone to Denver for a while, though."

Denver? That was where Sandi was, right? Maybe Sam and Sandi were one and the same. Maybe it was some kind of nickname. After all, Nate didn't seem like the cheating type. He seemed pretty honest. Straightforward.

She should just ask. It was natural to wonder who Sam was, with everyone talking about her. It wouldn't be nosy, or intrusive. And she usually wasn't one to beat around the bush. If she wanted information, she went after it, throwing etiquette and delicacy to the winds.

But she felt a strange reluctance to delve into the mystery woman's identity. Maybe it was because she really didn't want to know if Nate had been two-timing Sandi. After all, if he was a cheater, then he wasn't the man she thought he was. And if he was some kind of ladies' man courting a whole string of floozies, the sparks that flew between him and Charlie took on a whole different meaning.

Or rather, they took on no meaning at all.

She decided to ignore the whole thing, but the guy with the hat wouldn't cooperate.

"You'd better watch out," he said. "Pretty girl like that, she might never come back."

Nate shoved the cart farther down the aisle, kind of rudely, Charlie thought. Evidently Sam was a sore subject.

It was probably better not to ask.

"Hey," the man said.

Nate turned.

"Sorry. Kidding. I wasn't thinking," Len said. "You doing okay?"

Nate nodded, his mouth set in a grim line, his eyes fixed on the king-sized bottle of ketchup perched in the shopping cart's kiddy seat. He was a lousy liar. Whoever Sam was, he obviously missed her.

Yeah, right. Missed her so much he fell into bed with the first woman who came his way.

Charlie felt her cheeks warming up with a slow burn that was half anger, half shame. Swinging the freezer case open, she grabbed the last two boxes of veggie burgers and half a gallon of Rocky Road ice cream.

The flavor was the perfect metaphor for Nate's life, she thought. And hers, if she was totally honest about it.

She followed Nate toward the checkout, where the tattooed man had been replaced by a white-haired woman, stout and motherly.

"Nathaniel," she said. "I heard about Sandi and Sam."

Okay, so they were two separate women. This really was a small town. Everybody seemed to know Nate's business. And everybody seemed kind of worried about him. She felt a pang of envy. When she went shopping in Newark, nobody knew her name. Nobody asked how she was. Except maybe that "Saddle Up" chick. But Charlie had bought her friendship with the purchase of those stupid boots and that pricey jacket.

The checker leaned forward across the conveyer belt and looked up into Nate's eyes, her own filled with concern. "Are you doing okay, hon?"

Nate blinked a few times, swallowed, and nodded. The woman reached over and patted his hand. "It'll all turn out okay," she said. "Don't you worry." She turned to Charlie. "And who's this?"

"This is Charlie," Nate said. The woman nodded, as though seeing Nate with yet another woman was perfectly normal. Next time anybody mentioned small-town values, Charlie'd be able to tell them a thing or two. "Charlie, this is my Aunt Gwen."

Charlie nodded. "Nice to meet you." She went down to the end of the counter and bagged while Nate busied himself finding the bar code on each item in the cart and placing it facedown on the belt.

"You take care now," Nate's aunt said when they were finished. "If you need anything, just call me. You know me and Uncle Ted are there for you." She turned to Charlie. "That's a good man there. You take care of him."

A good man? With three women? All Charlie could do was swallow hard and nod. Obviously, Nate's family loved him unconditionally.

They loaded the bags in the back of the pickup and climbed in. "Feed store next," Nate said. He drove back to Bucky's in silence and put the car in park.

The feed store was a barnlike, cavernous structure stocked to the ceiling with feed, tack, tools, and even clothing. Nate stopped at the cash register to talk to yet another acquaintance while Charlie paused at a circular rack of Carhartt jackets, admiring the stiff, utilitarian canvas and wondering what kind of winter called for a coat that could stand up by itself. She moved on to the hats, trying on a felt Stetson like Nate's, then whipping it off before it could wreck her hair.

"Hey. Come on back here," Nate said, leaning around the corner of a tall metal utility shelf stacked high with sacks of feed. "I want to show you something."

Charlie followed him to the back of the store, where boxes lined the wall, each stack topped with a cowboy boot.

"Try these on," he said, handing her a boot. It was a soft shade of brown, with simple tooling decorating the leather. The toe was pointed, the heel slanted, but it wasn't nearly as extreme as her Jersey boots.

Charlie sat down on a bench and slipped her foot into the boot, but it wouldn't make the turn. Frowning, she tugged at the top and shoved her foot the rest of the way in.

"Comfortable," she said, surprised. "Really comfortable."

"That's how a boot should feel. Those things you're wearing are like torture devices."

"You got that right." She picked up the other boot and examined the tooling. "How much are these?"

Nate turned away. "Don't worry about it."

"No, really, how much? I think I might want a pair."

"Sure hope so, 'cause they're yours," he said, faking absorption in the label on a Western shirt.

"You bought them? For me?" Charlie touched his arm, forcing him to look at her.

"They're not very fancy," Nate said.

"No," she said. "They're *real* boots." She tugged off her other high-heeled absurdity and slid her foot into the other boot. "They fit," she said. "How did you know my size?"

"I looked," he said, flushing. "You left yours in the kitchen last night." He cleared his throat. "You have, um, little feet."

What was this fascination he had with her clothing? First he wanted to see her panties; then he was checking out her footwear. The man had some kind of fetish.

"I thought you were broke," she said. "I mean—sorry, but you don't have to buy me stuff."

"I have an account here," he said. "It's fine. And you'll need them for working with the horses." He turned away. "I—I need a fair amount of help out there."

He swallowed hard. Charlie knew that admission hadn't come easy. And while Nate might not talk much, buying the boots was a clear statement that he trusted her with the horses.

And that he wanted her to stay.

She wasn't sure how she felt about that, except that

she was moved by the gesture. She stood pigeon-toed in the middle of the aisle, looking down at her feet and admiring the pointed toes and the soft sheen of the new leather. She felt like a little girl wearing her first pair of grown-up shoes.

"Thanks," she said.

Nate looked so embarrassed she took pity on him and changed the subject. "What else do you need? I can help carry stuff."

"Nothing," he said.

"You just came in to buy me boots?" Charlie could feel her heart warming and melting in her chest.

"That's it," he said. "Let's go."

He charged for the doorway like a bull charging an open gate. Charlie could barely keep up with him.

She paused when they reached the truck, savoring the quiet. She could hear crickets chirping and the occasional hum of a passing car, but there were no blaring horns, no loud music, no shouts or sirens. The single stoplight flicked from amber to red to green, but there was no traffic to heed the signal—just empty streets lined with shop fronts. Several of the shops were closed for good, their show windows covered with pristine plywood. Charlie wasn't sure she'd ever seen a boarded-up window unmarred by spray paint.

This was nothing like New Jersey.

And Nate was nothing like the cowboy she'd expected. She watched as he shoved the truck in gear and stared straight ahead. Buying her a present should have broken the ice that had built up between them since the episode in the bunkhouse. Some men would have made a big deal of it, made her feel like she owed them something, but Nate seemed simply embarrassed by his own generosity.

She was starting to think her mother might be wrong. There were good men in the world—you just had to know where to find them.

But who the hell was Sam?

~~~

While he put the truck into gear, Nate could feel Charlie's gaze hot on the back of his neck.

"So who's Sam?" she asked as he pulled out of the lot.

Nate groaned inwardly. He'd have to get it over with. Spill his life story, and that would probably put an end to any chance of more intimacy between them. Once she figured out how much he'd messed things up—his life, and Sandi's too—she'd probably run away screaming.

"Sam's my little girl," Nate said. "She's seven."

"You have a daughter?" Charlie looked down in her lap, and he could see she was surreptitiously counting on her fingers.

"We had her in high school," Nate said, saving her the trouble of figuring things out. "That's why me and Sandi stayed together. We probably would have gone our separate ways otherwise."

Actually, there was no "probably" about it. Sandi had always made it clear he'd ruined her plans for the future. She'd been headed for beauty school, and after that, she was going to go to L.A. and be a stylist to the stars. The way she said it, you'd have thought she'd had a ten-pound line hooked onto fame and fortune if Nate hadn't come along and messed everything up with his renegade sperm.

"Got a picture?"

Nate gestured toward the keys dangling in the ignition, and Charlie reached over and fingered the Plexiglas fob. It held a school photo of a little girl with strawberry blond hair and a wide grin. Someone had tried to tame all that hair into a stylish girlie up-do, but it was cascading around the child's face as if it just couldn't be tamed. She looked like she'd just blown in on the Wyoming wind.

"She's adorable," Charlie said.

"Yeah," Nate said. "She sure is."

He blinked a couple times, cursing himself for being so transparent. As far as he was concerned, Sandi could go to Denver and stay there, but he had to get Sam back. Sam was the only person in the world who loved the ranch like he did. Who belonged there, like he did.

"You miss her," Charlie said.

Nate nodded, his throat tightening. "You have no idea." His voice came out sounding half-strangled at first, but then he picked up speed. "She's—she's really something," he said. He could feel the words building up inside him, spilling over. Once somebody asked about Sam, talking was suddenly no problem. He couldn't stop. It was like he'd released a pent-up horse from the corral and it had taken off at a gallop. "She loves the horses and the plains like I do. She does okay in school because she's really, really smart, but she hates it because she has to spend the day inside." His voice came easier as he talked, the lump in his throat disappearing. "She rides like she was born on horseback. Sandi has fits about it—says she doesn't act like a lady. Well, why should a seven-year-old act like a lady anyway?" He cleared his throat, suddenly feeling awkward. He'd said too much. "We can't seem to agree on how to raise her," he muttered.

"So you and Sandi aren't—I mean, you don't... you're just together because...."

He knew what she was asking. She was asking if he'd been in love with Sandi. That wasn't a question he wanted to answer.

And anyway, love didn't matter when you had a child to raise. He'd done what he had to do, and so had Sandi.

Until now.

"It seems like you and Sandi didn't have much in common," Charlie said.

"We had Sam," Nate said. "That was enough."

Chapter 17

THOSE TWO SENTENCES TOLD CHARLIE PRETTY MUCH everything she needed to know about Nate. The guy might not talk much, but he'd managed to define his whole adult life in six words. She spent the next ten minutes in thoughtful silence, readjusting her picture of her cowboy host. She'd seen him with his horses, kind and patient. Now she'd caught a glimpse of his love for his daughter.

Maybe cowboys weren't so bad after all.

Not this one, anyway.

She thought of her own father—which wasn't easy to do. She didn't even have a clue what he looked like. He'd never said she was "really something." He'd never known she was smart in school. And he obviously didn't give a damn if she acted like a lady or not.

Charlie had always told herself she hadn't lost much when her father walked out of her life. Most of her friends had awkward relationships with their dads, so she'd decided hers wasn't that different from other men. Men just weren't into kids.

But Nate was pulling that rug right out from under her firmly planted feet.

She looked over at his rugged profile. The checkout clerk at the grocery store was right.

This was a good man.

She'd known that, deep down, the moment she'd first met him, when he'd bent down to soothe his nervous horse with that gentle, tender touch. She remembered how he'd coached her through her encounter with Junior, helping her earn the frightened animal's trust. How he'd held her after the incident, squeezing her tight, as if he'd really cared about her safety despite how difficult she'd been.

And she remembered the hurt she'd seen in his eyes when she'd checked his pupils, looking for signs of a concussion and finding a pain that went way beyond a knock on the head.

"You're a good dad," she said softly. "My father—he left us when I was a baby. I don't even know what he looks like."

Nate shot her a look so full of pity she was tempted to pull up her tough-girl shield—toss her hair and throw out a joke, laugh the whole thing off. But she'd opened a long-closed door and the anger she kept locked behind it was bolting for freedom.

"Your daughter's lucky," she said. "There aren't many men who give a crap about their kids. It's like the parenting gene and testosterone cancel each other out or something. Men ditch their daughters all the time. They don't realize what a damn mess they leave behind, and they don't care, either. Men are…"

The truck lurched to a stop and she looked up, startled. Had she offended him? Scared him? She hadn't meant to get going like that, but once she started emptying the bitterness out of her heart, she hadn't been able to stop. It felt cathartic, like throwing up after too much tequila—only you generally did that in private. You didn't go spewing your poison all over some stranger you barely knew.

"I'm sorry," she said.

Sorry? Heck, she was appalled. She was screwed up and she knew it, but she didn't generally share her abandonment issues—not even with her best friends. And now she'd gone and dumped them in Nate's lap. He was probably wishing she'd get out of the car and out of his life. He was probably...

"Deer," he said quietly, nodding toward the side of the road.

A trio of big-eared does exited a copse of trees and minced across the road in front of them on impossibly slender legs, one pausing to regard them with enormous, long-lashed eyes before leaping gracefully into the brush on the other side.

"Oh," Charlie said, straightening in her seat, forgetting everything in the wonder of the moment. "Mule deer. I've never seen one."

Nate's knuckles whitened on the steering wheel. "You almost got to see one real close. You have to be careful driving at night. They seem to have a death wish."

"They're beautiful," Charlie breathed. Nate started to put the truck back in gear and she reached out and set her hand over his on the shift knob. "Wait," she said. "Let's watch them a minute."

The deer were picking their way up the bank on the left side of the road, turning occasionally to regard Charlie and Nate with their big brown Bambi eyes. When they reached the top, each one leapt over the barbwire fence, four-footed ballerinas *en jete*.

"Beautiful," Charlie said again.

"They are, aren't they?" Nate said, his voice hushed. "I forget to pay attention, sometimes. Forget to appreciate things."

He turned to her as the shadowy forms of the deer faded into the twilight. The moon, nearly full, had floated in her window like a silent companion all the way back from town, casting its dim silver light over the plains and calming summer's gold and tan down to black and white and gray. Now it lit Nate's face, creating soft shadows that gentled the hard line of his jaw and made his gray eyes glow with an otherworldly light.

Charlie started to reach up and touch the side of his face, but her fingers had somehow entwined with his on the gear shift. She lifted her other hand and started to say something about his concussion—about how his eyes looked almost normal now, and he must be feeling better—but the words caught in her throat when his hand mirrored hers, reaching up and tracing the line of her cheek. She tilted her head into his palm, then closed her eyes as he leaned in and touched his lips to hers.

The kiss started out like a question, hesitant and gentle. Charlie answered with a cautious but unmistakable "yes" and it grew more assured. Suddenly they were tangled together, lips and limbs and bodies, joining in that kiss like Charlie had never joined with any other man—not in bed, not anywhere.

The kiss said everything Nate had been hiding behind his wall of silence. It said he'd never loved Sandi. It said he'd been unbearably lonely all those years, trying to forge a family from a relationship that should have ended long ago. It said he missed his daughter. It said he needed comfort.

It said he needed love, and Charlie felt something in herself reach out to answer that call. There were empty places inside her, aching, painful places, and that kiss was filling every one. She kissed him harder, tugged him closer, and felt like she had in the bunkhouse, dizzy and happy and whole and full.

Too whole. Too full.

She pulled away. What was she thinking? Was she thinking at all? For some reason she'd granted a man she barely knew the status of a savior simply because he had his kid's picture on his key fob.

Her heart was getting ahead of her head. She had The Plan, she reminded herself. There was no time in her life for romance.

And anyway, she was going home soon. The sooner the better. Otherwise, she was liable to end up like Sandi, alone on this godforsaken ranch with a man who couldn't even carry on a conversation.

But he sure could teach her a thing or two about non-verbal communication.

―⁓―

Nate opened his eyes as Charlie pulled away. He could hardly believe he'd broken the rules again, kissed those sweet red lips again, buried his fingers in that wild, spiky hair.

He could hardly believe she'd let him.

And this time, it had been more than a kiss. It had been something infinitely better—like a complicated dance with a perfect partner who knew all the steps. A partner who followed your lead, then took her own turn, revving up the tempo until you lost control and your stately minuet turned into a wild hoedown free-for-all.

It had been one hell of a dance. And it was starting to become clear that the dance was leading somewhere—somewhere inevitable. That kiss held a promise neither of them could break.

Their tryst in the bunkhouse had been a mere taste, a test of what was between them. The kiss made it clear it was growing into something more. Was he ready for this? Was Charlie? He'd only just let Sandi go. And Charlie—hell, Charlie didn't even like him half the time.

Did she?

He looked away, clearing his throat, and shoved the truck into gear.

"Sorry," he said.

Charlie glanced over at him, then concentrated on the road ahead as if her life depended on it. He cursed himself. Should you apologize after kissing a woman? It seemed rude, somehow.

"I mean, I'm not sorry. I'm—I don't know what I am. But I shouldn't have done that. Not that I didn't like it. I did. A lot. I just…"

"I never thought I'd have to say this," Charlie said. "Never in a million years." She took a deep, shaky breath. "But—shut up, Nate."

Chapter 18

A DIM LIGHT BURNED AT THE DOOR TO THE BUNKHOUSE when Charlie and Nate reeled in from their shopping trip, but the building's windows were dark. Doris and Phaedra had evidently turned in early. The only sound was the faint scrape of cicadas and the whisper of a sage-scented breeze that tickled Charlie's cheek as she stepped out of the truck.

Once they'd lugged the bags inside, Nate pulled a six-pack of beer out and popped the top off two cans, handing one to Charlie. Then he grabbed a gallon of milk and put it in the fridge while she downed a generous glug of Bud Light.

"You don't have to do that," she said as he pulled a bottle of balsamic vinegar from another bag. "I'll put the stuff away. That way I'll be able to find it when I cook."

Nate tightened his lips into a thin line and shook his head. "You shouldn't have to do all the cooking. I could make something once in a while."

"Like what?"

"I don't know. Like, umm…" His voice trailed off into silence.

"It's okay. Gotta earn my boots." She kicked out one booted foot and grinned.

"You already did. Come on, I'll help. It'll go faster."

The guy did his best, but he clearly wasn't at home in the kitchen. He opened three cupboards before he figured out where the vinegar should go, and then stood in the middle of the room with a jar of thyme in his hand, scanning the cupboards for a likely home.

"The spices probably go somewhere near the stove."

Charlie reached past him and opened a narrow cabinet to the right of the oven. *Voila*. Spices.

"How do you know this stuff?" Nate grumbled.

"Girl power," Charlie said. "It's kind of like Spidey Sense, only better. More practical."

They worked in silence for a while. Charlie glanced sideways now and then, watching as Nate bent to put the cereal in a low cupboard or stretched to reach a high shelf. Occasionally their eyes met, and she glanced away, embarrassed to be caught looking, wondering if he could tell how that kiss still lingered warm on her lips. The memory of it filled the air, heating up the kitchen like a simmering pot on the stove. She downed the rest of her beer and felt suddenly dizzy, as if she'd downed the whole six-pack.

"'Scuse me." Nate nudged her hip with his as he reached over her to put away a bottle of cooking wine and she felt a spasm of lust shoot from her hip to her heart, then bounce around until her whole body was on red alert. The cupboard was high up over the microwave and his body pressed into hers as he slid the bottle home, turning the spasm into full-fledged convulsions. She clutched the oven handle, gritting her teeth to keep from backing up, pressing against him, instigating another kiss. Biting her lower lip, she squeezed her eyes shut and threw her head back, willing herself not to respond.

Big mistake. The movement brought her face close to his, made her hair brush his cheek. His breath warmed her neck just below her ear, sending shivers over her skin.

"Charlie," he whispered. "Hey."

Who knew her own name could sound so sexy? Or the word "hey." Right now, she was pretty sure she wanted the word "hey" engraved on her tombstone. It was so... expressive. Sweet, yet sexy, an irresistible invitation distilled into one whispered word.

His hand brushed her hip, then slid across her belly until he held her against him. He bent his head and did something to her ear—kissed it, breathed in it, something—and she sucked in a long, shuddering breath. Before she knew what was happening she'd turned her head, letting her lips meet his. And then the heat between them exploded again. The rockets' red glare, the bombs bursting in air... it would have given Francis Scott Key an orgasm. She turned, plastering her body against his, and he pressed her hard against the front of the stove and delivered a kiss so demanding and yet so pleading that she was stunned by his eloquence. Who knew passion like that could come from a laconic cowboy who could barely meet her eyes most of the time?

He pulled her hips to his, hoisting her off the floor. She wanted to protest, to pull away, but her body betrayed her, her lips too eager to taste his, her center craving the heat of him rocking hard against her. His hands started wandering, gliding over her body, savoring her breasts, her hips, all the usual places, but also the tender skin below her ear, the soft spot on the inside of her arm, the secret spot near her hip that sent ripples of pleasure pulsing like sonar to the parts of her that wanted him most.

She pulled her lips from his and buried her face in the crook of his neck, breathing hard. He wrapped his arms around her, holding her close, his own breathing shaky and shallow. She breathed in his scent and felt strangely comforted. Warm.

Safe.

She hadn't felt safe in so long.

More, please, she thought.

He kissed her again, and the two of them staggered across the kitchen and through the bedroom door. "The candles," she said, dropping onto the bed and kicking her shoes off. "Light the candles. *Hurry*."

He opened a drawer and pulled out a pack of matches. His hands shook so badly he stroked the match three times before it sparked into flame. He touched it to the candles, one after another, and the room leapt to life with wavering shadows and golden light.

Nate lit the last candle and glanced in the mirror. Charlie was sitting on the side of the bed, her green eyes glinting with golden reflections of the candle flames. He crossed the room in a single step and eased her down onto the mattress, holding her prisoner beneath him as he searched her eyes. She answered his look with her usual challenging gaze, but there was something behind it—something that lured him, taunted him, dared and double-dared him to brave her barriers and uncover the truth of her. His lips found hers and the dance began again, but with a few half-remembered steps from that first illicit tango in the bunkhouse. His hands dipped under her T-shirt, stroking her, soothing her, making her writhe and shiver as he swept a hand over her breast.

"Remember," he muttered against her lips. "I am *so* not your type."

"Good thing," she said. "Imagine what this would be like if you *were*."

He started to laugh, but he realized just in time she was serious. She hadn't expected this any more than he had.

They kissed and rolled and wrestled and the need in him rose to a frantic crescendo, a steady, burning desperation. Burying his hands in that crazy, spiky hair, he straddled her hips and tugged her shirt up and off, then fumbled with her belt while she tore at the buttons on his shirt, unbuttoning one, then another, then growling in frustration and giving the fabric a tug that sent the rest of the buttons shooting across the room.

He shrugged the shirt off and she turned her attention to her own clothes, unbuckling her belt and wriggling off her jeans to reveal another pair of those long-imagined panties. Actually, you could hardly call them panties. She was wearing a scrap of black lace with a white panel in front. A small red bow just beneath her belly button topped a row of tiny black buttons. It looked like a little tuxedo. In all his wild imaginings about her mysterious panties, he hadn't come up with anything quite that interesting.

Or quite that small. There was nothing to it, really. Just a film of lace, a little bit of nothing between his skin and hers.

There wasn't much to the matching bra, either. It was see-through lace, with a matching red bow in the center. He stroked a finger along the edge, savoring the swell and dipping into the valley of her cleavage, then cupped his hands under her breasts and ran his thumbs over the nipples clearly visible through the lace. She arched her back and moaned and suddenly, somehow, the lace was draped over the bedpost and she was naked.

Naked.

She arched her back and gave herself to him, closing her eyes and gasping as he moved his hand between her legs and felt the slick, wet warmth of her waiting for him.

"I need you *now*," she said, tugging at his belt. He groaned as she ran her hand up the hard length of him and tugged at the button fly on his jeans.

"Now," she said. "Please. Now."

She was practically whimpering. Dang. He'd never had a woman want him this much. He closed his eyes, calling up every ounce of self-control he could muster. Taking a deep breath, he scooted down the bed, out of her reach. She made a pleading sound and he reassured her, stroking her thighs before he parted them and bent to taste her, searching out the magic spots that made her shiver and moan. She tensed, closing her eyes, and he marveled as she tossed her head from side to side and buried her fingers in his hair.

Dang. He'd never thought he was any good at this. The last thing he wanted to think about was Sandi, but he couldn't help remembering how she'd stiffened and endured him, how he'd felt so clumsy, so inept and clueless.

But judging from Charlie's reaction, he was an expert.

She shivered, thrashing in his grip, and he pushed all those conscious thoughts out of his mind and did what felt right, losing himself in her until she tensed, going suddenly still, and let out a high, keening sound as she arched her back and shattered, her hips pulsing, riding the waves of her orgasm.

He'd never seen anything like it.

As the pulsing slowed, she pulled away, lifting her head to meet his eyes.

"Wow," she said.

"Yeah," he said. "Wow."

Well, he'd never claimed to be much of a conversationalist. Apparently, though, he had other skills that might go a ways toward making up for that. He laid down beside her, stroking a strand of hair out of her face, pulling her close.

"Thank you," he said.

"Thank *me*?" She laughed. "Oh, no. Thank *you*."

"I just—I never…" He could feel his face flushing. "You *like* it so much."

She stared at him and he cursed himself silently. What a stupid thing to say. He was going to mess this up again, he was sure of it. Why couldn't he keep his mouth shut? Stick to the nonverbal kind of communication?

She propped herself up on one elbow, resting her head on her hand. There. She was pulling away. He'd ruined it.

"Of course I like it," she said. "You're—dang, I don't know how to say it. You're *good* at this. You make me—well, you know." She was blushing now. "I think I made it pretty clear."

He nodded, swallowing. "It's just that Sandi—ah, shoot. I'm sorry."

He was really blowing it now. What man was clueless enough to bring up his ex-girlfriend in bed?

"Sandi didn't like it?"

She didn't look mad. She looked—interested. He'd kind of forgotten she was a psychology student. He was probably an interesting case study.

"No," he said. "I could never make her—you know." He gestured toward her, figuring she'd know what he meant.

"Then maybe you just weren't meant to be together," Charlie said. She took his hand in hers and met his eyes. "Because you are the best ever for me. I mean it. Maybe it's because you don't talk. It's like you saved everything up and put it into the way you touch me." She scooted down on the bed and kissed his hand before releasing it.

"So touch me again," she said. "Now. Please."

She wanted him. He was used to being the one who wanted, the one who begged, who risked rejection. But Charlie wanted *him*. She'd looked him in the eyes and said so right out loud. He felt his heart swell with pride—or maybe with something else. Something deeper.

She reached down and stroked him with one finger and the pleasure from her touch was almost painful. He closed his eyes, willing himself to hold on, to make it last as she touched and teased and finally tasted. Teetering at the brink, he managed to drag himself away from the swirl of sensation and back to the real world long enough to lunge across the bed and open the nightstand drawer. He pulled out a condom and she grabbed it, taking charge, pushing him down on the bed and ripping the foil open. Her fingers trembled as she smoothed it in place.

Straddling him, she set her hands on his shoulders and pinned him to the bed. She smiled into his eyes with a feral grin that was a little bit wicked and a whole lot sexy as she lowered herself slowly, just touching him before she pulled away, then dipped down to touch him again, again, again, letting him ease into the soft heart of her a little at a time. He rocked his hips up, straining for her, but she kept on teasing, letting him slip inside a little farther each time, a little deeper, and then finally he was there, inside her, and her heat wrapped around him and carried him away.

Charlie moved against him, building from a sweet, slow rhythm to an all-out rumba, watching his face as if to see how far she could go without taking him over the edge, slowing when he started to crest, speeding up again when his strength returned. He gripped her hips in his hands, wresting control from her before he lost it completely, and moved her in a slow circle. She threw her head back and closed her eyes and he watched her give in to the pleasure of it.

He wouldn't lose control, he told himself. He wouldn't. He wouldn't.

He would.

Arching her back, Charlie cried out and the sweet animal abandon of the sound carried him to a height he hadn't known he could reach. She tensed and drove herself down onto him just as he rose to meet her and let himself go, groaning with sweet, aching release.

She lowered her body to his, nestling her head in the hollow between his neck and shoulder. He could feel her breath warm on his neck, her body vibrating with subtle aftershocks. He sucked in a quick breath and started to speak, but she put her finger to his lips and stopped him.

He smiled. "You're telling me to shut up again," he said.

"Trust me," she said, closing her eyes. "You have nothing left to say."

Chapter 19

CHARLIE WOKE TO THE HIGH, WILD WHINNY OF A HORSE. Junior was up and at 'em. Turning her head, she glanced at the clock and shot out of bed.

Nine o'clock. Nate must have been up for hours. He'd gotten up and dressed while she lay beside him, sleeping. He'd probably given her that look again. Seen her with her defenses down. Caught her at her weakest.

Yeah, right. Like she'd had a shred of willpower last night. What the hell had been in that beer? She'd gone and slept with the guy again. She couldn't resist him. Couldn't say no. Once he got close, once he touched her, she was helpless.

That was okay—more than okay—as long as neither one of them took it seriously. She had a life to live, and it wasn't going to happen here.

If Nate lived a little closer to civilization, they might have made a real relationship work. For what they had together, she might have considered changing schools. Compromising. But there wasn't a university she'd consider within three hundred miles of Purvis.

She'd have to give up everything to be with him— and no man was worth that.

Not even Nate.

Besides, there were still some disturbing details about the man she didn't understand. That ever-present Stetson kept his eyes shaded from view through most of their conversations. And it wasn't just his feelings he kept hidden away.

There was something in the attic. Something he felt compelled to keep secret behind a locked door.

Slipping into a pair of jeans, she shoved her feet into her new cowboy boots, tugged the T-shirt she'd slept in down far enough to cover her midriff, and headed for the kitchen, pausing by the attic door on the way and rattling the knob.

Still locked.

She frowned at it for a moment, then turned and galloped out the front door to face the emotional fallout of the morning after.

Junior was in the round ring, bucking out his morning kinks, greeting the sun with another high-pitched challenge. Nate leaned against the gate, watching the big horse dance. As Charlie approached, the stallion stopped dead in his tracks, then bounced up on his hind legs and whinnied out a welcome.

"Mornin'," Nate said. The smile he gave her was loaded with shared secrets and promises.

"Morning." She pretended to be absorbed in the horse, but she couldn't help flicking her eyes sideways now and then, watching Nate. What did you say to a man after a night like that? *Thank you* hardly seemed appropriate.

But that was about all she had to say. She'd lost her head and shed her emotional armor with her clothes last night, and now it was time to suit up and defend herself. She'd almost broken her promise—to herself, to her mother, and to Sadie. She had to keep her distance. *Observe and report.*

She suppressed a smile. Sadie's glasses would slide right off her nose and onto her desk if Charlie observed and reported on last night. A paper on Nate's considerable nonverbal communication skills would lead to a very different kind of career. Probably a more lucrative one, but not quite what The Plan called for.

No, The Plan demanded that she should keep her head—even if she lost her panties. Nate was a fling, nothing more. A good time. A little break from real life.

But nothing serious. She should put the whole incident behind her. Maybe she could even find a way to regret it.

Cowboy, she told herself. *Stupid cowboy.*

It wasn't working. Some other voice inside her was overpowering the Plan-approved mantra with wild speculations on what might happen if she stepped a little closer, if she reached out and touched Nate's shoulder. She couldn't look at him without remembering how he'd touched her, how he'd looked at her, how he'd sent her into orbit with his hands and his mouth and his...

Damn.

"We need to talk," she said. She folded her arms on the fence rail and kept her eyes glued to the horse.

"We do?"

She nodded. "That was great last night. Really. But it was nothing serious, right?"

"Right," he said. "Sure."

He sounded disappointed. He must have thought they'd started something that would last. She glanced over at him, taking his body, his broad shoulders, his eyes and lips and talented hands, and wrapped all those gifts in one tidy package in her mind. Then she slapped a label on it: *Fling.*

The trouble was, she wasn't sure that word was in Nate's vocabulary. He seemed to take things so seriously. And the way he looked at her…

She wasn't ready for that. She needed to stop this now—before anyone's feelings got hurt.

"I'm sorry, Nate. It's just—I don't want to get involved right now. Not with anybody." She sighed. "It's not you. You… well, you're… you're fine." That was an understatement. "I'm the problem." Sheesh, she sounded like a seventh grader struggling through her first breakup. "It's just that I have a plan, Nate, and it doesn't include a relationship."

There. She'd said it, clearly and concisely. *Walk away,* she told herself. *Just walk away now.* But something kept her glued to the ground.

Maybe it was the fact that he deserved better. That he'd given her so much of himself, and she was tossing the gift away like it was some tacky bauble from the five-and-ten.

But he hadn't given her everything. He still had secrets.

"So what's in the attic?" she asked. "Ears? Fingers?"

"What?" Nate looked totally confused.

"I thought maybe you were a serial killer and you kept your trophies up there."

He laughed, sort of. It was more of a mirthless cough, really. He didn't sound amused.

She stepped back.

"No big secret," he said.

"Nate, the door's locked."

"You're impossible." He sighed. "It's Sam's room, okay? I knew you didn't want to take my bed—not that first night, anyway." He flashed her a faint smile.

"You'd have thought it would be better to sleep upstairs, and I didn't want anybody messing with her stuff. Sorry, but it's still just like she left it. I don't want her to come home and—well, you know. It's hers."

Charlie nodded. She and her mother had moved so often she'd never felt like she had a room of her own—just a series of cubicles that held her white-painted bed and matching dresser. Every one of them had neutral carpet and featureless walls, and not one of them had felt like home. But Nate protected his daughter's room as if it was a sacred space. Charlie could feel her armor crumbling again.

"That's nice," she said. "That you keep it for her, I mean. So when is she coming back?"

"I don't know." He kept watching the horse, his face impassive. "Soon, I hope."

He didn't sound hopeful. "Sorry." She took a step back, but she could feel something tugging her closer, something drawing her to the man. Something that grew stronger and stronger as she learned more about him.

Step away from the cowboy, she told herself.

"I didn't mean to get personal," she said.

Nate turned and braced his elbows on the top rail of the fence, crossing his ankles as he looked her up and down. The pose emphasized the breadth of his shoulders, the solid mass of his muscled chest, the narrow hips encased in his worn Wranglers. She dragged her eyes up to his face.

"Is that what you call it?" he asked. "Getting personal?"

Even to Charlie, that seemed like a weak definition for what had happened the night before. She looked away, shutting out the memories and bringing back her mother's lifelong litany of admonitions and advice.

"I need to get my life together," she said. "Finish school, get my degree—you know."

He nodded. But he didn't know. He couldn't. His life was so different from hers. He was right where he wanted to be, building the life he'd envisioned. She'd barely gotten started on her own dreams.

She couldn't stop now. Not for anything—or anybody.

"It's just that I want to do something meaningful with my life," she said. "Something important, that helps people. I don't want to just, you know, get married."

The corners of his mouth tilted up in a faint smile.

"Not that we'd ever get married or anything," she said. She could feel her face going red as Junior's nylon halter. How many times had she blushed since she arrived here? She'd never blushed before she met Nate. Never.

What did that mean?

She didn't want to know.

"I didn't mean I think you want to marry me or anything," she said. "I mean, we just had sex, right? Really good sex, and everything, but not, like, marry-me sex. It was more like crazy, hot, gotta-have-it sex. A fling, you know? So I... I don't..."

He put his hands on her shoulders and turned her to face him. "Charlie," he said.

"What?" She scanned his face, searching his eyes, knowing she should pull away but somehow helpless, fixed to the spot. He reached toward her and she flinched, but he only set his finger to her lips.

"Shut up," he said.

And then he kissed her, hard and thoroughly, bringing back all the heat and desire that had pulled them into bed last night, carrying her to the brink of collapse, tearing her armor to shreds in the space of a minute. When he stopped, she opened her eyes wide and stared at him.

"You can't do that," she said.

"No?" His shoulders relaxed and his lips flexed into a smile.

"No," she said.

"Okay." He shrugged and turned away, and Charlie suddenly hated herself. Why did she always make things so complicated? Why couldn't she just let loose and enjoy herself? Why was she so worried she'd break his heart when she finally got over him and left? He was a man, for heaven's sake. Men were good at good-byes.

"Well, good morning," a voice behind her said.

Charlie started guiltily at the sight of Doris and Phaedra approaching from the bunkhouse. She wondered how much they'd seen. Doris looked exactly like she always did, sparkling and chipper, but with a knowing smile that said she'd caught that kiss—and maybe even knew where Charlie had spent the night.

Phaedra, on the other hand, looked like death warmed over twice and pounded flat. Her black hair was snaking around her face in Medusa tangles, and her eyes were ringed with remnants of yesterday's makeup and mascara.

But when she saw the horse, her eyes widened and she almost smiled.

"Mornin'," Nate said. "Thought I'd just work the kinks

out of Junior, here, while you folks have your breakfast. Then we'll do some demos with the other horses."

"I thought we were going to *ride* the horses," Phaedra said.

"We are—eventually," Nate said. "But ground work always comes first, and we need to talk about conformation. It'll be a while before you're ready to ride."

Phaedra put her head down and muttered something about "bullshit."

Charlie offered a smile to offset the teen's sulky pout. "Well, I've got every kind of cereal you could think of. Frosted Flakes, Rice Krispies, and oh, Phaedra—you'd probably like Count Chocula. He's kind of a kindred soul, right?"

"Not hungry," Phaedra muttered.

"Well, come on anyway," Charlie coaxed. "Have some coffee, at least. Or orange juice."

Phaedra shook her head and set one foot on the bottom rail of the gate, determined to watch Nate put the stallion through his paces.

"You're not staying here," Nate said. "You'll be a distraction. I need Junior's full attention, and you're freaking him out." As if to demonstrate, Junior arched his back and crow-hopped across the ring like a spastic wind-up toy.

"Whatever." Phaedra slouched off toward the bunkhouse. The kid would probably go back to bed, Charlie figured. Hopefully she'd wake up in a better mood on her second try.

Two bowls of cereal later, Doris and Charlie headed for the round ring. Nate had finished with Junior, and was cleaning up the horse's leavings with a pitchfork.

"The romance of ranch life," he said, tossing a pile of road apples to one side. He rested the pitchfork against the fence and led the two women to the barn.

"Where's the princess of doom and gloom?" he asked.

Charlie shrugged. "I have no idea. I thought she'd gone back to bed, but she's not in the bunkhouse."

"I'm not sure that one's going to work out," Nate said.

"Maybe you should call her parents," Doris said. "See if they can clue you in. The child seems troubled to me."

"I know," Charlie said. "But we don't know how to get in touch with her parents. We don't even know her last name. The registration forms are, um, missing." She looked the older woman up and down, feigning suspicion. "For all I know, you're a wanted psycho killer."

"Nothing so interesting," Doris said. "Just an old cowgirl past her prime."

"I'd say you're right in your prime," Charlie said. "Right dead center."

Doris grinned, nodding. Charlie hoped she'd be as satisfied with herself when she was that age.

"Maybe you could talk to Phaedra," Nate said to Charlie. "She seems to like you. You could find out some contact information, like you want to keep in touch with her after the clinic. Then we can call her parents and have them take Witchy McSpook back home."

"Maybe," Charlie said. "Or maybe I can talk her into behaving herself. Give her a chance, Nate. I think she might shape up once we start working with the horses."

"Let's hope." Nate stopped in front of a generous box stall housing a handsome brown-and-white paint. The horse had a round brown circle over one eye in an otherwise white face, making him look like the dog in the old *Little Rascals* films. When they stopped, he tossed his head up and lifted his upper lip. Charlie could swear he was smiling.

"This is Razz," Nate said. "Short for Rascal, 'cause of that patch and his personality. I thought we'd start with him today."

Charlie reached out a tentative hand to pet the horse's muzzle, but he shied away. She sucked in a wondering breath. "Is he a mustang?"

Chapter 20

"A MUSTANG?" NATE TOOK A DEEP BREATH AND TRIED TO nod, but something in Charlie's trusting gaze wouldn't let him do it. "Not really," he said. "He's not wild, just difficult."

Shoot. He cursed himself silently. He'd planned to convince her Razz was a genuine wild pony, but she looked so serious, so sweetly enraptured, that he just couldn't trick her like that. Besides, he was lousy at lying. He'd get found out sooner or later anyway.

"He's just a troublemaker," he said. "But you'll use the same techniques to calm him that you used on Junior the other day. Only today we'll go one step farther." He handed her a woven rope hackamore. His fingers brushed hers and a thrill zipped up his arm and headed for the danger zone. Swallowing, he bent his focus to the task at hand. "Once he quiets down and lets you touch him, see if you can get this over his head. The knot goes under his chin, okay?"

"Okay." Charlie took a deep breath and stepped inside the stall.

Nate almost laughed as Razz scampered away. The paint had a wicked sense of humor that had tried Nate's patience from day one, but Charlie had learned her lesson well. She held the hackamore behind her back, moving slowly the way she had with Junior. The horse stretched his neck out and sniffed the air in front of her face with the delicacy of a wine connoisseur, lifting his lips up over his front teeth in his trademark smile.

"Oh, he's a character," Doris whispered.

Charlie and the horse stood nose to nose for half a second before the paint bunched his hindquarters beneath him, planted his hind feet, and spun to the other side of the stall.

"Get him to do that with a rider on him and you'll have yourself a reining champ," Doris said.

"He has his days," Nate said. "Good ones and bad ones."

"I'll bet," Doris said. "Looks like this is one of the bad ones—for humans. The horse is sure having a good time, though."

Nate had to agree. Razz was thrilled to find a new playmate, and he led Charlie around and around the stall before allowing her to stroke his long nose and bring the hackamore out from behind her back. She let the horse sniff it before slipping it neatly over his head.

"I did it!" Her eyes sparkled. "How was that?"

"Great," Nate said. "I think he likes you. He's usually a pretty tough customer." He tugged on the reins dangling from the bosal and Razz shied, dancing a little two-step at the barn door as if he didn't want to go outside. It was another one of his usual games.

"Come on, buddy, let's—hey," Nate said, glancing over at the stall by the door. "Where's Boy?"

The stall that had held the black gelding the night before was empty. Nate hadn't put him out this morning; he'd been planning to use him to show what a well-trained cutting horse could do.

"He must have gotten out," Charlie said.

Nate scowled. "Right. And then he closed the stall door behind him."

"Uh-oh," Charlie said. "He was the black one, right?"

Nate nodded, his face grim.

"Are you thinking what I'm thinking?" Doris asked.

Charlie nodded. "Yup. That black horse matches Phaedra's outfit, doesn't he? How much you want to bet the Ghoul of Goth took herself for a little ride?"

Before Charlie had time to answer, Nate flipped the reins over Razz's head and grabbed a handful of mane. Vaulting smoothly onto the horse's back, he spun the animal once, then twice, finally pointing him toward the open fields.

Charlie's eyes narrowed as he brought the horse under control with a slight tug of the reins. "Clinic's postponed," he said. "Sorry."

"Geez," she said. "I thought you said he was difficult."

"He knows I need him," Nate said, touching his heels to Razz's flanks and launching the horse like a rock from a slingshot.

Nate bent over the horse's neck and urged him on. He couldn't remember being this pissed off, ever. That little creep had basically stolen Boy—a horse that didn't even belong to him. If anything happened to the black, Nate was in deep trouble. Even for a seasoned rider, there were dangers out there on the open plains. If Boy stepped into a prairie dog hole, he could break a leg.

This was all Sandi's fault. She probably thought running a clinic was as easy as the ones you saw on TV, where a smiling trainer coached a cooperative group of experienced riders on the finer points of horsemanship.

Instead, she'd managed to get him a gang of greenhorns who couldn't even sit straight in the saddle.

Well, not really. Doris was obviously experienced with horses, and Charlie did have a gift, even if her riding skills were pretty much nonexistent.

She had a gift for something else too. He tensed as he remembered the night before, how she'd warmed and writhed, responding to his touch. He'd never forget that night, but he needed to change the way he thought about it. She obviously hadn't given him her heart—just her body.

And apparently, it was a limited-time offer.

He needed to calm down. Get a grip before Razz picked up on his tension. Gently, he pulled to a stop and scanned the horizon, stroking the horse's neck. As he calmed the horse, the horse calmed him. It was a give-and-take that had worked for him all his life.

His gaze swept right, then left, then right again, and paused. There. He shaded his eyes, focusing on a black dot in the distance that was climbing one of the ranch's rolling hills.

"There's your buddy, Razz," he said. "Let's go get him."

He clicked his tongue and Razz danced into a sprightly jog, then lifted into a pounding lope, angling across the field to cut off the distant rider.

It took them a good twenty minutes to catch up to Boy and Phaedra. To her credit, the girl pulled up when she saw them coming; Nate had been worried she'd take off and lead him on a chase, and he wasn't sure Razz could outrun the spirited Boy.

"I guess you want me to come back now," Phaedra said, pouting.

Nate bit back six or eight swear words and replied as mildly as he could.

"Yeah, let's go back," he said. "And then I'll call the sheriff and have your ass hauled off to jail for horse stealing." He reached over and grabbed Boy's reins just below the snaffle bit. At least the girl had used the right bridle.

"I can ride him," Phaedra said. "I'll follow you."

Nate ignored her, flipping the reins over the horse's head and clenching them in his fist. Wordlessly, he turned back toward the ranch, leading Boy at a slow walk with Phaedra sulking in the saddle.

The teenager sat the horse like some bizarre equestrian ghost. She'd left the stirrups pulled up and was riding with her knees up around the horse' withers like a racehorse jockey. To make matters worse, she'd taken the time to put on her full Goth trappings, makeup and all. She looked like something out of a Tim Burton movie. Maybe the Fifth Horseman of the Apocalypse, if the Fifth Horseman was a misfit teenager.

Maybe they all were. That would explain the Apocalypse.

"I don't know why you're so pissed off," she mumbled. "It's a riding clinic, right? I just went for a ride."

"On a horse that isn't yours. Or mine. This is a customer's horse. You mess him up, I'm the one who pays."

They plodded on in silence, Nate staring straight ahead, his jaw painfully clenched. It was all he could do not to turn around and knock her off the horse.

"You're a spoiled brat," he muttered.

"Oh, yeah, right," Phaedra said. "I'm spoiled. That's why I spend every minute I'm not at school alone in my mom's shitty apartment, watching my dad on TV while she's off with her latest beau. That's what she calls him. Her beau." She snorted. "Beau-beau the clown, that's what I call him. He wanted me gone, so he told her she ought to get my dad to pay for this camp. So now you're stuck with me. And you hate me too." She sniffed, and Boy caught her agitation, prancing sideways a moment before a glance from Nate settled him down. "Figures."

"So your dad's on TV? What is he, a newscaster or something?" Nate asked.

"Or something. Why do you care?"

Nate didn't answer, just stared at the route ahead through the space between Razz's ears. Beau-beau wasn't the only one who wanted this kid gone.

"Where do you live?" he finally asked, thinking he'd find her mother and send the kid packing.

"L.A.," Phaedra said. "We used to live out in the Valley, but then my mom decided she needed to live in the city. More opportunity, she said." She snorted. "She says she's an actress, but she's never worked a day in her life. Her idea of an 'opportunity' is finding a new sugar daddy to sleep with." She sniffed again and wiped her nose with the back of one black-nailed hand. "Guess my dad wasn't good enough for her."

"Maybe she didn't really love your dad," Nate said. "Sometimes relationships are complicated." The comment surprised him. What was he, Dr. Phil all of a sudden?

The kid snorted. "Everybody loves my dad. Besides, when we lived in the Valley, I had a horse and everything. Well, a pony, anyway. Then Mom left and fucked it all up."

"Watch your language," Nate said.

"You don't mind when Charlie swears," she said.

"Yeah I do. I just don't say anything because she's not a kid."

"Yeah, and 'cause you like her. But you hate me. Everybody does, because I'm such a freak."

"You're not a freak," Nate said. The kid's self-hate was starting to worry him. "You just dress different. It's like you try to look weird."

"Yeah, well, it's better than being pretty," she said. "This way, people leave me the hell alone."

Nate glanced back at Ghoul Girl. She was staring down at the horse, petting it, fondling its mane. Her eyes were bright with tears, and in that moment, she looked almost human. Like somebody's daughter. Somebody's child.

But most kids wanted to be pretty. Most kids didn't want to be left alone.

Unless…

"Does he bother you? That Beau, or whatever his name is, does he…?"

Phaedra shrugged. "I just don't like the way he looks at me. He never did anything."

Nate's anger deflated like a punctured balloon. He didn't like this kid, but that's what she was—a kid. He thought of Sam, down in Denver. For all he knew, his own daughter could be traveling the same road as Phaedra—living in some apartment with Sandi, gradually growing into a bitter teen while Sandi brought home men she barely knew and chased all those dreams she claimed he'd killed.

He pictured his daughter grown tall, dressed in

Phaedra's ghoulish getup, giving him that cold, hard-eyed stare that had seen way too much.

It could happen, he realized. Without him there to protect Sam, anything could happen. He had to get her back.

And that meant dealing with Sandi.

He tamped down the thoughts of Charlie that had been smoldering in the back of his brain. He'd been tempted to protest this morning when she passed off their union as a non-starter. Hell, he'd felt like falling to his knees, right there in the barnyard, and begging her to give him another chance. Her kisses, her passion, the stunning surprise of it, the way it made him feel—she'd made him realize what it was like to be with a woman who actually wanted him.

But she didn't want him—not for good. It was just a fling. What had she called it? "Crazy, hot, gotta-have-it sex."

That's all it was.

And that was all it could be. After all, they'd known each other less than a week. Nate had never been a believer in love at first sight, and yet he'd let this woman's exotic looks and spunky manner go to his head like a teenager with his first crush. It was crazy. Irresponsible. He had a daughter to raise, and he needed to be careful who he brought into her life. After all, "flings" didn't stick around. "Flings" went away, leaving a trail of broken hearts behind them. He couldn't let that happen. Not to him, and especially not to Sam.

He needed to stay away from temptation—away from Charlie—and concentrate on Sam. He'd get hold of Sandi as soon as he got back. Talk her into bringing his daughter home. There had to be something his ex wanted—something she hadn't already taken. He'd give her anything if she'd just let him keep Sam.

He'd even give up Charlie.

Chapter 21

CHARLIE COMMANDEERED THE RUSTING GAS GRILL AND played chef that night, flipping burgers and trying not to watch Nate too much. Doris was doing her best to stir up a little cookout camaraderie, but getting a conversation going with Phaedra was kind of like getting Butt to play fetch. Charlie had tried to give the dog some exercise that afternoon, throwing a tennis ball over and over, then plodding after it while the dog lay grinning and panting in the grass.

Doris lobbed a few conversational volleys onto the dinner table, trying to get the girl talking, but she wound up mostly talking to herself while Charlie and Nate avoided each others' eyes and Phaedra stared at her plate. The girl had been eerily silent all through Nate's demonstrations that afternoon.

"Wow," Charlie said as she cleared the table. "Those were, without a doubt, the best veggie burgers I've ever had." Usually the frozen ones were a gluey amalgam of unidentifiable soy products. These had been tasty, crisp on the outside and seasoned just right. "We need to get some more of those. Quick, before they run out."

Nate pushed back his chair. "I doubt they'll have many takers for them," he said. "This is beef country."

"They were good," Phaedra said, her eyes on her lap. "Thank you."

Charlie cocked her head and studied the teenager. The

girl was utterly miserable, her black getup obviously in sync with her psyche. Charlie's heart ached for the girl, but the most important thing right now was to keep everybody safe—humans and horses. They couldn't risk Phaedra taking off again. So she'd lit into the girl, chastised her to within an inch of her life. It seemed to have worked—maybe a little too well. The girl was all manners and no personality, trotting out her pleases and thank-yous like a brainwashed debutante.

"Help me with the dishes," Charlie said impulsively, grabbing Phaedra's hand and pulling her up from the picnic bench. Phaedra looked stunned, fixing her with those cool gray eyes as if considering a life-or-death decision, then nodded, biting her lower lip.

They cleared the table in silence, but once they were alone in the kitchen, Phaedra turned to her with urgency in her eyes.

"Nate won't tell my dad, will he?"

"Tell him what?"

"About me taking the horse, or—or anything."

Charlie cranked the faucet on hot and glanced over at her helper. The gray eyes were no longer expressionless. They were panicked. "I won't tell," Charlie said. "But Nate probably will. He was ready to send you home."

Phaedra gathered the silverware in her fist and let it clatter into the sink. "Don't send me home." Her voice was shaky and piped up an octave on the next words. "Please. I don't want my dad to know I'm not—I'm not *good*."

"Okay," Charlie said soothingly. "And you're not bad, hon. You just made a bad decision." She'd found Phaedra's weakness. As long as she feared they'd talk to her father, she'd behave. "We won't call your dad."

We. She'd done it again. There was no "we." There was just her, all on her own, driving straight toward the future she wanted.

No detours. No passengers.

She rinsed a plate, then handed it to Phaedra, who slipped it into the dishwasher.

"But he'll be here tomorrow," Phaedra said. "If he's on time. Mom says he's late a lot, if he even shows up at all." She ducked her head. "I hope he doesn't. Nate'll probably tell him, and then he'll hate me too."

"Your dad's coming here?"

The girl nodded. "He thought we could, like, bond over this horse training thing."

"Sounds good to me," Charlie said. "I mean, you like horses, right? It should be fun."

Phaedra nodded. "Yeah," she said. "I'm just nervous. I don't know my dad very well."

Charlie scrubbed the next plate a little harder than necessary, avoiding her helper's eyes. "Well, at least you know him," she said. "I never knew mine."

"You didn't?"

"Not really."

"But you seem so, you know, sure of yourself. I thought that would've come from your dad."

Charlie almost laughed. Whatever had happened to her parents' relationship, it hadn't been her dad who was the strong one. Charlie wondered sometimes if he'd really left on his own, or if her spunky, smart-mouthed mother had run him off.

"So what's your dad like?" she asked.

Phaedra shrugged. "He's a cowboy."

Charlie rolled her eyes. "Another one," she said.

"Yeah. Cowboys are so not cool," Phaedra said. "I wish he was a rock star, or a Mafia don or something. That would be so much better."

"Yeah?" Charlie almost laughed at the thought of Phaedra as a Goth Mafia princess. The rock star thing would fit, though. Except she'd probably end up like that Osbourne chick, a poor little rich girl flailing around for her own identity.

"Well, at least he can probably ride," Charlie said. "That'll make Nate happy."

"I don't know." Phaedra shoved a knife and fork into the dishwasher's flatware basket. "Mostly my dad just pretends to be a cowboy. I don't think he's really that good."

Charlie sighed. Wannabe cowboys were probably even worse than real ones. "How often do you see him?"

Phaedra shrugged. "It's been a while," she said. Her eyes lit on the countertop, on the window—everywhere but Charlie's inquiring eyes.

"How long?" Charlie asked.

"I think I was five," Phaedra mumbled. "I don't really remember."

Charlie almost dropped the dish she was washing. "You haven't seen your father for ten years?"

Phaedra shrugged. "My mom and I do okay," she said. "We don't need him." She delivered the line with a singsong quality that told Charlie she'd said it many times before. And no wonder, Charlie thought. She'd had ten years to practice it.

Ten years to build up a defensive façade against the fact that her father didn't give a crap about her. No wonder Charlie felt such a kinship with the girl. They were wearing matching suits of emotional armor.

"I'm sure you do fine," Charlie said fiercely. "No woman needs a man like that. But you deserve better." She put her damp hands on Phaedra's shoulders and turned the girl to face her, looking in her eyes. "You deserve much, much better, okay? You're smart, and you're your own person, and a real father would be proud to have you."

"You think?"

Charlie went back to the dishes. "I *know*," she said. She shrugged as if it didn't matter. As if this wasn't a topic that had haunted her own childhood. "It's just how men are. They don't love like we do." She handed Phaedra another plate. "That's why you have to be able to rely on yourself."

They finished the rest of the task in silence, but something between the two of them had shifted. When Phaedra slid the last spoon into the dishwasher, she turned to Charlie and actually smiled. It was a wan smile, sort of a sad clown thing, but it was better than her usual scowl. Charlie smiled back. For some weird reason, she kind of liked this kid.

"Do you think I should apologize to Nate?" Phaedra asked.

"Yes," said a voice behind them. It was Nate, tramping into the room, Butt trailing close behind.

"Okay." Phaedra took a deep breath, but she never got any further. A car horn blared outside, sounding a sharp nasal root-a-toot-toot, and Charlie whirled toward the window at the familiar sound.

It was her Celica. Her adorable little red Celica, miraculously healed of its wounds. It stood out against the gray and brown dullness of the ranch like a ruby in the dust, its wide, unblinking headlights fixed on the horizon like it couldn't believe where it had ended up.

"My car," Charlie whispered. It should have looked good to her. She was free to go now—free to leave Latigo Ranch and all its problematic denizens behind. Free to run away before her feelings for Nate got the best of her.

But for some reason, the sight of her car gave her a heavy feeling inside, as if she'd swallowed a rock.

She glanced over at Nate to see how he was taking it. He looked like he'd swallowed the same stone.

"Ray," he muttered. "He must have gotten it fixed somehow." He surveyed the clean kitchen counters, the floor, the ceiling—everything but Charlie's face.

Charlie stepped to the front door in time to see a child leap from the car almost before it came to a full stop and rocket toward the house, flailing heels kicking up dust. She turned to Nate. "He's got someone with him," she said over her shoulder. "His daughter, maybe."

The color drained from Nate's face. "His... oh," he said. He looked totally shocked. Scared, even. "His *daughter*?"

The door swung open and a miniature redheaded tornado spun into the room like a swirl of autumn leaves, pausing a moment at the door, then rushing over to Nate and enveloping him in a storm of affection.

"I'm back," it squealed. "I came back!"

Nate let out a noise, something between a grunt and a sigh, and the color flooded back into his face as he dropped to his knees and embraced the child.

The hurricane subsided a little, slowing enough to reveal a pale, freckled child with Nate's gray eyes, a tousled head of fervently auburn hair, and a grin the size of Latigo itself. Even if Charlie hadn't seen the key fob, she'd know this was Nate's daughter. The eyes were a dead match.

"I missed you," she squealed. "What happened to your head? How's Peach? Grandpa said she hurt her leg. How's Butt? Who's that lady? Why is that girl dressed funny? Are you glad I'm back? You have flowers on the table! Thanks, Daddy! Did you pick 'em yourself? Did you know I was coming?"

Nate wrapped the child in a bear hug, burying his face in her hair. He didn't answer her questions. He didn't speak at all. He just closed his eyes and clasped the child close, swaying gently from side to side as he held her. Charlie thought she saw his lips moving, as if he was praying.

Charlie watched through a blur of rising tears. Glancing over at Phaedra, she realized the girl was having the same reaction. Not all men were the same. There were fathers who loved their children. There were men who would never walk away—not willingly. The proof was right there in front of them.

Oblivious to Nate's emotion, the tornado pulled away from him and whirled toward the door.

"Can I go see Peach?" she asked. "I missed Peach too."

"Sure," Nate said. He looked a little bewildered—shell-shocked, almost, Charlie thought.

The little cyclone spun outside, almost trampling an older man who was just stepping up onto the porch. Sweeping off a battered cowboy hat, he turned and gently slapped at her receding form, grinning at Nate.

"Surprise," he said, running a hand through his

grizzled hair and setting the hat, crown down, on the table.

Nate stared out the door, still looking dazed.

"Yeah," he said. "Surprise. What the hell is going on?"

Chapter 22

THE GRIZZLED MAN GRINNED. "I HAD TO TAKE A TRUCK TO Dooley over in Lusk, and he had the part. So we don't have to wait." He turned to Charlie. "Your ride's all fixed, ma'am. Ready to go when you are."

"Great," Charlie said. A day ago she'd have meant it. But now—now, she didn't know what to feel.

"So what brings you here?" he asked. "You one of Sandi's friends?"

Charlie smiled. "No, I'm just a customer," she said.

"Well, you're a pretty one. I wouldn't say you needed any of that Mary Kay stuff, but Sandi could probably convince you to buy something if she was here."

"Oh, I'm not here for Mary Kay," she said. "I'm here for Nate." She blushed—again. What was it about Nate that kept her in a constant state of embarrassment? "I mean…"

The man chuckled and shook his head. "Always said he ought to get a stud farm going. But that wasn't quite what I meant." Charlie's blush intensified, but then he laughed, a slow, easy chuckle, and she instantly felt more comfortable. He offered her a calloused, blue-veined hand.

"I'm Ray Givens," he said. "Sandi's dad." He turned to Nate. "Now, what about that bandage for Peach?"

Nate was still standing in the middle of the kitchen, gaping like a grounded trout. "Sam," he said. "Sam's here."

"Oh, yeah," Ray said, as if he'd just remembered something. "Sandi dropped her off. She didn't tell you?"

"Tell me what?"

Ray sighed. "That girl. I'm sorry, Nate. We raised her to do better."

"It's all right," Nate said, but his lips were drawn into a tight, thin line.

"She needs you to take Sam for a while so she can go to beauty school. In Denver, I guess."

"Ray, I'm happy to have Sam. Heck, I'm thrilled. I missed her like crazy. But what the hell?" He shook his head. "She just dumps our daughter off like— like baggage?"

"You know how it is, Nate," the older man said soothingly. "Sandi gets a bug up her butt, there's no stopping her. I'm sorry. Lord knows, she should treat you better. Sam too."

There was an awkward silence. Charlie cleared her throat, figuring she might remind them they had strangers horning in on their family issues, but they didn't seem to notice her.

"So is she coming back?" Nate asked. "Or is this it?"

Ray started to answer, then paused as Charlie cleared her throat again. "Let's go see about that horse," he said.

———⁓———

Nate pressed his head against Peach's shoulder and held the mare's knee in his cupped hands while Ray wrapped a length of purple vet tape around the animal's pastern. "Don't know why you keep this animal around," Ray said. "Sam's ready for a full-sized horse, and this one's nothing but trouble anyway. You're lucky she didn't get to Junior. You'd have some pretty interesting offspring from that pairing."

"So what am I supposed to do? Send Peach to auction? You know where she'd end up."

"Alpo," Ray said. "The way of all flesh."

Nate could hear Sam's piping voice rising and falling out in the corral as she introduced Charlie to the other horses. At least he wouldn't have to explain anything later. Sam was probably giving her a somewhat skewed version of his life story, but what did it matter? Charlie had her car back. She'd be gone soon. And that was just as well. There was nothing between them. Nothing but sex. Crazy, hot, gotta-have-it sex. Nothing more.

Not to her, anyway.

He felt a ripple of regret. The picture of her pale face resting against the stallion's dark hide, lips parted, eyes closed in ecstasy, gave way to the image of her naked in his bed. He could still feel this morning's stolen kiss hot and hard against his lips. She'd been tense, surprised. Not like last night. Last night she'd kissed him like she was dying of thirst and he was the only water for a hundred miles.

Hell, she'd kissed him like she loved him. Or at least, like she maybe could. He pressed his forehead into Peach's warm flank and squeezed his eyes shut. It didn't matter. She'd be climbing back into that shiny red spaceship of a car any minute now, going back to Planet Jersey.

"So how many customers showed up for the clinic?" Ray asked.

Nate narrowed his eyes. "You knew about that?"

"Yep."

"Well, I didn't. You might have warned me." Nate set the horse's foot down and rested his arms on the animal's broad back. "How many of those brochures did Sandi send out?"

"You saying she didn't tell you about that either?" Ray shook his head. "Shoot. I wondered how she got you to do it. She had a hundred of 'em printed."

"Well, I guess they didn't work too well." Nate patted Peach's rump and sat down on a nearby hay bale. "We only got three takers."

"Hmpf." Ray stood up, brushing the straw from his pants. "Funny. She got four deposits."

"What?"

"Deposits. She got four of 'em. You've probably got another student on the way. The thing doesn't officially start 'til tomorrow, right?"

"I wouldn't know," Nate said. "I never even saw the damn brochure. You wouldn't happen to have one, would you?"

Ray pulled a crumpled pamphlet out of his back pocket and handed it over. "Live the Western Adventure at Latigo Ranch," it proclaimed. It was the same as the one he'd seen in Charlie's car.

Nate read the description of the various packages offered, then took a look at the rates Sandi had charged. Holy shit. For that kind of money, folks would be expecting miracles and gourmet meals.

He chewed the inside of his cheek, a habit he always turned to when he was nervous.

"What did she do with the money?" he asked.

"How do you think she paid for beauty school?" Ray said.

"You're kidding me."

Ray splayed his hands. "I'm sorry, Nate. I keep saying that. I don't know what else to say."

"Sorry isn't going to pay the bills, Ray," Nate said. "These people are going to want refunds." He nodded toward the far side of the barn, where Sam and Charlie were absorbed in earnest discussion. "That one already does. She's been cooking for the whole gang since she got here. Hell, I ought to be paying her, not the other way around."

"They won't need a refund if you give 'em what they came for," Ray said.

Nate folded his arms across his chest and glared at the old man. "I don't have what they came for."

"Sure you do." Ray eased to his feet, and Nate tensed in anticipation of a fatherly lecture. "Sandi just wants you to make something of yourself, Nate. For Sam's sake. You know you have the skills these people are interested in. All you have to do is take a few hours a day to teach 'em, and they'll go home happy."

"I don't know." Nate shrugged. "There's no way Charlie's going home happy."

"I don't know. She looks pretty happy right now." Ray gestured toward Peach's stall. Sam was holding up various grooming implements and demonstrating them on Honey. She was apparently explaining the fine art of grooming to Charlie, who was grinning with her head cocked to one side.

Damn. She was good with his horse, good with his kid—and a revelation in his bed. If only things were different.

If only she could stay.

He pictured her in the kitchen, helping Sam bake cookies. In the barn, helping him with the chores. In his bed, helping him… well, just helping him.

Ray spoke and Nate almost dropped the horse's leg. He'd been lost in thought and pretty much forgotten where he was.

"Sandi's just trying to give you a push in the right direction, son," Ray said.

Sandi was giving him a push, all right. She was pushing him away, just like she had for the past seven years. He'd just been too dumb to see it until last night. Charlie made him realize not all women were like Sandi.

He chewed the inside of his cheek, thinking. "So is Sandi coming back?"

"I guess that depends."

Nate splayed his hands. "On what? On which way the wind blows? On whether she has a bad hair day? I need to know, Ray."

"I'd say it probably depends on the clinic," Ray said. "You do it, and it works out, and maybe Sandi'll see you're trying."

"Trying?" Nate slammed the flat of his hand against the barn wall. "*Trying?* What have I been doing all these years, Ray, but *trying*? This place was a wreck when I took over, you know that. I've made something out of almost nothing, and I've provided a good home for my daughter. And for her mother too." He folded his arms across his chest and scowled. "Not that she appreciates it."

"It's not the kind of home she wants."

"It's a good home. Good for Sam. Maybe it was Sandi who needed to *try*."

"She has." Ray knelt and adjusted his pant leg over

the top of his boot. "She's tried for seven years, Nate. I think she figures it's time to try something new."

"Well, she's welcome to it," Nate said. "Tell her I said 'good luck.'"

"Give it a chance," Ray pleaded. "Just do the clinic."

"It's not like I have a choice," Nate said. "But what am I supposed to use for horses?"

"Mustangs," Ray said. "It's right there in the brochure, and there's a sale in Green River on Saturday. You have to admit, Sandi thought this through."

"All except one important detail, Ray. I don't have any money—not even enough for adoption fees. She took everything I had."

"Everything?" Ray looked surprised. It figured. Sandi hadn't even been straight with her own dad.

"Everything," Nate said. "Checking, savings—she cleaned it all out. I can barely feed these people. I can barely feed your granddaughter. She took the money that would feed her own child."

Ray sat down hard on a bale of hay and ran his fingers through his hair. "Oh, Lord," he muttered. "That girl."

He was a decent guy, and Nate knew he must be tired of making excuses for his only daughter. His wife Rhonda was a good woman too. How the two of them had raised a girl as impetuous and difficult as Sandi was a total mystery.

"I'm sorry, son. I didn't know," Ray said. "Look, if you want, I'll buy the horses. We'll call it an investment."

"I guess," Nate said—but he wasn't sure at this point that he wanted Ray's help. He'd about made up his mind that the situation was hopeless. Even if he got the money, he wasn't sure letting greenhorns work with wild horses was a smart thing to do. Somebody could get hurt. He could end up getting sued.

Besides, giving up was starting to sound like a sanctuary—like the only safe port in the storm Sandi had created.

"Let me help, son," Ray said. "There's no shame in it."

Nate nodded, his lips pressed into a thin line. First he'd had to ask Charlie to help out. Now he was taking money from Ray. He'd always taken pride in standing on his own two feet, but he couldn't seem to make this thing work on his own.

He looked over at Charlie just as she glanced his way and flashed him a conspiratorial smile. Maybe having help wasn't so bad. Maybe the fact that Charlie was working with him was one of the things that made their connection so strong. He and Sandi had been two separate people, with different needs, different visions of the future—but he and Charlie were a team. Partners.

"What do you say, son?" Ray asked.

"Okay," Nate said. "Thanks." He took a deep breath. "I could use the help."

"Dad!" Sam flew down the aisle ahead of Charlie, startling Peach and almost upending Ray, who was putting the finishing touches on the bandage. "Charlie and her friends are having a pajama party in the bunkhouse tonight, and I get to go if you say I can. We're going to paint our nails and talk about boys. Can I? Please?"

Nate ruffled her hair. "You're too little to talk about boys," he said, flashing Charlie a dirty look.

"I know. That's what I said," Sam said. "But Charlie said we can talk about how they're stupid and have cooties."

"Well, in that case…" Nate began.

"Yay! Charlie, I get to go!" Sam did an impromptu jig on the tips of her toes, then settled down and cocked her head, all seriousness. "Is there anything I can bring?"

Charlie suppressed a smile. At least someone had taught the kid some manners. Had to be Sandi, since Nate had all the social graces of a rodeo bull.

"Maybe some snack food," Charlie said. "You could check and see what's in the pantry. Maybe you could find chips or something. And salsa. Salsa would be great if you have any."

Sam ran off to check the snack supply and Charlie grinned at Nate. He gave her an answering smile, and she took a quick step back, almost falling into the feed trough. She could read that smile as clearly as if he'd spoken. He wasn't smiling about his adorable daughter. He was smiling about her. About the way they were working together, understanding each other.

He was smiling because he was thinking he'd get her back into his bed.

Well, that wasn't going to happen again. She tossed her head and turned away, hoping he couldn't see that his intimate smile had damn near sparked an orgasm all on its own.

"Pajama party," he said. "You going formal again?"

"No," she turned away, pretending to be absorbed in untangling Peach's mane. She felt like today's panties were burning their way through her clothes. They were blue, with big white stars on them. Wonder Woman panties.

"Stop it," she whispered. "Just—just stop it."

"I can't," he said. "I keep thinking about it. That little tuxedo thing… sorry."

"What?" Ray rose somewhat creakily to his feet and cupped one ear. "Not as young as I used to be. Did you say something, Nate?"

"Nope. He didn't," Charlie said. "Not a thing. What do I owe you for the car?"

Ray shrugged. "Not much. We took that axle off a wreck old Dooley had layin' around. That kind of car don't last long around here."

"It doesn't have to," Charlie said. "It'll get me back to Jersey, right?"

Ray gave the car a sidelong gaze and stroked his chin. "Maybe," he said. "If you can get as far as Purvis. I barely made it here. She looks good, but she's creaking and rattling like an old jalopy on these dirt roads. Think you might'a shaken a few other things loose."

"Great," Charlie said.

"What year is that thing? A '78?"

Charlie nodded.

"Well, she's an old lady then. You stop at the shop before you go. I'll give her a good once-over, tighten up what's loose," he said. "No point doing it now; it'll just rattle free again on the road to town."

Charlie nodded. She alternated between wanting to light out from Latigo that very minute and wishing she could stay forever. Right now, Sam had her leaning toward the forever side. Sam, and that smile of Nate's. Sam was adorable, and Nate—well, Nate was trouble. He had her so distracted she could barely observe, let alone report. If Sadie knew how she was mucking up this assignment, she'd have a fit.

"You sure are a hit with my granddaughter," Ray said. "She's awful excited about that party."

"She's a great kid," Charlie said. She glanced over at Nate. "Someone's doing a good job bringing her up."

"That's Sandi," Nate grunted. He looked down at his boots and shoved his hands in his pockets.

Wow. He'd gone from Casanova to caveman in less than sixty seconds. The mere mention of his ex shut him down like the push of a button.

"Sandi taught her all that about horses?" she asked. "I just got a whole grooming clinic over there. You should hire her on as your assistant professor."

"No, that had to be Nate," Ray said. "Sandi's scared of horses." He brushed his hands briskly. "Let me just get Sam's things, Nate," he said. "Then I'd appreciate a ride home."

Charlie watched him go, then turned to Nate. "Sandi was afraid of horses?"

He shrugged and turned his attention back to the pony's injured leg.

No wonder the girl left, Charlie thought. Nate's whole life centered on the horses, and Sam was headed down the same road. Sandi must have felt like an outsider in her own home.

But then why had she gotten together with Nate in the first place?

Charlie knew the answer to that one. She didn't even like the guy half the time, but after tasting what he had to offer, she was tempted to indulge herself on a regular basis. If she was a randy teenager, instead of a sensible, mature woman with plans and goals, she'd just haul him into a box stall and rip his clothes off so they could go at it like they had the night before.

She glanced his way. He was bent over, cradling Peach's injured foot. His blue chambray shirt was stretched tight over his broad shoulders, and those Wranglers fit his lean backside just right. The randy teenager inside her squirmed, wanting out.

Yeah, she could see how Sandi wound up here.

The sooner she bounced her poor little car down that rough dirt road, the better.

Chapter 23

"YOU'RE KIND OF NICE, BUT YOU LOOK REALLY SCARY," SAM told Phaedra. "Like my teacher."

Phaedra glanced up from Sam's fingernails, which she was painting with Nate-approved pink polish. Sam had wanted to try out Phaedra's Urban Vampire Black, but her father had threatened to cancel the pajama party if Phaedra tried to turn Sam into Junior Goth Girl. "Your teacher dresses Goth?" Phaedra asked.

"Oh, no," Sam shook her head. "But she wears these slanty-eyed glasses that make her look really mean, and her hair's real curly and red, like a scary clown. You want to scream and run away when you first see her—but she's nice. She helped me after school with my subtraction."

"So what's nine minus four?" Phaedra paused, holding the brush inches above Sam's fingers.

"Five."

"Right." The polishing resumed. "So do you want to grow up to be a beautician like your mom?" Phaedra asked.

"No." Sam shook her head. "I want to go to regular college. You know. In the daytime."

Charlie lifted her head from filing her own nails. "Your mom goes to night school?"

Sam nodded solemnly. "Mostly Fridays and Saturdays. Sometimes she has to stay over."

Charlie's filing stopped mid-rasp. "Who stays with you when Mommy's at school?"

Sam shrugged. "A sitter. Usually Mrs. Bennett from across the hall, but sometimes Cara. Cara's cool. She's seventeen." She invoked the pinnacle of adolescence like a prayer.

"Seventeen! What is that woman..."

Doris interrupted, casting a sharp look at Charlie. "We'll have to ask your mom about that. That sounds kind of—different."

All heads turned as a sound like a pride of roaring lions thundered out of the darkness beyond the windows. Lights flashed across the far wall and Doris bounded to the window.

"Pickup," she said. "A big ol' diesel. More students, I bet."

A cowboy whoop pierced the darkness and the truck skidded to a stop outside the bunkhouse. Phaedra applied one last stroke of polish to Sam's pinky nail and sighed.

"I think that's my dad," she said. Charlie wouldn't have thought the girl could get any paler, but she went white as a marble statue under her pancake makeup.

"Then you were right," Charlie said. "He sure sounds like a cowboy."

She sighed. Now she was in for it. She felt like she'd dodged a bullet, coming out here to the Wild West and avoiding all the wild Westerners. But judging from the din outside, her luck had just run out.

Boot heels sounded on the bunkhouse steps, and the new arrival filled the bunkhouse door. With his craggy face and rangy build, he could have stepped right off a Marlboro billboard. Charlie took one look at the ice-blue eyes peering out from under his white felt hat and was struck dumb.

"Well, I'll be," Doris said. "Chance Newton."

The newcomer grinned, perfect teeth gleaming in his tanned face. "Taylor Barnes," he said. "I just pretended to be Chance Newton for a while there."

Charlie let out a strangled croak in lieu of a greeting. Taylor Barnes was a cowboy, all right—or at least Chance Newton was. That was the character the actor had played for a hit movie Roger Ebert defined as "Little House on the Steroids."

Of course, the Chance Newton character was a family man too, with a passel of daughters he cared deeply about. Taylor Barnes, on the other hand, hadn't seen his own daughter for ten years—and the moment he'd walked into the room, Phaedra had ducked into the bathroom in a panic.

The guy was obviously a hell of a lot better at acting than parenting.

"I'd sure appreciate it if you folks'd call me Taylor instead of Chance," he said. "Gets old after a while, being fictional." He glanced around the room, his eyes lighting on the bottles of polish on Sam's nightstand. "Do I have to get my nails done too? Because I can tell you right now, that shade of pink doesn't work for me. I'm more a fuchsia kind of guy."

"We might let you off the hook this time," Doris said. "But we take our cowboy hygiene real serious around here."

Taylor chuckled and Charlie glanced toward Phaedra, who stepped out of the bathroom wiped clean of any trace of Goth makeup. Fresh-faced and clean, she looked like a different child.

An ordinary child.

Charlie grimaced as the newly scrubbed teenager sat down on the bed against the far wall and folded trembling hands in her lap. The kid was obviously desperate to please her father, but a man who'd abandon his daughter for ten years probably wouldn't change his ways for a pretty face and good behavior. Phaedra might have had better luck with the Goth strategy. She could have scared him into staying.

Taylor's eyes settled on her and his handsome face lit up with his trademark grin. "You must be Phaedra."

"Good guess," Charlie muttered. The last time the guy had seen his daughter, she'd been a kindergartner. There was no way he could recognize her now, any more than Charlie's own father could have picked her out of a crowd.

"Hi, honey." He stepped forward, obviously expecting a hug, but the girl just settled onto the side of her bed and fixed him with those uncanny gray eyes, her face expressionless. Charlie gave the girl an encouraging smile. She wasn't going to let the guy off easy. Good.

Taylor crossed the room in two long strides and settled down beside his daughter.

"How are you, sweetheart?" he asked. "You look nice. You've grown up real pretty."

Phaedra smiled down into her lap, and Charlie realized she wasn't snubbing the guy. She was struck dumb by shyness.

"Are you doing okay here so far?" Taylor asked.

The girl tossed her hair in the time-honored gesture of ultra-cool teenagers. "It's okay," she said. "Charlie's been nice to me."

Taylor smiled and gave Charlie a nod. "Thanks," he said.

While Charlie tried to think of a suitably snippy response, Sam stepped up beside her holding the bowl of chips. "Would you like some chips and salsa, Mr. Newt—I mean Mr. Barnes?" She was smiling bashfully, holding out the bowl of chips as if she was offering frankincense and myrrh. The kid was obviously a Chance Newton fan.

"Well, thanks." Taylor took a chip and bit into it appreciatively. Charlie was relieved he didn't call Sam a "little lady" or anything. Evidently he saved the corny cowboy shtick for the movies.

"You're welcome," Sam said, her voice hushed with awe. "This is *amazing*," she breathed. "It's really *you*."

Taylor grinned and took off his Stetson, setting it on Sam's head. She giggled as it fell down over her ears, then tilted it back with one pink-tipped hand and gave Taylor a luminous smile.

"There," he said. "You look like one of the good guys now."

Charlie marveled at the perfect placement of every hair on Taylor's head. The man evidently had access to an anti-hat-hair vaccination available only to movie stars. Either that, or he'd been born without the hat-hair gene.

Nate stepped into the room to check out the new arrival, and Charlie smiled to see a cowlick spring up at his crown as he pulled off his hat. He raked his hand through his hair in a reflexive gesture, but the cowlick stayed stubbornly sprung.

Now that was a real cowboy.

"Holy shit," he said when he spotted Taylor.

Oh, yeah. He was real, all right.

Taylor stood and stepped forward, one hand extended. "Taylor Barnes," he said. "I'm pleased to meet you, Mr. Shawcross. I've heard great things."

Nate blushed to a shade of crimson that almost matched Charlie's old boots. "Excuse me," he said. "I just—I wasn't expecting…"

"We had no idea you were coming, Mr. Barnes," Doris said. "So excuse us for being a little, er, flummoxed."

Barnes shrugged one shoulder in a gesture that was simultaneously eloquent and casual. Still watching his every move, Sam flexed a shoulder in imitation, her wide eyes never leaving the actor's face.

"Sorry," Barnes said. "Sometimes I think I should sign everything Chance Newton. People don't always recognize my real name."

"It's not that," Charlie said. "It's…"

"It's nothing. We're glad you're here," Nate said, cutting her off. She couldn't blame him. She'd been about to confess to Taylor Barnes that the clinic was a hoax perpetrated by an ex-lover—hardly a situation that showed Nate in the best light.

And this was the time for Nate to shine, if ever there was one, Charlie thought. If he could make a good impression on a star like Barnes, his stock would rise into the stratosphere. With a recommendation from the world's most wildly popular cowboy actor, he could land endorsement deals. Consultations on movie sets. The opportunities were limitless.

Maybe the lonesome cowpoke's luck was about to turn.

Chapter 24

NATE'S MIND WAS RACING, SEARCHING OUT SOLUTIONS TO ALL the problems Taylor Barnes's arrival had created. The man obviously couldn't sleep in the bunkhouse, although judging from the way he was looking at Charlie, he'd be more than willing to volunteer. Nate felt a hot snake of jealousy slither up his craw, but he swallowed it down. He had no real claim on Charlie. None at all.

She'd made that clear this morning.

But Barnes would have to sleep in the house. Nate winced, remembering the hot-cha bordello atmosphere of his bedroom. Well, he couldn't change it now. Besides, maybe that was what Barnes was used to. He was from Hollywood, after all.

"I need to settle a few details in the house," Nate said as smoothly as he could. "I'm sure the girls will keep you entertained for a while,"

Taylor grinned. "No rush," he said. "Phaedra and I have a lot of catching up to do."

"Yeah," Charlie said. "A lot."

Nate was surprised by her tone. She evidently wasn't a fan.

Good.

Spinning his hat in his hands, he turned and strode toward the house, making a mental to-do list. He'd have to tidy up the bedroom, maybe put some of those candles away. And he'd need to change the sheets. He'd also have to read Butt the riot act; a Hollywood star would be used to far more attractive bedmates than an overweight, smelly blue heeler who snored like a fat man with the flu.

He pulled a set of sheets out of the linen closet, then opened the door to the bedroom and groaned aloud. The place really did look like a bordello. A messy one.

He scooped a week's worth of spare change and pocket lint off the dresser, along with a hoof-pick and his Leatherman. Opening the closet, he started stowing candles, one by one, on a shelf in the back.

"What are you doing?"

Nate jumped at Charlie's voice as if he had a guilty conscience. "Thought I'd, uh, clean up."

"The candles are nice, though," Charlie said. "Leave them."

"They're just, um, kind of embarrassing."

Charlie grinned. "Well, they don't leave much doubt that you use the bedroom for something more interesting than sleeping."

"You thought that was… interesting?"

She couldn't help smiling, but her eyes were darting around the room, looking at everything but him. "Well, yeah. Kinda."

Now there was a rave review. If it wasn't for the heat he could feel simmering between them, he'd figure she hadn't had a good time. Her eyes finally lit on his face, and they stared at each other half a beat too long before turning back to the task at hand.

"Taylor's a cowboy, anyway," Charlie said, rearranging the candles. "He probably won't even notice what the room looks like."

"He's not a real cowboy," Nate pointed out. "Just a movie one." He shrugged. "He's probably gay."

"Well, if he is, he'll love this bedroom." Charlie laughed as Nate's face colored. "Never mind. Just change the sheets and run a feather duster over stuff and it'll be fine." She looked down at the carpet, where Butt had tracked in a trail of mud and God-knows-what. "Maybe run a vacuum," she said. "You want help with the sheets?"

She leaned over the bed and grabbed the blankets, yanking them back in one swift graceful movement. Nate went around to the other side and helped. He knew the drill. He'd helped Sandi make this bed a hundred times. Sandi hadn't been much of a house-keeper, but she'd tear the bed apart the morning after they did the deed, every time. He'd always felt like she was erasing what they'd done. Like she was ashamed or something.

They peeled the sheets back, and a picture of himself and Charlie climbing into bed the night before flashed across his mind. He imagined her peeling off her clothes and tossing them aside like she was tossing the sheets now, remembered how her skin felt under his fingers, the sweet scent of her, the way she'd writhed and moaned with pleasure. He could still feel her hands on him, the sparks that leapt from her touch, the way she'd…

He looked up and their eyes met. He could have sworn he felt a faint crackle like static as their thoughts met and meshed. He glanced away. Much as he wanted to pull Charlie down on the bed and have his way with her, Nate knew he needed to attend to business. He looked away, trying to ignore the glimpse of cleavage as she leaned over the bed, and concentrated on shaking the pillows out of their cases and tugging the fitted sheet off.

It was too quiet, he thought. There were two people in this room, and the silence felt awkward. They should be having a conversation—about something light. The weather. The horses. Sex.

No, wait, not sex. He scrambled around for an appropriate topic and felt the familiar ache paralyze his throat. If he tried to say anything, he'd croak like a frog.

That might be a good thing. Maybe she'd kiss him on the off chance he'd turn into a prince.

Charlie grabbed a pile of sheets from the corner of the dresser. "These?"

Nate nodded, swallowing.

"Maybe you're right," she said, picking up the fitted sheet and snapping it in the air, shaking it out so it ballooned over the bed. "Taylor can't be a real cowboy. He can actually talk."

Nate couldn't let that pass. "Only when somebody tells him what to say," he said. "You give me a script, I'll charm your pants off too."

Oh, man. What a thing to say. No wonder he didn't talk. Every time he opened his mouth, he embarrassed himself.

"I'm not taking my pants off for anybody," Charlie said. A mischievous smile tweaked her lips. "Not tonight, anyway. And certainly not for Mr. Barnes."

"I should hope not," Nate said. "The guy's practically a senior citizen."

"He's not that old," Charlie said. "Forty-eight."

"How do you know that?"

She shrugged. "I don't know. Read it somewhere, I guess."

"You a fan?"

She shrugged again. He pictured her with a bunch of other women, lining the red carpet, pressing against the velvet rope and begging for autographs.

No. Charlie wasn't like that.

Besides, judging from the way Barnes had looked at her, she wouldn't have to beg for anything. Nate was pretty sure he'd gladly give her something much more significant than an autograph.

That conjured up another picture Nate didn't want to see.

Charlie shook out the top sheet, letting it settle gracefully onto the bed. Looking down at the over-hang, she said, "I've got about a foot. How much do you have?"

"'Bout that."

"Yeah, that's what I figured." She laughed and he floundered around for a snappy, sexy response. Damn. If he could just keep the conversation moving that way... But he couldn't. Couldn't think of a thing to say. He was good at the looks and the touches. The talking? Not so much.

Together, they hoisted the bottom of the mattress and tucked the sheet underneath. Charlie folded a neat miter into the corner, then came around to his side and matched it.

Nate cleared his throat. "Wow. Military corners."

"Hospital corners." Charlie quirked a faint smile. "I was a candy striper."

Nate pictured her in the uniform—the red and white striped dress, the little white shoes, the cap—and a new fantasy was born.

"I bet you were good at it," he said. "Really good."

He smoothed the sheet, bending over the bed just as she did the same. His hand slid over hers and he instinctively gripped her wrist and pulled her toward him. The two of them stopped, staring at each other, still as the deer that had paused to watch the truck the night before. He half expected Charlie to leap away like the deer had, but she leaned in and touched her lips to his for one brief, warm kiss.

"Sorry." She pulled away, flustered. "I mean—sorry. I know we shouldn't—should we?"

He couldn't answer. He had no idea what to say. But he knew what to do.

"Just once," he said. "Just one more time."

Charlie climbed up onto the mattress and knelt there, looking up at him, but there was no challenge in her eyes this time. She looked worried, reluctant. He sat down beside her.

"Nate, we can't," she said. "I—I'm going back to Jersey."

"I know," he said. He reached up and swept her hair back from her forehead. "But you're here now. I know it's not forever, Charlie. I can handle it. But it's—it's so *good*." He gave her a smile. It was meant to be reassuring, but he was pretty sure it came across more wolfish, since he had no doubt she could read his thoughts in his eyes. Thoughts of touching her, kissing her, stripping off that shirt and jeans… "There's no reason not to enjoy it while we can."

She looked past him out the window, her expression troubled.

"It's just for now, Charlie. No strings."

He tugged at her waistband, revealing a slice of

bright blue cotton decorated with white stars, and the smile broadened.

"Wonder Woman," he said. "Perfect." He cupped her head and pulled her close, kissing her gently on her cheekbone, the curve of her jaw, her neck, the blade of her collarbone. She breathed in a shaky breath and tensed, then relaxed into him and exhaled, her breath soft against his ear.

"Okay," she said. "No strings."

He kissed her lips again, cupping her tush with both hands while she pressed her breasts into his chest and kissed him back. For a moment there was nothing but the two of them, alone in the universe with nothing between them but the sensation of his hands on her skin, her lips on his.

But just for a moment. Just as he started to ease one hand up under her shirt, just as his fingertips sensed the soft, untouched skin of her breast, the door opened.

"Daddy! What are you doing?"

Charlie jumped as if she'd been electrocuted, stumbling off the bed while Nate fell onto it, abruptly conscious of his flushed face and mussed hair.

"Sam," he said, smoothing his hair. He stood and tried to look innocent. Damn. Wasn't that supposed to be the kid's job?

Sam looked from Nate to Charlie and back again. "You're not supposed to do that, you know. Mommy said."

Nate felt all the air leave his lungs in a whoosh. Mommy was the last thing he wanted to think about right now. What had she said? What had she told Sam? Did the kid think she had to be a watchdog, making sure her dad didn't fall for some strange woman?

Was the kid right?

Charlie was tugging her shirt down as if she could stretch the fabric to her knees. "Sorry, honey." She brushed an invisible fleck of lint from her shirt. "Sorry."

Sam waggled a cautionary finger as Nate struggled to stay composed. What had she seen? How could he have done this—risked his daughter catching him with a woman other than her mother so soon? Was she scarred for life?

Probably.

He knelt on the floor. "I'm sorry, honey. Sometimes grown-ups do—bad things. They get carried away." He glanced over at Charlie. Her back was turned toward him, so he couldn't see her reaction to his calling their kiss a "bad thing." But what was he supposed to say?

"That's okay, Dad," Sam said. "But no more, okay?" Her tone mimicked Sandi so closely it was uncanny. Nate swallowed hard and the little girl nodded sharply— just like her mother.

"Jumping on the bed just *ruins* the mattress," she said. Mission accomplished, she spun around in an energetic pirouette and trotted out of the room.

Charlie turned to him as Sam left, her smile tight as she suppressed a laugh. But it wasn't funny. Not funny at all. He'd almost let Sam see him kiss another woman. No way was she ready for that.

He turned away, pretending absorption in their task, smoothing the rumpled top sheet.

—∿∿∿—

Charlie watched Nate run his hands over the sheet, flattening every wrinkle as if he could erase what had just happened between them—as if he could erase it from his own mind, and Sam's too.

She was nothing but relieved when he turned away and followed Sam out of the room. Or at least, that's what she told herself. Actually, it would have been nice if he'd said something reassuring—something that would convince her that he wasn't once again "sorry" that he'd given in to the undeniable attraction between them. Something that would indicate their kiss wasn't really a "bad thing."

She pulled the burgundy comforter back onto the bed and fluffed the pillows, arranging them in an inviting mound, then set her hands on her hips and looked around the room. It would do. It probably wasn't quite as plush as Taylor Barnes's usual accommodations, but it was acceptable.

She glanced over at the mirror and tugged her shirt down self-consciously. She hadn't noticed this morning how it rode up, exposing her jeweled belly button and the top of her flaming horse tattoo. Scowling, she assessed her spiky hair and bold makeup. No wonder Nate was embarrassed for his daughter to see them together. She fit into this room just fine, with its fur and feathers, its candles and fluffy pillows. But on the rest of the ranch? She was as out of place as a dance-hall girl in a sod hut.

No matter how much she loved the place—and the animals, and hell, even the people—she really didn't belong in Nate's world.

Chapter 25

FOR A GUY WHO HADN'T PLANNED ON TEACHING A CLINIC, Nate had plenty of material to cover the next day. Charlie felt like her head was bursting with information on horse conformation—uphill and downhill builds, shoulder and croup slopes, high and low pasterns, throatlatch flexion. She'd absorbed a whole new vocabulary—gaskins, cannons, and hocks; collection, impulsion, and balance. Then there were the problems to look out for—bandy legs, buck knees, calf knees, splay feet, sway backs, mutton withers, cow hocks, and sickle hocks. Nate used his own horses, photographs from books, Sam's plastic ponies—everything he could find to teach them how to judge an animal's strengths and weaknesses. It got to the point where Charlie found herself analyzing the finer points of the sofa versus the kitchen table. She might not know how to ride a horse, but she could sure as heck pick one out.

And she was about to get her chance. Saturday morning, Nate and Sam headed for the pickup, along with Taylor and Phaedra. Charlie was riding with Doris in the Ford. She couldn't help wondering if Nate was trying to keep her away from Sam.

"Where's the sale, anyway?" Taylor asked.

"Green River," Nate said. "At the prison."

"The *prison*? Hey, I think I broke the seat belt law once, but…"

"I've read about that program," Doris said. "The prisoners train the horses. It's a skill they can use when they get out. Some of them get jobs on ranches—that kind of thing."

Judging from Nate's situation, Charlie figured bank robbing and drug dealing were probably more secure professions, but what did she know?

"Yeah, and the prisoners learn a lot from working with the horses too—patience, give and take, that kind of thing," Nate said.

Charlie figured she could use a lesson in patience. She was still waiting for Nate to mention that little to-do in the bedroom. Still waiting for him to tell her their kiss wasn't really a "bad thing." And she wasn't waiting very patiently.

Still, she wasn't about to bring it up. If he really believed kissing her was a mistake, she'd never let him know it mattered.

And it wasn't like he was being rude, or giving her the cold shoulder. In fact, she'd caught him looking at her a couple times as if he was eating her up with his eyes and maybe pondering an encore of their bedtime romp.

But they hadn't been alone together since Sam had caught them kissing, so she had no idea what he was thinking.

"Aren't you nervous, taking Sam to a prison?" she asked.

"I've been before," Sam piped up. "The men are nice. And Dad says everybody deserves a second chance."

"Good for him," Doris said. She climbed up into the truck and cranked the ignition, slamming the door as she started the truck moving. "Well," she said as they bounced down the driveway. "It's about time we had a chance for some girl talk. How are things going with that cowboy?"

Charlie swallowed. She wasn't ready to talk about Nate. Not at all. And she sure as hell wasn't ready for Doris's practical take on her love life.

"Fine," she said. "I think he's happier now that his daughter's here."

Doris gave her a hard look. "That's not what I meant, and you know it. You two did the deed, didn't you?"

A dozen responses rose to Charlie's lips. *I'm sorry, that's private. Hey, that's none of your business. I don't want to talk about it.* But Doris's shrewd eyes bored straight into her brain, demanding an answer, and all she could do was nod.

"He any good?"

Charlie choked on her next breath and lurched into a coughing spell.

"That's what I thought." Doris settled back into the driver's seat and grinned. "When you find the right man, it's always good."

"He's not the right man," Charlie spluttered. "It was just a fling."

"Yeah, right," Doris said. "Don't tell him that."

"I already did."

"He believe you?"

"I think so."

"Then he's a fool," Doris said.

"No, he's just practical," Charlie said. "I mean, he's got his daughter to think about. The last thing that poor kid needs is a stepmom."

"I'd say it's the first thing she needs." Doris shook her head and braked on a sharp turn. "You heard her talking about her mother and that so-called beauty school, right? The kid needs something better. So does the man."

Charlie shrugged and faked absorption in the landscape. The first part of the ride was hardly scenic—just a long stretch of scrubby wasteland, marked only by occasional twisted pines and boulders left behind by the long-ago glacier that had scraped the earth smooth. But somehow, the primal roughness of the land had its own beauty, rugged and stern, a challenge to anyone who might try to tame it and turn it to use.

Doris dropped the truck into low gear as they headed up a hill. Charlie looked back over her shoulder, catching the same view she'd seen from horseback that first day with Nate—the distant ranch nestled in its hollow, with the silver stream making a long arc around it. But where the place had looked forlorn and deserted on her first sighting, it now looked completely different. The buildings seemed to be embraced by the long arm of the stream rather than cut off by it, the house protected by the hills, not dwarfed by their looming silhouettes.

Nate's pickup edged over to the side of the road and stopped. Doris pulled in behind him and rolled down her window.

"What's up?" she asked as he stepped out of his truck, Sam tumbling behind him.

"Nice view from here. Thought you might want to take a look."

His eyes lit on Charlie, as if this place, this view, was a gift meant for her eyes in particular. She gave herself a mental slap. She was assigning all kinds of romantic intentions to his casual glances and accidental touches—but deep down, she knew it didn't matter.

She'd be gone soon, and whatever they had between them would be over.

She slid down from the truck. The panorama below made her forget about Nate and everything else, hitting her like a blow to the heart. The land undulated away from them like a rumpled blanket, hill upon hill, dotted with trees and sage. The late summer grass was dry and coarse, but in the morning sun it took on a golden glow, with silvery highlights that glittered in the ever-changing breeze. In the distance, a rock cliff reared up against the clear blue sky, the ruddy red wall slashing like the broad swipe of a child's crayon across the scene.

"It's beautiful," Charlie said.

"Down there's where your car broke down," Nate said. She hadn't even noticed he'd come around the truck to stand beside her. "Remember?"

Charlie nodded. "But it looked so—so different then. So bleak."

"It wasn't home then," he said.

Home?

What the hell did that mean?

It didn't matter. She wasn't staying. But he was standing close to her—really close—and as he watched her, waiting for a reaction, the truth swept over her.

This *was* home. She'd never felt so part of a place. She could feel her roots snaking down into the hard dry soil, deeper and deeper the longer she stayed. However unlikely it seemed that a city girl could feel at home in such a godforsaken place, she felt like she belonged here. Part of it was Nate, but he wasn't the only thing binding her to Latigo. There was the land, the animals, the big, broad sky, the hard bright sunshine, and the clear gray dawns.

She loved it here.

She cleared her throat and glanced around, looking for a neutral subject of conversation, and pointed toward the clusters of showy white blossoms that dotted the landscape.

"What are those flowers down there?"

"Prairie roses. I'll show you." He took her hand and led her down the steep slope that fell away from the road. She shook her hand loose, glancing back at Sam.

"It's okay," he said. "Listen, I'm really sorry. I've been wanting to talk to you, but all these people... I just couldn't. We need to go slow, okay? For Sam's sake. I can't let her see us—you know."

"Then we need to drop it," she said, trying to ignore the surge of disappointment that washed over her. "I'm not going to sneak around."

"I don't mean that. I just..." He slumped his shoulders. "I just don't know what to do."

Charlie knelt to examine a clump of flowers. The blooms were enormous, bobbing on slender stems and bunched together like a bridal bouquet. "These are pretty," she said.

"Charlie, I'm not asking you to sneak around. I'm asking you to take things slow. But I'm serious. Serious about—us."

"Serious?" She glanced up at his face.

He took a deep breath. "I want you to stay."

Stay. She pictured herself living at Latigo, rising every morning to care for the horses, working side by side with Nate all day and tumbling into bed with him at night. It was a nice fantasy—but that's all it was. A fantasy.

It'll never happen, she thought. Graduate students didn't live in places like Purvis, Wyoming. If she wanted to do real work—meaningful work, the work her education had prepared her for—she'd have to go where her career took her.

Besides, she already had a home back in Jersey. Her apartment.

Yeah, right. 228 South Broad, Unit B was hardly a home, with its threadbare furniture and bare-bones kitchen, where the windows opened onto a stretch of cracked concrete as stark and barren as her love life and the night was filled with the shouts and curses of strangers and the blare of distant sirens.

She'd always pictured *home* as something more—a white frame house with a kitchen steeped in family memories, smelling faintly of some long-gone grandma's fresh-baked cookies; a cozy, old-fashioned place with a fireplace and a woodshed. Now she wanted home to have a barn too, sweetly scented with hay and horse. And most important, she wanted to wake up every morning to a look like the one she'd caught in Nate's eyes that morning on the sofa.

He was giving her that look now.

No one had ever looked at her like that before. And maybe nobody ever would again—unless she was lucky enough to find a place like this to call home.

And a man like this to… *no*.

She wasn't ready. She had work to do, a life to build. She wasn't going to shuck all her ambitions for a man.

Not even this one.

Maybe someday she'd come back to Wyoming—but now was not the time.

She could feel Nate's gaze on her, waiting for a response. "I can't, Nate," she said. "I can't."

He held out his hand to her, but she rose on her own and they climbed the hill in silence. She could feel him watching her as she hiked herself up into the seat of Doris's truck, but she refused to look back, even though her body warmed under his gaze as if he'd touched her.

Chapter 26

THEY TURNED OFF THE HIGHWAY IN RIVERTON AND stopped at a glass-enclosed guardhouse. Nate presented some paperwork and a uniformed woman waved them through to a parking lot. Piling out of the pickup, they were met by an extravagantly mustached man in a cowboy hat standing beside a short bus.

"I'm Archie, from the BLM Wild Horse and Burro Program," he said, handing out paperwork. "Need your signatures on these release forms. Basically says we're not liable if y'all get yourselves killed in there."

"Is that likely to happen?" Doris asked.

"Not really," he said. "Not unless you do something stupid."

Charlie snorted. She'd been doing stupid things ever since she arrived at Latigo. Falling for Nate. Kissing him. Sleeping with him.

And now that he'd asked her to stay, she realized how foolish she'd been. There was no happy ending for the two of them. She'd leave, and he'd find someone else. Hopefully, she would too—someday.

They handed in their forms and climbed onto the bus. Charlie was the last to climb on, and the only seat left was beside Nate and Sam. She sat stiffly, clutching the back of the seat in front of her, feeling suddenly claustrophobic. She'd been on a bus like this once before. It was back in New Jersey, but it was the same kind of bus, headed for a similar destination.

It hadn't been a good trip.

Archie, who was doubling as their driver, eyed her in the rearview mirror, assessing her top to bottom.

The driver in New Jersey had done that too.

"Hey, Shawcross," Archie said. "Is that the one who…"

"Uh-huh." Nate nodded.

"Hmm." The man's eyes scanned her in the mirror. Scanned her slowly. Thoroughly.

"What did you tell him?" Charlie hissed at Nate. Surely he hadn't blabbed about their tryst. The guy could barely put a sentence together. Maybe he was different with his friends, though. Maybe when men got together, they talked about…

"I didn't tell him anything," Nate said. "But I guess the State of New Jersey gave him an earful."

"What?"

"It's a prison," he said. "They do background checks."

"Oh, shoot." Charlie sank down in her seat, hiding her face in her hands.

"Don't worry," Nate patted her shoulder. "You've already paid your debt to society. Although I think society probably should have paid you."

She flushed. "I was young," she muttered. "And besides, that wasn't me. It was my evil twin."

"Huh," Nate said. "We ought to invite her for a visit."

Charlie glanced meaningfully at Sam. "I'd rather not discuss it," she said. The "Naked in Newark" PETA protest was hardly a topic for a seven-year-old. She'd felt like a crusader, out on the street in nothing but her "I'd

Rather Wear Nothing Than Fur" sign—but now she just felt like an idiot.

Nate grinned. "Guess not," he said. He leaned forward and whispered, his breath tickling her ear. "Almost makes me want to mistreat an animal, though, just to get you to protest me."

She turned away, folding her arms across her chest and lifting her chin while he laughed.

"What?" Sam asked. "Charlie failed a background check? Is she from a bad background?"

"You bet," Nate said. "Bad right down to her, um, bare bones."

"That's okay," Sam said. "Everybody deserves a second chance, right, Dad?"

"You bet," Nate said, grinning. "And I'll give her one." He slid a sly look toward Charlie. "Anytime she wants."

--- ∞ ---

Nate watched Charlie's eyes widen in wonder as they crested the hill that overlooked the compound. Dozens of corrals covered acres of ground below them, every one filled with milling horses of every conceivable color and build. He'd seen the facility before, but he'd never seen it so full.

"Wow," Phaedra said. "How are we ever going to decide?"

"Just remember what you've learned and stay rational," Nate warned. "Don't go picking a horse you feel sorry for. Pick one that has a future."

"They all have a future," Charlie said sharply. "They don't euthanize them, do they?"

Nate shook his head. "Nope. But some of them have

a future with humans, and some end up in holding facilities for the rest of their lives."

Charlie figured life in a holding facility was probably a lot like living at 228 South Broad, Unit B. She'd been in holding for a while now.

They stepped off the bus and followed the mustachioed driver to the first corral. "These are from the Rock Creek herd," he said. "Been here about three months."

The horses, about twenty of them, were bunched in a tight group on the far side of the corral. They shifted nervously, watching the humans with flared nostrils.

"Let's see some long-term residents," Nate said.

"Okay. This is a good group," Ernie said. He opened a gate and they stepped inside a large enclosure. Thirty-some horses were munching hay that had been spread on the bare ground in the center of the enclosure. "From Nevada. Been here a while." He scowled over his clipboard, flipping pages. "Five months, most of 'em."

The horses lifted their heads, watchful, still chewing their hay. One or two stepped forward cautiously, stretching their necks toward the visitors.

"Oh," Charlie whispered. "They're so tame."

"Not really. Just curious," Nate said. "Remember what you've learned. Don't look right at them. Turn your body away a little bit. Sam, go ahead. See if you can make a few friends."

Sam edged away from the group along the fence, studiously avoiding the horse's curious gazes. The horses seemed to sense she was harmless and a few mares approached, their heads low, their steps cautious. She extended one arm slowly, her hand curled into a loose fist, fingers toward the ground. One of the horses sniffed carefully, mumbling its lips over her hand, and Charlie could see Sam suppressing a giggle as she turned and walked back to the group, still ignoring the horses.

Several more joined the group following Sam. Charlie looked away as they approached, avoiding their eyes. A skinny buckskin took a cautious step toward her and eyed her curiously. Slowly, she held her hand out, following Sam's example, then reached up and stroked the horse's nose with the back of one finger. The horse stood stock-still for a heartbeat, then snorted and wheeled away.

"Wow," she said.

"Their capture was long enough ago that they've forgotten any rough treatment—or forgiven, anyway," Nate said. "They forgive easy."

"Sweet things," Charlie whispered.

Taylor and Phaedra were befriending a black gelding in the far corner. Phaedra's eyes were shining as the horse took a fistful of hay from her hand.

"I like this one," the girl said.

Nate eyed it critically. "Not bad," he said. "But we'll look at a lot more before we decide."

—⁂—

The last pen held horses from Oregon. Like the others, they lifted their heads and watched warily as the humans approached—all but one, who jerked her head up and took off, running in wild circles around the perimeter, kicking and bucking in a high-spirited display that reminded Charlie of Junior. She was a bay with long legs, a graceful neck, and a delicate, slightly dished profile.

"Wow," Charlie said. The horse arched her neck and carried her tail like a flag streaming out behind her. She looked like the flaming horse in Charlie's tattoo. As she neared the humans, she slammed on the brakes and skidded to a stop, tossing her head, then pivoted and dashed away.

Nate watched her go. "Trouble," he said.

Charlie eased away from the crowd while Archie explained the meaning of the freeze-brands on the horse's necks. Moving to a corner of the pen, she knelt down and watched the bay horse. It was still running, but slower now, and as it circled, its orbit kept straying closer and closer to Charlie's corner.

"Pshhhhh," Charlie whispered, looking away.

The horse stopped and lowered its head, watching her, curious.

"Pshhhh." The mare took one step closer, then another, mincing forward. Stretching her neck out, she sniffed the air in front of Charlie's face. Charlie breathed out slowly, and the horse sniffed again. Charlie dared to meet the animal's eyes and the mare stood stock-still for a long heartbeat, then turned and trotted away, quiet as a circus pony. When she reached the center of the pen where the hay was spread out, she shoved a few other horses away, then bent her head to eat, still watching Charlie from the corner of her eye.

"Mine," Charlie whispered to herself. She got up and rejoined the group.

"Okay, folks, this is it," Nate said. "Phaedra, you still want that black from the first pen, right? And Taylor, you're set on that paint gelding?"

The two nodded.

"Doris, you want the buckskin from the Rock Creek

herd, right? So the only one who still has to choose is Charlie."

"I chose." Charlie gestured toward the mare who was nipping at another horse that had dared to step into its space. Nate watched as she bucked and set off running again, galloping around the enclosure.

"Look at her tail carriage," Charlie said. "And her muscling. She'll make a great reining prospect, right?"

"Not with that temperament," he said. "She's impossible."

"So am I," Charlie said. "You said so."

"I didn't mean it as a compliment," he muttered.

"We're kindred souls," Charlie said. "We'll understand each other. You'll see."

"You're crazy," Nate said.

The horse jerked to a halt ten feet away, breathing hard, then spun and galloped away.

"See? She's crazy too. We're just alike, me and Trouble."

Nate groaned. "You named her?"

"No, you did," Charlie said. "It's perfect. Thanks."

Nate shook his head. "I don't want her on the ranch. She'll be disruptive. Fire up the other horses."

"I love her more every minute," Charlie said.

Nate stared at her and she stared back, arms folded over her chest, jaw squared. He looked away first.

"All right," he said. "You're here to learn, and I guess she'll teach you a thing or two."

The BLM required one-horse trailers for each animal, so only Trouble and Phaedra's black gelding were coming home on the first trip. Both horses braced themselves at the foot of the ramps, refusing to climb into what they probably saw as a Dark Box of Doom—but after much coercing and a little tugging and shoving, the horses seemed to sense their resistance was futile. At some mysterious tipping point, each one suddenly thundered up the ramp and into the trailers to stand shivering in the unaccustomed confinement, facing the wall. Naturally, Trouble took the longest to get to that point.

"Won't they freak once we get moving?" Phaedra asked.

Nate shook his head. "Generally not. Once they make up their mind to accept a situation, they resign themselves to whatever comes."

"A pretty good philosophy, really," Taylor said.

Charlie tossed him a scornful glare. He'd evidently resigned himself to abandoning his daughter ten years ago. She wasn't sure what had changed his mind and brought him around, but it surprised her how readily Phaedra forgave him. She'd given up more than the Goth makeup; she'd given up her surliness and sulking as well, and become a model child.

Charlie thought it was tragic. She missed the old Phaedra. And it made her wonder if she'd have sold her soul for a father at that age.

Probably. Watching Taylor sling an arm around his daughter's shoulders, she thought maybe she still would.

"So horses are kind of like Buddhists," Phaedra said. "They forgive easy, and they accept their situation and live in the moment."

"Pretty good summary," Nate said.

"Shoot." Phaedra kicked at the ground. "I'm, like, the opposite of a horse, then. I carry a grudge, and I never settle for the status quo. And I live for the future. For when I'm done with school and stuff."

"Me too," Charlie said.

It was true—especially the last part. She'd spent all her life preparing for some unknowable future, when she'd put her education toward some kind of meaningful work. But maybe it wouldn't be with horses after all. Maybe she wouldn't be able to truly understand an animal whose philosophy was so different from her own.

Maybe she should work with kids instead—teenagers, like Phaedra, who thought more like her.

Or maybe she should just grow up. Grow up, and stop wishing for things she couldn't have.

Chapter 27

CHARLIE LEANED ON THE PADDOCK GATE, WATCHING THE mustangs munch their morning hay. Nate and Taylor had picked up the last two horses, and the group seemed to have worked out new family roles already. Phaedra's black gelding and Doris's buckskin were the kids, eating greedily, focused entirely on the food. Trouble was more watchful, munching contemplatively, lifting her head occasionally to check out her surroundings, her ears twitching forward and back as she scanned the paddock and the pasture beyond for threats. She was obviously taking on the matriarchal role.

Meanwhile, Taylor's big paint gelding stood watchfully by. Suddenly he stiffened, widening his stance and raising his head, then lifted his tail and unleashed a torrent of pee into the dust of the corral.

"Some nice nonverbal communication for you there," Nate said, grinning. "That's how stallions say hello to unwelcome company. Guess he still remembers what it's like to be a man."

"I'm not sure that's a technique that would transfer well to people," Charlie said. "Kind of messy."

"But so handy when that obnoxious neighbor shows up at dinnertime," he said. He stepped up beside her and jostled her shoulder. It was a friendly, joking gesture, the kind of thing a guy might do to his kid sister—but it sent a jolt of lust through Charlie that made her clutch the railing and take a deep breath.

Nate nudged her again, gently this time, and she turned and met his gaze. The look he gave her was anything but brotherly. One more second and they'd be rerunning that kiss—or that scene in the bedroom.

She looked away and gazed off across the plains. She'd miss Nate when she went back to Jersey. She'd miss all this open space too. Plucking a few leaves from a nearby sagebrush, she crushed them between her fingers and breathed in its sweet, surprisingly strong scent. It permeated the air here, combining with the ranch scents of horse and hay and leather to create a sort of Eau de Latigo that seemed heady and exotic compared to the smoggy scent of New Brunswick.

A plume of dust in the distance drew her eye. She pointed it out to Nate. "Looks like a Jeep. A red one."

Nate peered at the dust cloud, then paled. "Trouble," he muttered.

"My horse?"

"Your horse is a baby lamb compared to what's coming. I have work to do." Nate practically ran into the barn. That was evidently how cowboys said hello to unwelcome company—or avoided saying hello.

At least he hadn't peed in the dirt.

She watched the oncoming car bounce up the driveway with a mixture of envy and admiration. It was a red Jeep Cherokee, the perfect mixture of style and sense—every bit as cute as the Celica, and tough enough to take anything the rocky road to Latigo dished out.

Cute and tough. That was a pretty good description of Charlie herself—or at least, she liked to think so. She was no great beauty—her figure was too bony, her features too bold—but she knew from the reactions of men like Nate and Taylor that she had a certain appeal.

She squinted into the sun as the jeep pulled to a stop in the wide dusty delta fanning out from the end of the driveway. Shading her eyes with one hand, she watched as the driver's door opened and a long, denim-clad leg eased out, capped with a pointy-toed black cowboy boot tooled with twining red roses. Charlie could almost hear the wah-wah soundtrack as the long leg was followed by slim hips and a shapely butt.

Funny. There weren't supposed to be any more students. Ray said Sandi had four deposits, and all four were accounted for.

So who was this?

Backlit by the setting sun, the new arrival swept off an Aussie-style cowboy hat and tossed her head, spinning out a golden halo of glossy blond locks. Charlie was a firm believer in female solidarity, but she couldn't help feeling an evil stab of envy as the woman propped an elbow on the top of the jeep and struck an artful supermodel pose to consider the rickety ranch house. Tall and slim, the woman was a dead ringer for Heidi Klum—only younger, and possibly prettier.

Unclenching her teeth and smacking down her inner bitch, Charlie pasted a welcoming smile on her face. The newcomer's svelte figure was encased in slim silver-washed jeans, a crisp white fitted shirt, and a fringed black suede jacket that shimmied with every graceful movement. She looked like she'd just stepped out of a Western wear catalog, or left some exclusive Denver soirée. Not only was she attractive; she had the

suave self-possession that always graces women gifted
with beauty.

"You must be a friend of Taylor's," Charlie said,
proud of her deduction. Women like this didn't soil
themselves with messy stuff like horseback riding.
Women like this found themselves a rich guy—pref-
erably a film star or rock singer—and agreed to func-
tion as the ultimate decorative accessory, thereby
earning him the envy of every man on the planet. In
return, said woman was offered a life of languorous
ease that consisted mostly of displaying her incredible beauty at poolside, in limos, and at exclusive,
high-toned parties.

She was obviously slumming today.

"Taylor who?" The woman gave Charlie a blank, empty
look that still managed to be a seductive masterpiece—
lips slightly parted, eyes wide, head cocked at a quizzi-
cal twenty-degree angle.

Charlie wasn't fooled. She was sure the woman had
followed Taylor here, nose to the ground like a hound
dog, following the seductive scent of money.

"Taylor Barnes," Charlie said. "You know, Chance
Newton."

The woman's perfect lips tipped upward in a faint
smile. "Oh, so that's why that name sounded so familiar."

"Familiar?" It was Charlie's turn to try on the blank
look. She did the wide-eyed part okay, but she had a
feeling she'd muffed the head-cock.

"I knew I'd heard that name before when I saw it on
the check."

The check. Charlie felt as if some demon had wrapped
a black hand around her heart and squeezed. This perfect

creature, this goddess of the Western plains, had Taylor's check. Who had the check? Sandi.

Therefore, this perfect, stunning creature was Sandi.

Nate's girlfriend. Sam's mother.

No wonder she'd left. Standing in front of the ranch house, she looked like an exotic bird of paradise that had been torn from her exotic emerald jungle and tossed into a dusty, dilapidated henhouse.

And no wonder Nate looked so mournful all the time. He'd had this goddess for a consort—and now he was reduced to bedding ordinary mortals like Charlie.

Charlie resisted the impulse to box her own ears. The inner jealous bitch was bad enough. Now her insecure geeky teenager was running wild. She tamped them both down and lifted her chin, looking Sandi straight in the limpid blue pools God had given her for eyes.

"I'm Charlie Banks. One of Nate's students."

"Oh. I'm Sandi. Sam's mom."

Sam's mom. Not Nate's girlfriend.

Hmm.

Having dispensed with her psychologically challenged alter egos, Charlie turned her attention to wrestling with the writhing tentacles of the green monster that was wrapping itself around her subconscious. She had no right to be jealous. She and Nate had a fling. Nothing more.

"So where is he?" Sandi asked.

"Nate? He's in the barn," Charlie said. "He'll be glad to see you." It was tough to get the words past her clenched teeth, but she managed it.

"No, he won't." Sandi laughed, a high, melodious tinkle. "And I wasn't asking about Nate. Where's Taylor Barnes?"

She pronounced the name as if it tasted good—as if Taylor was a sweet chocolate truffle waiting to be plucked from the box and popped between those perfect lips. No doubt the truffle himself would go willingly. Charlie felt a stab of sympathy for Nate.

"Taylor's in the bunkhouse with the other students," she said, setting off across the yard. She narrowed her eyes. "Don't you want to know where Sam is?"

"She's with her dad, right?" Sandi rolled her eyes with even more drama than Phaedra could muster. "She's always with her dad when we're here."

Charlie nodded. She'd guessed right. Nate and Sam were a unit, while Sandi, lovely as she was, was the third wheel in the household. She swallowed her jealousy and resolved to be kind.

"I'll introduce you to the other students," she said, giving Sandi a friendly smile.

Sandi nodded. "Doris Pederson, right? And Paulette Barnes?"

Charlie glanced back. "Paulette Barnes?" She blinked. "Oh. That must be Phaedra. Our token adolescent."

"She's a teenager, yeah," Sandi said. "Phaedra?"

"That's what she calls herself," Charlie explained as they mounted the steps to the bunkhouse. "She uses just one name. You know, like Madonna."

"Like Cher," Phaedra—or Paulette—said as they stepped inside. But nobody heard her. Taylor looked like he'd been pole-axed, and even Doris stopped mid-story with her mouth half-open when Sandi sashayed into the room.

The only person unaffected by the woman's poise and beauty was Phaedra. Well, not unaffected—just affected differently. The appearance of the Goddess of Blondness seemed to have short-circuited whatever part of the teenager's brain housed her manners.

"Who the hell are you?" she asked.

"I'm Sandi. Your hostess."

Phaedra scowled. "Charlie's our hostess," she said.

Sandi whirled to face Charlie, her eyes narrowed and hard as a snake's, but the expression was so fleeting Charlie almost thought she'd imagined it as the woman's face smoothed into its customary serenity with disconcerting ease. It was like watching a shape-shifter.

"I've been helping out," Charlie said. "Nate couldn't take care of everything on his own."

Sandi sighed. "Nate can't take care of anything on his own. Can't, or won't." She shook her head as if she was talking about a fractious two-year-old. "I figured he'd manage to swim if I threw him in the deep end. Looks like he conned some other sucker into bailing him out, though." She looked around the bunkhouse. Her eyes paused on the wildflowers in their blue glass jars, the neatly made beds. "Looks like he's doing all right."

"Yeah, he's doing great," Charlie said. "His ranch got inundated with strangers who expect him to spend all day every day teaching them about horses. They also expect him to feed them and clean up after them. Then he hit his head and practically killed himself, and then his kid showed up out of nowhere with no warning. And now you're here. Oh, yeah. He's doing terrific."

Sandi shrugged, tossing her head as if to discount Nate's issues, then turned a radiant smile on Taylor.

"Well," she said. That was all she said, but her tone said a lot more. Charlie couldn't help bristling. She remembered the way Nate had stared down at Honey's reins when he first mentioned Sandi, the muscle that had flexed in his jaw as he'd wrestled with his inner pain.

Judging from the way Sandi was looking at Taylor, that pain was going to get a lot worse. And there was nothing Charlie could do about it. There'd been a time when she'd felt like she could make Nate feel better—at least for a while.

Now that she'd seen Sandi, she realized she'd been wrong.

This wound was going to leave a scar.

Chapter 28

Nate was sweeping the long alleyway that fronted the horse stalls, gathering loose straw and dust into a tidy pile at the doorway. The barn didn't need sweeping, and all his work would be undone as soon as he led the horses back in from the pasture, but he had to do something. He had to keep his mind busy, and he had to have something in his hands, because they were shaking.

A hot stew of anger and resentment boiled in his stomach. Sandi had told him she never wanted to see the place again. Why was she back? To see if he was doing the clinic? To gloat over the predicament she'd put him in? To ruin whatever relationship he might build with someone else—someone like Charlie?

Or had she come to take Sam back?

She couldn't. He wouldn't allow it. Sam needed stability—a home she could count on. Shuttling her back and forth between Denver and the ranch would only confuse her.

He dragged a few stray strands of hay into the pile. A shadow fell over the floor and he looked up to see his ex standing in the doorway.

"Hi," she said.

She didn't sound glad to see him, but she didn't sound upset either. Last time he'd seen her, she'd been screaming at him, stuffing her clothes and cosmetics into a suitcase, and calling him every name she could think of. Now she seemed reasonable. Rational. In control.

What was *that* all about?

"Hi," he said. "What are you doing here?"

"I live here," she said. "Thanks for the big welcome."

"You left. You said you were done with the place. Done with me."

"I am. Well, almost." She leaned in the doorway, crossing her long legs. Backlit by the sun, her hair glowed like a golden crown. She really was beautiful, he thought. On the outside.

Inside was another matter.

"So what are you doing here? You hate this place, re-member?" He quoted her own parting words. "You hope you never see it again. Or me. So why are you here?"

"We need to settle some things."

"Like what?"

"Like how we're going to split things up."

Split *what* up? She'd already taken everything he had. Everything but the ranch—and she sure as hell didn't want that. She'd always hated it. He went back to sweeping, raising a cloud of dust with short, angry strokes of the broom. "Take whatever you want, Sandi. You know I don't care about stuff. Just leave me what I need to keep the place going, okay? And if you want any furniture, maybe you could wait until the clinic's over. It was your idea, after all."

She stepped into the barn, brushing the dust off her arm where she'd leaned against the wall. "I don't want any furniture," she said. "Place is full of junk."

"It was my grandmother's," he said. "It's not junk to me."

"Well, you can keep it, then. All I want is my half of the ranch."

"What?"

"You heard me."

"Sandi, the ranch isn't yours. It's mine. And besides, you hate it."

"I've been here seven years, Nate. That makes me your common-law wife."

He let the broom clatter to the floor. "I offered to marry you—how many times? And you said no. And now all of a sudden you want to be my wife?"

"No. That's the last thing in the world I want to be."

"Thanks," he muttered.

"But since we're married in the eyes of the law, I get half of everything. And I want my half of the ranch."

He leaned against the wall, assessing her the way he'd assess any enemy before a fight. Somehow, she didn't look so beautiful anymore. There was a sharpness to her face he'd never noticed before, and a hard, greedy glint to her eyes. He narrowed his eyes and she looked away, faking interest in the view from the doorway.

"What the hell are you going to do with it?" he asked.

"Sell it."

"It's not for sale."

"My half is."

He kicked the pile of dust, stirring up a cloud that wafted down the aisle and settled over her fancy tooled boots. Picking up the broom, he went back to work as if she wasn't there, forcing her to back out of the barn as he flung dust and straw toward the doorway.

"Nate," she said. Her voice was taking on that hysterical edge he'd heard so often over the last few months. "Nate, talk to me. Dammit, don't you have anything to say?"

"Just this," he said, straightening and leaning on the broom. "You've taken everything I have. There's nothing left—no money, no nothing. But that's okay. All I want is for you to leave me alone. Me and Sam."

"No problem," she said. "Just sell the ranch, and give me half. You'll never see me again."

"No," he said. "You can keep the money you already stole. But I'm not selling the ranch. It's not mine to sell. It's Sam's."

"Okay," she said. "Then I want Sam." Turning, she strode off to the house without a backward glance.

Sandi was leaving the house when Nate walked in an hour later. He stood back and she stalked down the steps, avoiding his eyes to stare haughtily across the yard. Taylor sat at the kitchen table, drinking a glass of water and reading a book. He looked up as Nate walked in.

"You're a lucky man, Nate," he said. "I envy you."

Nate barked out a mirthless laugh. Well, at least Sandi wasn't sharing their little drama with the clients. Taylor obviously had no idea what was going on in his life.

But even if he didn't know about Sandi's ultimatum, Taylor had no reason to envy him. The man was a movie star, rich beyond reason, with his pick of women. He probably only worked a few months out of the year, and he only had to pretend to be a cowboy, so he never had to deal with horse poop, drought, or, heaven forbid, a bunch of greenhorns descending on him demanding riding lessons.

Why the hell would he envy Nate?

Oh. Yeah.

"She's pretty on the outside, I know," Nate said. "But if it makes you feel any better, she's not all flowers and sunshine."

Taylor laughed. "No, I wouldn't expect Charlie to be the flowers and sunshine type. But I'll bet you're never bored."

Nate could feel warmth flooding his face. How did Taylor know he'd been with Charlie? Was the tie between them that obvious?

Could Sandi tell?

He swallowed. "I meant Sandi," he said. "She's my girlfriend. My ex, I mean. Charlie and I—Charlie and I aren't together. Half the time, she can't stand me."

"Could've fooled me," Taylor said. "But I wasn't talking about either one of them, actually. Or that cute little half-pint you've got, although I wish I had the chance to start over with Phaedra at that age."

"Yeah," Nate said, pleased. "Sam's a good kid."

"What I was talking about was Latigo," Taylor said.

"What, the ranch? Yeah, I love it, but what do you see in it?" He glanced out the window, where the sunbaked outbuildings tilted like a drunken chorus line in the direction of the prevailing winds. There didn't seem to be a straight wall or a square corner in the whole place, but it was home, and always had been.

"It's not exactly a picture postcard," Nate said.

Taylor shrugged. "I don't know. The place has a lot of potential."

Nate nodded. "It does," he said. "I'm glad you can see it. God knows Sandi can't, and neither could the folks at the bank. The place has supported my family for four generations, but the loan officer almost didn't… oh, hell, you don't want to know about that."

Taylor looked puzzled. "You mortgaged it?"

Nate nodded, feeling a familiar headache set in as he clenched his teeth. "Sam was a preemie," he said. "Born more than two months early. The doctor bills—well, it was crazy. I had to mortgage part of the place to pay them off."

"That's a shame," Taylor said.

The pity in the actor's tone made Nate clench his teeth even harder, and the dull ache in his head began to throb, swinging into a thumping cha-cha beat.

"We're making it," he said. "Sometimes it's touch and go, but obviously Sam's worth every penny. I just hope I can hang onto the place for her, you know?" He remembered Sandi's threats and felt a heavy dose of dread settle in his stomach. "She loves it, and I want to make sure she's generation five living off this land. It's her heritage."

"Maybe I could help," Taylor said.

"No need," Nate growled. "We're okay."

Taylor grinned. "I wasn't offering charity."

"Good," Nate said. "I'm not taking any."

"I figured that. Look, here's the deal. I'd like to partner up with you. Buy into the ranch. I have some ideas to make it pay."

Nate looked down at his lap. First Sandi, now Taylor—it seemed like everybody wanted a piece of what was his. "Can't do it," he said.

"I figured you'd say that. You're not exactly the kind of guy who deals well with change, are you?" Taylor said.

"Guess not." Taylor must have been talking to Sandi already. She was always saying he was afraid of change. Always trying to get him to turn the ranch into some kind of modern factory farm, or a dude ranch. Always trying to kill the traditions that had supported his family for generations. And now she was trying to take the place away.

He clenched his teeth. No way. The ranch had belonged to his grandparents, and their parents before them. It was his birthright, and, more important, it was Sam's.

"Well, think about it," Taylor said. "The offer stands. And if you ever decide to sell…"

"That's not going to happen," Nate said. "Not ever."

"That's not what your ex says," Taylor said. "Sounds like she's got you over a barrel. I'm just trying to help out. I've got a couple of solutions for you when you're ready to listen. Unless you change your mind and want to sell the whole place."

Damn. The girl ought to quit that beauty school and go into real estate.

"Thanks, but no thanks," Nate said, shoving his chair back from the table. He knew he should be more gracious, but anger was burning a hole in his gut. "I'm not selling."

Chapter 29

JUNIOR NICKERED SOFTLY WHEN CHARLIE SWUNG THE STALL door open. "Buddy," she said, setting down a plastic bucket full of grooming gear. "How you doing today?"

She approached him cautiously, breathing down his nose in a slightly speeded-up run-through of their first encounter. When he calmed and accepted her presence, she ran one hand down his neck, then massaged the whorl on his forehead. The horse closed his eyes and blew out a long, contented breath.

"I don't know what to do, Junior," she said. She slipped her palm under the currycomb's backstrap and began massaging his gleaming bay coat with the slow circular motions Sam had demonstrated on Honey. "I should leave, huh? Get out of Dodge before this gets any worse."

The horse let out a falsetto whinny that sounded distinctly negative.

"I know," Charlie said. "I hate to leave Nate with Sandi. It's like, I don't know, like leaving an animal with an abusive owner. Same with Sam." The stallion lowered his head and cocked one foot, letting his lashes drift down to cover his eyes. Sighing, he leaned into the pressure of her hand.

"I don't think she treats them right, Junior. It's not just that I'm jealous."

The horse tossed his head and rolled his eyes.

"No, really. It's just that I—I've gotten so I care, I guess." Charlie worked her way down the horse's muscular shoulder and across his back, then set a hand on his rump and stepped slowly around to the other side. "And how the hell did that happen? He's a cowboy, for God's sake. But he's different, you know?" she said. "I mean, you like him. And you should know. You're a horse."

Straightening to work a cloud of dust and dander from Junior's back, she began singing the low blues song that had soothed him the day before. Gradually, her concern for Nate, her worries about Sam, and her fears for the future gave way to peace. There was only herself, the stallion, and the song, spotlit by a shaft of sunlight in the sweet-smelling hay-filled barn.

She'd crooned out the second verse and was rounding the corner into the chorus when Junior opened his eyes and lifted his head, his ears flicking nervously backward and forward. Whinnying softly, he stamped a heavy front foot.

"Nice singing."

Blinking as if she'd just awakened from sleep, Charlie turned to see Taylor Barnes resting his forearms on the rough wood edging the stall. He'd rolled up the sleeves on a striped Wrangler shirt, and she couldn't help noticing the ropy muscles flexing when he shifted his grip.

"Nice horse too," he said.

She almost said "nice arms," but she stopped herself just in time.

Junior nodded his head, and for a minute, Charlie thought he was agreeing—but what the horse was really doing was expressing his unease at the nearness of this stranger. He stamped again, this time dropping one black hoof perilously close to Charlie's own foot.

"Nice, but feisty," she said, keeping her voice soft and low. "He's a little scared of strangers. Could you back off just a little? Like over there?" She nodded almost imperceptibly toward the hay bales stacked against the wall a few feet behind Taylor.

"Sure," Taylor said. "Keep on doing what you're doing. I just didn't want to poke around in here without letting you know I was around." He settled onto the bales and rested against the wall, his long legs crossed at the ankles. "I've had some pretty private conversations with my own horse. Shared a lot of secrets."

Wondering how much he'd heard, Charlie finished up Junior's broad rump, then bent to trade the currycomb for a brush. With long, gentle strokes, she smoothed Junior's gleaming coat. "They're good listeners," she said.

"Yeah," Taylor said. "But it's more than that. There's something wise about them. I mean, Teaspoon doesn't say a word when I tell him my troubles, but somehow, whenever we finish one of those one-sided conversations, I end up with everything all figured out."

"Teaspoon?" Charlie smiled at the odd name.

"He's a retired barrel horse. Girl who had him called him Sugar. Couldn't let that stand. Figured Teaspoon was kind of related. Close enough, and he seems to prefer it."

"Right," Charlie said, holding back a smile and turning back to her work. "But I'm not sure even Junior can straighten out the mess I'm in."

"Want to talk about it? I'm just a human, but maybe I could help."

To Charlie's surprise, she felt a sudden urge to spill her story to this stranger. Of course, she felt like she knew Chance Newton—everyone who'd ever seen *West with the Wind* felt the same way. But Chance was just a character in a story, she reminded herself. This was Taylor Barnes. And she didn't know a thing about the man under the movie star façade—except that he'd abandoned his daughter, just like her own father. He was hardly qualified to give advice to anybody.

"Let's see," Barnes said. "I'll wager it's got something to do with Blondie out there." He grinned. "Something to do with how she's got our favorite cowboy jammed up against the wall."

Charlie shook her head, heat stealing over her face. "It's not my business," she said flatly. "Or yours."

"Nope. Probably not. But just so you know, he's got some issues you might not know about. That little girl was born premature. Medical bills just about ruined him, I think."

"I wondered," Charlie said slowly. "I knew the ranch had been in the family, so I couldn't figure out how he could be having so much trouble making a go of it."

"Guess it's mortgaged to the hilt," Taylor said.

Charlie turned back to the horse. "Like I said—none of our business. Besides, shouldn't you be out there bonding with your daughter?"

Taylor shook his head. "We're taking it slow," he said.

"I guess you could say that." Charlie couldn't keep the bite out of her voice. "Ten years between visits is pretty slow, all right."

"There's a reason for that."

"I'm sure there is," Charlie said evenly. She tried to swallow her anger, but it stuck in her craw like a piece of dry cake. When she looked over at Taylor, it was like she could see her own father, living out his life somewhere else, with barely a thought for his abandoned daughter. What would she do if he turned up and wanted a reconciliation?

She'd walk away. That's all men like that deserved. It would just about kill her, but she'd walk away. Show him how it felt.

"I'm sure there's a reason," she said. "But there's no excuse."

"You're right," he said. "But I was wondering if you could help me out. You're in psychology, right? I really want to fix things with Phaedra, but I don't even know where to start."

"I can tell you where to start," Charlie said. "About ten years ago." She shifted, turning her back on the actor.

"Look, that wasn't my choice," Taylor said. "Her mother's done everything she can to keep me from seeing her. Including telling her I'm a first-class bastard who doesn't care about her."

"And you do?" Charlie asked.

Taylor nodded, accepting her sharp tone as if he deserved it. That gained him a few points, but still...

"It's going to take a while to convince her I'm sincere," he said.

"And you are?"

"I am," Taylor said. "I've wanted to see her. I really have. But her mother made some—some threats. Said she'd make—accusations—unless I sent the check every month and stayed out of her life."

Charlie gave Junior a final stroke with the brush and set it back in the bucket, then carried the whole kit out of the stall and sat down beside Taylor.

"What kind of accusations?" she asked.

"The worst kind." Taylor was staring down at his hands, chewing the inside of his cheek. "Look, I shouldn't talk about this. No offense, but every time I confide in somebody there's a risk it'll end up in the tabloids. So until I know you better…"

All of a sudden, Charlie realized what kind of accusations Taylor's wife was talking about. Taylor had money and influence, but he was a public figure, and gossip travels fast. One whisper and he'd be the next Michael Jackson.

"I guess I can understand that," she said. "But I'm not sure Phaedra will. You have a lot of fence to mend."

When had she started talking in cowboy metaphors? She tried to think of something Jersey-ish to say, but swearing didn't seem appropriate.

"I sure do," Taylor said. "It's going to be a long road, and I don't even know where to start. I know more about horses than about teenagers. I should be going to a parenting clinic, not a horse training one."

"Well, maybe you can apply the same theories," Charlie said. "That's kind of what I'm going for with my research. How to learn from our interactions with animals, use them to enhance our relationships. I'm thinking their cues are more subtle, harder to pick up on. They bring out instincts we've forgotten how to use."

Taylor nodded, pressing his lips together and looking down into his lap. "I could try that," he said. "But it's so different. I mean, I'm not going to put a halter on her and lead her around, you know?"

Charlie laughed. "Good thing, because I don't think she'd let you. But you can't push her. Not after all this time."

The angled shaft of sunlight creating a dance hall for dust motes above the golden hay dimmed, then brightened as someone stepped into the barn.

"You're right," Sandi said. "You can't push me. Not after all I've been through with Nate." She tossed her hair and shot Taylor a teasing glance. "But when I get tossed off a bronc, I just climb right back on again."

"I thought you were afraid of horses," Charlie said. "Besides, we weren't talking about you." Grabbing the grooming bucket, she stood up. "Believe it or not," she muttered.

Sandi instantly took her seat beside Taylor and graced him with a luminous smile before turning back to Charlie. "You know not to get anywhere near that stallion, right? He's vicious."

"I just got done grooming him," Charlie said.

Sandi's eyes widened. "You did?"

Charlie nodded. She told herself to stop there, but she couldn't resist a childish urge to one-up Sandi. "Nate showed me how," she said.

"Charlie's a good hand with the horses," Taylor said. "Got a real gift."

Sandi sniffed and looked away. "Well, it's almost time for dinner," she said. "So I guess Nate needs your help again."

Charlie narrowed her eyes. "He doesn't need my help," she said. "This whole dude ranch thing was your idea, so I guess the cooking and cleaning is *your* job now." She grinned. "Got yourself just what you wanted, right?" She punched a fist in the air in a mock feminist salute. "You go, girl."

Chapter 30

Sandi frowned, and a deep crease appeared between her brows, a crack in the gleaming façade of her beauty. "I took a look at all that dreck you stowed in the kitchen," she said. "I haven't got a clue what to do with it. I mean, eggplants? Brown rice?"

"For ratatouille," Charlie said.

"Rat-a-what?" Taylor grimaced. "There aren't actually rats in it, are there?"

Charlie shook her head. "Nope. Just onions, tomatoes— you know. It's good. And besides, Phaedra's a vegetarian. So am I."

"So we all have to suffer?" Sandi scowled. "I don't know how to cook that stuff."

"Guess you'd better figure it out, 'cause it's all we've got," Charlie said. "Unless you know what to do with a brisket, or a boneless shoulder from some poor deformed cow." She turned to Taylor. "I think our break's probably over now. Time to get cracking on the horse whispering." She slanted her eyes toward the blonde. "You know, those lessons we paid Sandi all that money for."

She gave the woman an imperious wave. "Do me a favor, would you? Go tell Nate we're ready for him," Charlie said. "I sure am glad you showed up to help. The place was a little understaffed, you know? Compared to what you promised in that brochure." She grinned. "You coming, Taylor? Nate said I might be able to get a saddle on Trouble today."

"Well, good luck with that," Sandi said. "I'd say you'll be dealing with trouble, all right."

Charlie whirled. "What does that mean?"

Sandi widened her eyes. "Oh, nothing. That's the name of your horse, right? Trouble. So appropriate."

—⁓—

"Okay," Nate said, opening the gate to the round pen. "Charlie, Trouble's ready for you."

Trouble didn't look ready. In fact, she was doing her damndest to kick the round ring apart, rearing up and hitting it with her front hooves, then turning and kicking with her heels. When that didn't work, she took a fast turn around the perimeter and slammed into the gate once, twice, three times, then stood trembling, staring at the immovable wall. Throwing up her head, she let out a high, desperate whinny that pierced Charlie's heart like the wail of a baby.

"What do I do?"

Nate handed her a flexible pole with a scrap of fabric on the end. "Get in there and keep her moving with the flag."

"You don't want me to do like I did with Junior?" Nate had explained today's strategy before they started, but Charlie still hoped she could somehow make it easier.

"Nope. This is different. You're going to ride her today. You need to be the boss, not her best friend."

Charlie sighed. She was already Trouble's best friend—well, her best human friend, anyway. The horse ate from her hand, let her stroke her velvety muzzle, and even allowed her to tease the tangles out of her mane. She was more than willing to give the horse time—to let her get accustomed to people before putting her to work.

But Nate was adamant. "The quicker she learns to trust you, the easier her life will be," he'd said. "And she won't trust you until she respects you. It's not harsh, Charlie. You're not going to hurt her. Just push her a little."

Charlie slid off the fence and into the soft raked dirt of the ring, taking her place in the center as Trouble took off and galloped around the perimeter, then arched her back and crow-hopped a few times before kicking up her heels and taking off again.

"You have got to be kidding," Charlie said. "I'm going to ride her *today*?"

"Don't let her see you doubt it," Nate said.

Charlie took a step toward Trouble, then danced away as the horse flailed her back legs. "She'll kick me."

"She can't kick you when she's running away," Nate said. "Holler at her."

"She'll be scared of me."

"Okay. Guess you can't do it." Nate sighed and turned toward the rest of the group. "Phaedra, you want to try?"

"No, wait," Charlie said, feeling panic rise in her chest. "I can do it."

"Really?" Nate raised a doubting eyebrow. "You were just listing all the reasons why you couldn't. Trouble seems to believe every one of them."

The horse backed up and slammed into the fence again, as if to demonstrate her faith in Charlie's reasoning.

"No, I can do it."

"Don't tell me. Tell her."

"But I'm driving her away. I don't get how that helps."

Nate stepped into the ring and stood beside her. Taking the flag, he tapped the ground behind the horse and set her in motion.

"Trust me. Sometimes when someone pushes you away over and over, it makes you want nothing more than to be with them."

Charlie gave him a sharp look. "That doesn't make any sense."

But maybe it did. She'd pushed Nate away—after their first kiss, that morning after they fell into bed together, and the day they picked up the horses. She'd pushed him away over and over, but he hadn't given up. If anything, he seemed to want her more.

She hoped he didn't think her behavior was a calculated strategy. She wasn't manipulating him. She genuinely didn't think a relationship between the two of them was a possibility.

Well, she thought that most of the time. But once in a while, joining up with Nate seemed like the only way to set her universe on the right path.

"Trust me, it's working." Nate handed her the flag. "Just keep pushing. You'll see."

Taking a deep breath, Charlie took the flag and turned her attention to the horse. Waving the flag, she took a quick step forward, and the mare set off at a gallop.

"That's the first thing you've done right," Nate said. "With the horse, I mean." He grinned. "Other than that, you've done lots of things right, but never mind. Keep her going."

Charlie set her jaw and kept the flag moving behind the horse.

"Keep the flag behind her shoulder and don't let her stop."

Trouble kept running, sweat glistening on her dark coat, one rolling eye focused on Charlie. She slowed and Charlie let the flag touch her rump.

"Go," she said.

"Sound like you mean it," Nate said.

"Yah! Go!"

The horse kept running, but she slowed, and her circle grew smaller. She lowered her head, still watching Charlie, still running.

"She's tired," Charlie said.

"That's what you want," Nate said. "Keep her going."

Charlie felt tears heating the back of her eyes as she flicked the flag to keep the mare running. Trouble's eyes were softer now, begging Charlie for a break as clearly as if the horse had spoken. She worked her mouth and dropped her head, as if pleading to be allowed to stop.

"That's what you're looking for," Nate said. "See how she's chewing and dropping her head? That's submissive. And she's watching you, paying attention. Ease up now."

Charlie stilled, lowering the flag, and the horse slowed, then stopped, facing her from just a few feet away.

"Touch her with the flag."

Charlie cast a doubting eye toward Nate, then gently brushed the mare's shoulder with the flag. Trouble started and dodged away, then stood still, watching Charlie.

"Again," Nate said. "All over."

Charlie touched the horse again and Trouble stood still, trembling as Charlie stroked her back with the scrap of fabric, tickled her legs, her belly, even her ears. The horse stepped aside once or twice, but finally submitted.

Nate smiled. "Now you get to pet her."

Charlie smoothed the horse's damp coat with her hand. "Sorry, baby," she said. "So sorry. It's okay."

"Don't apologize to her," Nate said. "Praise her if you want, but you're doing her a favor, and you need to show that with your attitude. She can read you like a book, so be confident. It'll be easier for her if she sees you as a leader."

He slid from the fence and handed Charlie a lead rope. "Now you're going to take her out and snub her to that post over there." He pointed. "Tie her high and close, so she can't get a leg over the rope. She's going to struggle, but she'll be okay."

Charlie did as she was told, clipping the rope to Trouble's halter and tying the horse to the post with a quick-release knot. Trouble's mood changed in an instant. Setting her hooves, she pulled against the rope, twisting her head every which way in an effort to escape.

Charlie tried to stay quiet, but she couldn't help herself. "She'll hurt herself."

"She might," Nate said. "But not much, and only if she fights. It shouldn't take long for her to figure that out."

It shouldn't have, but it did. Charlie watched Trouble from the corner of her eye as Doris ran through the same procedure with her buckskin. Trouble's fiery nature flared up and she fought the rope through Doris's whole session before she gave up and stood trembling at the post. Charlie watched, feeling every tug of the rope. By the time the horse stilled, she felt like she'd been through the torment herself.

"Now the tarp." Nate tossed a blanket to Charlie. "Wave it over her back, over her head, around her feet— get her used to it. You're almost there."

Charlie flashed him a doubting look, but she did as she was told. Surprisingly, Trouble stood patiently while Charlie flicked the blanket all around her body.

"Okay," Nate said. "She's ready. Saddle up."

Chapter 31

An hour later, Charlie ran a brush over Trouble's damp coat.

"I can't believe it," she said. "I can't believe I just rode a wild horse."

"I can't believe it either," Nate said, grinning. "What would your PETA friends think?"

"If they could see it, they'd know it was okay. Trouble's not scared anymore." She untangled a knot in the mare's mane. "She seems calmer."

"How about you?"

"I'm calmer too. Mostly because I'm exhausted."

"Ready for dinner?"

Charlie gave Trouble a final pat and a kiss on the muzzle. "I guess."

She almost groaned when she sat down at the dinner table. Sandi had ignored the eggplants and onions and raided the freezer instead. A huge pot of stew occupied the center of the table. There was no ratatouille—although as far as Charlie was concerned, the chunks of meat floating in the pot might as well be rat. Rat, cow, cat—it made no difference. Meat was meat, and Charlie wouldn't eat any of it.

She scanned the table for something she could eat. A faint wisp of fragrant steam rose from a napkin-lined basket in the center of the table. Charlie reached over and pushed the cloth aside. Biscuits.

She took one and split it open. It flaked apart in delicate layers, releasing another cloud of delicious fresh-baked scent. Sandi might not know how to cook vegetarian, but she obviously had Charlie beat when it came to baking. When Charlie tried to make biscuits, they came out dense as hockey pucks and hit the plate with an audible thunk.

"Great biscuits," Taylor said, slathering one with butter. "Good stew too. You sure it's not rat, though?"

"I'm sure." Sandi flashed him a flirtatious grin. "Pure Angus beef. I was worried I wouldn't be able to keep up with what you're used to in L.A."

"This is fine," Taylor said.

The two of them spent the rest of the meal discussing Hollywood, with Sandi listening breathlessly as Taylor spun tales of movie sets and stars. Finally, Nate pushed back his chair and set his napkin on the table.

"Got to feed the horses," he said.

Charlie stood too. "I'll help."

Sandi frowned. "No. You're a paying guest, remember?" She tossed her hair and tilted her annoyingly perfect nose in the air. "I'll help Nate with the horses." She gave Nate a significant look. "*Our* horses."

Charlie would have laughed at the look of horror on Nate's face if she hadn't felt so sorry for him—and for the horses.

"I'll be okay," he said. "Don't worry about it, Sandi."

"I'm not worried," Sandi said. "I want to help with Junior. You said he was vicious, but you let *her* pet him."

"Charlie knows how to handle him, that's all," Nate said. "It's part of what I'm teaching."

"Well, if Charlie can do it, I can do it. Teach *me*." Sandi set off for the barn, slender hips swinging.

Nate turned to Charlie and scowled. "Why'd you have to tell her I'd let you handle the horse?" He waved her away. "Go play cards or something. I'll see you tomorrow."

Feeling dismissed, Charlie left without a word, the other students trailing behind. Only Sam was unaffected by the tension. Trotting ahead, she stopped on the steps and swept a bottle of polish from her pocket like a magician unveiling a rabbit from his top hat.

"Look, Mr. Barnes," she said. "Mom had fuchsia! Your favorite!"

"Sam, I don't think…" Charlie began.

"Do you think Mom should do it?" Sam fingered the bottle, biting her lower lip. "I mean, she's going to beauty school and he *is* a movie star. But she's busy with the horses now, helping Dad. I thought maybe I could surprise her."

Charlie nodded, casting a teasing smile toward Taylor. "Well, I bet she would be awfully surprised if she came in here and found out you'd painted Mr. Barnes's nails fuchsia."

Taylor made a mournful face, as if he'd been sentenced to the scaffold, but he sat down on the side of Charlie's bed and held out his big, square hands. "Go for it, pardner," he said. "But no cameras, okay? I don't want to turn up in the *National Enquirer* with my nails painted pink. They'd probably say I was sporting ladies' panties too."

Charlie stifled a giggle while Taylor's face turned a shade of pink that just about matched the nail polish.

Sam, who had been shaking the bottle as they talked, knelt in front of Taylor and had just unscrewed the top when a high, panicked scream rent the air outside. Every head turned toward the barn.

"Junior!" Charlie said.

———∿∿∿———

Nate dropped the bucket of sweet feed he was dumping into Boy's feed bin and vaulted the stall door, dashing toward the sound of Junior's panicked scream. He was about to fling the stall door open and hurl himself onto whatever was hurting the stallion, but the scene inside the barn stopped him dead in the doorway.

Junior was backed into the corner of his stall, eyes rolling like loose marbles, lather coating his neck. A panicked grimace pulled his skin tighter than a Hollywood facelift, highlighting every vein and muscle and drawing his lips back from his teeth. As Nate watched, the horse stretched his neck out in a sinuous snakelike motion, snapping his teeth, then repeated the motion twice more. Something had him riled up way beyond sanity.

And that something was crouched in the center of the stall.

Sandi.

Nate thought he might never breathe again. She was crouched in the straw, her hands covering her face, knees drawn up to her chest. Her shoulders heaved with sobs.

"He kicked me," she said.

He unlatched the gate, careful not to let it click too loudly, and slid inside the stall. Edging toward her, he dodged away as Junior snapped again, his face a mask of panic.

"Can you walk?" Nate asked.

Sandi shook her head. Nate wanted to run to her and drag her out of harm's way, but he knew better than to move too fast. Breathing slowly, he calmed himself. Hopefully, the horse wasn't too far gone to connect and feel the soothing vibrations Nate was sending his way.

A soft voice behind him broke his concentration.

"I could help."

Charlie had entered the barn so quietly Nate hadn't heard her. Neither had Junior, but he heard her now and rolled his eyes her way, a shiver rippling his skin from his neck to his heaving ribs. "Tell me what to do," Charlie said.

Nate remembered Sandi's argument. *You let* her *pet him.* This whole thing was Charlie's fault. This was what happened when you let outsiders mess with your animals.

Of course, Charlie wasn't really an outsider. Or at least, he hadn't thought she was.

Maybe he'd been wrong. Too quick to trust.

Pulling in a long breath, he struggled to retain his composure. "Just go," he said. "You've done enough."

He'd tried to keep a mild tone, but something in his voice sent Junior into another round of hysterics. Bunching his hindquarters, he lifted his front hooves and spun toward Sandi. Nate lunged from the side of the stall and slammed into the horse's shoulder, shoving the stallion sideways so his striking hooves hit the straw a bare six inches from where Sandi crouched in the straw.

"Mom," squeaked a small voice.

Sam. Nate blanched.

Sam. The horse. Sandi. Sam. His mind was scrambling, his protective urge dodging from one thing to another. He squeezed his eyes shut and focused hard on the horse under his hands. He was leaning into Junior's shoulder, his fingers buried in the damp strands of the horse's mane as he tried through sheer force of will to hold the animal steady. It wasn't working. He could feel muscles twitching under the animal's damp coat, threatening to explode into action. If the horse reared, Nate would be tossed off as easily as a rag doll. He didn't have the physical strength to hold the animal in check. Only his mind could hold the horse steady, and his mind was spinning with panic. *Sandi. Sam. Sam. Sandi. Junior.* He sorted the threats in his head, and one rose to the surface.

"Sam," he said, through clenched teeth.

"I've got her," Charlie said. "Come on, honey. Daddy's got the horse. Don't worry."

Nate felt some of the tension leach out of his muscles as the barn door closed behind them. He rested his forehead against the horse and willed himself calm while he flicked through his options in his head. He needed to get Sandi out of the stall. But if he focused away from the horse, anything could happen.

"Sandi," he said. "Hey. Sandi."

She opened one eye, peering through the fan of hair that almost obscured her face. Her expression was blank and distant. Could she even understand him?

"Where did he kick you?"

She just stared at him.

"You have to get out," Nate said. "Can you get up?"

Sandi's face was unreadable. Had she been kicked in the head, or what? She needed his help, but if he left the horse, they were both liable to get hurt.

"You have to get out if you can," he said. "I can't leave him."

Her expression shifted, grogginess giving way to stunned understanding and then outrage.

Nate had never been so glad to see her get mad.

"The damn horse kicked me right in the butt," she said. "Get away from him. Help me up."

"I can't," Nate said. "You'll have to get out yourself. I'm sorry."

"Nate, I practically passed out. I'm still dizzy." She covered her face with her hands. "I'm not sure I can walk."

Keeping his grip on the horse, he struggled to speak. Sandi finally tossed her hair back and gave him a look that held more anger than pain.

"Are you *sure* you can't walk?" he asked.

Glaring at him, Sandi struggled up onto her hands and knees and crawled slowly to the stall door, fumbling with the latch while Nate concentrated all his energy on holding the horse steady, sending surges of stolid concentration from his mind to his hands. Finally, she opened the gate and stumbled out of the stall. Turning, she kicked the gate closed behind her—hard. It slammed shut, the clack of the latch echoing like a gunshot. Junior stumbled backward, dragging Nate with him, one heavy hoof glancing across Nate's boot.

"Easy," Nate muttered, wincing and trying not to react to the pain. "Take it easy, boy."

The horse didn't want to take it easy. He arched his back and kicked the back of the stall, then reared up. Nate threw himself across the stall like an action hero fleeing a bomb blast, flinging himself at the gate. He fell out of the stall just as Junior's hooves hit the boards with a force that almost splintered the heavy plank door.

Nate turned and watched the horse, who stood trembling in the stall. He'd come so far with Junior. The horse had been doing so well, getting better every day. He'd even recovered from the setback he'd suffered from Charlie's foolishness on her first day.

But if Sandi hadn't done anything to provoke him—if the horse had simply lashed out at her—Nate was going to have to admit he'd failed. Junior would never be stable enough to breed. He might not even be stable enough to keep.

He turned to face Sandi, who was sitting on a hay bale with her head in her hands. Nate bent over her to brush her hair back from her eyes. The gaze he uncovered was almost as murderous as the look the horse had worn—but Junior's look had been born of fear. Sandi's was lit by anger, pure and simple.

"I'm surprised you didn't just let him kill me," she said. "That would solve all your problems, wouldn't it?"

"I couldn't let him go. I had to hold him," Nate said. He floundered through his mind, searching for the words that would make Sandi understand he'd had no choice. "I had to," he said.

Even to him, the words sounded weak.

"The damn horse kicked me," she said. "Knocked me down. I've probably got a bruise the size of a dinner plate on my ass." She shook his hand off her shoulder and grabbed the stall door, pulling herself to her feet. "My back hurts," she said, pressing one hand to her tailbone. "I told you that horse was vicious. You should have it put down."

Nate set his hand under her elbow and guided her from the barn. As they staggered down the alley between the stalls, he looked back to see Junior pawing at the straw with one frantic foot while he repeated the snakelike motion of his head and neck over and over. Snapping his teeth again and again, the horse trembled and pawed the straw, his body racked with shivers.

All that work, those long days, the trust Nate had built between himself and the horse—it was gone.

Sandi was already starting to take the ranch away, piece by piece.

Chapter 32

CHARLIE SLOUCHED ON THE SIDE OF THE BED, LISTENING TO THE crunch of tires on gravel as the ambulance trundled down the driveway. There were no sirens, no emergency lights. Sandi seemed fine; in fact, she'd managed to light into Nate with a diatribe that almost set the barn on fire once the EMTs arrived. She'd insisted she was gravely injured and would never walk again, but the fact that she was limping theatrically toward the ambulance as she said it made her claim a little suspect. Still, the ambulance workers had insisted on strapping her to a gurney and transporting her to the hospital to be checked out and Nate had gone along, leaving Charlie in charge of a very worried Sam.

And thank God she had Sam to worry about. If she'd been able to think of anything else, she'd have remembered the tone of Nate's voice, the hard sheen of his eyes when she'd offered to help. Clearly, he blamed her for Sandi's accident.

She spent the next two hours settling Sam into bed. The attic bedroom was a perfect child-sized aerie under the eaves, decorated with pictures of horses, horse figurines, stuffed horses, and a comforter set decorated with cowboys and bucking broncs. Charlie read her one story after another to distract her from the events of the evening. The fact that every book the kid owned was about horses didn't help any. Charlie did her best, assuring the child over and over that her mother was fine, pointing out that Robert the Rose Horse would never hurt anyone and Blaze always rescued Billy, even when there was a forest fire. Finally Doris poked her head into the open door.

"Your dad called," she said. "Your mama's going to be all right, honey."

Charlie heaved a phony sigh of relief and left the room. She hadn't heard the phone ring—not once. Doris was lying, probably trying to make the kid feel better. A kick in the butt might be just what Sandi deserved, but lower back injuries were no joke, and while Sandi's theatrics hadn't fooled the adults, Sam had watched anxiously, her forehead wrinkled with concern, as her mother was loaded into the ambulance.

Standing in the hallway, Charlie gave way to the guilt that was nibbling at the edges of her consciousness, telling her the whole incident was her fault.

But it wasn't. It couldn't be. Sandi had insisted on approaching the stallion despite Nate's advice. Charlie didn't have anything to do with that.

Right?

In a flash, she relived the past few hours. Sandi's warning about Junior. Her own flippant response.

It *was* her fault.

Deep down, she knew she'd set Sandi up on purpose. She'd resented the woman from the moment she'd met her. She'd known when she flaunted her own success with Junior that the woman would try to compete. She'd used the horse to hurt Sandi, surely as if she'd picked up a weapon and clubbed her over the head.

Which would have been infinitely more satisfying.

But what if Junior had *killed* Sandi? No matter how much Charlie disliked Nate's ex, there were people who loved and needed her. And was Sandi really that bad? Or was Charlie just jealous?

And what would happen to Junior if he really *was* a monster killer stallion? She remembered the odd, compulsive way Junior had twisted his neck, the way he'd drawn his lips back and snapped at the air as if he was seeing devils floating in the dusty air of the stable.

What she'd done was selfish, petty, and wrong. She'd never forgive herself—and judging from the look Nate had given her, he wouldn't forgive her either.

Well, that solved one problem. She could stay now and concentrate on doing her job for Sadie. Maintaining an objective perspective around Nate Shawcross had just become a major survival skill—because even if she wanted him, he wouldn't have her now.

Of course, it was that certain knowledge that made her realize just how much she really did want him.

Charlie woke hours later to Phaedra's light breathing and Doris's now-familiar snoring. The first time she'd heard the woman sleep, Charlie thought Bigfoot was on the loose, but she'd gotten used to it. It hardly scared her at all now.

Rubbing her eyes, she found her feet and padded across the floor to the bunkhouse door. Easing it open, she looked toward the ranch house.

No lights.

No pickup.

Nate and Sandi were still gone.

She glanced down at her wrist, squinting to see her watch in the pale light of dawn. Four a.m. Surely they would have been back by now if Sandi was okay. Tugging her T-shirt down and brushing the seat of her jeans, she headed for the house. She needed to call the hospital. Taylor was sleeping in there, probably on the sofa. She wasn't sure what Nate had planned to do with Sandi as far as sleeping arrangements went, and that was just as well. In any case, she'd try to sneak in and use the phone without waking Taylor.

Yeah, right. Once she reached the front door, she realized sneaking into the house wasn't a possibility. For one thing, the door stuck, and when it finally burst open it hit the wall with a solid thump. For another thing, Butt heard her coming and jumped off the sofa, hitting the floor with a mighty thud and woofing out a greeting. Taylor stumbled out of the bedroom, rubbing his eyes.

"Something wrong?" He squinted at her, his eyes bleary, his jaw shadowed by the day's growth of stubble.

"I don't know," Charlie said. "They're not back yet. I'm calling the hospital." She waved him back toward the bedroom. "Go get some sleep."

Frowning, Taylor shuffled over to the kitchen table and sat down. He obviously wasn't used to following orders.

Charlie found a phone book and flipped to the emergency numbers. Crooking the old-fashioned wall phone between her shoulder and chin, she punched the Cheyenne hospital's number into the keypad.

"Cheyenne Regional Medical Center. How can I help you?" said a robotic voice.

"I'm calling about a patient," Charlie said. "Sandi—um,

Sandi Givens." She'd almost said Shawcross. "She was brought in earlier. In an ambulance."

"I'm sorry, there's no one here by that name." Charlie could hear the clicking of a keyboard over the static of the phone line.

"Was she released? Or did they…" She swallowed. "Did they have to take her to Denver?"

"Are you family?"

Charlie sighed. "No. Just a—a friend." *Yeah, right,* she thought. *I'm Sandi's pal. We're regular BFFs.*

"I'm sorry, all medical information is confidential," the voice informed her. "I'd recommend you call your friend. Or try a family member."

"I'll do that. Thank you," Charlie said.

She sat down at the kitchen table and covered her face with her hands. "They won't tell me anything," she said. "It's confidential. I wonder what's really going on. I wish Nate would call. I wish…"

She wished so many things—but most of all, she wished she could relive the past six hours. Change the course of her life, and Sandi's, and Junior's. Keep Sam from seeing her mother crouched in the stall with the furious stallion looming over her. What if the incident made Sam afraid of horses? She thought of the horse-themed room upstairs. The kid would have nightmares up there.

Taylor shoved his chair back and shuffled to the refrigerator. Hauling out a gallon of milk, he poured two glasses—one for himself, one for her. He sat down across from her and they sipped wordlessly for a while.

It was a little awkward. Charlie felt like she should say something, but she was afraid of what might come out if she opened her mouth. She could feel sobs building up in her chest, and worse yet, a self-pitying wail. She wondered what Taylor would do if she burst into tears and cried like a baby. He'd probably run. Maybe lock himself in the bedroom.

The actor shifted in his seat, fooling with a napkin. His lips were tight, his chin tucked. He glanced at her, then glanced away. Finally, he reached over and patted her hand. It was a fatherly gesture that almost set her sobs free. Sympathy was always her undoing.

"It'll be okay," he said.

Charlie shook her head. Swallowing, she struggled to talk, the words squeezing through the ache tightening her throat.

"It's my fault," she said. "I knew she'd be jealous. I knew she'd try to handle the horse."

"You didn't know she'd hit him," Taylor said.

Charlie stilled, her back going rigid. "She *what*?"

"She hit him. That's what Nate told me. Junior snapped at her and she smacked him on the nose." He shrugged. "You couldn't have known she'd do that."

"No," Charlie said, pulling away. "How could she? She has to know he's fragile. She has to know his history."

"She didn't care," Taylor said. "He made her mad. So, see? It's not your fault."

"Thanks." Charlie said. "That's a relief." She leaned back in her chair and groaned. "There you go. What kind of person am I? It's like I'm glad she abused him, because it gets me off the hook. I'm a freaking monster."

"No you're not," Taylor said. "You're just a woman." He gave her a wry smile. "Although sometimes that's mighty close to the same thing. Besides, that got Junior off the hook too. Nate was about ready to give up on him until he found out Sandi whacked him one."

They lapsed into silence again, sipping their milk, listening as the clock over the stove ticked the minutes away. They were still sitting there when Nate's truck pulled in an hour later.

Sandi laughed at nothing as she stepped out of the truck. It was a high, tinkling laugh, obviously intended for an audience. Nate looked around the barnyard and groaned inwardly. The only audience was Charlie, standing in the open front door, looking like she hadn't slept a wink.

Damn. He'd gotten so involved dealing with Sandi, he hadn't thought to call the ranch. Charlie looked like she'd been up all night worrying.

Maybe she deserved it, though. Well, sort of. There was no doubt she'd played a part in tonight's events. A big part. But he knew she hadn't realized how Sandi would respond to her baiting, or how serious the repercussions might be.

"Oh, hi, Charlie," Sandi said. "We're back!" She spread her arms and did a quick shuffling dance step, making it obvious there was no real injury to her back. The girl wasn't just better; she was giddy. You'd have thought getting kicked in the butt by a horse was the next best thing to winning the lottery.

In her mind, it was. She'd read Nate a whole new set of rules and taken his silence for submission when he was just being nice because he felt bad about the accident. She'd misinterpreted everything he said—and even managed to misconstrue what he *didn't* say. She'd heard what she wanted to hear, and when she didn't hear anything, she'd figured he agreed with her. She always did that. He could never tell if she did it on purpose, or if she was so focused on herself she couldn't wrap her mind around the notion that someone might disagree with her.

In any case, she'd made two things clear: she was taking Sam back to Denver, and she was going after the ranch. She said she'd already seen a lawyer and she had a right to half.

He might not like change, but it was coming no matter what he did. When he'd tried to protest, she hit him with a bombshell—a secret she'd been keeping for years.

A secret that changed everything.

Charlie scuffed a foot in the dusty driveway and looked up at Sandi. "You okay?" she asked.

"Oh, I'm fine." Sandi laughed again, and the sound scraped up Nate's spine like ragged fingernails. What the hell was so funny, anyway?

Nothing, obviously. The laugh was fake. It was a perfect imitation of some actress on a TV show they used to watch. Sandi's laugh was about as real as her acrylic fingernails. As real as the hair extensions Nate had caught his hand in while she lay on the gurney at the hospital. One of the extensions had come off in his hand, and he thought for a moment he'd ripped her hair right out of her head. She'd laughed then, too, at the look of horror on his face.

"So you're really okay?" Charlie asked.

"Oh, yes." Sandi tossed her golden hair. "I'm better than just okay. We had a good talk, didn't we, Nate?" She threw him a lash-fluttering look and a saucy smile.

"Things are going to change, aren't they?" She tossed her hair. "Well, I have to go pretty up."

———※———

Charlie resisted the urge to make a gagging gesture as Sandi stepped into the bathroom and closed the door. The woman looked fine, but she was probably one of those women who stayed in the bathroom for hours, putting on mascara one eyelash at a time, or whatever it was they did that made their beauty routines take up half their lives. Charlie liked to look nice, but she tried to limit her mirror time to twenty minutes in the morning.

Nate cleared his throat. "I need to feed the horses," he said, heading for the door. Charlie wondered if she should follow. Judging from the way he avoided her eyes, she should probably stay right where she was.

But then she'd be alone with Sandi—and that was the last place she wanted to be. As the door swung shut behind Nate, she lunged for it—but she was too late. Sandi burst out of the bathroom, letting the door slam back against the wall. She stood in the doorway, the fluorescent light over the sink making her golden hair glow like a shining halo. Her expression was hardly angelic, though. Setting her fists on her hips, she glared at Charlie.

"What are you doing with my husband?"

"Your husband?"

Sandi rolled her eyes in the universal high school language for *I can't believe how clueless you are*.

"Nate," she said. "You know, the dumbass cowboy you've been fooling around with."

Charlie spun around, her hands on her hips. "He's not

a dumbass, and I don't fool around. And he's not your husband either."

"Yes he is," Sandi said. "I've put up with him for seven years. That makes us married. Common-law husband and wife."

Charlie felt a stab of sympathy for Nate. What kind of miserable, empty relationship did the two of them have?

"I thought you left," she said. "I thought you guys broke up."

"He might have thought so, but he was wrong," Sandi said. "I'm not done with him yet."

Chapter 33

TAYLOR WAS SITTING AT THE KITCHEN TABLE WHEN NATE came in from the barn. The actor was finishing off a bowl of the sugary cereal Charlie had insisted on providing for the duration of the clinic. She'd claimed everybody enjoyed reliving their childhood once in a while, and she'd been right. The sugary treats had made serving breakfast a whole lot easier, and infinitely more PETAfied. No eggs, no bacon, no animal products except for milk. Just Fruit Loops, Frosted Flakes, and an assortment of sliced fruit.

"Wife okay?" Taylor slurped up a spoonful of pink-tinted milk.

"She's not my wife." Nate kept his voice low. "Though she might tell you different. But, hey, I wanted to talk to you."

Taylor wiped his mouth, then folded his napkin in half and laid it beside his bowl. "You got the wrong guy," he said. "You want advice about girls, you're better off asking just about anybody else."

"It's not about girls," Nate said. "It's about real estate."

Taylor lifted his eyebrows. "You're selling the place?" He looked stunned, as if he hadn't been fishing for a deal the day before, and Nate wondered if the actor's offer had been serious. Maybe he didn't really want to buy the ranch. Maybe the guy was all talk.

"Yeah, I am. I have to," Nate said. He pulled out the

chair across from Taylor and sat down, folding his hands on the table. "Sandi wants her share, and she's taking Sam to Denver either way. I need to move closer."

"Nice to know she has her daughter's welfare in mind," Taylor said dryly.

"Well, I do," Nate said. "So Sam will be okay. And Sandi thinks it would be better for her to grow up some- place more civilized."

"And what do you think?" Taylor asked.

"Well, I don't know about civilization," Nate said. "Seems to me what few people there are out here are a whole lot more civilized than the folks in Denver. You know they have 'drug-free zones' around the schools? Makes you wonder about the rest of the town." He shook his head. "But I'll tell you, there's not much of a hospital here. I mean, if Sam had been hurt like Sandi was, I wouldn't want to have to drive an hour just to get to a hospital. And I wouldn't want to trust her to the doctors here either. Doc Rafferty drinks, and his partner's just incompetent."

"It's good enough for Sandi, though," Taylor said, suppressing a smile.

"Kids are more fragile," Nate said. "You don't want to take risks."

"That little spitfire of yours is tougher than any of us," Taylor said. "She's not afraid of anything."

"That's part of the problem," Nate said. "Sandi doesn't want her around the horses. Says she's not care- ful enough. Especially with Junior being the way he is."

"Junior's not the problem and you know it," Taylor said. "Besides, that kid handles animals a lot better than her mom handles anything."

Nate looked away, his jaw working. Taylor was right. Sam was good for the animals, and the animals were good for her. Junior would never hurt Sam, because Sam knew her way around horses—and she knew enough to stay away from the stallion until her dad had worked with him some more.

But Sandi was scared, and she'd always wanted a different kind of life for Sam. She wanted her to live in what she called a proper house, and if he sold the ranch, she'd be able to buy one. Something in a neighborhood near Denver, with other kids for Sam to play with. Kids needed that—or at least, that's what Sandi said.

And Sandi had always been the boss where Sam was concerned. After all, she was the kid's mom. Carried her in her body for nine months. Sandi always said Sam was a part of her, so she knew what was best for her.

But lately, Nate was starting to wonder. Sandi seemed to want Sam to be her own little mini-me—a carbon copy of her own perfectly groomed, fashionably dressed self. And that wasn't Sam. Not at all.

Of course, that was Nate's fault. The way Sandi told it, you'd have thought he'd kidnapped the kid every morning and dragged her out to the stables kicking and screaming. Sandi just couldn't face the fact that Sam had always chosen to go with him. That she loved the ranch life. That she belonged there.

But none of that mattered. Not to Sandi. She'd laid down the law, and Nate was going to have to toe the line.

Toe the line, or lose Sam.

"Why don't you just sell half of it?"

Nate shook his head. "I can't. One half has the house and barn and the stream. The other half's pretty much desert—worthless on its own without the water." He sighed. "Besides, shuttling Sam back and forth over that distance would just be wrong. Sandi wants her to go to school in Denver, so if I don't move closer, I'll only have her every other weekend. Maybe a month in the summer."

"So you're moving to Denver? What are you going to do with yourself?" Taylor asked. "Get a desk job?"

"No way." Nate shook his head, suppressing a shudder. "I'll try and get one of those little ranchettes in the suburbs with my half the money from the ranch," he said. "That way I can hang onto some of the horses, teach kids to ride, maybe do some clinics—just on a smaller scale." He relaxed his shoulders, thinking of the one positive thing in all this. "The good part is, I'm thinking maybe I can talk Charlie into moving there. She could maybe find work in Denver. Or finish school there, or whatever."

"Did you ask her?"

Nate sucked in a deep breath and looked down at his hands. "Not yet. But I'm going to do my best to talk her into it."

"That's the one smart thing you've said so far," Taylor said.

"Yeah." Nate looked down at his lap, then shifted in his chair and looked directly at Taylor for the first time that morning. "So do you want it?" he asked.

"The ranch?"

Nate nodded, then held his breath, waiting for Taylor's answer. If all his talk about buying the ranch had been just that—talk—it could take a year for Nate to sell the place. A year apart from Sandi and Sam. A year where Sandi would maybe meet someone else, force a stepdad into Sam's life. If he had to stay on the ranch, Nate wouldn't be able to keep an eye on his daughter.

Anything could happen.

He flushed, realizing the actor was watching his face. Sandi always knew what he was thinking, and sometimes he thought everyone else could see through him just as easy.

"You're getting jacked, aren't you?" Taylor eased back in his chair with the confidence of a man who had the whole situation figured out. "She's making you sell the ranch, or she'll take the kid."

Nate didn't answer.

"Fight her," Taylor said. "Sam's your child too. You have a say in her future."

Nate shook his head. "No, I don't."

"You do," Taylor insisted.

Nate shook his head again. "No." His throat tightened. "I don't have any rights at all. Sandi says Sam's not mine."

Chapter 34

CHARLIE STRAIGHTENED A SHEET AND SWEPT A FEW crumbs off the corner of a nightstand, then stood back and surveyed the bunkhouse. Cleaning was really Sandi's job, but Charlie knew she wasn't fit company for horse or human. She figured she'd better keep busy or she'd start screaming and throwing things. She didn't know what had happened between Nate and Sandi, but whatever it was, it had gone Sandi's way.

And that had to be bad news.

She took a deep breath and headed for the corral. Class had apparently started for the day. Doris was up on her buckskin, trotting figure eights while Nate tossed out instructions and the rest of the class watched. Taylor and Phaedra stood side by side.

Spotting her, Taylor whispered something in Phaedra's ear, then strolled over. His interactions with his daughter had grown easy, natural. The guy was turning into a real father. And Phaedra had suddenly turned back into... Phaedra. She was decked out in full Goth regalia, with pale makeup accentuating the dark rims around her eyes.

"Looks like the Cowgirl of Death has been resurrected," Charlie said.

Taylor grinned. "Yeah, and believe it or not, I'm glad. She kept wearing the same outfit, and when I asked her why, she said she didn't have anything 'appropriate.'

Just school stuff, she said. When I pushed her, she admitted she'd 'cleaned up' for me."

"Yeah, that bothered me," Charlie said.

"Bothered me too." He shook his head. "Her mother used to change identities like a chameleon changes colors." He scowled. "The whole time we were together, she dressed like a dudette in all these crazy cowgirl duds. She tried to convince everybody she was a gen-u-wine range-ridin' cowgirl, even though she'd never been on a horse in her life. Then after we broke up, she started dating a singer from some band and did the whole grunge thing—flannel shirts, ripped jeans, the works. When she moved on to a producer, it was all red carpet gowns and designer stuff."

"Ugh," Charlie said.

"Exactly. I don't want my daughter changing to please some man—not even if the man is me. I might think she looks better without all that goop, but she has a right to express who she is. Her mother was pretty much willing to sell her soul to the highest bidder. And *her* mom—Phaedra's granny—was a socialite, all diamonds and furs, with a husband who looked like a troll. We're ending that cycle right here, right now."

"Good for you," Charlie said. She thought of her own mother, battling issues of abandonment and betrayal and passing her fears down to Charlie herself. She knew all about cycles.

"Sandi about had a fit when she saw Phaedra this morning." Taylor mopped his forehead. "Wanted to give her a makeover. I put my foot down, and I swear to God the woman growled at me."

Charlie almost smiled for the first time that day. "You don't like Sandi, do you?"

Taylor grimaced and shook his head. "I like Nate. And I don't like what she's doing to him."

"What's she doing to him?"

"What pretty women always do to a man," Taylor said. "Manipulating him to get what she wants."

"What's she after?" Charlie asked.

"His everlasting soul," Taylor said. "She's making him sell the ranch."

Charlie laughed. She couldn't help herself. The idea that anyone could tear Nate away from any part of this land was ludicrous. Sandi wouldn't get her way this time, that was for sure.

She felt suddenly hopeful. Maybe the woman would get a clue and leave. Things would never work between her and Nate. Not until she accepted the stone-hard fact that he was, and always would be, a cowboy.

A stupid, stick-in-the-mud, stubborn cowboy. A week before, that fact had made Charlie want to toss her cookies. Now it made her want to stand up and cheer.

If Sandi thought Nate would sell the ranch, she was bound to be disappointed. And then she'd leave. And then...

And then Charlie would have to go home, and that would be the end of it. But at least she wouldn't have to think of Nate snared in Sandi's web for the rest of his life.

"He won't do it," she said. "She'll never talk him into it."

"I think she's about got it done," Taylor said.

Charlie waved him away. "He won't sell the ranch. He can't. It's part of him, and it's part of Sam too." She shook her head. "He'll never go for it. She might as well ask him to cut off his—well, you know."

Taylor set his lips in a thin grim line. "He offered to sell it to me this morning," he said. "I'm thinking about accepting. Starting up a sanctuary for abused horses." He looked down at Charlie's shocked face. "You want a job?"

Charlie shook her head and quirked a smile.

"Yeah, I know. Your future's not with me," he said, smiling like he could see something good in front of her. She felt a sudden burst of affection for the man. For all his fame and wealth, he was really a nice, down-to-earth guy. A nice, down-to-earth but totally deluded guy.

"Look, I don't want to burst your bubble, but you might need to hold off on your plans," Charlie said. "I think you're jumping the gun. Nate won't sell the ranch. No way. He wouldn't…"

Her voice faltered as she caught sight of Nate standing at the corral gate. He was staring off across the prairie toward the horizon, where a faint line of blue hinted at mountains in the distance. His face wore such a naked look of sorrow that Charlie suddenly knew, sure as if Nate had admitted it himself, that what Taylor was saying was true.

"No way," she whispered. "How could he? How *could* he?"

"I guess she's got him," Taylor said. "She may not have asked him to cut 'em off, but the woman's definitely got that boy's balls in a vise."

Charlie leaned against the bunkhouse wall and watched the setting sun paint the sky with gleaming strokes of coral and gold. For a city girl, the unobstructed view across the prairie made the evening light show a spectacular treat. Only the dark form of the barn and the silhouette of a cowboy standing at the paddock gate obscured the sky.

Nate was utterly motionless. He'd taken his hat off and was holding it over his heart, watching the sunset as if he was trying to absorb it into his soul.

"Seems like your cowboy's going to ride off into that sunset soon if you don't stop him," Doris said, plopping down beside Phaedra on the bunkhouse steps. "Why'nt you go talk to him, Charlie?"

"About what?" Charlie kicked a stone and sent it skittering across the path. "He looks to me like a man who's made up his mind."

"Or had it made up for him."

"If Sandi's got that much power over him, I can't help him." Charlie sighed. "This place is everything to him—and to Sam. I thought he cared."

"He does." Doris nodded sharply. "So there must be something going on."

"What? What's going on?" Phaedra asked. Her eyes were fixed on the spectacular sunset, and she sounded like a girl awakening from a dream.

"Nothin', honey." Doris said. "Nothin' important."

Charlie smiled down at the teenager. The ranch was good for Phaedra in the same way it was good for Sam. What would life be like for Phaedra if Taylor bought the ranch?

Better. Much better.

And if Taylor bought the ranch, his financial resources would turn it into a thriving operation. He'd be able to save hundreds of horses like Junior, where Nate could only rescue a few. And best of all, Taylor's celebrity would bring the place a ton of publicity, turning a spotlight on the plight of abused and aging horses.

Maybe she should just keep her mouth shut. Walk away. Let it happen.

But Taylor could buy some other ranch. In fact, Taylor could probably buy any ranch he wanted.

Charlie watched Nate prop one foot on the bottom rail of the fence and rest his arms on the top. Something about the way he was standing—the slump of his shoulders, the loose, hopeless way his arms were draped over the fence—twisted her heart and wrung it out, flooding her body with memories of the night they'd spent together. Her nerve endings twitched and wriggled, sending frantic messages to her brain. *Touch him,* they said. *Talk to him.* She could ignore those urges, but her heart joined in with a message of its own. *Help him.*

The dry grass crunched under her boots as she made her way across the yard. It was only mid-June, and already what little vegetation had managed to withstand the glare of the summer sun was crisp and nearly dead. How did he manage to make a go of ranching in this climate, anyway? It had to take incredible determination. He must have survived droughts, storms that destroyed the hay crop, horses going lame or getting sick—but he'd persevered through every difficulty fate threw his way.

So why was he giving up now?

Doris was right. Something was going on.

Charlie leaned on the fence beside Nate and watched the mustangs pluck at the scant grass, but she couldn't think of a damn thing to say. Maybe she was turning into an honest-to-God cowgirl. Maybe talking was the first thing to go.

—∿—

Nate couldn't tear his eyes away from the sky. Sunsets at Latigo were always a wonder, and he didn't dare miss a moment of the magic. If he wound up in Denver, his sunsets were numbered, and he needed to memorize every one. He was so absorbed in the color and the light and the beauty of it, he didn't notice Charlie until she rested her arms on the fence beside him.

"What are you doing?" she asked.

"You heard?" He suddenly felt ashamed. How could he have messed up his life bad enough to lose the ranch? He kept his gaze glued to the sky. He couldn't even look at Charlie.

"I talked to Taylor," she said. "What's going on?"

"I'm selling the ranch," he said. "I have to."

"What about Sam?"

"Sam *is* what it's about," he said.

"Really?" Charlie snorted. "If you think that kid would be better off anywhere but here, Sandi's really got you snowed." She leaned forward, scanning his face intently. "Funny. I can't see the ring in your nose. So how's she leading you around?" She let out a frustrated growl and walked away.

Nate gave her a few minutes, then followed her into the barn. He knew she'd head for the horses. Being with them calmed her like it did him.

Animals had been his therapists since he was a kid. He'd come out here to the barn at night and just sit, listening to the soft breathing of the big animals, smelling the sweet earthy scents of hay and horses, getting over whatever bad days and hard times came his way. He remembered discovering that magic as a kid, that calming, comforting aura even the wildest animals put out.

Sandi had never understood it. She'd never been able to feel that bone-deep connection with animals. She'd never even been willing to try—but this crazy spike-haired city girl had found the magic in just one week.

Charlie could hardly be more different from him. She faced the world with fists clenched and feet planted, ready for a fight; he confronted it with a clenched jaw and an unshakable determination to keep his emotions under control. But when it came time to recover from their battles, they each reached for the same shelter. For all their differences, they were alike where it really mattered.

Charlie stood at the gate to Junior's stall, standing quietly with her head down—but Junior had lost the magic. The stallion stood with his back to Charlie, trembling in the corner of his stall. He wasn't kicking, or hollering, or making a ruckus. He was just enduring her presence, watching her with wary eyes.

She opened the gate and stepped into the stall. Alarmed, Nate started toward her, then eased back into the shadows. He'd only make her angry, rile her up—and the horse too. Better to stand back.

"Junior," she said. "Hey, boy."

He whinnied and spun to face her, slamming his butt into the corner. Twisting his neck like a striking rattler, he snapped his teeth a foot from her face.

Charlie didn't flinch, didn't move a muscle.

"Easy," she whispered. "It's me. It's okay, boy."

But it was obvious nothing would convince Junior that anything was okay. He made that odd, compulsive gesture with his neck twice more.

Charlie didn't persist. She had enough horse sense to know Junior's recovery from the incident with Sandi wasn't going to happen in a day, and there was no point in pushing him beyond his comfort zone.

She stepped out of the stall, closing the gate quietly behind her, and dropped onto the hay bales set against the wall. She watched Junior a while, her eyes filling with tears, then overflowing.

Nate couldn't stand it. Charlie didn't cry. She was the kind of girl who raged, pouted, stamped her feet, or yelled—but she didn't cry. And Junior—Junior behaved pretty much the same way. Just like Charlie, the horse was impossible, intractable, and fearless.

Now Charlie was crying, and Junior was scared.

Nate's world was falling apart.

Chapter 35

CHARLIE HEARD FOOTSTEPS AND SWIPED HER EYES, SETTING her face in a dead-eyed mask to hide her despair, but it was too late. As Nate approached, she glanced around the barn. Maybe she could thunk herself over the head with a manure shovel, or strangle herself with a piece of baling wire. Anything to avoid letting Nate see her cry. He'd already seen too much of her weak side. Wiping her eyes, she gave him a hard stare, daring him to pity her as he sat down beside her.

The guy might not be much for talking, but everything he felt showed in his eyes. Her crying demolished him, but the way he looked at her didn't make her feel pitied.

It made her feel loved.

Gulping in a totally unlovely way, she swallowed and wiped her mouth with the back of her hand. There was no point in hiding how she felt. Working with the horses had taught Nate the subtle signals of body language, and she was sure her every move had been telegraphing her feelings ever since Saturday night.

She watched him lean back against the wall, lacing his hands in his lap. Together, they watched Junior shift from one leg to the other, shudders rippling his gleaming coat.

"He's scared," Nate said.

"Me too."

"I know," Nate said. "You and Junior are a lot alike."

They sat there side by side like strangers on a train, staring straight ahead. Finally, Nate reached over and took her hand.

"What are you scared of?"

"You, mostly," she said. "And Sandi. And Sam."

"You shouldn't be scared of me," he said. "Sandi—now that I understand. But Sam?"

"You guys are dangerous," she said. She looked down at his hand and clasped it between hers.

"Oh, yeah. We're real killers. 'Specially Sam." His mouth twitched. "She's a desperado, that one."

"I think I might be falling in love with you," she said. "Both of you."

He brought her hands up to his chest, then bent and kissed them. "You don't have to be afraid."

Charlie met his eyes. Was that the cowboy version of a declaration of love? She knew she should hold out for the right words, the Big Three, but from Nate, this was enough. The meaning was in his eyes, in his touch. He'd told her so many times, without a word.

Hadn't he?

"I need to tell you something," he said.

Charlie shook her head. "You don't have to. It's okay."

"No, I do," he said. "You deserve an explanation."

She met his eyes. "I deserve a lot of things. So do you," she said. "But it doesn't look like either of us is going to get them."

Nate stared down at her, marveling at the way her fine features and razored hair looked oddly exotic, yet totally at home in the rustic setting. He remembered an old movie poster, or maybe it was some famous pinup—a busty, dark-eyed brunette sprawled in a cinematic hay-stack. Even when she wasn't trying, Charlie issued the same wanton invitation the actress had given the camera. He wanted to accept that·invitation more than anything— but they had business to take care of. Kissing her might show her how he felt, but she needed some cold hard facts before she could understand what was driving him to sell the ranch.

He dropped her hands and moved away, just far enough to break the magnetic force that stretched be-tween them.

"There's something you don't know about Sam," he said.

He coughed. His voice hardly sounded like his own. It was hoarse, raspy. His throat was dry, and it felt like it would close up any minute. He was surprised he could breathe—let alone talk.

"No, it's okay," she said. "I already know."

"You do?" He was about to tell her the truth anyway, so why did he feel such a rush of alarm at the thought that Taylor might have told her he wasn't Sam's real father?

He knew why. The minute Sandi told him Sam be-longed to another man, he somehow ceased to be himself. Nate Shawcross was a lot of things—horse trainer, rancher, friend, lover—but most of all, he was Sam's father. If Sam wasn't his, he'd lost the biggest part of himself.

He didn't know who he was anymore.

And the ranch, the horses, the clinic—even Charlie and whatever was starting up between them—lost all its meaning if Sam wasn't there to share it.

"Yeah," Charlie continued, oblivious to the fact that

all the air had whooshed out of the barn. "I know she was premature. Taylor told me. I know you had to mortgage the ranch, and I know she has health issues." She fluffed her hair with her fingers. "So now I get why this might not be the best place for her. I guess you're afraid she'll get hurt, right? Or overtax herself or something. Is it her heart?"

"No," Nate said. She didn't know, then. He felt a surge of relief, followed by a cold rush of dread. Now he'd have to tell her. "Her heart's fine," he stammered.

His own, however, was breaking into a million pieces. It was a lot easier to deal with Charlie when she was being her usual combative self. When she was kind and understanding, he felt like he might start crying himself.

He cleared his throat. "Sam's a little delicate, but she's so active—the life here is good for her. She loves the horses, and the fresh air's so healthy…" He couldn't seem to get to the point. "So, um, it's not that anything here is bad for her. In fact, it's good. Really good."

Charlie turned toward him with an incredulous stare, as if he'd suddenly grown horns and a tail.

"Then why the heck would you leave? Why would you let it go?" She edged away from him and folded her arms protectively over her chest. Judging from the expression on her face, he'd suddenly gone from an object of desire to a loathsome bug.

"I don't have a choice," he said.

"Is it money?"

Nate shook his head. "It's Sandi."

Charlie stiffened. He could have smacked himself for being so clumsy. Why couldn't he think before he spoke?

"Everything's about Sandi, isn't it?" She stood up and brushed a stray strand of hay off her jeans with a swift swipe of her hand. "I guess I can understand that. She's Sam's mother, after all." He watched helplessly as more tears welled up in her eyes. "Just forget what I said, okay? Just forget it. I got—I got carried away. All that love stuff—I didn't mean it."

He opened his mouth to answer, but she turned away before he could find his voice and strode down the barn's long alleyway and out the door, her boot heels clicking out a militant drumbeat.

"Stop. Wait. Let me explain. It's not what you think," he said. He lurched to his feet and followed her.

"Charlie, listen," he said. "You don't understand. She's not mine."

Chapter 36

THE WORDS PUT A HITCH IN CHARLIE'S STEP, BUT SHE CAUGHT herself and kept walking. Of course Sandi wasn't his. No woman belonged to a man. Maybe that was part of the problem between him and Sandi.

Maybe he felt he owned her.

Maybe he was controlling.

Maybe Charlie had just made a lucky escape from one of those guys who thought he had the right to tell you how to wear your hair and which panties to wear on Sundays.

"Sam," he said when they reached the door. "Sam's not mine."

She couldn't have heard him right. She stopped and turned to face him slowly, lifting her eyebrows. "What?"

He swallowed hard and nodded.

"Nate, that's impossible," she said. "The kid looks exactly like you. It's almost spooky—like your face on a seven-year-old girl."

He lowered his head, staring down at the ground, and mumbled something she couldn't make out. When he looked back up, his face was flushed. "She's not mine," he said.

Charlie ran through a litany of emotions, searching for something appropriate to feel. Shock? Surprise? Sorrow?

No. Maybe anger. That was always her fallback

position, and mostly, it seemed to work. Anger with a couple shots of distrust kept her safe and uninvolved.

Of course, she was already involved with Nate. The times they'd kissed, the times they'd… She'd been treasuring those memories, but now they were just painful. She shoved them out of her mind and put up a shield of anger, setting her fists on her hips and cocking her head.

"So you lied?" she demanded. "You didn't get Sandi pregnant in high school?"

"I thought I did," he said. "She only just told me different. I had no idea there was anyone else." He shook his head, staring down at the floor. "No idea."

She relaxed and let her shoulders slump. Being mad at Nate was impossible. There was something helpless about the guy, and the combination of vulnerability and virility was almost irresistible.

But being mad at Sandi was easy.

"Nate, she's lying," Charlie said. "Sam looks just like you."

"So did my cousin," Nate said. "Cody looked so much like me everyone thought we were brothers."

"She slept with your *cousin*?" Charlie tried not to shriek, but the question came out sounding like the screech of an outraged chicken. "And how can she know, anyway? Did she get a DNA test or something? Because if that tramp was sleeping with both of you, there's no reason you couldn't be the father."

"Why would she lie?" Nate spread his hands. "If Sam really was mine, she could leave anytime and get child support. There's no reason for her to lie. She says Sam's Cody's, she's Cody's."

Charlie rolled her eyes.

"I could never figure out how it happened, because we always used—we were careful, you know? But she and Cody... I guess they didn't... you know. She said he was drunk." He sighed. "She's really ashamed, you know. It was hard for her to tell me. Sandi might be kind of difficult, but she's pretty honest."

"Oh, yeah," Charlie said. She kicked at the ground and sent a stone skittering across the yard. "A real stickler for the truth. That's why she was banging your cousin without a condom while you were paying your dues with romance and flowers." She hung her head. "I'm sorry. It's just—that *bitch*. I could kill her. Just *kill* her."

"It wasn't her fault," Nate said. "You didn't know Cody. He was—he was really something, like I said. All the girls wanted him."

Charlie imagined Nate in high school, with those broad shoulders and that tight cowboy butt, making his way down the hallways between classes with his loose-hipped cowboy swagger. She had a feeling he hadn't been anyone's second choice.

"So why isn't *he* taking care of them?" Charlie asked. "Why doesn't Cody send her to beauty school?"

"Because he's not alive to do it," Nate said, his voice flat and expressionless. "He died before Sam was even born." His eyes shifted away, staring into a past she couldn't share. "He was coming back from a rodeo. He'd been drinking." Lowering his head, he put one hand to his forehead and covered his eyes as his voice roughened again. "He hit a semi head-on. Died instantly, they said."

He turned away, his eyes shining in the half-light from the night sky. "Nobody knows about Sam. I don't think Cody's mom even knows."

"Your Aunt Gwen, from the store? Is she—was she his mom?"

Nate nodded. Leaning into the wall, he rested one forearm on the rough wood and turned his head away. When he spoke again, his voice was hoarse. Charlie couldn't see his face, but she suspected he was crying.

"Cody was older than me. A bull rider. Fearless." She could hear the pride in his voice. "He could ride anything. Bring up a demon out of hell, and he'd strap a saddle on it and ride it like a pony in a petting zoo." He cleared his throat. "When I was a kid, I thought the sun rose and set on that guy. He had a wild streak a mile wide—riding bulls, drinking, driving fast, getting in fights—but he was more alive than anyone I ever knew."

Charlie thought of Sam's eyes, the line of her jaw, the way she moved, the way she laughed. The kid was a carbon copy of Nate. If Cody had been his twin, she might believe it. But a cousin?

"No way," she said. "The kid is yours."

Nate took off his hat and swept his hand through his hair. "There's more to the story, Charlie. She and Cody—she was always kind of flirting with him, and he didn't seem to mind. It used to piss me off. I always felt left out when the three of us were together." He cleared his throat. "Still, it never crossed my mind they might have been more than friends. I never would have believed Cody would do that to me. That hurts almost as much as losing Sam."

"There has to be a way to fix this," Charlie said. "There has to be a way."

—⁓—

Nate nodded, staring down at the toe of his boot. She was right. There had to be a way to fix it—but danged if he knew what it was. The only solution he'd been able to find was to toe Sandi's line and sell the ranch. Sam was worth it.

"If I sell the ranch and give Sandi half, she'll let me adopt Sam. If I don't, she'll do a DNA test that proves I'm not Sam's father and she'll take her away."

"So she's selling her child."

He tightened his lips and nodded, looking down at the floor. "I guess that's about right."

"And you're going to pay."

He refused to meet her eyes. She couldn't possibly understand how important Sam was to him. She couldn't possibly understand that the ranch didn't matter anymore if his daughter wasn't there.

The ranch was his inheritance, but it was hardly a gold mine. Someone had once told him that the best way to make a small fortune in ranching was to start with a large fortune—and they were right. When he'd had to put his grandfather in a home weeks after his grandma passed, he'd figured he'd have to sell the place. He hated to do it, but he was headed for college and the ranch needed full-time management. More than full-time. It had run down in the years since Granddad had started his slow slide into dementia.

But then Sandi got pregnant, and college suddenly became an impossibility, while the ranch looked like salvation. He'd moved them into the old house and struggled to build a horse operation and make it pay. He'd done it too. And as Sam grew and flourished, he realized it had been the right decision. He was creating a legacy for his daughter that would sustain her all her life.

His daughter? No. His cousin. If Cody was her dad, Sam was his first cousin, once removed.

Yeah, right. Nate didn't feel removed from Sam at all. And blood didn't matter—not when it came to Sam. Whether she was his or Cody's or the milkman's, she was the one thing in his life that mattered. He'd hoped to pass the ranch on to her—but if it had to go to keep her, then it had to go. He couldn't let Sandi take her away.

"What are you going to do? The ranch is your livelihood."

"I figure I'll get a smaller place," Nate said. "Maybe do more clinics, teach riding—that kind of thing. It'll have to be near Denver so I can watch Sam while Sandi goes to school." He took a deep breath. "Denver's got a lot going on, you know."

She looked at him like he'd just grown an extra head. "You can't live in Denver. Neither can Sam. You belong here." She shook her head. "Denver might have a lot going on, but what's there for Sam? Do you really think she'll be happy there?"

"Sandi says…"

"Sandi doesn't give a rat's ass about that kid. She doesn't care about anybody but herself."

Nate turned away. Charlie was right, but he didn't have to acknowledge that. He'd already said too much— to her, to Taylor, to Doris. Heck, even Phaedra was in his business. They knew he'd screwed up his life and Sandi's, and they knew his family was a train wreck.

Well, no more. A man kept his own counsel, ran his own life. He didn't drag a bunch of strangers into his problems—especially when those strangers were paying clients. He'd see a lawyer on Monday, figure out his rights and Sandi's, and take it from there. In the meantime, the less said the better—even to Charlie. For all he knew, their relationship would endanger his right to keep Sam.

If there was even a relationship left. Judging from the expression on her face, whatever they'd had was over.

He turned away and headed for the house. He had nothing left to say.

Chapter 37

CHARLIE NEEDED A DISTRACTION. THE ANGER SHE'D SUMMONED up to face Nate was still simmering, building up pressure, threatening to burst out any moment. She wasn't sure she could control it, so she needed to find an appropriate target.

That was easy.

The idea of being anywhere near Sandi made her sick to her stomach, but with any luck she could pick a fight and get some relief from the rage that was clawing at her throat.

She climbed the porch steps two at a time. Maybe she could get the woman talking about her special weekend overnight beauty school. That would be interesting.

"Need some help?" She tried to act casual, leaning one hip against the doorjamb and scanning the countertops. They were strewn with debris—onion skins, paper towels, a half a green pepper canted on its side.

"I sure do." Sandi threw herself into a kitchen chair like she'd just finished making a seven-course meal. As far as Charlie could see, all she'd done was chop an onion and slice a pepper in half.

"What are we having?"

"I put a brisket in the slow cooker this morning."

"Great." Charlie didn't bother asking if she'd prepared anything for the vegetarians. For all Sandi cared,

Charlie and Phaedra could go out and graze in the pasture with the horses.

"You want me to cut up some carrots? Potatoes?"

"Sure," Sandi said, wiping a hand across her forehead. "I'm taking a break."

Charlie busied herself washing potatoes, then rummaged through the utensil drawer for a peeler. She didn't dare use a paring knife; she might be tempted to turn around and stab the bitch.

"Seems like you're all recovered from your accident," Charlie said.

Sandi nodded. "Yup. Tougher than I look."

That was for sure.

"So you're okay? They ran tests and everything?" Charlie sliced a length of peel from a potato and let it dangle into the sink. Carefully, she edged her peeler round and round, keeping the long spiral intact.

"No." Sandi was still sitting at the table, totally unconcerned with the fact that Charlie was doing all the work. "I got out of there as fast as I could. I hate hospitals."

"Oh," Charlie said.

Sandi and Nate had been gone all night.

Now she really felt nauseous.

"You were gone a while," she said.

"Yeah. We went and parked down by the quarry, like we used to in high school. Nate and I had a lot of talking to do." Sandi simpered and tittered out one of her annoying giggles. "A lot of *making up* to do."

Charlie's peeler slipped and she sliced through her careful spiral. It dropped into the sink, the neat coil splaying in disarray. "What?"

"We got things all worked out." Sandi tossed her hair. "We're back together now. We're selling the ranch. Moving to Denver. Didn't he tell you?" She grinned. "I can't wait. This is what I've always wanted."

Charlie turned her attention back to the potato, but her hands were shaking. Nate *had* told her. He'd said he had to move to Denver so he could watch Sam while Sandi went to school.

She hadn't realized what that meant. She hadn't realized they were moving there *together*.

She remembered her halting confession of love and winced. She'd completely misinterpreted Nate's reaction. What had he said? *You don't have to be afraid*. In the clear light of the kitchen, she realized that was hardly the declaration of love she'd taken it for. What else had he said?

You deserve an explanation.

He'd been trying to break up with her.

She tried to picture Nate and Sandi in the dark pickup by the quarry, talking things out. She couldn't. No way could Nate carry on a conversation that long.

No, while she'd been sitting in the night-shrouded kitchen with Taylor, picturing her cowboy weeping over a body bag, he'd been doing some serious bimbo-busting down on Lover's Lane.

And tonight, he'd found her crying in the barn and said a few kind words she'd totally misinterpreted—just as she'd misinterpreted all his looks and touches over the past week.

A week. That's all it had been. How could she have thought she was anything but a rebound fling—a roll in the hay to help him forget the woman he really loved?

How could she have been so worried that *she* would hurt *him*?

She'd been delusional.

"Oh, hold on. I almost forgot." Sandi rummaged in her pocket. "He wanted me to give you this." She pulled out a slip of paper and handed it to Charlie. "Here." She narrowed her eyes. "He said I should give it to you so you can go."

It was a check—reimbursement for the full amount of Charlie's deposit, plus an extra hundred dollars.

"I don't know what that extra hundred's for," Sandi said. "Nate said you'd done some… special things." She winked and Charlie felt a blush warming her face. Surely Nate hadn't told her what had happened between them.

And surely he didn't want her to leave. This had to be Sandi's idea.

She looked down at the check, figuring she'd see feminine handwriting, but it was penned in masculine block letters, with Nate's signature neatly scripted below. That was bad enough, but the memo line struck her like a knife in the heart. "For services rendered," it said, in those same neat block letters.

Charlie took a step backward and grabbed the back of a chair. Nate never would have come up with those words on his own. He would have written "thank you," or, more likely, nothing at all. Charlie pictured Sandi shoving the check at Nate, telling him what to write.

She pictured him dutifully obeying. He had to know those three words would sting like a slap in the face.

Taking a deep breath, she steadied herself. She didn't know which emotion was going to win—anger, regret, or embarrassment—but she wouldn't let Sandi see any of them. She wouldn't let Nate see them either. She'd swallow this bitter medicine and count herself cured.

"Thanks," she said, shoving the check in her pocket. "I've been waiting for this. Waiting about a week too long."

Had it really been just a week? She counted back. Yup. It was a week ago she'd kissed her first cowboy. A day later she'd ended up in his bed. Two days ago, she'd started to think she loved him, and tonight she'd bared her soul and told him so.

She felt as naked and exposed as the peeled potato in her hand. Hacking it in half, she tossed it into the slow cooker and stalked out of the room.

Chapter 38

CHARLIE FLOUNCED INTO THE BUNKHOUSE, SLAMMED HERSELF down on the bed, kicked off her shoes, and punched the pillow as hard as she could.

Taylor looked up from the table where he was playing Texas Hold 'Em for pennies with Doris and Phaedra and grinned. "What's got into you?"

She hated it when men did that. For some reason, she was apparently vastly entertaining to the opposite sex when she was angry. She felt tears start in her eyes and dug her fists into the sockets to push them back where they'd come from. She'd probably just smudged her mascara into a raccoon mask, but at least Taylor wouldn't get to see her cry.

"You were right," she said. "He's selling out."

"And you're surprised."

"You bet I'm surprised." Charlie bounced up and paced the length of the floor, her fists balled at her sides. "I mean, the guy has his flaws, but I thought he loved this place." She'd thought he loved her too, but she wasn't about to air that piece of information. The thought of what she'd said to him—her confession—made her want to hide under the bed until the embarrassment blew over in about twenty years. "I thought he'd fight for it, at least for Sam's sake. But he's going to lay down and let that woman run roughshod over both of them." She whirled and paced the other way. "I mean, he can sell his own soul for Sandi. Whatever he wants. But I can't believe he'd do this to Sam."

"What's he doing to Sam?" Phaedra asked, looking up from her cards.

Taylor gave Charlie a subtle shake of the head. "He thinks he's doing what's best for her. What he has to do."

"Then cowboys are even stupider than I thought," Charlie said, then blanched as Doris let out a throaty chuckle. "Present company excluded." She shot the actor a hard look. "Maybe."

She glanced around the room at the matching coverlets and the daisies in their glass jars, and remembered giving in to her nesting instinct, foolishly making herself at home. Then Nate had come in, and she'd given in to another instinct altogether. She felt her face warm again, and muttered a curse under her breath. She'd never blushed before coming to Latigo. She'd always been solitary and self-possessed—but now she was an embarrassment to herself, and probably to Nate too.

She'd done nothing but screw up since she'd arrived. She loved the ranch, but now she had to admit the place was toxic. There was no way she could stay and watch Nate and Sandi together, patching up their relationship.

Pulling her suitcase out from under the bed, she grabbed a few scattered pieces of clothing and shoved them inside.

"Well, I'm out of here," she said, hoping they couldn't tell she was holding back tears. "I've had enough."

She kicked off the boots Nate had bought her and shoved her feet into the old metallic red torture devices she'd brought from Jersey. Her toes protested, but it felt good to punish herself. After all, the boots were a perfect symbol of her mistake. She'd actually begun to think she could belong here, but she didn't know a damn thing about it.

"Whoa, girl," Doris said. "Slow down. Don't you have a job to do?"

"To hell with it," Charlie said. She glanced over at Phaedra. "I mean heck. To heck with it."

"Aren't you overreacting a little? Did you talk to him about this?"

"Talk to him? Yeah, I talked to him. He just… never mind." She swallowed, remembering just how much she'd talked. How she'd bared her soul to a man who'd just made up with the love of his life. Maybe Nate didn't talk enough, but she had the opposite problem.

She didn't listen.

She grabbed her luggage, scooped her car keys off her nightstand, and headed for the door.

Phaedra shot to her feet. "No," she said. "Don't leave. You belong here, remember? Nate said so."

"He was just being nice," Charlie said. "He didn't mean it."

Phaedra looked wounded and Charlie felt a pang of regret. Setting down the suitcase, she gave the girl a hug. "I'm sorry," she said. "I have to go. But we'll keep in touch."

"You sure you're okay to drive?" Taylor called after her.

"I'm fine," she said, breezing out the door.

Sure. She tossed her suitcase into the Celica's hatch.

Just fine. She slumped down into the driver's seat and slammed the door behind her.

A light drizzle was falling, and the windows were pebbled with rain. She hit the steering wheel with the palm of her hand and swore as a sob exploded from her chest. It hurt. If she hadn't been able to look down and see her intact T-shirt, she'd have sworn her heart had just torn itself in two and fallen out of her chest.

Stupid, she told herself. *Stupid, stupid, stupid.*

How could she have fallen for a cowboy? The two of them were so different—such total opposites. They should be oil and water.

But they weren't. No matter how much she tried to hate him, she knew they were two pieces of a puzzle, meshing perfectly, completing a picture. Her strengths were his weaknesses, and what he lacked was what she had to give. Sure, he didn't talk much, but she prattled on enough for both of them. And she tended to go off like a firecracker at the slightest touch of a flame, while he was steady and unchanging as the eternal Wyoming plains.

Except when it came to love, or sex, or whatever it was that had happened between them.

She sighed. She couldn't blame him. She'd pulled him close, then pushed him away. She'd told him straight out he had no place in her life. She'd been scornful rather than supportive when he was devastated by Sandi's news about Sam's parentage. Why would he want to have anything to do with her?

Why would anyone?

All her life, she'd been a fighter, not a lover. She'd pushed away every man who'd tried to get close, for fear he'd abandon her like her father had. She'd nurtured her combativeness, built up an impenetrable shield, and now she was upset because she'd finally fallen in love and the man she wanted couldn't hack his way through the thicket of thorns that surrounded her heart.

It had never mattered before. But she'd never met a man like Nate before either—a man who put his daughter first, who would give up everything he loved to keep his child safe. A man who was clearly the opposite of her father.

Whatever woman ended up sharing Nate's life would always hold second place to Sam in his heart. That was as it should be—but it made Charlie the loser in Sandi's high-stakes game of tug-of-war.

And the loser needed to clear the field.

Chapter 39

THE PITTED DIRT ROAD RATTLED THE CELICA TO ITS CORE, pummeling out some of Charlie's anger. By the time she reached the paved road, there was an ominous grinding sound coming from the right front tire and a rattle somewhere in the back. It sounded like the car was going to self-destruct, leaving a trail of nuts and bolts all the way to Jersey.

But it would make it. It had to.

She putt-putted onward, pausing at Purvis's one-and-only streetlight, then gunning the motor to head east. The car shot through the intersection—but some crucial part of it stayed behind, tumbling with a loud clang to the pavement.

Judging from the 50-decibel lawn-mower growl emanating from the Celica's chrome tailpipes, that crucial part was probably the muffler. Charlie spun a wide circle in the empty intersection and pulled over next to the sidewalk. Throwing the shifter into neutral and giving the parking brake a vicious yank, she stomped out of the car and retrieved the runaway hunk of metal from the middle of the road. She didn't know much about cars, but this thing looked like it was Celica's liver, or maybe its kidney. Something crucial, anyway. Muttering a soft but heartfelt string of obscenities, she pitched it into the hatch and collapsed into the driver's seat. Setting her hands on the wheel, she laid her forehead on top of them. What was she going to do now?

She could keep going. She hadn't seen a cop for a good two hundred miles before she hit Purvis, so it wasn't likely anyone would care if her car sounded like a convoy of three hundred Harleys running wide open. But that also meant she couldn't count on any help if the Celica gave out in the middle of nowhere.

It looked like Ray Givens was her only hope. She'd have to stay the night, and have him look at the car in the morning.

She stood on the sidewalk, glancing left and right. She could sleep in the car, but a hotel would be better—if Purvis had such a thing. She tried to remember her drive through town with Nate. Had there been a hotel? A bed and breakfast? Anything?

Glancing to the right, she caught a flash of neon—an arrow, pointing down toward a dimly lit one-story building that crouched in by the sidewalk. "Vacancy," it said. And no wonder. The place looked like the last refuge of the homeless.

Sighing, she stepped out of the car and hauled her suitcase out of the backseat. The kidney, or whatever it was, would have to stay. If someone stole it, fine. It wasn't working anyway.

She jerked the suitcase handle to its full length and squared her shoulders. Sighing, she headed down the street, the suitcase trailing behind her like an obedient rectangular dog. She stared down at the cracked concrete as she walked, lost in a sea of self-pity.

Suddenly, the suitcase tilted and lurched. A metallic *ping* sounded behind her and the right wheel popped off and rolled into the gutter.

Damn. Couldn't anything in her life go right?

She was struggling to collapse the handle when the sharp toot of a horn almost made her look up, but she kept her eyes firmly pinned to the sidewalk. Probably some cowpokes out on the town. Next they'd whistle and holler suggestive comments.

"Hey!"

Sure enough. She flipped them the bird and kept wrestling with the suitcase. A little New Jersey sign language should get them out of her hair.

"Charlie!"

She turned to see Doris's enormous truck barreling down on her, angling across the street to pull to a stop at the curb. The door opened and the wiry ranch woman jumped from the cab, landing right in front of her like a wizened leprechaun dropping from the sky.

"Doris?" Charlie felt her face go hot. "Sorry I flipped you off."

"That's okay." The woman grabbed Charlie's arm. "But come on," she said. "We need to talk. I'll buy you a drink."

"Hold on." Charlie gestured toward the suitcase. "My suitcase threw a shoe."

Doris picked up the wheel and scrutinized it. "Bet a good mechanic could fix that. Nate's father-in-law, maybe." She grabbed the suitcase's handle and slid it home in one smooth motion. "I've got it," she said, hoisting the heavy case with one hand. "Now come on."

"I don't want a drink." Charlie set her jaw. "And sorry, but I don't really want to talk either. I need to get going." Doris would try to convince her to stay, but leaving was the right thing to do—Charlie was almost sure. It was clear she wasn't ready to trust a man, and besides, she had a life to live in Jersey.

A picture flashed in her mind of Sandi haranguing Nate at the dinner table. Bossing him around in the barn. Making demands. Issuing ultimatums. She shook her head. She couldn't save him. He'd have to save himself.

"I didn't ask what you wanted to do." Doris tugged Charlie's arm, dragging her forward. "We're drinking. We're talking." She scanned the street. Three bars shed squares of yellow light on the sidewalk, but every other business was shuttered and dark. "Pick a bar," she said. "I'm buying."

Charlie eyed the various establishments. Hogs 'n' Heifers was ruled out by the convoy of Harleys parked out front. Doris was obviously feeling pugnacious, and the woman would probably end up in a fight with some 300-pound tattooed hog driver.

At first glance, The Snag looked interesting, with concert posters plastered in the front windows and a blinking "Live Music" sign over the door. But when they stepped closer, Charlie saw the posters advertised mostly country acts, including a selection of washed-up Opry stars that could have formed the cast of one of those D-list reality shows—*Nashville Rehab* or something. No doubt the mood music would reflect the owner's taste, and Charlie was sad enough without listening to the sorrowful twang of Loretta Lynn or George Jones. After all, her own life had turned into a country song. "My Baby's Baby Ain't Really His Baby, so I Can't Be His Baby No More." It was so pathetic it was bound to be a top forty hit.

Next came The Crown Bar. That looked about right. Its storefront window was almost completely covered with planks of rough, dark-stained wood so only a small rectangle of glass remained, barely big enough for the neon Budweiser sign. Hardly any light seeped from the place, so it would probably be dingy and dimly lit. Perfect for her mood.

"The Crown," she said.

Doris nodded sharply and headed for the lighted doorway. Swinging open the door, she stepped inside, dragging Charlie behind her.

A scarred, stained oak bar fronted by a row of red vinyl-topped stools stretched the length of the room. A few men crouched over drinks, and several others occupied the booths lining the opposite wall. Heads turned as Charlie and Doris stepped up to the bar and ordered two Bud Lights.

The two of them sat down, Charlie hunching over her beer like a noonday alcoholic. Doris perched beside her and fixed her bright eyes on Charlie's face.

"You ought to give Nate another chance. Boy's miserable with you gone."

"I don't think so." Digging in her pocket, Charlie pulled out the check. Thrusting it at Doris, she stabbed a finger at the bottom line. "Look at this and tell me if you think he deserves another chance."

Doris scanned the check and her lips tightened when she reached the memo line. "Services rendered? That doesn't sound like our boy," she said.

"No, it sounds like his girl," Charlie said. "But our boy let it happen. They're back together."

"That can't be true," Doris said. "I sure haven't seen 'em together." She sighed. "He loves you, honey. Anybody can see it."

"He doesn't love me," Charlie said. It was true. She should have known it from the start. What kind of love stayed so silent and stoic? Cowboy or not, he would have said something. "He loves Sandi. I guess it's one of those toxic relationships, but that's not my problem." She sighed. "Anyway, I'm done with him."

She stared down at the check, scanning his neat handwriting, his tidy signature, and that bottom line: *services rendered*. Doris looked over her shoulder and scowled.

"He didn't write that," Doris said. "I'm willing to betcha. Look at the letters."

Charlie squinted down at the words. They were written with the same pen, in the same block lettering—almost. But Doris could be right. They slanted a little differently. Charlie leaned across the bar and held the check under the lamp.

"Look at 'd' in *rendered*," Doris said. "It's different from the 'd' in *dollars*. The 's' is different too."

Charlie traced the letters with her finger and felt a surge of hope. Doris was right. The letters were clearly different.

"Sandi wrote that," Doris said. "She knew it'd piss you off. And you're playing right into her hands, running away." She smacked Charlie's thigh with one bony hand. "She's a devil and a liar, that one. She's manipulating you, and you're lettin' her get away with it." She shook her head, staring sadly down into her beer. "I can't believe you'd just turn tail and run. I had you pegged as somebody stronger than that."

"I'm not running away."

"Looks like that to me. Why are you so anxious to believe Nate wrote that on the check? You know him better than that. You're just looking for an excuse to run." She pointed an accusing finger. "You're scared. What the hell happened to our kick-ass princess?"

Charlie stared down at the check. Doris was right. She *was* scared.

"And if she lied about him writing that, what else did she lie about? The beauty school, for one. What else? The woman's psycho. A pathological liar."

Charlie nodded. Doris was right. Sandi was lying about everything else. Why was Charlie so willing to believe she and Nate were back together? She was probably lying about that too. Maybe it was just a ruse to get Charlie out of the way. The woman was probably gloating at this very moment, glorying in the success of her scheme. Charlie pictured Sandi rubbing her hands with satisfaction, like a wicked witch contemplating her next evil spell.

Downing the rest of her beer, Charlie slid off the barstool and stood up. "You're right. I can't let her get away with it."

Doris grinned. "Atta girl," she said. "I knew you'd stay."

"I'm not staying," Charlie said with a toss of her head. "But I'll go back and straighten things out before I go."

Doris tightened her lips disapprovingly. "You belong here, girl."

"No I don't." Charlie stared down into her beer. "I'm a city girl born and bred, Doris. I'd never fit in here."

Doris grinned. "I was a city girl too," she said. "I think I fit in okay."

"You?" Charlie scanned Doris from her windblown, sun-dried hair to the toes of her battered cowboy boots. The woman didn't just fit in; she was practically a part of the Wyoming landscape. "Thought you were a native species."

"Nope." Doris grinned. "I'm from Boston."

"No shit." Charlie blinked. "I mean, no kidding."

"Came out here on vacation with my folks when I was eighteen years old. Met my Eddie and never went back. I loved the wide-open spaces, the animals—I just felt at home here. And I loved my Eddie. So I stayed."

They swung out of the bar and headed for the truck. Charlie knew her red metallic cowboy boots looked ridiculous, but the heels made a gratifyingly authoritative sound as she clicked out of the bar and down the sidewalk. She almost wished she had spurs, just for the tough-guy clanking sound they'd make as they hit the concrete. She'd sound like a legendary gunslinger stalking the mean streets of Purvis, spoiling for a fight.

Which wasn't too far from the truth.

She paused beside her car and looked back at Doris. "Follow me, okay? I'm not sure this thing'll make it back to the ranch."

Doris grinned. "Sure. I'm your wingman. Let's go kick Sandi's ass and get you a cowboy."

Charlie grimaced. "I didn't say I was staying," she said.

"No, you didn't." Doris started up the truck and pulled into the street. "But you're headed in the right direction."

Chapter 40

Nate clutched his pillow and tried to turn over, but his legs were pinned down. He was trapped. Trapped in the dark.

He flailed a hand out and hit the end table, swearing under his breath. Butt snorted and hit the floor with a loud thump.

Now he could move his legs.

Not that it helped much. He couldn't get comfortable no matter what position he slept in, and flipping from one side to the other like a burger on a fast-food grill wasn't helping any. All he could think about was that morning he'd woken up on this same sofa with Charlie in his arms, tucked against him.

He sat up and rested his elbows on his knees, staring out the window. He'd heard a car door slam hours before and looked out to see the Celica bouncing away down the driveway.

He wondered if Charlie was gone for good.

No. She'd leave eventually, but not like this. She'd say good-bye to Sam, and to the horses. To Doris and Phaedra and Taylor. She'd probably gone to Purvis to indulge her wild city-girl side in one of the bars that lined the main street. He hoped she hadn't gone to Hogs 'n' Heifers. She'd likely rile up some biker and get in a fight.

She'd probably win, though. She was sure kicking his

ass six ways to Sunday. He felt like he'd been run over by a truck, followed by a locomotive leading a herd of stampeding buffalo that finished off the job. Charlie's quick switch from fiery passion to white-hot anger left him feeling like he had emotional whiplash.

But whatever she dished out, he deserved it. He'd dragged her into his complicated life, enmeshing her in Sandi's net. He should have left her alone. What was he thinking, fooling around with a woman he barely knew when his daughter's future was at stake?

The dog snorted again, and Nate had to agree. That hadn't been fooling around at all, and Charlie was no stranger. That had been making love to a woman he wanted more than Butt wanted biscuits.

Hopefully Charlie would have the sense to stay in town if she drank too much. He closed his eyes, and immediately a picture of her slipping into bed in some anonymous hotel room flashed across his mind. She'd shuck off her jeans and crawl into bed in her T-shirt and panties, and look sexier than a Victoria's Secret model in skimpy lingerie, just because she wasn't trying.

Panties. A T-shirt and *panties*.

Nate squeezed his eyes shut and pressed his temples with one hand, trying to wring out the images of Charlie in that tuxedo thong. In the Wonder Woman panties. He decided he'd better imagine she was wearing something sensible tonight. White cotton granny panties, maybe, a size or two too big.

Saggy-ass panties.

Damn. That got him thinking about Charlie's ass. Now he'd never get to sleep.

He swung his feet to the floor and levered himself out

of bed. Sleep was impossible. He ached all over—his legs, his back, but mostly his heart.

He stepped into a pair of jeans and slipped a T-shirt over his head. He'd go check on the horses. It wouldn't be the first time he'd sought their company in the middle of the night, and it wouldn't be the last. With all that was happening, he'd need the peace of the barn more than ever—the soothing warm darkness, the quiet hush of the animals breathing slow and easy, their sweet, musty scent.

He shuffled quietly across the bedroom, through the kitchen, and eased the front door open. On his way to the barn, a sound caught his attention—a low growling, like a car without a muffler. He shaded his eyes with one hand, squinting. A truck was bouncing along the road to Latigo.

Doris. But what was that in front of her? A car?

Yep. A red car. And that seemed to be where all the racket was coming from.

Charlie was back.

He jogged to the barn. It wouldn't do to be caught standing in the middle of the yard with his mouth half-open and his heart in his hand, waiting for her. And what would he say, anyway?

He ducked into the barn. Maybe she'd come in here too to see the horses. Stopping at Honey's stall, he leaned on the gate. The horse was standing quietly, watching him through half-shuttered eyes. Outside, Charlie's car door slammed and he heard her boots hitting the dirt driveway as she headed for the bunkhouse.

The bunkhouse, not the barn.

Dang.

He proceeded down the alleyway, trying not to wake

the horses, but they blew and shifted from left to right, catching the quick rhythm of his nervous breathing, the slight shaking of his hands. He struggled to control himself, but that only made it worse. Behind him, Junior let out a faint whinny and kicked the side of his stall.

There was a window at the end of the aisle and he couldn't resist glancing outside. Charlie was sitting on the bunkhouse steps staring up at the sky like she was lost in thought. He wondered what she was thinking about.

Maybe she was thinking about him. Maybe she was trying to figure a way through this problem too. Maybe she was searching her mind for a way to hang onto what they had.

Yeah, right. More likely she was thinking up fifty ways to kill a cowboy.

The bell for round one of the Charlie vs. Sandi Championship Fight would ring any moment, but with the deafening racket the car made, Charlie hadn't had a chance to work out a solid plan of attack. All she'd done was work herself into a state of nerves.

In fact, now that she was here, she wasn't sure fighting was such a great idea after all. She should have kept driving. Turned the Celica east, gunned the accelerator, and gotten the hell out of Dodge, or Purvis, or whatever you wanted to call it.

But here she was, back at the OK Corral. She'd dreamed up a dozen ways of confronting Sandi on the drive, but now that she'd arrived she realized it was Nate she needed to talk to—because it was Nate who needed to confront Sandi. After all, he was the one who had the most to lose.

Charlie stepped back inside the bunkhouse and tiptoed over to Doris's bed. The woman was already asleep, releasing an escalating series of snores that sounded like the entire New York Philharmonic's wind section tuning up.

"Doris." Charlie shook the woman's shoulder.

"Huh?" Doris shot upright with a snort. "What?"

"I need your help."

Doris rubbed her eyes and ran one hand through her hair, swinging her legs out of bed. She waggled her feet, fishing around for her slippers. "Okay," she said.

"I'm going to try to talk Nate into confronting Sandi. I'll show him the check, tell him she said they were back together, but I need you to back me up about what Sam said. You know, about those overnight classes at the beauty school. Once he sees how much she's lying, maybe he'll call her bluff about Sam."

"Sure," Doris said. She slid her feet into a pair of beaded moccasins and stood up. Her T-shirt was rumpled and her hair was flat on one side, but vanity apparently wasn't an issue for ranch women.

Charlie wondered if she'd get like that if she stayed in the West. Would her skin brown and wrinkle in the sun? Would she stop wearing makeup and let her hair grow out?

She'd never know. She wasn't staying.

A horse neighed from the barn.

"Come on," Charlie said. "Let's go." She squared her shoulders and headed across the lawn, Doris trotting along behind her.

Ding. Round one.

"Let me do the talking," she said to Doris. "Just back me up if he doesn't believe me."

Nate looked up as they entered the barn. He was bent over Peach's leg, unwrapping the bandage, moving his hand up and down the pony's leg, checking for swelling.

"Hi." Charlie shifted her weight from one leg to another. She'd nursed her anger all night, but now that Nate was right there in front of her, she knew she needed to calm down. She needed to find a smooth way to show him what was written on the check. A tactful way to tell him what Sam had said about the weekend beauty school.

No problem, right? She was a psych major. A student of interpersonal communication. She should be able to find precisely the right words to use, the right approach to take.

"Um," she said.

Nate looked up expectantly.

"We need to talk to you," she said. "Can we, um, sit down somewhere?"

"Okay." He rewrapped the bandage, taking his time, making sure no wrinkles would irritate the horse's skin, then led her down the aisle to the feed area, where two battered folding chairs leaned against the wall. He unfolded them and settled into one, then rested his elbows on his knees, folding his hands in front of him.

She sat down beside him, folding her hands so she wouldn't be tempted to reach over and touch him. Doris stood behind her, her hands on the back of the chair.

Nate cleared his throat and looked off to the side as if he was studying the lettering on the old broken chest freezer where he used to store the grain.

"Okay," he said. "Go ahead."

—~~~—

Nate couldn't look at Charlie, or Doris either. He'd screwed up everything. Everything. He knew they were trying to help, but he was starting to think he was hopeless. His life was a lost cause, now that Sandi had her claws in the ranch, and in Sam—the two things he cared about most.

And then there was Charlie. He watched as she took a deep breath, like she was about to plunge into the deep end of a bottomless swimming pool. "Sandi's lying," she said. "She's lying about all kinds of stuff. Like... she said you were back together."

"No," Nate said. He looked up at Charlie, his eyes wide. "Dang, Charlie, no. Never. She's lying."

"She's lying about Sam too. I'm sure of it."

He shook his head.

"You and Cody were close," she said. "Like brothers. Would he really do that to you? Do you really believe that?"

Nate stared down at the barn floor, shaking his head. "No," he said. "The idea he'd sneak around with Sandi behind my back hurt almost as much as losing Sam. I trusted him."

"He didn't do it, and you know it, deep down," Doris said. "Call Sandi's bluff. The girl's lying. And you've got too much at stake to let it pass."

Nate nodded. They were right. He should confront Sandi. But what if he was wrong? What if she took the test, and he wasn't Sam's father?

What if Sandi took her away?

"That woman's an unfit mother," Doris said. "And

even if you're not Sam's dad, you're family. You've taken care of her all her life. If Sandi's declared unfit, the court would give Sam to you, whether she's your daughter or not."

He sighed. "Sandi's selfish, I know. She's probably not the best mother in the world. But she's not unfit. She doesn't beat Sam or anything."

"No. She just neglects her. That woman's not going to beauty school."

"Yes she is," Nate protested. "She's—"

"She's lying," Charlie said. "And she's lying about other stuff too. She told me you wrote this."

She dug a slip of paper out of her pocket and handed it to him. It was the check he'd written to reimburse Charlie's deposit. He'd been surprised when Sandi said he should make it for a hundred dollars extra. Usually she was so tight with the money, but she'd had a flash of generosity. A hundred dollars wasn't much, but he figured it would show Charlie he was trying.

"Read the bottom line," Charlie said.

He looked down at the memo line and felt like he'd been clonked on the head all over again. "*Services rendered*?" He shook his head. "I didn't write that, Charlie. I swear I didn't."

"I know," Charlie said.

"But that doesn't mean she's lying about school. She always wanted to go. She always said—"

Charlie interrupted, her tone harsh, "We were asking Sam if she wanted to go to beauty school like her mother," she began. "She said no. She wants to go to a regular school. One where you don't have to spend the night."

"What?"

Doris jumped in again, telling Nate about the week-end overnights, the teenaged babysitter.

"She's not going to school, Nate. She's kickin' up her heels like those *Sex in the City* gals. And she leaves Sam with people she barely knows while she does it."

Nate thought of Phaedra, remembering the girl's sullen recounting of her life in California. He'd worried Sam might be on the same road, and now it turned out he'd been right. "She wouldn't," he stammered. "Sandi wouldn't do that."

"Do you need us to draw you a picture or what?" Doris asked, splaying her hands. "She did it. And there's more."

"There is?" Charlie turned and stared at Doris. She looked as surprised as he felt.

"There sure is. I talked to Sam the other day, while we were in the barn. She was telling me about some of her mother's pajama parties. Her mother used to invite Uncle Joe, but lately Uncle Ted comes instead. And one time there was another guy, but Sam never found out his name."

Nate blanched.

"She didn't find out his name because she doesn't get to go to the parties," Doris continued. "They're for grown-ups. So Sam has to stay in her room so she doesn't get in the way." She set her hands on her hips. "Now, come on. Even if you weren't the kid's father, do you think that woman would take off and leave a full-time babysitter behind? She'll never take full responsibility for that child. She's got too good a deal going right here."

"Talk to Sandi, Nate," Charlie said. "You owe it to Sam."

Nate pictured Sam shut in her room, playing with

her Barbies and trying not to listen while Sandi messed around with some stranger, then glanced over at Charlie. He'd expected to see triumph and smug gloating, but she looked pained, as if she was sharing his dismay. He felt that connection again, stretching between them, stronger than ever.

He stood up. Tugging her toward him, he planted a firm kiss on her lips and looked her in the eye. "I owe it to you too. Thank you. I have to go." He balled his fists and thinned his lips into a hard line. "I'll take care of Sandi. Don't worry."

"Kick her ass, cowboy," Doris said.

"I will." Turning, Nate grabbed Doris and wrapped her in a bear hug. "Thank you too," he said, squeezing her hard and tight against his chest. "You're the best."

"Well." Doris grinned at Charlie, patting her hair and straightening her glasses as Nate left the room. "I can see why you like him."

Chapter 41

NATE TOOK THE PORCH STEPS TWO AT A TIME. HE COULD SEE his ex at the window rinsing out a glass. He opened the door and got ready to rumble.

"Have a fight with your girlfriend?" Sandi turned and leaned against the counter, crossing her arms over her chest. "She took off out of here like she was mad or something."

"She was," Nate said. "Me too." Pulling out a chair, he sat down at the table. "We need to talk," he said.

Sandi turned and opened a cupboard, then slammed two cereal bowls down on the counter. "Good." She bent to rummage through a lower cabinet, pulling out a box of cereal and shaking a portion into each bowl. "I agree. Because you have a lot to do today, and I want to make sure you've got your priorities straight."

"I always have a lot to do," he said. "Especially now, with this clinic thing you set up."

"You can take some time off from that," Sandi said. "You need to call a realtor. Get this sale going."

"No."

"What?"

"No. I'm not selling."

"You most certainly are. I've waited long enough." She jerked the refrigerator open and grabbed a jug of milk. "You need to get to town and hire a realtor. Today."

"I don't think so. I have some other stuff I need to do." He was starting to enjoy this.

Sandi spun to face him, splashing milk over the counter. "You listen to me, Nate Shawcross. You…"

"Sandi." Nate felt his control slipping away as Sandi spun into shrew mode. "I said no. Stop telling me what to do."

"I'll leave, then. I'll take Sam and I'll leave."

He took a deep breath. It was time to call Sandi's bluff. "Sam's not going anywhere. Not until she has a paternity test. You know, that test that'll prove I'm her father."

She stared at him, her mouth half-open. For once, she was speechless and he had something to say. He let the words out in a rush.

"I know you're lying about Cody, Sandi."

Amazingly, his eternally poised ex was losing her composure. Clearly, Charlie and Doris were right. Sandi's face had gone tense and tight as Junior's. His ex was pretty, and she was devious, but she wasn't particularly smart or quick-witted. She hadn't expected this, and without a scheme laid out beforehand, she couldn't figure out how to fight back.

Finally, she mastered her emotions and forced her lips into a smile to frame one of her phony high-pitched laughs. "Sorry. I'm sure you'd like to believe that. But it's true."

"Quit lying, Sandi."

"I'm not."

"Yeah, you are. So let's schedule that test." He picked up the phone. "Monday okay?"

She turned to face him, her chin tilted up, her fists clenched.

For a minute there, the fight in her eyes reminded

him of Charlie. It was the first time in years he'd seen something in Sandi to like.

But when Charlie fought, she fought for what was right. Sandi only fought for what she wanted.

"I'm not taking any test," she said, swinging her purse off the counter and onto her shoulder. It was hideous, a brand-new piece of high-fashion garbage with some hotshot designer's initials all over it. He wondered how much it had cost him. "I'm leaving."

"You're leaving because you're lying," he said.

She didn't answer, pretending she was too busy rummaging for her car keys to listen to him. Finally, she fished them out and stalked to the door. Turning, she dangled the keys in the air.

"I'm going back to Denver. And I'm staying this time. It's over."

"It was over a long time ago," he said. "And you're not taking Sam." He liked the sound of that so much, he said it again. "You're not taking my daughter."

Sandi whirled. "Damn right I'm not," she said. "You want her so bad, you keep her. You see what it's like being tied down with a kid when you could—when you could be…" Her mouth stretched, struggling to form the words she'd been holding inside for seven years. "All I ever wanted was to fulfill my potential. Everybody thought I'd be famous. And then you went and got me pregnant."

"Right," Nate said. "I went and got you pregnant. And, of course, you had nothing to do with it. You were just an innocent bystander."

"It was your fault," Sandi said. "It was." She shoved her lower lip out into a decidedly unattractive pout. "And I was stuck here, stuck with you and her, and I couldn't…"

"You couldn't do what you wanted," he said. "Well, now you can. Go live your life, Sandi. I'll take care of Sam. I don't mind a bit."

Sandi swiped at her eyes and looked up at him, her lower lip trembling. A month ago that look would have undone him. He'd have done anything to stop her from crying. Now he just wanted her gone. Hell, he was practically paying her to leave.

"But you owe me. You have to sell the ranch. I get half."

"I'm not selling the ranch," he said.

"You have to pay for my beauty school," she said. "That's what I always wanted. My—my dream."

The half-open kitchen door swung inward and Doris stepped in from the front porch, with Taylor close behind. Nate suddenly realized he and Sandi had been shouting. He wondered how long his clients had been out there and what they'd heard.

And Sam. Had Sam heard what her mother had said?

Hopefully not. Her bed was at the far end of her attic bedroom. She was probably still sleeping under the slanted eaves under her bucking-horse comforter, her ratty stuffed pony clasped in her arms. Just thinking of her made his heart swell until he thought it would burst. He'd take care of her. Always. No matter what Sandi did.

And he'd never tell her the truth about her mother. He'd never let her know what Sandi was really like. Kids needed their moms—needed to love them. He'd have to deal with Sandi somehow, get her to be a part of Sam's life.

But not his. Not anymore.

Doris set her hands on her hips, then pointed a finger at Sandi like an angry schoolmarm. Like the girl had screwed up her times tables or forgotten the capital of North Dakota.

"You know that's not true," she said. "Beauty school's not what you want. What you want is the ranch. What's it worth? If Nate sells it, how much does he get?"

Sandi paled. Tossing her hair, she looked away, out the window, as if scanning the acreage around the house. "How would I know?" she said.

"You had it assessed. You gave me a price," Taylor said. He looked at Nate and said slowly, "One-point-two million."

"That much?" Nate felt like he'd been hit on the head again.

"What would that kind of money do for you, Sandi?" Doris asked. "You wouldn't use it for beauty school, would you? You wouldn't bother with that."

"Yes I would," Sandi said. "I'm already going to school. I wouldn't quit."

"Really?" Nate asked. "What's the name of that school, Sandi? I'm going to check it out, so you'd better tell me the truth."

"It's... it's..." Sandi's voice trailed off.

"It's a special school, isn't it? One that meets only on the weekends, at night. Sometimes you have to stay over, don't you?" He gripped the counter behind him, holding his rage in check. "Sam doesn't understand, but I do. You're not going to any school. You're living the high life in Denver, and you left your daughter with a seventeen-year-old high school kid while you hunted for a new sugar daddy."

Sandi covered her face with her hands. Her nails were perfect, each a gleaming red claw. "You don't understand," she said. She pulled her hands away from her face and looked up at Nate. Her eyes were bleary and red-rimmed. Tears streaked her makeup. She looked like Britney Spears in meltdown mode.

"All my life, I've been the good girl," she said. "Because everybody was watching. And when I got to the city, I just—I could finally do what I wanted." She stamped a foot and clenched her fists. "I deserved it. I'd done everything for everybody else all my miserable life. It was finally *my* turn." She stormed out the door, tossing the last line over her shoulder.

"You're a mother," Doris called after her. "*That's* your turn."

Sandi hiked her purse farther up her shoulder and turned away. "That's what *you* think," she said. "My turn's coming. You'll be hearing from my lawyer." She spun back to hurl the last word. "I'm getting half the ranch, Nate. It's mine, and I'm taking it."

Chapter 42

DORIS LOOKED FURIOUS, BUT TAYLOR, STEPPING UP BEHIND her, looked almost elated. He held up one hand and Nate gave him a half-hearted high five.

"I'm sorry," the actor said, stifling a smile. "I know this is serious. But as soon as you people get done, I'm writing it all down." He grinned. "I've been working on a new screenplay, and let me tell you, this is better than anything Sam Shepherd ever dreamed up. I'm thinking I'll call it *Cowgirls Gone Wild*."

Doris turned and focused her wrath on Taylor. Nate took in her aggressive stance and her peeved expression and was glad he wasn't in her sights.

"Can you maybe quit gloating over other people's misfortunes and do something useful?" She jabbed a finger toward Nate. "Talk to him, will you? Help the guy out."

Taylor sighed and sat down at the table. "I'll do better than that," he said. He folded his hands and faced Nate. "You want to talk business?"

"Not really," Nate said. "I need to go find Charlie."

"Just wait," Taylor said, pulling out the chair beside him. "Sit. Listen. I had an idea that'll work for both of us." He ran a hand down his face as if he was wiping off his expression, turning serious. "I've been watching Phaedra. The clinic's changing her—teaching her a lot of skills and something more—a sort of sensitivity, a new outlook. She's learning how to live from the horses. That stuff you said at the sale—she took it to heart. She's learning to accept things. To forgive."

Nate nodded. "Good. I'm glad."

"So what about starting up a camp that teaches troubled kids to train horses?"

Nate laughed. "I don't know anything about kids."

"No, but Charlie does," Taylor said. "And with her psych degree she'd give you some credibility."

"I don't even know if she'll stay," Nate said.

"She'll stay for this," Taylor said, rubbing his hands together. "It's just the kind of work she wants to do. Besides, you know more than you think. You're a good dad—the kind of dad I wish I'd been. You're even good with Phaedra."

Nate snorted. "Hardly."

"She told me about the time she took the horse," Taylor said. "You handled it right."

"What? I turned her over to Charlie."

"It's a wise man who knows when he's beat," Taylor said, grinning. "And delegation is a valuable skill. Think about it, Nate. You could do a lot of good."

"I don't think so," Nate said. "I don't want a lot of messed up kids around Sam."

"Thought you told her everybody deserves a second chance," Taylor said.

"I did," Nate said. "But I didn't say we had to be the ones to hand it out."

Taylor shrugged. "You're going to have to do something." He nodded toward the door. "You heard Sandi. She'll put a lawyer on it. She'll end up making you sell the place. If we partner up, you can give her a lump sum. Enough to get her out of your life for good."

Nate stared off across the kitchen, chewing the inside of his cheek. Taylor was right. Sandi couldn't take Sam away now. Sure, she'd probably pick her up on weekends once in a while—Nate hoped so, for Sam's sake—but she couldn't take her away permanently, or use her as a bargaining chip. He'd won that battle, thanks to Charlie.

But the money was another matter. Sandi would fight hard for a half million.

"Let me buy in," Taylor said. 'I'd be an investor in the program, not the ranch itself, so the land would still be yours. You could pay off Sandi with a settlement and start fresh. It would take her years to win in court, and she needs money now, so she'll take a lot less." Taylor stood up. "Think about it. Talk to Charlie. You don't have to make a decision right away."

—∿∿—

Nate wandered through the barn, then checked out the bunkhouse.

No Charlie.

Her car was still in the driveway, so she had to be around somewhere. He circled the house, then wandered out back of the barn. Looking up the hill, he saw a small figure perched on the park bench, her dark hair silhouetted against the sky. She hadn't styled it like she usually did. It was smoother, framing the heart-shaped curves of her face. Without the jagged spikes, she looked softer. Sweeter.

Dang, he'd better not tell her that. She'd hack it all off if she knew how soft and womanly she looked.

He made his way up the winding path and sat down beside her. The two of them looked down at the barn, at the horses whisking their tails in the corral, the dog prostrate in a patch of sun by the door.

"You need to replace a couple shingles," she said, pointing at the barn roof.

"Yeah," he said. He reached over and took her hand. "We do."

She stiffened and looked down at their joined hands, then slowly eased hers away.

"We?"

He nodded. "Sandi's gone. You were right." He picked up her hand again and kissed the back of her fingers. "I don't know how to thank you. You pretty much saved my life."

She pulled her hand away. He started to reach for it, then set his hands on his thighs. "I'm sorry," he said. "I don't blame you. I've been an ass." He glanced at her, and she met his eyes. That was all the signal he needed to reach over and push a lock of hair out of her face, his hand lingering, trailing tenderly down her cheek. "Let me make it up to you."

He wasn't sure how he'd do that, except in bed. There he could make her forget Sandi ever existed. Heck, he was pretty sure he could make her forget her own name.

She reached up and took his hand, but only to pull it away from her face. "I need some time, Nate. I need to figure out where I belong."

He nodded. "Okay. I understand. But you belong here. I hope you know that."

"I'm not sure." She looked down at her lap, twisting her hands, biting her lower lip.

"What's wrong?" he asked.

She looked up, her eyes probing his. "Did you go to the quarry with Sandi that night she got hurt?"

He hung his head and nodded. "She wanted to talk. She said we'd work out custody for Sam. Then she told me that lie about Cody." He felt hot anger bubbling up like a hidden spring at the thought of it. "She said she'd take Sam and leave. Forever. I was petrified, Charlie. I thought I was going to lose my daughter. I wasn't thinking straight."

"I guess I can understand that." She slid her gaze sideways. "Just how panicked were you? What did you do?"

"I didn't sleep with her," he said. "Honest. I didn't. I couldn't." He paused and took her hand. "Not after you. She tried, but I—I couldn't even imagine it. It was never any good with her. With you it's—it's beyond good."

That was lame. He sat there, struggling to find the right words. "Please stay," he finally said. "Please. I love you."

He'd said it. Said it out loud. Charlie couldn't doubt his feelings now. But what could she do? She had a life to live, a degree to finish, a career to start. "I love you too," she said. "But I can't just stay, Nate. Not even if I want to." She sighed. "I have school to finish, and then I need to find a job in my field. There's nothing here for me."

"There's me," he said. "And Sam, and the horses."

"I know. And that's a lot. But I want to make a difference in the world, Nate. For more than just a few people."

Nate stared down at the ranch buildings scattered below them. His brows were drawn, and he was biting his lower lip, as though he was pondering some momentous decision.

"I have a proposition for you," he finally said.

"A proposition." She steeled herself to say no, but her renegade heart was tap-dancing in her chest. She tensed and lowered her voice. "Nate, we need to wait on that, okay? I'm not ready."

He laughed, a low chuckle that lit up every nerve ending in her body with a slow, smoldering flame.

Maybe she *was* ready.

"Not that kind of proposition," he said.

"Oh. Good." She straightened, hoping he couldn't sense her secret disappointment.

"It's a business proposition," he said.

"Hmm," she said. That wasn't what she'd expected at all.

"I'm thinking about keeping on with the clinics," he said.

She nodded. She'd figured that. He actually seemed to enjoy sharing what he knew.

"And I was thinking I might open the place up to troubled kids. Teenagers like Phaedra. Teach them to train the horses, help them work stuff out."

Charlie nodded. It was a good idea.

"I want you to help me run it," he said.

Her eyes widened. This was the kind of work she'd always wanted to do. It might deviate from The Plan a little, but the whole point was to find meaningful work, and what could be more meaningful than helping kids and horses? A job like that would fulfill her dreams of working with animals. It would let her stay on the ranch with the man she loved, living a life that fit her like a custom boot.

But she'd have to quit school. She'd be letting down her advisor, and her mother.

She took a deep breath. Maybe she should follow her instincts. Deep down, staying felt right. Sometimes a woman had to go with her gut—and Charlie's gut told her, loud and clear, to take the deal.

Trouble was, lots of other body parts were telling her to do that too. She had a lot of good reasons to say yes, but her mind kept churning its way into forbidden territory. A partnership with Nate would let her stay with him. Sleep with him. Wake up to him every morning.

She shook off the memory of his hands on her skin, his lips on hers, telling herself it was time to stop thinking about those long, steamy nights and think about her future. Love didn't always mean forever. She'd learned that from her mother. And if their relationship didn't work out, she'd have to cope with her feelings for Nate every day.

And besides, what did she really know about him? He was kind to animals, he loved his daughter, and he was drop-dead fantastic in bed. Was that enough?

She ignored the parts of her body that were screaming "*yes*" and looked out across the paddock to the mist-shrouded mountains in the distance, then back at Nate. He was looking at her expectantly, waiting for an answer.

"I need to think about this, Nate," she said. "It's a big decision. I need time."

He nodded, looking away, and she knew he was hiding disappointment by the way his shoulders tightened. "Okay," he said. "But decide soon, okay? I want…"

She could see that muscle in his jaw working, like he

was nervous. Like he was working up the courage to say something that didn't come easy.

Maybe this was more than a business deal after all.

"I want to do this," he said. "I really do." He cleared his throat. "With you." He set his hand on her arm, his touch warm and persuasive. "I need you, Charlie."

She felt herself warming, melting, the word "yes" rising in her heart—but she couldn't say it. She wasn't ready.

Poor Nate. From day one she'd bucked worse than the rankest rodeo bronc, throwing him in the dirt over and over. Maybe she'd never be broke to ride when it came to relationships. Maybe she'd always spook and shy. Maybe she'd jump the fence and run off the minute something went wrong.

In a way, she'd been trained to buck. Her mother had taught her from an early age to balk at commitment. But maybe it was time to shake off her mother's issues and grapple with her own.

Maybe it was time to grow up.

"Let me think about it," she said. "Give me some time."

Chapter 43

SHE WATCHED NATE MAKE HIS WAY DOWN THE HILL, HIS hands in his pockets, his shoulders slumped. Pulling her phone out of her pocket, she speed-dialed home.

"Mom?" she said. She took a deep breath. "I might be changing The Plan."

Her mother lit into her just like she'd expected, but Charlie talked over the protests. "Now wait. I still end up meeting the same goal. I just get there different. Listen, Mom."

Her mother was still protesting.

Charlie held the phone an inch from her mouth and hollered.

"*Listen!*"

"All right."

Charlie described Nate's proposition, and for once, her mother listened without interrupting, without objecting. "I'd be doing the kind of work we talked about, Mom," she said. "Helping people. Kids *and* animals. It's perfect."

"But your degree. Oh, Charlie, you're almost there. Don't let it go."

"Mom, I have to write a few papers. Maybe teach one more class. Then I have to do my practicum, and this is perfect."

As she said it, she knew it would work. The program would be a perfect practicum. She could interview the kids at the start, note their progress, then assess the therapeutic outcome at the end.

Her advisor would say yes. She was sure of it.

She didn't have to give up one dream for another. She could have them both.

"It's perfect, Mom. It's really what I want to do."

Dead air thrummed through the line, and Charlie knew her mother was reading the bullshit-ometer, that secret device known only to mothers.

Apparently it still worked, even long-distance. Mona Banks cleared her throat in a no-nonsense way that didn't bode well for the rest of the conversation.

"Charlie, this is about a man, isn't it?"

Charlie clenched her fist and punched it into her thigh. *Busted*.

"He's part of it." She hated the way her voice came out—surly and defensive, like a little girl caught with her hand in the cookie jar.

"Can you trust him?"

Charlie thought back, remembering everything that had happened. "Yes," she said. "He's never lied to me. Not even when it might have been a smart thing to do."

"Well, that's good." Her mother lapsed into silence and Charlie waited for the verdict. She didn't let her mother run her life, but she knew this deviation from their shared goal would hurt. The Plan had been a bond between them—maybe not a particularly healthy one, since Mona Banks was clearly living vicariously through her daughter's success, but it was essential to both of them. They'd been a team for so long—a mother/daughter partnership that faced the world united.

"Have you committed to this yet?" her mom asked. "Signed anything?"

"Of course not. I'm just thinking about it."

"Well, think hard," her mother said. "I understand why you want to do it. It does sound like good work." She sighed. "It sounds like the kind of thing I would have liked to do. Helping kids like that…"

Charlie's heart ached for her mom. "Well, maybe if I do it, you could come out and visit, or even help. It's beautiful here, and I'd be making money—not a lot at first, but I wouldn't have any expenses. Maybe I could send you a ticket."

"Maybe." Her mother sounded wistful for a moment, but she cleared her throat and got back to business. "But don't let that influence your decision, honey. Be rational. Make sure it's what you really want."

"Okay, Mom."

"And don't sleep with him."

Charlie didn't answer.

"Oh, honey." The long sad sigh of a martyred mother whispered over the miles. "It's too late, isn't it? Just be careful. Use protection."

Charlie rolled her eyes.

"Don't roll your eyes at me. Even smart women screw up."

Charlie laughed. "How'd you know I rolled my eyes? I'm two thousand miles away."

"I know you. And I love you."

"I love you too," Charlie said. "I'll call you when I decide, okay? And don't worry. I'm not stupid."

"No," her mother said. "I know you're not stupid. You're just human."

Charlie said good-bye and clicked the phone shut, then called her voice mail. She had three unheard messages. Two from her advisor, and one from someone with a Wyoming number.

Skipping over the first two, she listened to the Wyoming message. It was Brock, from the grocery store. He'd gotten in more veggie burgers.

Hallelujah, she thought. Between that and the salad, she and Phaedra would be set.

She just needed to run into town. She could stop at the garage too. Maybe Ray could tighten up the bolts on her car and fix her suitcase. Whether she stayed or not, she'd need it to go back and tie up loose ends.

Besides, stopping at Ray's would give her time to think. Time on her own, away from the ranch. Away from Nate, where she could think clearly.

She slid the phone in her pocket and stared down at the ranch. She pictured herself sitting on this bench, surrounded by teenagers struggling to surface from various emotional crises. She'd draw them out, steer them toward solutions, teach them to tackle problems with logic, determination, and optimism. She pictured Nate, leading the kids on trail rides, with herself and Trouble bringing up the rear to make sure no one fell behind. She'd watch them as they rode, assess their body language and identify the ones that were hurting, the ones whose self-esteem needed a boost.

She pictured herself lying naked in bed with Nate on a hot summer night while a sage-infused breeze whispered through the window, cooling their flushed skin. In winter, she'd snuggle up to him while the wind whipped around the ranch house and poked icy fingers through the gaps in the doors and windows.

Something rustled at the bottom of the hill, interrupting her thoughts. Standing up, she craned her neck to see Taylor making his way up the winding path.

"How's it going?" he asked.

"Good." Charlie glanced down at the barn and outbuildings, wondering where Nate was. "Really good."

"Nate must have told you about my idea," he said.

"What idea?"

"About the kids. The clinics." He sat down beside her. "You know Nate would never ask for help. But I've been looking for something like this—something meaningful to do with my money."

"Your money?" Charlie felt the elation inside her slow and stop dead. "What are you talking about?"

"The ranch," Taylor said. "I offered to stake Nate—partner up with him—if he'd open it up to kids like Phaedra. Didn't he tell you about it?"

"Noooo," she said slowly. "Not really. He told me a little."

Taylor eased down beside her with a sigh. "Sandi's trying to get him to sell the ranch. Calling in a lawyer, says she should get half. But I figure she'll go for a settlement if it's big enough. So if I invested…"

She stared straight ahead and intoned the words, "…then Nate could keep the ranch."

Taylor nodded. "Right. And I really think a riding camp for troubled kids would be a winner of a business plan."

Charlie nodded.

"And it would be perfect for you. You love it here,

right? And with your psych degree, you'd give the place credibility. Combine that with my endorsement—we'd do great." He paused, then eyed her with concern. "You're going to do it, right?"

"I don't know.

"I sure hope so." His tone was casual, but his posture seemed tense. "I don't know how we'd do it without you."

"Did you tell Nate that?"

"Sure." Taylor nodded eagerly. "Without you, we've just got a horse trainer and a celebrity. It's the psych expert that would make it work."

"So if I don't stay, you won't do it?"

Taylor shrugged. "I don't know. Maybe not."

Charlie gripped the edge of the bench, hanging on for dear life as her emotions spun and crashed, dropping the bottom out of her brand-new future. Taylor had offered Nate money—but only if he could get her to stay.

So did he really want her for herself?

Of course he did. He'd told her he loved her, and coming from a man who barely spoke, that was huge. Surely he meant it.

Or was she just believing what she wanted to believe?

She needed to think this through, and she needed to do it somewhere else—somewhere far from the ranch, where Nate wasn't always around, fueling her fantasies.

She headed for the house, breathing a sigh of relief when she found the bunkhouse empty. Grabbing her suitcase, she headed for the car. She'd stop at Ray's first and get that broken wheel fixed. Then the grocery store, to pick up those veggie burgers.

By the time that was done, maybe she'd be able to make a rational decision.

Chapter 44

NATE WAS JUST FINISHING UP IN THE BARN, CLOSING THE DOOR behind him, when Charlie crossed the barnyard. She was carrying her suitcase.

Her suitcase. Was she leaving? His heart started thumping like a step-dancer on speed. She couldn't leave. She couldn't. They fit together. They were made for each other. And she'd be helping kids and horses, fulfilling all her dreams—it was perfect. *They* were perfect.

"Did you decide?" he asked. He wasn't sure he wanted to hear the answer.

"Nate, I don't know," she said, shoving the suitcase into the backseat of her car. "I just don't know, okay?"

He grabbed her arm and spun her toward him, making her stumble and fall against him. He loved her. He needed her. He'd told her, but maybe that wasn't enough. Maybe he needed to show her. Trapping her in a fierce embrace, he crushed his mouth to hers and set his instincts free.

She was wrong. It would work. They'd proved it that night, and now they were proving it again. She was kissing him back, devouring him as fiercely as he was consuming her.

Then she stiffened and pushed him away, twisting in his arms and shooting him a furious glare. He'd expected to see heat in her eyes, but a heat that answered his—not one that repelled it.

"Nate, no," she said. "No. I have to go."

Nate staggered to the kitchen and slumped into a chair, resting his head in his hands. He was still sitting that way when Taylor walked in ten minutes later. The actor pulled out a chair and sat down.

"What's got your girlfriend riled up?" he asked.

"What girlfriend?" Nate asked bitterly.

"The one that just peeled out of the driveway."

Nate shrugged.

"You have a little trouble with this kind of thing, don't you?" Taylor said, grinning.

Nate sat back down and shook his head, resting his elbows on his knees, his hands hanging limply between his legs. "You might say that," he said. He looked over at Taylor, who was still grinning. "Glad you find the whole thing so damned entertaining."

"I'm telling you, this place is better than *One Life to Live*," Taylor said. "You want some help planning out the next scene in your soap opera?"

"I'd appreciate it," Nate said. "I sure as hell don't know what to do myself."

"You love her?"

Nate shrugged again.

"Well, do you?"

Nate nodded.

"Let's use our words," Taylor said in the same tone he might use with a toddler.

"Yes," Nate mumbled.

"So what do you want to do?"

Nate gave him a scornful glance. "Keep her from leaving, of course. But it's a little late for that."

"No, I mean what do you want to do, long term? Where do you see this relationship five, ten years down the road?"

Nate paused—not because he didn't have an answer perched on the tip of his tongue, itching to jump off and make itself known. He just wasn't sure he wanted to confide in the man who held his future in his hands. If Taylor knew what an emotional wreck he was, he might change his mind about investing in the ranch.

Right. Because up until now, Nate's behavior had been so professional. Hell, he'd already screwed things up so badly, he might as well go for broke. He should be out there in the arena, helping Taylor and Doris tame their horses. Instead, they were in here helping him tame his screwed-up life.

"So what do you want to do?" Taylor repeated.

"What I want to do is marry her," Nate said. "But where do I see it long term? Over. I mean, she's gone."

Taylor sighed. "You dumbass," he said. "She's only gone if you let her go. Did you tell her you want to marry her?"

"I haven't gotten that far yet," Nate said. "But she knows. She knows I want to—to be with her forever, and all that."

"Does she?"

"Well, yeah. I think so."

"You think so?" Taylor looked at Nate like he couldn't believe what he was hearing. "Did you tell her?"

Nate shifted in his chair. "Well, not really. But I—I kind of showed her."

Taylor rolled his eyes and sighed. "Yeah, I'll bet you did. Women like to be told, though, okay? How 'bout you give that a try? The girl can't read your mind, you know." He laughed. "Not even when you're naked."

Nate shook his head. "You don't get it. She's gone, suit-case and all. I'll never see her again. I don't even know where she lives. Sandi has all the registration forms, and cashed all the checks. And she's not liable to give me Charlie's num-ber." He splayed his hands helplessly. "She's gone."

"You know where she goes to school, right?" Taylor asked. "There's this thing called the Internet, you know. Great for finding people."

Nate nodded. Taylor was right. He could track Charlie down, try again. But what could he say that he hadn't already told her?

"I don't know how to do this, Taylor. I don't know what to say," Nate said. "And Charlie needs—more than some women. Not that she needs anything. She's fine on her own—so *complete*, you know? But still, she's delicate." He looked down at his hands. "She's been hurt. Her dad…" He stopped. Charlie wouldn't want her secrets spilled, not even to Taylor.

"Sounds like you've got it figured out. What you need is a script."

Taylor grabbed a notebook off the end table in the living room, along with a ballpoint pen, and sat down across from Nate. Flipping open the notebook, he clicked the pen and gave Nate a questioning look.

"Okay. What do you want to say?"

Nate ducked his head and mumbled.

"What? Speak up, son."

"That I love her. That I want to marry her," Nate said. He still couldn't meet Taylor's eyes. This was embar-rassing, that's what it was.

"Okay. That's a good start, but we need more. How much do you love her?"

"A lot. A—a whole lot."

Taylor rolled his eyes. "That's not going to cut it," he said. "You need to be more original. Speak from the heart."

Nate shifted in the chair, wishing he hadn't let this business start. "My heart doesn't have much to say, that's all." He shrugged. "It says I love her. A lot."

Phaedra emerged from the bathroom, along with a cloud of steam. She was dressed in a black silk bathrobe with a red-eyed bat embroidered on the lapel. A towel was wrapped around her hair like a turban.

"Hey," she said. "Sorry, the shower's nicer in here. Dad said you wouldn't mind."

Nate shrugged.

"And it's lucky I'm here, because I'm good at this stuff. My teachers all say I should be a writer. So." She pulled out a chair and sat down, folding her hands on the table and leaning earnestly toward Nate. "Tell me what else you love."

"What?" Nate couldn't believe this misfit teenager thought she could help him.

"What else do you love?"

"Sam," he said. He didn't even have to think about that one.

"Okay, but you can't compare your love for Charlie to how you feel about your daughter," Phaedra said. "That would be ooky. What else do you love?"

Nate thought a moment. "The ranch."

"Okay." Phaedra pulled the notebook away from her father and wrote down, "The ranch." She drew a bulbous heart above it, then looked back up at Nate. "What about it?" She slashed a line through the heart and tipped it with an arrowhead, then sketched feathers onto the other end.

He shrugged.

"You are hopeless," Phaedra said. "What's the best thing about it?"

"Sunrise," Nate said. He didn't have to even think about that one.

"Why?"

"I don't know." He looked off across the kitchen, avoiding her gaze, and it was almost like he could see the peachy sky at sunrise reflected on the wall. "It's like, first one bird sings, and then all the others join in, and the song gets bigger and bigger, and louder and louder. And it's like they're all celebrating that the sun came up again, like it's some kind of miracle, and it's a new day, and everything's—I don't know—fresh." He blushed. That sounded dumb, coming from a cowboy. More like some sissy poet guy or something.

"Okay. That's good." Phaedra tapped the pen, staring down at the notebook, then started writing. "How 'bout this?" She spoke slowly as she wrote. "When I see you, it's like the sunrise—like when the birds start singing, and everything's new, and no matter what happened the day before, you know you're going to get a fresh start. You're my fresh start, my rising sun, and I want to wake up to you every day."

"That's kind of corny," Nate said.

"No shit," Phaedra said. "It's a love letter, not a literary masterpiece. And besides, it has to sound like you—and frankly, you're kind of a corny guy."

Taylor laughed.

"Well, he is—always mooning around after Charlie like a lost puppy or something. It's pathetic."

"Thanks," Nate said.

Phaedra looked down at the notebook. "This is a good start," she said. "I'm going to go back to the bunkhouse and work on it a while. Maybe Doris has some ideas."

Nate rolled his eyes.

"Hey, she's got a lot of life experience," Phaedra says. "And we should use all our resources."

"I've got a better idea," Taylor said, pushing his chair back. "How 'bout we go for a ride?"

Phaedra clutched the notebook to her chest, shaking her head. "I want to work on this."

"Okay." He turned to Nate. "You and me, bud. Let's saddle up and take off for a while."

"But the clinic…" Nate began.

"Forget the clinic. You need a break," Taylor said. "Besides, we're partners now. And a ride'll do you good."

Nate nodded, picking up his hat and tipping it onto his head. A ride would do him good.

It was the one thing he was still sure of. He could definitely ride a horse.

Chapter 45

CHARLIE SLOWED DOWN ONCE SHE'D MADE THE TURN OUT OF Nate's driveway. She didn't want to shake the car apart before she'd even gotten to Purvis. So far, the rattletrap Celica seemed to be holding up, despite the racket the engine made.

Nursing the clutch and accelerator, she steered carefully between the potholes, avoiding the jagged rocks that thrust themselves out of the dirt every twenty feet or so and easing the car across the dips where runoff had carved crooked channels in the dirt.

She dropped the car down into second when she hit the hill. She remembered Nate saying this was the halfway marker—ten miles to town, ten miles back to the ranch.

The ranch. She missed it already. She missed the long view from the kitchen window, the sound of locusts clicking in the grass. She missed the silvery twilight, the ruddy sunsets, the long afternoon shadow stretching from the barn across the yard. She missed Doris, and Phaedra, and Junior.

She missed Nate.

She crested the hill and the view spread out below her like an open book. Stopping the car, she opened the door and propped one foot on the rocky ground so she could hike herself up to rest her elbows on the car's pockmarked roof and admire the landscape.

The hills undulated endlessly toward the horizon like the rippling surface of a windblown lake, the sun flecking the grass with golden highlights. It was almost midday, so no shadows broke the glittering carpet of summer color. The red cliff reared like a painted wall over the waves of gold and rust and umber, rising to meet a sky so blue that the contrast with the bright rock was almost painful.

Charlie sucked in an admiring breath. Nothing in her previous life could ever compare to the primitive beauty of this arid, inhospitable land and the animals that wrestled out a living from its parched grass and scant water.

She stared off into the sage-flecked valley and knew she'd remember this view forever, whether she wanted to or not. She remembered how Nate had watched the sunset when he'd thought the ranch was lost, imprinting the scene on his mind so he could carry it with him, and she knew exactly how he'd felt.

If she left, she'd always remember Latigo, and she'd remember it with a sense of regret that would wound her every time the image came to mind. She'd curse herself, knowing she'd been too scared to take a chance and stay in the one place where she felt at home.

All of a sudden, the veggie burgers didn't matter anymore. Neither did getting the car fixed, or her suitcase. What the hell did she need a suitcase for, anyway?

She wasn't going anywhere.

Her eyes filled with something suspiciously like tears, and her heart felt like it was going to explode—but with happiness this time. She had to tell Nate she'd stay.

She had to tell him *now*.

She climbed back into the car and motored down the

hill, but she wasn't watching the view anymore. She was looking for a place to turn around.

Spotting a gravel-strewn turnout, she slammed on the brakes and cranked the wheel to the right, figuring it offered space enough for the Celica to spin on its short wheelbase and head back to Latigo.

Back home.

The car jerked, balked, then lurched forward. Charlie cranked the wheel to the left, but she was too late; the damage was done. The steering wheel fought her hands, pulling her hard to the right and into the turnout, as if the car agreed with her decision and wanted to turn back toward home like a barn-sour horse.

She stopped the car and sighed. Flat tire. She knew it without even looking. At least she'd been going slow. If she'd broken another axle, she'd have had to throw herself down in the dirt and give up. They'd find her bones later, picked clean by coyotes.

But a flat tire she could deal with. She stepped out of the car, rounding the front bumper with a profound sense of déjà vu.

Yup. A pointy rock jutted up just behind the tire. She must have hit it just right. Or rather, just wrong.

Reaching across the passenger's seat, she yanked the hatch release and hobbled to the back of the car. Fishing out the jack, she propped it under the car's frame just behind the wheel and cranked the car up off the ground.

She pried off the hubcap and levered the lug nuts loose with the tire iron, then spun them in her fingers until they dropped to the ground. Setting them carefully inside the hubcap, she pulled the wheel off, grunting as its weight dropped into her hands, letting it thump down onto the ground before she realized her mistake.

Now that she'd taken the jack out, the back of the car was empty.

She'd had the axle repaired. She'd had Ray tighten up the bolts and belts. She'd filled up the tank, and she'd even thought about washing the car, but she'd decided to wait until she was done with dirt roads and dust. All in all, she'd been very sensible.

Except that she hadn't bought a new tire. The old one, slashed beyond repair during her first trip to the ranch, hadn't been worth keeping. She was driving on the spare.

Sighing, she lifted the tire she'd just removed back onto the wheel and spun the lug nuts tight. Maybe she could drive just a little ways on it—get up over the hill, at least, so she could hoof it back to the ranch. It wouldn't be a very dramatic entrance, but she had a feeling that once she told Nate what she'd decided, it would be dramatic enough for him.

She drove twenty feet before she realized it was hopeless. The car listed so far to starboard that it was all she could do to keep it from plunging off the shoulder in an impromptu off-road excursion. She pulled over and rested her forehead on the steering wheel, closing her eyes.

Maybe the coyotes would pick her bones clean after all.

A thought struck her and she lifted her head. The hill. The hill was even higher than the one behind the barn. Maybe she could get a cell signal there too.

She trudged back the way she'd come, staggering up the hill in the hot midday sun, feeling sweat prickle on the back of her neck. When she reached the highest point, she took her phone out of her pocket and turned it on, whispering a soft prayer to the cell phone gods.

It worked. She only got two bars, and the battery was almost dead, but it worked. She could make one call. She paged through her contacts to the only number with a Wyoming area code.

Sighing, she highlighted Nate's number and pressed "send." She'd spent her whole life learning to be self-sufficient at her mother's insistence, so she wouldn't need a man. Learning to change her own tires, to do well in school so she could make her own living, to be prickly and independent and sure of herself. And now, despite all that preparation, here she was, calling a man to come rescue her.

She listened to the tinny, repetitive ring and pictured the phone ringing in the empty ranch kitchen, the light slanting through the window over the sink, the curtains shifting in the breeze. She could almost call up the homey smells of it—a little bit of musty old house, a touch of lemon dish soap, and that hint of fresh baked cookies.

The phone rang, and rang, and rang again.

Chapter 46

"HELLO?"

It was Phaedra. Charlie tapped her thigh nervously, hoping the phone's battery would last long enough for her to talk to an adult.

"Phaedra, it's me. Charlie."

"Hey! I thought you left."

"Just to go to town."

"Oh, geez." Phaedra laughed. "Nate thought you left for good."

Charlie spun around and stared toward the ranch. "What?"

"He thought you were going back to Jersey."

"Why would he think that?" She thought back to their last exchange. What had she said?

I have to go, Nate.

"He misunderstood," she said. "It's a long story, though, and my battery's low. Is he around? I need him."

"Nope. He went riding. But he really wants you to stay. He had me write a speech."

"He *what*?"

"He had me write a speech so he'd know what to say. It's really good. There's some nice imagery and symbolism and stuff. I asked him what he was feeling, you know, and then I made it, um, better. Prettier. He's kind of basic, you know?"

Charlie almost laughed. Basic was right. Nate was

definitely not a fancy, flowery kind of guy. He was a cowboy, through and through—quiet, comfortable, more at home with animals than with people. Better at nonverbal communication than giving speeches.

"So you'll come back? And hear the speech?"

"If somebody comes and gets me," Charlie said.

"Score. I'll tell him as soon as they get back." There was a sharp click, and suddenly the line sounded vacant, empty.

"No. Wait. Tell him…" Charlie pulled the phone away from her ear and stared at it. Putting it back to her mouth, she said, "Hello? Hello?"

Phaedra was gone.

Her battery warning beeped, and she snapped the phone shut. Sighing, she turned and headed down the hill toward the car.

———

Nate slid off Honey's back and led the horse to the paddock on the shady side of the barn. Doris and Taylor followed suit, along with Sam. Taylor was bending to help Sam unsaddle Peach when Phaedra tore out of the house.

"Hey! Nate!"

Dang, she was probably going to read him that speech she'd written. It was good, sure, but he had a feeling it wouldn't sound good coming from him. He just wasn't the speechifying type. Charlie would probably laugh at it.

No. Charlie would never get to hear it. Charlie was gone. He pulled off Honey's saddle and slung it onto the fence.

"Charlie called," Phaedra said.

Nate felt a rush of energy go straight to his head,

making him dizzy, almost faint. He turned and stared at Phaedra, dumbstruck, clutching Honey's saddle blanket in both hands.

"Charlie?" he finally managed to say.

"Yeah. She said to tell you she needs you."

The dizziness turned to elation, which made him even dizzier. He felt like he was either going to fall down or float up into the sky—he wasn't sure which.

"She said what?"

"She said she needs you." Phaedra was grinning like she'd won the lottery or something. "Her car broke down, and I think if you go out there and help her, she'll come back."

"I knew it," Doris said. "That girl was meant for you." She grinned and punched him in the arm. "Go get her, cowboy."

Nate draped the blanket over the fence and stepped up on a rail, tossing a leg over the horse's bare back. If the car was busted, Charlie would need a ride. She'd probably want to go to town, get Ray. But if she had to ride up behind him on Honey, they'd have to go back to the ranch. Maybe it would remind her of that first day. That first ride.

And if it didn't work, at least he'd get to feel her close to him again, with her arms around his waist, her breasts pressed up against his back. He hadn't fully appreciated that the first time.

He hadn't realized what he had.

Charlie sat in the back of the Celica's hatch, dangling her feet over the bumper. Leaning back, she lay down and closed her eyes, wondering how much longer she'd have to wait. She might as well take a nap.

A cloud wafted over the sun, and a cool breeze swept through the car's open doors, soothing her hot skin. She let herself drift into a drowsy half-sleep, enjoying that semi-conscious, wishful dreaming state where her mind loosed itself from her conscious control and frolicked through unlikely scenarios. Most of the scenarios involved Nate. Nate, and Nate's bedroom, with all those candles. Nate, and Nate's bed. Nate, and all those beds in the bunkhouse, one after the other. Nate and her own sweet self, naked and willing.

Stop, she told herself. *Just knock it off.* She could feel her body waking to new possibilities, softening, anticipating. At this rate, she'd end up dragging the guy into the back of the car and having her way with him the minute he arrived.

That sparked enough new fantasies and logistical speculations to fill the time until she heard the drum of hoofbeats cresting the top of the hill, galloping into a crescendo, then slowing to a broken, stumbling halt as Nate pulled the horse to a stop. He looked just like he had the first time she'd seen him—pure cowboy, rough and dangerous and sexy as hell.

Dangerous. Yeah, he was that. Dangerous to her peace of mind, dangerous to her precious Plan, and dangerous to her heart. But she could deal with danger.

It was danger that made life worth living.

"Hey," he said. He looked down at his hands, fooling with the reins, that muscle in his jaw pulsing, his eyes hidden by the shadow of his hat. "Phaedra said you needed me."

She stepped out of the car and smiled up at him. "Phaedra's right," she said. "I need you like I never needed anything in my life."

He slid off the horse and dropped Honey's reins. "What made you decide?"

She pulled him down beside her. From their seat in the back of the car, they could see all the way down the hill and across the valley.

"This," she said, gesturing toward the land below them. "And this." She leaned into him, closing her eyes, and kissed him with every ounce of eloquence she possessed, moving from tenderness to passion and back again. When she finally opened her eyes, he was staring at her and she felt like she could read his soul.

"I need you too," he said. He kissed her again, pressing her backward until she lay beneath him in the back of the car. She was helpless, pinned under his weight, but she'd never felt more powerful.

He kissed her again, his hands moving down her body, slipping under her shirt, fumbling with her belt buckle.

"Um, Nate?" Charlie tensed. "There's just one thing."

His eyes scanned her face, as if he was worried she was going to change her mind.

She gestured toward the road. "We're kind of, um, outside. Like, in the middle of the road. Don't you think we should wait?"

His lips tilted up in a grin. "I can't," he said.

"Sure you can. You just…"

"I have to know what you're wearing."

He unclasped her belt and tugged at her jeans. Sighing and rolling her eyes in mock despair, she helped him, sliding her loosened jeans down one hip to reveal a leopard-printed slip of silk.

"Mmm," he said. "Catwoman."

"Later," she said. She heaved him off her and sat up, smoothing out her hair.

"But you need me." He grinned.

"I need a ride first," she said.

"Well, you know the drill."

She nodded and took off her boots while he backed the horse over to the car. She slid into place behind him and wrapped her hands around his waist.

"Thanks for rescuing me," she said.

"You're welcome." Nate leaned back against her, his broad back warm against her chest. "But you're rescuing me too." He sighed, his breath shaking as he struggled for words. "I've always loved the ranch. Loved it more than anything except Sam. It was home, you know? The one place in the world I belonged. I used to look off across the land and see possibilities—new pastures for fencing, new horses, a new barn. But there was always something missing." He swallowed. "And then when I saw you pull away this afternoon, it changed. All I could see was how empty it was. It looked so—so bleak." He took a deep breath. "I never felt so alone in my life." There was a hitch in his voice she'd never heard before, except when he'd thought he might lose Sam. "It never would have been the same with you gone. I never would have been whole."

"I'm sorry," she said softly.

"Don't be. I learned something." They moved along in silence, Honey's ears flicking forward as she sensed the nearness of home. "You know how they used to call it 'breaking' horses? Well, I was broken."

"Sandi broke you," Charlie said. "You did everything she wanted, and she still whipped you just to keep you scared."

"Maybe. I don't know. But when you go to gentle a horse, you push him away, right? You won't let him close. And then he just wants more than anything to be with you, and next thing you know, he's whole again, ready to join up even if he's been hurt."

Charlie nodded. That was what she'd done with Trouble. Had she done it with Nate too?

He kissed the back of her neck and a thrill ran down her spine. "If we could stop pushing each other away—if we could learn to trust like the horses do, I think we'd both be better off."

Charlie smiled. "Wow. The kid's really good."

"What?"

"Phaedra. She told me she wrote you a speech. That was great."

"That was me," he said indignantly. "Hers was all poetic, about sunrises and stuff."

"Oh." Charlie felt her heart soften and glow. "That was you?"

"Uh-huh."

"Oh."

So that was Nate. The real Nate, spilling his heart out unedited, unrestrained. Telling her, as best he could, that he loved her. And his best was pretty damn good.

She bit her lower lip as the horse moved on, then tilted her chin, looking up at the cloud-strewn sky. Making a silent resolution, she took a deep breath. It was time to unclench her fists and step out of the ring. Time to drop her guard and risk hitting the mat.

"You're rescuing me too," she said. "I didn't know where I was going, but I thought wherever it was, I had to go there alone. I didn't think I could let anyone into my life until it was all set up—until I had everything I wanted. But you *are* what I want." Her throat ached, reluctant to let the words out, wanting to hold her secrets close, and she realized how Nate must feel. Sure, she talked a lot, but she never really brought her true feelings into the open. Nate did—and it was difficult and painful. Quiet as he was, he gave more of himself every day than she ever had.

"You, and Sam, and the ranch, and the horses—you're what really matters," she said. "I was going along just fine, doing what I thought I had to do, but I felt broken too. Because it was just me. Everything was all about me and where I wanted to go." She cleared her throat as tears stung at the back of her eyes. "And now I don't want to go there alone. I—I want you with me. You and Sam."

She let the words go, and it was as though she'd unlocked a door in her padlocked heart and let her real self out. She'd never noticed the ache of loneliness, but now that it was gone, she realized she'd been hurting all along.

She'd been broken ever since the day her father left, since a day she couldn't even remember, and now she was starting to heal.

Chapter 47

THE RANCH SEEMED STRANGELY SILENT AS CHARLIE AND Nate stepped into the kitchen. There was a note on the counter.

"Took the girls riding," it said in an almost illegible scrawl. "Sam's chores done. Horses fed and watered. See U later. MUCH later. Taylor."

"Guy should have been a doctor, not an actor," Nate said. "Got the handwriting for it."

"Should have been a shrink," Charlie said. "He knows just what people need." She pointed to the words "*way later*" and gave him a sultry smile. "Now, guess what *I* need?"

"Same thing I do."

"Well, let's see if I can help you with that." Charlie led him to the bed, pulling him down beside her. Bringing one hand up to brush her hair out of her face, he gave her a look of such tenderness the room seemed to warm and she could swear the mattress softened beneath her. "I thought I'd lost you," he said. "I thought you'd given up on me."

Charlie smiled. "We Jersey girls are fighters."

"You sure are," Nate said. "You're like a superhero." He stretched out, propping his head up on one hand, and somehow, it seemed natural to join him, to lie down beside him. He turned toward her, then hiked himself up on his elbows. Suddenly he was looking down on her, his body pressed against hers, his face inches away. "The Girl Avenger," he said. "That's you."

"I'll pick up my gold cuffs and a mask tomorrow," Charlie said.

"I think it's time to take the mask off, don't you?" Nate murmured. He kissed her, gently at first, then more insistently, his tongue seeking hers, his fingers buried in her hair. She reached up and tugged his shirt open, the pearl snaps clicking open one by one, and ran her hands down his bare chest, savoring the way the skin flowed so smoothly over his muscles. Stroking the fine hair that flecked his chest, she let her fingers skim over his nipples and stroke his ribs.

He deepened the kiss and she felt him gather power, his muscles swelling under her hands, his gentle touch firming as he cupped one breast and stroked the tip with his thumb. She arched her back, yielding, helpless, unable to hold back. She wasn't sure her heart was ready for this. But it was as ready as it would ever be, and she was willing to take the risk. And her body?

It was all set.

They thrashed through the awkwardness of shedding their clothes, Nate tugging her T-shirt over her head, momentarily trapping her arms and taking advantage of her brief helplessness to duck his head and take her breast into his mouth, his tongue teasing while she pretended to struggle against the folds of fabric. When she finally pulled her hands free, she moved them to his chest, signaling with her own touch what she wanted from him, and he took the hint readily, giving her all she'd asked for and more. And more. And more.

Obviously, cowboys were *not* stupid. Not this one, anyway.

She moved her hands down to his belt, fumbling with the buckle, clawing at the snap on his Wranglers. He shifted his hips, making it easy for her to peel the rough denim down so he could kick his way free.

Charlie pushed him down on the mattress and sat up, straddling his hips. She just wanted to look. Just wanted to see him as she'd remembered him so often since the last crazy time they'd fallen into bed. That had been an accident—sort of. This time, she wanted to savor every moment. She wanted to see his muscles shifting under his skin, the solid mass of his chest, the fine hair trailing down that ranch-raised Grade A six-pack.

That trail led straight to where she wanted to go. The all-American cowboy wore appropriately all-American Fruit of the Looms.

"These have to go," she said, slipping a finger under the elastic and giving it a gentle snap. He shook his head, despite the fact that his body was doing its best to stretch the white cotton to its limit. She ran her hand over him and he groaned. She paused and played a while, looking straight into his eyes, resisting his efforts to pull her down against him.

Grabbing his wrists, one in each hand, she lifted them above his head to hold him prisoner.

"You're in no position to be bossy," she said.

But that brought her body down to his, close enough that he could hook his leg across her and roll, pinning her to the mattress in an MMA move straight off of Spike TV. Before she could recoup, he had both her small hands in one of his large ones, leaving the other free to roam her body, stroking and smoothing, making its way over her breasts and down to her barely-there panties.

"I like these," he said, flicking the elastic in gentle retaliation. "Are these the emergency panties?"

She laughed. "No. But this is definitely an emergency."

He slipped his hand beneath the sheer fabric, teasing and touching everywhere but where she wanted him most. Her skin tingled, nerve endings shimmering with electricity, coaxing her to rock and writhe while his mouth covered hers, stifling her moans as her hips bucked up to meet his hand.

Nate shifted to one side so he could see Charlie's face. He wanted to watch as she closed her eyes and her body responded. She was so ready for him, so warm and wet. She tilted her pelvis, begging for more, and he answered, stroking longer, deeper, harder as she tipped her head back, bracing her heels on the bed and lifting her hips.

She was right. The Fruit of the Looms had to go. He skinned himself out of them in a floundering rush, his hands fumbling as he shoved them down his legs and dipped his body to touch hers. There was no thought, no planning, no strategizing to get where he wanted to go; she was with him, carrying him on the tide of her own need.

The tide ebbed and surged and surged again. He didn't want it to end. Squeezing his eyes shut, he strained to hold on, but she clenched around him, threw her head back, and let out a silent scream and he joined her, crashing into her like a high wind battering the wheat, riding her as she rose and broke and broke again.

—◌◌◌—

Charlie was going to die. She was sure of it.

Her head was going to explode, her pelvis was shattering into a million pieces, and her arms and legs were about to fly off to the four corners of the room.

Nate would have to call an ambulance to peel her off the ceiling. And if they ever managed to put her together again, it wouldn't matter.

She wouldn't be good for anything but sex ever again.

And that was fine with her.

Strong arms swept around her, *his* arms, and held her together. She closed her eyes and slept, safe, secure, and whole.

Chapter 48

CHARLIE OPENED HER EYES TO MORNING LIGHT. ROLLING OVER, she smiled at… nothing.

"Dang," she said to the empty bedroom and almost laughed. She was starting to swear like a cowboy now without even thinking about it. "When did he get up? And why didn't I hear him?"

She didn't know the answer to the first question, but the second one was easy. She hadn't heard him because she'd been sleeping off the effects of the night before, when he'd turned her knees to Jell-O and her brain to sweet butterscotch pudding.

She climbed into her jeans and slid a T-shirt over her head, then padded to the kitchen and peered out the window. The sun had barely risen over the distant mountains, and the whole ranch was lit with a pinkish glow. An empty glass on the counter held a puddle of orange juice, the only evidence of Nate's presence.

She refilled the glass and gulped down a slug of juice, then headed out the door. It started to swing shut behind her, but she caught it before it slammed.

She'd surprise him.

She crossed the yard as quietly as she could, then eased the barn door open and tiptoed down the aisle. She peered around the corner. He was in front of Honey's stall, kneeling on the barn floor.

"When I see you, it's like the sunrise," he mumbled.

Honey scarfed up a mouthful of hay and chewed contemplatively, tilting her head to watch Nate with the
equine equivalent of a puzzled expression.

"Like when the birds start singing, and—oh, dang it."
Nate lurched to his feet and pulled a scrap of paper out
of his pocket. "Sorry."

The horse must have forgiven him because she
kept on eating as he set off down the aisle, reading the
words scrawled on the paper, his lips moving, his brow
creased with concentration. He stopped at Razz's stall
to shake a flake of hay into the feed box, then fell to
his knees again. "Like when the birds start singing, and
everything's new, and no matter what happened the day
before, you know you're going to get a fresh start,"
he said to the horse. "You're my, um, my rising—no,
wait—you're—oh, damn." He rose again and fished for
the paper.

He moved over to Junior's stall. "When I see you,
it's like the sunrise—like when the birds start singing,
and everything's new, and no matter what happened the
day before, you know you're going to get a fresh start.
You're my fresh start, my rising sun, and I want to wake
up to you every day."

He dropped to his knees again and looked up at
the horse.

"Will you marry me?"

Charlie clapped her hand over her mouth, but she
couldn't hold back the whoop of laughter that escaped
her lips. Nate spun to face her, his face crimson.

"I've heard about you cowboys and your fondness for
livestock, but I never thought it was true," she said, grinning. "And I thought sheep were the critters of choice."

She slanted her eyes over toward Junior. "Ambitious, aren't you?"

"No," Nate blushed as he grabbed the edge of the stall and hoisted himself to his feet. "I was just, um, practicing."

"Is inter-species marriage legal in this state?" Charlie asked, touching a finger to her lips and looking up to pantomime deep thought. "It's the 'Cowboy State,' so I guess it would have to be." She softened her smile and took a step toward him. "Wouldn't you really rather marry a woman? Like, a human one?"

Nate nodded and swallowed. No wonder he'd been practicing on the horses. Now that she was in front of him, he was tongue-tied again.

"So, did you have a woman in mind?"

He nodded. "I, um…"

She stepped in close and wrapped her arms around his neck. "Show me," she whispered.

He bent down and kissed her, and the kiss was a proposal in itself—soft and yielding, then firm and masterful, it carried her through every conceivable facet of a marriage, from panting need to tender longing and back again. She tightened her arms around him and proposed right back.

Junior let out a frustrated nicker. "Jealous brat," Charlie muttered. She looked up at Nate, who still held her close, his eyes saying even more than the kiss.

"Yes," she whispered. "Yes."

Epilogue

SAM SHOOK HER HEAD, AND THE CAREFULLY ARRANGED flowers decking her hair tumbled to the floor for the third time.

"Oops," she said.

"Sam!" Phaedra gathered the flowers and set them aside, then smoothed Sam's hair with a comb and rebraided it. "Sit still," she said to the fidgeting child. "You want to look nice for the wedding, don't you?"

Sam sighed and nodded, banging her feet against the rungs of the kitchen chair she'd been forced into when she'd snuck out to visit Peach and streaked dirt on her lacy pink dress.

"I wish Mom could have come," she said.

"She had to work," Phaedra said. Sandi had gone to beauty school after all. Sam went down to Denver every other weekend and "helped" her in the salon she shared with three other graduates.

"I know. It's okay," Sam said. "She likes her job a lot better than she likes the ranch anyway."

In the next room, Nate shifted his weight nervously from one foot to the other and picked at a loose thread on the sleeve of his black dinner jacket.

"Leave that thing alone," Taylor said. "You'll have the whole thing unraveled if you don't watch it. I'm not standing up as best man to a naked cowboy, I can tell you that. That'd be sure to hit the tabloids."

Nate grinned. In the year they'd been in business together, he and Taylor had built up a solid friendship—a friendship, not a partnership. He hadn't really needed Taylor's money. One trip to a lawyer had revealed even more lies on Sandi's part. There was no such thing as common law marriage in Wyoming.

Sandi didn't have any claim on the ranch at all.

But Charlie had talked him into teaming up with Taylor anyway, and it had worked out fine. Together, they'd trained a half-dozen reining horses for film work, and Taylor had kept a steady stream of actors, friends, and wannabe wranglers coming to the clinics.

Then there were the kids. Nate felt like a father to every one of the long parade of high school misfits that had arrived at the ranch, their spirits broken and bruised. Every one of them had left stronger—not healed, not totally, but well on their way.

Who knew you could care so much about kids that weren't your own?

Charlie. She'd known. And she'd taught him, and enriched his life beyond anything he'd ever dreamed of.

"How's the work on the house going?" Taylor asked. Nate knew Taylor was just trying to distract him. He didn't know why he was so nervous. It wasn't like he didn't want to marry Charlie. The past year had been perfect—except that they hadn't had time to make their relationship official. Nate wanted everything nailed down so their life together would never change.

"It's going okay," he said. "Charlie won't let me change that wallpaper in the kitchen, though. Or the cabinets."

Taylor shook his head. "That is not a normal woman you've got there," he said.

"Nope," Nate said. That was the best thing about Charlie. He couldn't believe he'd ever thought of her as girlie. Working by his side in her battered Wranglers and ripped T-shirts, her hair grown long and her nails cut short, she looked like she'd been ranching all her life. Beautiful still, but healthy and wholesome. The perfect rancher's wife.

He wondered how she'd look today. The gown had been guarded like a state secret.

An organ chord resounded through the church. Nate licked his lips and straightened his tie.

"Here we go," Taylor said. The two of them covered the aisle in seconds; Purvis's tiny church wasn't exactly geared toward long processions. Taking his place before the daisy-decked altar, Nate turned to watch as the organ reeled into the "Wedding March" and Sam trotted out of the apse strewing flowers from a woven basket. Behind her walked the most beautiful creature Nate had ever seen.

Charlie had brought the best of her old Jersey girl self back for the wedding. The gown was a fitted white sheath that hugged every curve. Her hair was up in an elaborate 'do that brought to mind her old, spiky style, and she'd painted her lips scarlet and made her eyes look smoky and mysterious. He was reminded of the exotic creature he'd first seen standing beside the crippled Celica, but the smile tilting her lips was a far cry from the scowl she'd worn that first day.

The woman beside her was smiling too. It was a hard-won smile. Mona Banks hadn't been pleased when her daughter gave up her education to "play cowgirl," but a visit to the ranch had changed her mind.

It had changed the ranch too. Charlie's mother had fussed so much about her daughter's cooking that Nate told her to do it her own danged self, and she'd gone and done just that. She was the center of the household now, ruling the ranch kitchen, churning out massive amounts of food that kept the clients almost too full to ride. She'd outlawed sugary cereal for breakfast, but she'd made up for it with fluffy omelets and the best pancakes Nate had ever had.

She'd never pull another waitress shift in her life if he had anything to say about it.

The preacher was talking. Charlie's mother was giving her away, but all Nate could do was stare at his wife-to-be through a haze of happiness. Charlie stepped up beside him, and he couldn't stop smiling. He probably looked like the dumb cowboy she'd taken him for that first day. Well, now she was taking him again, for better or for worse. For richer or for poorer.

Forever.

His soon-to-be-wife lowered her lashes modestly, then glanced up at him and smiled.

"Love me?" she asked, cocking her head to one side.

He nodded.

He'd always been better at nonverbal communication.

THE END

Acknowledgments

It's a good thing I had a two-book contract, so I can thank all the people I left out of my first attempt at acknowledgments. Practice should make perfect, but I still feel like a drunken starlet blinded by the bright lights at an awards ceremony.

It takes six things to make a romance writer: a supportive family, a critique group, good friends, a brilliant agent, a great publisher, and a heart-stopping, samba-dancing, rock-'em, sock-'em relationship for singin'-hallelujah, take-your-breath-away inspiration.

I covered that last item in the dedication. Now for the other five:

My family: My parents, Don and Betty Smyth, gave me the support I needed to finally, finally become a writer. My sister, Carolyn Smyth, inspired me with her creative spirit. Web genius Scott McCauley proved you can combine family and work. And Alycia Fleury and her family have continued to enrich my life.

My writing groups: Thanks to Jeana Byrne, Mary Gilgannon, Heather Jensen, Liz Roadifer, and Mike Shay, who helped me through some tough times and offered the perfect balance of advice and encouragement. I love you guys! And to the Saturday Writers—Amanda Cabot, Tina Forkner, Pam Nowak, and Marjie Smith—I admire you all so much, and your support means everything.

My friends: Belated thanks to Cheyenne's illustrious Barnes & Nobility, including Linda Herget, CRM extraordinaire, as well as B^2 and the entire management crew for putting up with my whining. And to the staff and the regulars—thanks for making my first publishing experience such an event! I'm also grateful to Laura Macomber and Jeff Brown for their never-ending support, and to Mike and Amy Bell for their friendship.

My brilliant agent: Thank you, Elaine English, for always being there when I need you. And thank you to Naomi Hackenberg and the fabulous interns, for making this very solitary job feel like a team effort. If you're a writer, trust me—you need an agent, and if you're lucky, you'll find one like mine.

My great publisher: Editor Deb Werksman, publisher Dominique Raccah, and publicist Danielle Jackson. You are an awesome all-girl A-team of publishing superwomen. Thank you for helping my books be the best they can be.

Okay, I know I said five. But evidently, I'm still in drunken starlet mode because I forgot what is possibly the most important element of all in any writer's success: the readers. Thank you, thank you, thank you to all the readers and reviewers who helped make *Cowboy Trouble* a success. I hope you enjoy this next book, and the one after that—because really, they're for you. And if there's anything else you want, let me know at www.joannekennedybooks.com.

About the Author

After dabbling in horse training and chicken farming in Pennsylvania, Joanne Kennedy ran away to Wyoming twenty years ago and was surprised to discover that real cowboys still walk the streets of Cheyenne. Her fascination with Wyoming's unique blend of past and present leads her to write contemporary Western romances with traditional ranch settings. She lives in Wyoming with two dogs and a retired fighter pilot. The dogs are relatively well-behaved.

Joanne loves to hear from readers and can be reached at joanne@joannekennedybooks.com.

For more from Joanne Kennedy,
read on for an excerpt from

COWBOY
Trouble

Now available from Sourcebooks Casablanca

Chapter 1

A CHICKEN WILL NEVER BREAK YOUR HEART.

Not that you can't love a chicken. There are some people in this world who can love just about anything.

But a chicken will never love you back. When you look deep into their beady little eyes, there's not a lot of warmth there—just an avarice for worms and bugs and, if it's a rooster, a lot of suppressed anger and sexual frustration. They don't return your affection in any way.

Expectations, relationship-wise, are right at rock bottom.

That's why Libby Brown decided to start a chicken farm. She wanted some company, and she wanted a farm, but she didn't want to go getting attached to things like she had in the past.

She'd been obsessed with farms since she was a kid. It all started with her Fisher Price Farmer Joe Play Set: a plastic barn, some toy animals, and a pair of round-headed baby dolls clutching pitchforks like some simple-minded version of American Gothic.

A Fisher Price life was the life for her.

Take Atlanta—just give her that countryside.

Libby had her pickup half unloaded when her new neighbor showed up. She didn't see him coming, so he got a prime view of her posterior as she bent over the tailgate, wrestling with the last of her chrome dinette chairs. The chair was entangled in the electric cord from the toaster, so he got a prime introduction to her vocabulary too.

"Howdy," he said.

Howdy? She turned to face him and stifled a snort.

Halloween was three months away, but this guy was ready with his cowboy costume. Surely no one actually wore chaps in real life, even in Wyoming. His boots looked like the real thing, though; they were worn and dirty as if they'd kicked around God-knows-what in the old corral, and his gray felt Stetson was all dented, like a horse had stepped on it. A square, stubbled chin gave his face a masculine cast, but there was something soft about his mouth that added a hint of vulnerability.

She hopped down from the tailgate. From her perch on the truck, he'd looked like the Marlboro Man on a rough day, but now that they were on the same level, she could see he was kind of cute—like a young Clint Eastwood with a little touch of Elvis.

"Howdy," he said again. He actually tipped his hat and she almost laughed for the first time in a month.

"I'm Luke Rawlins, from down the road," he continued. The man obviously had no idea how absurd he looked, decked out like a slightly used version of Hopalong Cassidy. "Thought maybe you'd need some help moving in. And I brought you a casserole—Chicken Artichoke Supreme. It's my specialty." He held out a massive ceramic dish with the pride of a caveman returning from the hunt. "Or maybe you could use a hand getting that chair broke to ride."

Great. She had the bastard son of John Wayne and

Martha Stewart for a neighbor. And he thought he was funny.

Worse yet, he thought she was funny.

"Thanks." She took the casserole. "I'm Libby Brown. Are you from that farm with the big barn?"

"Farm? I'm not from any farm." Narrowing his eyes, he slouched against the truck and folded his arms. "You're not from around here, are you?"

"What makes you say that?"

"You calling my ranch a farm, that's what." A blade of wheatgrass bobbed from one corner of his mouth as he looked her up and down with masculine arrogance. "There's no such thing as a farm in Wyoming," he said.

"Well, what do you call this, then?" Libby gestured toward the sun-baked outbuildings that tilted drunkenly around her own personal patch of prairie.

"A ranch."

"That's not what I call it. I call it 'Lackaduck Farm.'" She pointed to the faded letters arched over the barn's wide double doors. "That's what the people before me called it too. It's even painted on the barn."

"Yeah, well, they weren't from around here either. They were New Yorkers and got smacked on the bottom and sent home by Mother Nature. Thought they'd retire out here on some cheap real estate and be gentleman farmers. They didn't realize there's a reason the real estate's cheap. It's tough living." He looked her in the eye, no doubt judging her unfit for a life only real men could endure. "You think you're up to it?"

"As a matter of fact, I am." Libby hoped she sounded a lot more confident than she felt. "This is what I've always wanted, and I'm going to make it work."

She didn't mention the fact that she had to make it work. She didn't have anything else. No career—not even much of a job. And no boyfriend. Not even a dog.

The dog died in September, right before the boyfriend ran off. Lucky couldn't help it, but Bill Cooperman could have stuck around if he'd only tried. He just had a wandering eye, and it finally wandered off for good with a hotshot editor from the *Atlanta Journal-Constitution*. The hotshot editor was also Libby's boss, so she basically lost everything in the space of about six weeks. All she had left was a broken heart, a cherry red pickup, and the contents of her desk in a battered cardboard box.

Since her professional and romantic aspirations were a bust, she'd sold her one-bedroom condo in downtown Atlanta and literally bought the farm. She was now the proud owner of thirty-five acres of sagebrush and a quaint clapboard farmhouse in Lackaduck, Wyoming. At the moment, tumbleweeds were her primary crop and grasshoppers her only livestock, but the place was as far from Atlanta as she could get, and she figured a fresh coat of paint and a flock of free-range chickens would make it her dream home—one utterly unlike the one she'd left behind. So far, Wyoming was like another planet, and that was fine with her.

"I'm definitely going to make this work," she repeated, as much to herself as to her new neighbor.

The cowboy reached over the truck's battered tailgate for the dinette chair, which freed itself from the toaster cord the minute he touched it.

"Guess you'll be glad to get some help then."

He swung the chair over his shoulder and headed for the house.

Libby sighed. She had her pride, but she wasn't about to turn her bad back on an able-bodied man who was willing to tote furniture for her. Beggars can't be choosers, and Luke Rawlins wasn't really such a bad choice, anyway. She wasn't in the market for his brand of talent, but it sure was fun to watch him move furniture. Those chaps, with their swaying leather fringe, must have been designed by the early cowboys to highlight a man's best assets.

—✦—

Luke set the chair in the kitchen, then traipsed back out and scanned the contents of the truck bed. He'd been worried when they sold the Lackaduck place, but the new neighbor seemed all right. More than all right. When he'd first seen her, tussling with her furniture in the back of the pickup, he'd thought love might have finally come to Lackaduck. Then he'd realized all he could see was her backside and decided it was probably just lust.

Besides, her sofa was definitely a deal breaker.

It was enormous. And hideous. Once they wrestled the dang thing inside, it dominated the homestead's tiny front room like some evil crouching monster. Carved cherubs on each corner lofted a complicated scrollwork banner in their pudgy fists. They were probably supposed to be cute, but Luke thought they looked like evil leering babies, preparing to strangle unsuspecting sofa sitters with their long wooden ribbon. He made a silent vow to stay as far away from that piece of furniture as he could.

"Careful," Libby said as they swung it into place. "It's an antique."

"Antique?" He did his best not to sound judgmental.

She tipped her lightly freckled nose in the air and flashed him a hard look. "French Victorian Baroque Provincial," she said. "That's what the dealer said."

French, he could believe. And Victorian, and all that. But mostly, the thing was plain ugly. It seemed like a city girl should have better taste—especially one who was obviously educated. There were at least fourteen boxes of books in the bed of the truck. It took him a good twenty minutes to haul them all into the house and stack them in the front hall.

"You a schoolmarm, or what?" He set down the last box and parked his Stetson on the newel post.

"I'm a journalist. I have to read a lot." She picked up his hat and tipped it onto her head for a half-second, then whipped it off and plopped it back on the banister.

"A journalist? Well, good luck finding a job around here," Luke said. "We've only got one newspaper, and it's barely surviving, because there isn't any news at all." He picked up the hat and set it back on her head, adjusting it to a rakish angle. "Don't take that off," he said. "It suits you."

"No thanks." She took it off and shook her springy brown curls back into freeform disarray, and he had to agree the wild, untamed look suited her way better than the hat.

"So I guess my new job will be a challenge," she said.

Oops. He'd stepped in it, as usual. Said precisely the wrong thing. "You're going to work for the *Lackaduck Holler*?"

"That's the plan."

He couldn't think of any response to that. *The Holler*

was the most pathetic excuse for a newspaper he'd ever seen. The most exciting headline of the past six months had been the one about Chet Hostetler's freak heifer. That one had made the wire services—popped up in papers coast to coast, and all over the Internet. It was pretty sad when your hometown's only claim to fame was a two-headed cow.

But Libby didn't need to know that. Judging from that sofa, she was accustomed to something a little more cosmopolitan than Lackaduck had to offer. Once she figured out that one day in Lackaduck was pretty much like the next, she'd probably move on, and that was a shame. Interesting women were in short supply in this town.

It was time to turn on the charm. He gave her a grin that had melted the hearts of half a dozen rodeo queens, then turned and scanned the tiny hallway, stacked high with book boxes. "Well, I bet you're a real smart lady."

She shot him a scowl. "You know, I can tell you're not John Wayne. When you're not thinking about it, you drop that hayseed accent and talk almost like a normal human being."

Yikes. Most women fell all over him when he channeled the Duke, but this one was a mite on the prickly side.

"Yeah, well." He slumped back against the post. "Most of the women I meet from back East are pretty hot for the cowboy type."

"Not me," she said. "No cowboys for me. No boys of any kind at the moment. I'm on my own and staying that way. Got it?"

"Got it." Luke straightened up and gave her a pitying look. "So are you gay or heartbroke?"

She looked up at him, her brown eyes taking on a teary sheen, and for one terrifying moment he thought she was going to cry. He glanced over at the door, planning an escape route, but she just blinked a couple times, then stiffened her back and straightened her shoulders. Somehow, that was even harder to take than tears.

"None of your business," she said. A lock of that crazy hair flopped over her forehead and dangled over one eye. He reached over and flipped it into place.

"Sorry," he said. "Forget I asked." Her hair was surprisingly soft, with none of that sticky spray stuff all the local girls used. Of course, the locals knew about the Wyoming wind. Those thirty-mile-an-hour gusts would tangle Libby's hair in a hurry. She'd end up looking like she'd just gotten out of bed.

His bed.

Now where had *that* come from? He brushed her hair back again, savoring its softness, surprised when she didn't swat him away. Maybe he hadn't blown it yet. Maybe she liked him.

"Sorry. It's just that you're awful pretty to be out here on your own," he said. "It doesn't seem right." He spun one corkscrew curl 'round his finger, then let it spring back into place. "What are you running away from?"

Libby could feel her face flushing at Luke's touch—and her backbone stiffening against temptation. Despite a tragic case of hat-hair, something in his green eyes was turning her insides to warm, wobbly Jell-O, and she had to rein in a sudden urge to spill her whole life story.

"Nothing," she said. "I'm not running away. I'm running toward."

"Toward what?"

"This, I guess."

He glanced around the shabby hallway. "This?"

Libby followed his gaze and winced. The house had obviously stood empty for months. Cobwebs spanned every corner, and it needed a good coat of paint and a lot of scrubbing. It hardly looked like anybody's dream home, but it was hers.

All hers.

"Yeah, this." She squared her shoulders. "I might have to fix it up a little, but it's what I've always wanted. And anyway, even if I was running away—and I'm not—but if I was, at least I'm moving. Getting somewhere." She set her hands on her hips. "How long have you been at that ranch of yours?"

"All my life," Luke said. "I got lucky. I was born right where I belonged."

He was lounging against the newel post, his pose casual and relaxed, the ridiculous cowboy duds looking perfectly natural on his angular frame. The thighs and inseams of his jeans were worn almost white from riding, and his eyes were framed by faint crow's feet, etched by the Wyoming sun. He was right, Libby thought. He belonged here. He was a cowboy, pure and simple.

She hadn't had any idea such a thing still existed. It was like moving to Austria and finding your neighbors decked out in lederhosen.

"You are lucky," she admitted. "Sometimes I'm not sure where I belong. Maybe I have to build a place myself. Start from scratch." Hoisting a box in her arms, she struggled to set it on top of the stack he'd started against the wall.

"Whoa there," he said. Libby had a feeling that corny cowboy line had tamed more women than horses, but she was relieved when he leaned over and helped her slide the box into place.

"So are you going to live out here all by yourself?" he asked. "No boyfriend? No dog?"

She looked up, startled by the realization the guy was a total stranger. For all she knew, he was the latest heir to Ted Bundy. She looked down at his hands, square and strong and calloused from work, and imagined them clenched into fists. Then she studied his face, searching his eyes for some sign of sociopathic mania, but it was tough to get past that smile and come to any rational conclusion.

"I've got a dog," she lied. "I just didn't bring him yet."

"Well, good. I hope he's a big one for protection."

"Oh, yeah, he's a big one, all right." She searched her mind for a really good name—one that would discourage even the most depraved serial killer. "Nobody messes with Ivan."

"The Terrible?"

She nodded. "Right."

"Well, I guess you'll be okay then." He tipped the hat back on and started toward the door, then turned. "Be careful, though. A gal went missing from around here a while back."

She thought of Ted Bundy again and her stomach flipped over. "What do you mean, she went missing?"

"She disappeared." Luke's easy smile was gone.

"They think she might have been abducted—maybe even murdered, but they never figured out what happened."

Libby sat down on a box of books and tried to ignore the *Jaws* music thudding through her subconscious. "They never found her?"

"Nope. The sheriff just about lost his mind over it. Now it seems like he's given up." He slapped a streak of dirt off his jeans. "It's been almost three years."

"So somewhere in this town is a kidnapper, or a murderer. It could be anybody." She shook her head. "And you say there isn't any news. Good thing you're not a journalist."

"Well, it was a long time ago. And it was probably a transient, or a tourist. Somebody passing through."

"Wow." She traced a line across the dusty hardwood floor with the toe of her sneaker. "I'll bet I could figure it out."

"You?" He looked doubtfully at her torn jeans and ratty sweatshirt, and she realized she wasn't exactly dressed like a superhero.

"Yeah, me." She sat up a little straighter. "I covered crime stories for the *Atlanta Journal-Constitution*. My boyfriend—ex-boyfriend, I mean—was a police detective." She cleared her throat. Despite Bill's betrayal, her voice still went all husky every time she tried to talk about him. "He was a jerk too, but he was good at his job, and he taught me a lot. I don't mean to brag, but I'll bet I know more about tracking down killers than your average small-town sheriff."

Luke shrugged. "Our sheriff doesn't know much about anything. He's kind of a good ol' boy."

Libby pictured a Boss Hogg type, narrow in the mind

and big in the belly. "Guess this place really is perfect, then." She stood and tore the tape off one of the boxes. It was full of reference books: *Games Criminals Play*, *Why They Kill*, *Crime Scene Investigation*. "*The Holler* hired me to write features and local political stuff, but what I really like to do is crime stories." She waved a forensic textbook in the air. "Maybe this case just needs some city smarts."

Luke reached into the box and pulled out a copy of *Profiling Today*. "Looks like you know what you're talking about," he said, flipping through the pages. "Maybe you could find Della."

"Was that her name?"

He nodded. "I could give you some background if you want. We could get together sometime."

The *Jaws* music was starting up in Libby's head again. Either this guy really was a Bundy brother, or he was dangerous in some other way. She looked at the laugh lines around his eyes and the dimple that flashed when he smiled and decided he probably wasn't a Bundy.

"I'd like to hear more about it," she said. She wasn't about to bounce into a rebound relationship, no matter how fetching that dimple was, but she wanted to know more. Besides, she thought she might enjoy another look at the fine Wyoming scenery—as presented by Wrangler.

Luke brushed the dust off his hands. "Tomorrow?"

"Sure. I'll be home all day." Libby gestured vaguely toward the boxes stacked in the hallway, then waved toward the dilapidated outbuildings. "I've got plenty to do."

"Great." He adjusted the brim of his hat and glanced

back at her from the doorway. "Make sure you let that dog of yours know I'm coming, though. Wouldn't want to cross old Ivan."

COWBOY

Trouble

BY JOANNE KENNEDY

*All she wanted was a simple country life,
and then he walked in...*

Fleeing her latest love life disaster, big city journalist
Libby Brown's transition to rural living isn't going exactly
as planned. Her childhood dream has always been to own
a farm—but without the constant help of her charming,
sexy neighbor, she'd never make it through her first
Wyoming season. But handsome rancher Luke Rawlins
yearns to do more than help Libby around her ranch.
He's ready for love, and he wants to go the distance...

Then the two get embroiled in their tiny town's one and
only crime story, and Libby discovers that their sizzling
hot attraction is going to complicate her life in every way
possible...

"I'm expecting great things from Joanne Kennedy! Bring
on the hunky cowboys." —Linda Lael Miller, *New York
Times* bestselling author of *The Bridegroom*

"Everything about Kennedy's charming debut novel hits
the right marks...you'll be hooked." —*BookLoons*

978-1-4022-3668-6 • $7.99 US / $9.99 CAN / £4.99 UK

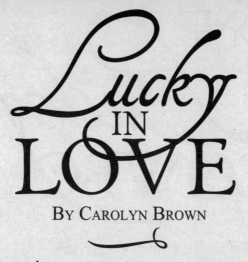

Lucky
IN
LOVE

BY CAROLYN BROWN

BEAU HASN'T GOT A LICK OF SENSE WHEN IT COMES TO WOMEN

Everything hunky rancher "Lucky" Beau Luckadeau touches turns to gold—except relationships. Spitfire Milli Torres can mend a fence, pull a calf, or shoot a rattlesnake between the eyes. When Milli shows up to help out at the Lazy Z ranch, she's horrified to find that Beau's her nearest neighbor—the very man she'd hoped never to lay eyes on again. If Beau ever figures out what really happened on that steamy Louisiana night when they first met, there'll be the devil to pay…

Praise for Carolyn Brown:

"Engaging characters, humorous situations, and a bumpy romance… Carolyn Brown will keep you reading until the very last page." —Romantic Times

"Carolyn Brown's rollicking sense of humor asserts itself on every page." —Scribes World

978-1-4022-2435-5 • $7.99 U.S. / $9.99 CAN

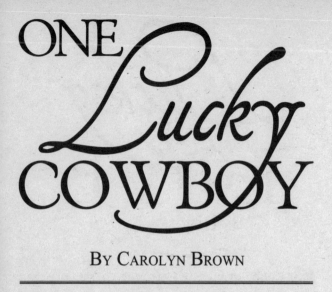

ONE *Lucky* COWBOY

By Carolyn Brown

No big blond cowboy is going to intimidate this spitfire!

If Slade Luckadeau thinks he can run Jane Day off his ranch, he's got cow chips for brains. She's winning every argument, and he's running out of fights to pick. But when trouble with a capital "T" threatens Jane *and* the Double L Ranch, suddenly it's Slade's heart that's in the most danger of all.

Praise for *Lucky in Love*:

"I enjoyed this book so much that I plan to rope myself some more of Carolyn Brown and her books. Lucky in Love is a must read!" —Cheryl's Book Nook

"This is one of those rare books where every person in it comes alive… as they share wit, wisdom, and love." —The Romance Studio

978-1-4022-2437-9 • $7.99 U.S. / $9.99 CAN

GETTING

Lucky

BY CAROLYN BROWN

Griffin Luckadeau is one stubborn cowboy...

And Julie Donovan is one hotheaded schoolteacher who doesn't let anybody push her around. When Griffin thinks his new neighbor is scheming to steal his ranch out from under him, he's more than willing to cross horns. Their look-alike daughters may be best friends, but until these two Texas hotheads admit it's fate that brought them together, running from the inevitable is only going to bring them a double dose of miserable...

Praise for Carolyn Brown:

"A delight to read." —Booklist

"Engaging characters, humorous situations, and a bumpy romance... Carolyn Brown will keep you reading until the very last page." —Romantic Times

"Carolyn Brown's rollicking sense of humor asserts itself on every page." —Scribes World

978-1-4022-2436-2 • $6.99 U.S. / $8.99 CAN

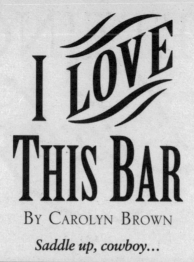

I LOVE THIS BAR

By Carolyn Brown

Saddle up, cowboy...

She doesn't need anything but her bar...

Daisy O'Dell has her hands full with hotheads and thirsty ranchers until the day one damn fine cowboy walks in and throws her whole life into turmoil. Jarod McElroy is looking for a cold drink and a moment's peace, but instead he finds one red hot woman. She's just what he needs, if only he can convince her to come out from behind that bar, and come home with him...

Praise for *One Lucky Cowboy:*

"Jam-packed with cat fights, reluctant heroes, spirited old ladies and, of course, a chilling villain, Brown's plot-driven cowboy romance...will earn a spot on your keeper shelf."

—*Romantic Times*, 4 stars

"Sheer fun...filled with down-home humor, realistic characters, and pure romance."

—*Romance Reader at Heart*

978-1-4022-3926-7 • $7.99 US / $8.99 CAN / £4.99 UK